Mystery in Mind

a collection of stories of the paranormal

ISBN: 0-9727494-0-3

Table of Contents

Foreword

By Dr. Sally Rhine Feather

I want to thank each and every one of the authors of this book for the generous donation of their time and creative talent that makes this collection of short stories such an entertaining success! This book presents the winning entries submitted to the first Mystery Stories Contest ever sponsored by the Rhine Research Center (RRC). These stories were selected from a large number of entries submitted by both well-known and novice authors, and they are published as much-appreciated contributions to aid in the fund-raising efforts of the RRC, a nonprofit organization.

The RRC is renowned for first introducing laboratory research into the realm of the paranormal, beginning with my father J. B. Rhine's card-guessing tests in the early 1930s at Duke University. Today, the RRC is an independent organization located off-campus in Durham, North Carolina. It continues a program of serious scientific research to better understand the paranormal, while providing educational opportunities for the general public. Our internationally attended Summer Study Program, begun in 1974, is an intensive 8–week course for professionals and college students who want to learn about parapsychology, the scientific study of psychic (psi) phenomena.

With *Mystery in Mind,* the RRC is embarking on an entirely new venture— the publication of a collection of purely fictional stories, all with a paranormal theme. We emphasize that this collection of stories does not represent reality, as we know it, in regards to parapsychology as a legitimate science. Yet, a few of these chilling tales come close to the more than 14,000 actual reports that we have collected from the general public over the years. Realistically, these stories represent ideas spun off from reality in the way that imaginative writers have been creating good fiction throughout history. We present these stories purely for your entertainment as many of us might have enjoyed listening to ghost stories around the campfires of our youth.

Income from a modest endowment has supported the RRC since 1965, but that endowment has not kept pace with the requirements of quality research or the demand for our educational programs. The RRC's ability to continue its vital programs depends critically upon the growth of the endowment and upon specific, project-oriented grants and donations. To meet these challenges, we also rely upon the generous support of those individuals who wish to share our mission.

We hope that you will continue your interest into the real world of the paranormal by visiting the RRC Web site at www.rhine.org and by joining the real worldwide network of Rhine Research Center Association members. We invite you to send in your reactions, questions, or suggestions for future books to the addresses given on the Web site and to contact us for more information.

Acknowledgments

The Rhine Research Center would like to thank the following individuals for their generous donation of time and creativity that helped to make this project a success. First and foremost, a special thanks to all the authors for their imaginative stories: Skye Alexander, L. L. Bartlett, Nicole Burris, Jordan Carpenter, Margaret DiCanio, Amanda Dickerson, Lee Driver, Rosemary Edghill, Jon Fabris, Sarah E. Glenn, Jan Holloway, Patricia Harrington, Elorise Holstad, Nicholas Knight, Michele Lassig, Martha Lawrence, Scott Nicholson, Helen Rhine, George M. Scott, David Terrenoire, and Didier Quémener. The Center also extends gratitude to Chris Pugh for permission to use his artwork throughout the book and on the cover.

We also wish to thank the panel of judges who were instrumental in selecting the stories to be included in this collection: Jo Carpenter, Maggie Blackman, Lynette Minnich, Libby Parish, and Sally Williams. A special thank you is extended to Carolyn Nuhn for her vision. And to Libby Parish for her commitment while working as an agent on this project as well as to Beth Basset for her assistance in editing.

Finally, we wish to thank the entire staff of the Center for their exhaustive assistance on this project and their continued dedication to the Rhine Research Center.

Author Biographies

Martha C. Lawrence

Martha C. Lawrence's "remarkable first novel" (*Library Journal), Murder in Scorpio,* introduced psychic detective Elizabeth Chase and won nominations for three of America's most prestigious mystery awards: the Edgar, the Agatha, and the Anthony. The acclaim continued with her second mystery, *The Cold Heart of Capricorn,* hailed as a "superior shocker" (*San Diego Union Tribune*) "that offers a truly intelligent heroine to solve it" (*Denver Post). Kirkus Reviews* called Lawrence's explosive third novel, *Aquarius Descending,* "gripping, believable . . . distinguished." Lawrence's fourth novel, *Pisces Rising,* won the *San Diego Magazine* award for best fiction in the year 2000 and was nominated for the Nero award. Her fifth novel, *Ashes of Aries,* was published in the fall of 2001 and praised by *Publishers Weekly* as a "riveting . . . fascinating page-turner."

Inspired by her own real-life psychic experiences, Martha's novels have been published around the world. A former book editor for Simon and Schuster and Harcourt Brace Publishers, she reviews fiction for *The San Diego Union-Tribune* and has made numerous television and radio appearances. She lives in Escondido, California, and can be reached through her Web site at www.marthalawrence.com.

L. L. Bartlett

L.L. Bartlett, a 2002 finalist in the Malice Domestic Contest for Best First Traditional Mystery, has done it all—from typing scripts in Hollywood to drilling holes for NASA—and like the characters in Cold Case, makes a life of crime in Western New York.

Skye Alexander

"Hidden in Plain Sight" is the prequel to Skye Alexander's first astrological mystery *Hidden Agenda,* which launched her Magical Mystery Series featuring astro-sleuth Charlotte McCrae. *Hidden Agenda* won the 1998 Kiss of Death Award, given by the Romance Writers of America's Mystery Chapter for the year's best book of romantic suspense. *Devils in Disguise,* the second book in her "Magical Mystery Series," is in process.

She is also the author of four nonfiction books, *Magickal Astrology, 10–Minute Fend Shui, Planets in Signs,* and *Enchanted Secrets & Magickal Spells.* Her stories have been published in various literary magazines and anthologies and translated into German and Korean. Alexander is a regular contributor to many magazines and newspapers and has published more than 1,000 articles on metaphysical subjects.

Like her protagonist, Alexander is a professional astrologer and has worked with police across the United States to solve crimes. A magickal practitioner for two decades, she was filmed performing a ritual at Stonehenge for a Discovery Channel TV special, which aired in October 2001.

Alexander can be reached through Mojo Publishing at POB 7121, Gloucester, MA 01930 or mojo@shore.net.

Margaret DiCanio

Margaret DiCanio, a freelance writer, has published nine non-fiction books, including the Encyclopedia of Violence: Origins, Attitudes, Consequences, and several mystery stories. A former academic with a Ph.D. in Sociology and an M.A. in Psychology, she served as executive director of two mental health centers. She is past president of the New England Chapter of Mystery Writers of America and the chapter's newsletter editor. She lives north of Boston.

Lee Driver (Sandra Tooley)

Lee Driver is the pseudonym for author Sandra Tooley. Tooley is the five-time women's club champion at her home course. She can be reached via her Web site at www.sdtooley.com.

Mystery author Sandra Tooley is the creator of the Sam Casey Series and the Chase Dagger Series (written as Lee Driver). She has held a number of interesting and diverse jobs such as administrative assistant to a local mayor, car salesman, sales assistant, assistant to the president of a franchise consulting firm, seminar coordinator, and her most recent and enjoyable job as a casino dealer. The author is particularly fond of the unusual and has carried her interests in the unknown and unbelievable to her writing. Her Sam Casey Series features a Native American detective with the unique ability to hear the dead speak, mixing mystery with paranormal. Her Chase Dagger

Series (written as Lee Driver) includes a young Native American woman who is a shapeshifter, combining mystery with fantasy. The second in the series, *Full Moon-Bloody Moon,* combines mystery with horror.

She has written a number of articles for *Mystery Readers Journal* and is a frequent speaker at area libraries and local mystery reader groups. She is a member of Mystery Writers of America/Midwest Chapter, and Sisters in Crime. Website: www.sdtooley.com

Jon Fabris

Jon Fabris was born and reared in the suburbs of Boston during the Brady Bunch era of the 70s. He graduated from Bentley College in Waltham, Massachusetts, with a computer degree. Presently he lives in rural North Carolina, in a Civil War–era farmhouse next to a log cabin he restored by himself. In addition to being a sought after computer programmer, he is also a skilled sculptor, potter, animator, woodworker, builder, game designer, filmmaker, and writer.

Jan Holloway

Jan Holloway is the author of several mystery genre fictions, most of which have been published in online electronic magazines. Her stories focus on real world paranormal events, a subject that has fascinated her since childhood. Jan has recently relocated from the isolated coast of northern California to her home state of Texas where she lives with her husband and phantom dog, Patti Tzu.

Helen Rhine

Helen is a native Texan, software engineer, and mother of a Navy JAG (he also flies jets and has a marksmanship medal). She currently is attempting screen writing. Perhaps the most obvious question about Helen is whether she is related to the Rhines of the Rhine Research Institute. The answer: She has no idea. Rhine is a fabricated surname, given willy-nilly to people in a group of immigrants from the Rhineland whose "real" German surnames were deemed to be too difficult for the natives to pronounce. Descendants of this group don't know if it was a family group, unrelated people, or a mixture. Only a DNA test would prove it one way or another.

David Terrenoire

David Terrenoire was born in a steel town best remembered for industrial pollution that killed more than 20 people in a single night. That incident is what inspired this story. In 1969, Terrenoire learned how to light cigars in the rain and fish with hand grenades. After the service, he worked as a carpenter, a railroad worker, and a short order cook; now, he writes. He wrote his most recent novel, *Man Down,* for the FBI profiler John Douglas. *Man Down* is due to be released by Simon and Schuster in November, 2002.

Nicholas Knight

Nicholas's stories can be found in anthologies such as The Hour of Pain, The Midnighters Club, The Witching Hour, and Rembrandt is Great, as well as magazines such as Underworlds, Whispers From the Shattered Forum, Futures Mysterious Anthology, and Black Petals, among others. He can be contacted at *knight@darktales.zzn.com*

Elorise Holstad

Elorise is an artist and writer living in Michigan. Her short fiction, which often explores the fascinating subject of paranormal experiences, has appeared in publications as diverse as "Thema" and "Crimestalker Casebook." She's currently at work on a suspense novel.

Patricia Harrington

Patricia Harrington has written mystery fiction that has appeared in *Woman's World, Mystery Time, Futures Mystery Anthology Magazine, Gateway S-F,* and *Orchard Press Mysteries,* as well as on Mystery.Net, Mystery International.com and other Web sites. Her first mystery novel, *Death Stalks the Khmer,* about the murders of a Cambodian couple living near Seattle, was released in trade paperback in 2001. Harrington also is co-editor of *Bullet Points,* an anthology of micro-mystery stories that will be released by Wildside Press in 2003.

George M. Scott

By day, George teaches cultural anthropology at California State University, Long Beach, and by night (and quite often day), he writes in the genres of mystery, suspense, horror, and science fiction. His short fiction has appeared in *Futures Mysterious Anthology, Nefarious: Tales of Mystery, Aphelion: The Webzine of Science Fiction and Fantasy, Without a Clue, deathlings.com,* and *HandHeldCrime.* Following novelist Tim O'Brien's recommendation, George continues to value "story-truth" over "happening-truth." Visit his Web site at www.georgemscott.com.

Nicole Burris

Nicole Burris is a writer, a wife, a stay-at-home mom, and a talk show host for a public radio station who lives in the middle of the United States. She keeps her sanity by cooking, crocheting, and writing every story or poem that comes out of her mind. Her writing has seen publication in many magazines, including, *The Blue Review*, *The First Line*, and *Quantum Muse*. A complete list of her published works can be found at http://hardengnome.dyndns.org/biblio.html.

Sarah Glenn

Sarah is the former editor of Rainbow Wind Magazine and The Trellis.

She works as a database wrangler at the University of Kentucky.

Her interest in psychic phenomena stretches back to her childhood, when she ordered her first deck of ESP cards from the Institute and learned the language of statistics from J.B. Rhine's books. She wanted to grow up to be Kolchak: the Night Stalker, but would settle for Scully.

Jordan Carpenter

Jordan is a student at the University of North Carolina in Chapel Hill, studying screenwriting and psychology. He has had a short piece performed off Broadway in New York, and one of his poems will be included in a CD to be released soon by Poetry.com. He has also worked for over two years as a research assistant in parapsychological studies, rating aspects of experience of hundereds of persons taking part in Ganzfeld ESP sessions, and had an excellent "hit" himself as a ganzfeld subject at the Rhine Center.

Scott Nicholson

Scott Nicholson lives in the Appalachian Mountains of North Carolina. His first novel, *The Red Church*, was inspired by an actual haunted church near his home. His novel *The Harvest* will be released in late 2003. He's also published the story collection *Thank You for the Flowers*. Nicholson's Web site at www.hauntedcomputer.com contains fiction, articles, and author interviews.

Didier Quémener

Didier Quémener is a writer, photographer and psychic-medium. He has lived and worked in his native France and the United States. He holds a bachelor's degree in literature and linguistics from The Sorbonne in Paris. He currently lives in Paris with his wife Adria and their cat Valentine.

Michele Lassig

Michele Lassig holds a Bachelor of Arts degree in English Literature from the California State University at Long Beach. She has won various awards for writing both fiction and non-fiction but is most comfortable with the supernatural/horror genre.

She currently resides in Temecula, CA. with her husband, Don, along with two Bengal cats and a Labrador Retriever. This is the first time one of her works has been anthologized.

Amanda Dickerson

Amanda and her husband live with three cats, one of which is present only in spirit now. In addition to fiction, Amanda also freelances for the gaming industry under the name Amanda Dickerson. Her first RPG adventure book, Dead Sea Murder, is available from Rogue Publishing www.roguepublishing.com). A second one, A Tangled Web, is due out in late 2002 from the same publisher.

Rosemary Edghill

Rosemary Edghill was born long enough ago to have seen Classic Trek on its first outing. As she aged, she put aside her dreams of taking over from Batman, and returned to her first love, writing, where, among other light classics, she is the author of three novels featuring the Wiccan amateur detective Bast. Between books and short stories, she's held the usual writer jobs, including book store clerk, secretary, and grants writer. She can truthfully state that she once killed vampires for a living, and that without any knowledge of medicine has illustrated half-a-dozen medical textbooks. Find her on the web at: http://www.sff.net/people/eluki

Chapter 1

A Little Light on the Subject

By Martha C. Lawrence

Being a psychic investigator has its pluses and minuses: On the upside, you occasionally get the opportunity to shed new light on a dark crime. On the downside, you have to endure the inevitable teasing from the cops. At the moment, I was getting an earful from Detective Callister.

"I thought you psychics didn't like to hear too much about the case ahead of time," he was saying. "Thought maybe the facts interfered with the vibes or something." He widened his eyes and made a rippling motion with his hand. I put a mental caption under the scene: Skeptical Cop Pantomimes Aura Emanations.

"Guess I'm one of those psychics with a penchant for facts. It would help me if you'd lay out what you think's important here."

Most days are sunny in San Diego, and this Wednesday afternoon was no exception. Callister and I were traveling over a winding road that snaked through the scrubby backcountry northeast of the city limits.

"The first thing to know is that this is a kid-glove case," Callister said. "We're talking high profile. Don Shaw owned a big chunk of this town at one time, so a murder at the Shaws' isn't just any old residential homicide—these people are different."

"Different how?"

"Eight-thousand-square-foot house at the top of the hill. A Beemer, Mercedes SL, last year's Acura Legend, and a brand-new Cherokee in the driveway. Nobody's working nine to five, and there are four adults living there. Well, three since the body was found." He shook his head. "Rich people. I'm telling you, they're different from you and me."

"Yeah, they have more money."

Callister took his eyes off the road just long enough to glare at me. "That supposed to be a joke?"

"A very old one. Sorry. Go on with the facts."

"Okay, facts: A 911 call comes in last night. A girl with a fancy foreign accent, Christine somebody, says she just got home and found Natalie Shaw in the backyard. Between the hysteria and the accent it's hard to understand her, but we get that she's pretty sure Natalie Shaw is dead. We drive up there and find a 22–caliber pistol in the bushes and a corresponding hole in the back of Ms. Shaw's head. You can read the report in the file there."

He nodded toward a pocket-style folder in the middle of the seat. I pulled out the report and skimmed the narrative section.

"So the victim was dead when you got there?"

"For at least a day—a stiff in the true sense of the word. And while we were dusting for prints and trying to make sense out of this Christine woman, the other two housemates came home."

"Kaye Shaw and Alex Arno," he said, remembering from the report.

"Yeah. Victim's sister and fiancé."

A traffic light at the intersection up ahead changed from green to red and Callister stomped on the brake. That was the first moment I saw. How do I describe such moments? It's as if time comes to a sudden stop and I'm the only living thing, sole witness to a frozen world. These moments speak to me: Pay attention, Elizabeth; something's important here. But pay attention to what, I wondered now—traffic lights?

Then the moment was over, and everything returned to normal.

" . . . no prints on the gun," Callister was saying, "and everyone has enough alibis to keep us digging for weeks."

"What alibis?"

"The medical examiner narrowed down the time of death to sometime late Monday afternoon or early evening. The boyfriend claims he was driving to L.A. at the time; no witnesses. The sister, Kaye Shaw, claims she was at the barn with her horses; no witnesses. The foreign girl who called in, Christine, claims she was on her way to a class at the university. When we asked her if her classmates could corroborate the story, she said that after she got there, she found out the class had been canceled—likely story, right? But we tracked down the professor this morning, and it turns out she's telling the truth."

"Okay, so everybody's got an alibi. How about physical evidence?"

"Nothing. Like I said, no prints on the gun. At first we thought we had a robbery/homicide, since the victim was missing a pricey engagement ring, but nothing else was taken. The murder weapon was a family heirloom kept under lock and key in an upstairs cabinet. We're pretty sure this was an inside job."

"So you have three likely suspects. Sounds like this is a case you could easily handle without my help."

Callister looked at me as if I'd said something sensible for the very first time.

"No doubt; but like I said, this is high profile. Lieutenant Gresham wants to close the case pronto—like today. We're short on manpower right now, and he seems to think we'll save a lot of time by bringing you in. Says you can quickly point us in the right direction."

I smiled. This was the third case the lieutenant had thrown my way. I was a little concerned that he was expecting instant results, though. Ten years as a research guinea pig at Stanford had proven to me that although my psychic ability is undeniably real, I can't turn it on and off at will, which is why I have a private investigator's license. With most cases, I devote as many hours to methodically poking around as I do to chasing down psychic flashes.

"Who am I to argue with the boss, right?" Callister said. "But I still can't believe I'm going out on a call with a psychic investigator." He shook his head. "Does the department actually pay you for this?"

"Yep. I may be different, but I'm not that different. I work for my wages just like you do."

We rode the next 3 miles in silence as Callister's car climbed the sage-covered foothills surrounding the San Pasqual Valley. At the crest of the range he turned onto a private drive. The luxury cars must have been tucked away in the six-car garage, because the circular driveway was empty when we pulled in and parked. I stuffed the case file into my all-purpose tote and walked with Callister toward the sprawling two-story hacienda.

"You exaggerated," I said as we neared the front door. "This house can't be an inch bigger than 6,000 square feet."

We stopped under the towering entryway, and Callister pushed a lighted button on the wall. The grand scale of the place was intimidating; I was half expecting the wizard of Oz to poke his head out and demand to know who was ringing that bell. When the door opened, I saw that my wizard theory had been way off.

Alex Arno was a thinking woman's version of tall, dark, and handsome. Six feet two or three, he wore understated clothes that nonetheless announced a great body. His light-green eyes were as striking for their intelligence as for their unusual color. Right now they stared steadily at Callister.

"Hello again." His voice, deep and soft, put his sex appeal over the top. "You brought a friend, I see."

Callister glanced sideways at me. "This is Dr. Elizabeth Chase. She's working with the department on the case."

Alex's eyes met mine, and one of his eyebrows went up a notch.

"Special investigator," I said, as if that explained anything.

He stepped back and opened the door wider. "Please, come in."

Once inside, I went about my usual routine. I always begin with a walk-through, checking for psychic impressions such as visual images and gut feelings. My rational mind argued that the ritual would take hours in a house this size, but I pressed on, trusting that my feet would take me where I needed to go.

My initial instinct was to go to the back of the house; it might have been simple curiosity, since this was where the body had been found. I stood at a sliding glass door, looking out at a swimming pool surrounded by a wide, brick terrace. Beyond the terrace, the valley opened up in a magnificent three-dimensional backdrop. Although I had the vague sense that something was significant about this spot, I saw no inner images, felt no gut feelings. As I say, I can't turn my psychic ability on and off like a faucet.

In time, something pulled me to the center of the house and up the stairs. I felt drawn toward an open door at the end of the upstairs hallway. I popped my head inside and found Alex Arno. I wasn't surprised; it didn't take psychic powers to realize a lot of women must be drawn to him.

Alex was kneeling on the floor, disassembling an entertainment system. Around him were several boxes, some taped shut, others half full. Most of the shelves on the bookcase along the wall were empty.

"Go ahead—ask me anything. I'm operating on about 2 hours' sleep, so I can't promise I'll be coherent, but I'll try." His attention was fixed on the back of an amplifier, where he was twisting a long, slender screwdriver.

"What do you do for a living?" I asked.

He looked puzzled. "Seriously? You really don't know?"

"No. Should I?" Perhaps Callister had told him I was a psychic and he was expecting omniscience on my part.

"I'm an actor." He pulled a wallet from his back pocket, flipped it open and handed it to me. Inside was a laminated card from the Screen Actors Guild. "I play Jason on *Malibu Shores.*"

Maybe it wasn't exactly a nine-to-five job, but a role on *Malibu Shores* certainly qualified as gainful employment. I recognized the name of the show but had never seen it.

"Sorry; I'm afraid I don't watch much television."

He smiled. "That's okay. To tell you the truth, it's kind of refreshing not to be recognized."

His smile disappeared, and suddenly my heart began to feel as heavy as if I'd just received news of a death in my family: I felt shock and depression. These weren't my own emotions; they were Alex's, coming into my body loud and clear. I examined the feelings for remorse, guilt, or anything that would point to Alex's part in the murder. I found nothing but grief. Painful.

I handed his wallet back. "So you were engaged to the victim."

He put the wallet back in his pocket and stared at the carpet, nodding slowly. In the silence that followed, I watched his face and reminded myself that Alex Arno was an actor. Was the tear forming at the corner of his eye induced by some method technique? I doubted it but couldn't be sure. I broke the silence with the obvious question.

"Do you have any idea who might have killed Natalie?"

When he looked up, his features were tight and anguished.

"I have a perfectly excellent idea who killed her: Kaye did. I assumed you people were here to arrest her. You are going to arrest her, aren't' you?" He searched my face and, when he didn't see an answer, pressed his eyes shut. "Please don't tell me she's getting away with this. That cocky little———."

"Why would Kaye kill her sister?"

"She hated her." He picked up the screwdriver and resumed twisting. "The kind of hate you only see in families—know what I mean? Like psychotic sibling rivalry. Anything Nattie got, Kaye wanted for herself: attention, money, even me. I always knew Kaye had a thing for me. She finally came on to me a few days ago; I turned her down. Maybe she flipped over that. Who the hell knows."

"You've mentioned your thoughts about Kaye to the police?"

"Of course I have. I'm sure they think I had a better reason to kill Nat than Kaye did." He coiled some electrical wiring and tossed it into a box.

"What would that be?"

"Isn't the boyfriend or husband always the first suspect?"

I shrugged.

"Natalie and I were having problems." His shoulders sagged. "We'd had a big fight." He gestured across the room with a sweep of his arm. "Hence the moving boxes. I have a place in North Hollywood, but off-season I lived here with Natalie."

"Did she break off the engagement?"

"No. At least, she was wearing her engagement ring the last time I saw her."

"What was your fight all about?"

"There's not a simple answer to that. Basically, Nat wasn't ready to make the compromises marriage requires. She was used to being independent, traveled around the world alone." His smile returned. "Talk about a stubborn redhead. The engagement ring's a perfect example: She wouldn't let me give her a diamond. She had to get the ring on her own. She said it had to be a special stone." Alex reached into his back pocket and retrieved the wallet. This time he flipped to a photo and handed it to me.

I studied the picture. Alex and his former fiancée were posed in classic engagement-photo stance. Framed by a full head of shining red hair, Natalie's face was interesting but by no means classically beautiful. She was smiling warmly, her left hand resting on Alex's shoulder. My eye was immediately drawn to the gem on her ring finger, extraordinary for its size as well as its ruby-red color.

"Did that bother you, Natalie's independence?"

"No, what bothered me was not being together enough. I wanted her to marry me and move to Los Angeles. I was sick of this house meaning more to her than I did."

"This was her house, then?"

"Hers and Kaye's. Inherited from their father. Their mom died several years ago. Their dad left them the house and a portfolio worth God knows how much."

"All Kaye's now?"

"Until you arrest her."

"I won't be arresting anybody. I'm just an investigator."

I wandered from Alex's room out into the hallway. As I neared the stairs, a door opened and a woman with pale blond hair stepped into my path. She looked directly at me, and her dark-blue eyes widened. She was young, nowhere near 30 yet.

"I'm with the police," I said. "You're the one who found the body?"

She nodded and gripped the banister.

"Are you all right? You look as if you don't feel well."

"I feel horrible. I've never lost anyone this close to me before." Her European accent was heavy. Although she spoke excellent English, understanding the words required active listening.

"Were you related to Natalie Shaw?" I asked.

"No, but she was like a sister to me. We were very close."

"How did you meet?"

"Natalie was setting up a business in Denmark. That's what Nat did; she helped American companies get established in Europe—Madrid, Paris, Oslo, even Moscow. I worked for the company she set up in Copenhagen 3 years ago."

"How did you end up here?"

"I'd always dreamed of studying in the U.S. We talked about it a lot. Last year she offered to let me live here while I earned my college degree."

"So you've lost a friend."

"More than a friend. I'll probably return to Denmark now. Kaye doesn't like me, and I can't afford to stay on my own."

We stood in silence for a few moments, looking down at the first floor below. I opened myself to Christine's energy. This time I picked up physical sensations: a rapid heartbeat and quick, shallow breathing—fear. Brought on by the shock of discovering her friend's body? Or was Christine afraid because she had something to hide? I turned to face her.

"What do you think happened to Natalie?"

"I don't know." Her blue eyes locked onto mine. "I'm trying to accept that either Alex or Kaye shot her, but I can't believe it." She looked down the hallway toward Alex's room and lowered her voice. "Maybe Alex did shoot her. The day before yesterday, they had a terrible fight."

"Alex and Natalie, you mean."

She nodded. "I'd heard them fight before, but not like that afternoon on the terrace. I was watching from that window." She pointed to the other end of the hallway, where a bay window looked out onto the backyard.

"Could you hear what they were saying?"

She shook her head. "Not really. Just their loud voices." But something registered in Christine's mind; I saw the memory flicker in her eyes.

"What was that?" I asked.

"What?"

"That thought. The one that crossed your mind just now."

She looked surprised but answered willingly. "I was just thinking that I did hear the last thing Alex yelled as Natalie walked away. He said, 'The *hell* with her!'"

"Do you know who he was talking about?"

Again she shook her head, more slowly this time. "No. After that I saw Nat get in her car and drive off. Alex went back inside, and then I heard him drive away, just before I had to leave for school."

"When did you find the body?"

"Not until a whole day later, yesterday around sunset. I went out to do a few laps in the pool and————." She put her fingers to her mouth. Her voice turned to a whimper. "I saw her leg first, under the azalea bushes. I knew it must be Nat . . . I recognized the shoe she wore, but her skin was gray."

"What did you do then?"

She cleared her throat and steadied her voice. "I ran into the house and called 911."

"Were Alex and Kaye home?"

"I hadn't seen Alex since the day before, when he'd been fighting with Nat. He came back last night just after the police and the ambulance got here."

"How about Kaye? Was she at work?"

"No, Kaye doesn't have a job. She came home about 15 minutes after Alex did. She'd been at the stable all day. She often is, with her horses."

"Was Kaye home the afternoon Alex and Natalie had the fight?"

"No. She didn't get home until after I left for school."

"So it's possible that Kaye could have killed Natalie while you were at school."

"I don't know." Christine shook her head. "I just don't know."

Detective Callister appeared in the downstairs hallway and called up to us.

"Could the two of you come down here a minute?"

When we reached the bottom of the stairs, Callister led us into the living room. He glanced at Christine and pointed to the coffee table.

"Do you want to explain what these were doing in your room?"

Christine and I walked over for a closer look. On the tabletop were a blue topaz necklace and a pair of pearl drop earrings. Callister stared hard at Christine.

"Kaye Shaw says she found them in your dresser drawer this morning. Says they belonged to her sister."

Christine looked up, dazed.

"They did belong to Nat. She lent them to me. Kaye doesn't think I stole them, does she?" Callister didn't answer. "You don't think—" She looked to me, then back to Callister. "Am I in trouble?"

Again he didn't answer her. He simply walked out of the room.

Christine and I watched him go. I hadn't liked the look on his face, and again I felt Christine's fear. I had the sense of a frightened animal, injured and unable to fend for itself.

"You might want to get a lawyer," I said.

"What? Is that policeman saying he thinks I killed Natalie over a pair of pearl earrings? That's ridiculous. Everyone knows how much I loved her. Besides, if I was going to kill and rob her, don't you think I'd take something of real value, like her engagement ring?"

A similar thought had crossed my mind. I knew a little about jewelry, and the baubles on the coffee table weren't worth pilfering, let alone killing for.

A phone rang in the next room, and Christine excused herself to answer it. I took a seat on the sofa and pulled the case file from my tote bag. I turned to a list of the evidence that had been gathered from the crime scene last night and reviewed the personal effects found on the victim's body: two diamond-stud earrings and a gold-plated hairclip. No engagement ring.

That was the second moment I *saw*. The evidence list was printed on a pale green police department form. As if I'd been staring too long, the paper suddenly turned a translucent, glowing red. Most people would chalk up that experience to eyestrain; I knew better.

I walked through the kitchen area to the sliding doors at the back of the house. Through the glass I could see Detective Callister talking with Kaye Shaw on the terrace. She was unusually petite and prettier than Natalie was in Alex's engagement photo but somehow not nearly as attractive. She was listening to Callister with her slender arms crossed over her chest. She nodded, and Callister started back toward the house. I slid the door open for him.

"If you're going to interview her, I'd like to listen in," he said.

I closed the door behind him.

"I'd rather you didn't." I made a rippling motion with my hand and gave him a smile. "Interferes with the vibes, you know?"

He rolled his eyes. "Whatever," he said as he left the room.

For the next few moments, I watched Kaye, standing at the edge of the terrace. Rigid as a statue, she stared across the valley.

I slid the door open and walked out to join her. Kaye's close-cropped hair was a fiery, chemical-induced red. Her features in profile were stern.

"I'm sorry about your sister," I said as I approached.

"Thank you." She didn't turn to look at me when she said it.

"I'm with the police."

"I figured."

The air was temperate, but at that moment I wanted a jacket. I rubbed my arms to warm them up. I didn't feel safe standing next to Kaye Shaw. I picked up a reckless, volatile energy that made me jittery, the way you might feel walking past a downed power line that could suddenly snake your way. I didn't know where to begin, so I started in the middle.

"I've been talking to your housemate, Christine. She thinks that perhaps Alex Arno killed Natalie."

Kaye was shaking her head before I'd even finished my sentence.

"That's ludicrous." She thrust her hands into her jacket pockets. "No, I've already told the police that I'm certain Christine shot my sister." Kaye was a terrible liar. Her eyes darted away from mine like cockroaches scuttling from the light.

"Why would Christine do a thing like that?"

"She lost her head in a jealous rage." Kaye directed her comment to the sky overhead.

"She was envious of Natalie's possessions, you mean? Her jewelry and whatnot?"

"Christine is in love with Alex." Kaye looked up at me through mascara-coated lashes. "She couldn't bear the thought of losing him to Natalie."

More likely Kaye couldn't bear the thought of losing Alex to Natalie, I thought.

"Christine says Alex and your sister had a bad fight the day before her body was found. Isn't it possible that he could have shot her in anger?"

I could see Kaye's hands balling into fists inside her jacket pockets.

"Alex? Never. Christine was desperate. She knew she couldn't stay on here once Natalie got married."

"Have you asked Christine to leave?"

Kaye wrinkled her nose. "I assume the police will arrest her. She stole my sister's jewelry, you know."

"Is that right?" I tried but failed to catch her eye. "What about Alex? Will he be leaving too?"

Kaye's fingers worried the contents of her right-hand jacket pocket.

"There's absolutely no reason for Alex to leave. He'll always be welcome here."

The front Kaye put up was as brittle as icicles. I wondered if rattling her would break something loose.

"If your sister had married Alex, they would have moved to Los Angeles. Isn't that right?"

"Possibly. I don't really know." Her fingers continued to fidget.

"Now Alex is leaving here anyway, isn't he?"

Kaye didn't answer. Her attention was fixed on a hawk circling over the valley. Hard questioning wasn't getting me anywhere, so I followed her gaze and tried some flattery.

"This is such a beautiful spot."

"I grew up on this property," Kaye said dreamily. "I'll never leave it." She set her jaw firmly and the hint of a smile played on her lips.

"I suppose if Natalie had moved to Los Angeles, she would have wanted to sell the property and split the proceeds."

Kaye crossed her arms over her chest again and shrugged. My eyes were drawn to her jacket pocket. That was the third moment I saw. The insight came as a vivid mental image of Alex and Natalie's engagement photo. The picture appeared in exact detail, right down to the victim's ruby-colored engagement ring.

Years of experience had taught me to trust these unbidden visions. I thrust my hand into Kaye's jacket pocket. She turned to defend herself, but too late. My fingers found the hard metal and brought the ring into the light. The stone glittered in the rays of the setting sun, but my confidence was quickly replaced by bafflement. To my utter disbelief, the gem wasn't ruby; it was a clear, bright green. Kaye looked at me with disdain.

"Do you always go around picking people's pockets?"

Feebly I handed the emerald back to her. "I'm sorry. I thought. . . ."

I expected her to throw a fit and demand that I leave the premises at once. Instead, her enigmatic smile reappeared, and she turned back toward the view.

Why wasn't she angry with me? Her reaction was odd, as though she were trying to protect our mutual dignity by pretending the scuffle had never happened. She pointed toward the east.

"That's the San Diego Wild Animal Park over there," she said in the same dreamy voice. "Sometimes at night the wind carries the sound of the lions' roaring all the way up here from across the valley."

Clearly something wasn't right with Kaye Shaw. Last night paramedics had dragged her sister's corpse out from under the azalea bushes, and now she was waxing poetic about lions. I played along.

"Isn't it strange the way the big cats are so lethargic in the daytime? It's as if they change into entirely different animals in the darkness."

I thought about what I'd just said, and about how the changing light affects all living things: plants, animals, and human beings. That was the final instance I *saw,* only this time it came as a flash of understanding—about change, about light.

"Kaye," I said casually, "would you come inside with me for a moment?"

She turned to me slowly. "Why?"

"I'd just like to finish talking inside. It's so beautiful out here it's distracting me." I smiled. "Humor me. I'll only take a moment or two more of your time, I promise."

"Well, I'd rather. . . . Here, let's sit on the bench over here. That way you can turn away from the view if you want to."

"I really need to go inside." I took her by the arm and guided her gently toward the house. "Please, this won't take but a minute."

She followed along complacently enough at first, but the closer we got to the house, the more she resisted. As we neared the back door I could hear her heels scraping across the bricks.

"You have no right to be handling me this way!" she snapped.

But tiny Kaye was no match for me, and pulling her into the house was almost too easy. I flipped the light switch on the wall and led her into the center of the kitchen. Again I reached into her pocket and brought out the ring. Under the glow of the incandescent lights, the stone that had been bright green in the sunlight glowed red as a live coal.

"Alex was right," I said. "You *are* cocky, holding your sister's engagement ring right under our noses."

Her perfectly painted mouth formed a little O, but she recovered quickly and started talking fast.

"Natalie's engagement ring was a ruby—everyone thought so. You're making a mistake. This clearly isn't Natalie's ruby."

"Everyone thought so?"

She tried to snatch the ring from me. "I'm telling you that's not Natalie's ruby!"

I held the ring high above her reach and studied it through squinted eyes.

"No, it's her alexandrite," I said. "Catherine the Great's favorite gemstone, named for the czar Alexander of Russia. Natalie bought it to honor her own

Alex, didn't she? Alexandrite looks red indoors and in photographs, under artificial light; but out in the sunshine it turns green. Only the finest stones make such a complete color change. This is an exceptional specimen. Natalie probably found it on one of her trips to Moscow."

"It doesn't prove I killed her."

"The last time anyone saw this ring, Natalie was wearing it, and she was alive. How did a dead woman's ring get into your possession?"

"It doesn't prove I killed her," she repeated. Kaye's eyes were no longer darting away. They bored into mine, radiating hate and determination.

Someone coughed. I looked up to see Detective Callister in the doorway. Kaye whirled around at the sound.

"I think we'd better discuss this at the police station, Ms. Shaw." He stepped forward and took Kaye by the arm. "Let's go."

As he led her away, Callister caught my eye. He made a rippling motion with his free hand, gave me a thumbs-up, and winked.

Chapter 2

Cold Case

By L. L. Bartlett

"You're not the first psychic to come through Paula's apartment, Mr. Resnick."

Hands on hips, Dr. Krista Marsh stood before me. Her heels gave her an inch or more on me. Blond and lithe, and clad in a turquoise dress with jet beads resting on her ample breasts, she was the best-looking thing in that lower–middle class apartment.

"I don't use that term. Con artists, liars, and frauds take advantage of people with problems. I'm just someone who sometimes knows more than I'm comfortable knowing."

Truth was, I hadn't wanted to be there at all, giving my impressions on the fate of four-year-old Eric Devlin. He'd gone missing on an early-autumn evening some 8 months before. One minute he'd been there—riding his Big Wheel in front of the apartment building—and the next he was gone. Like every other good citizen, I'd read all the stories in the newspapers and seen the kid's picture on posters and on TV. The only place I hadn't seen it was on the back of a milk carton.

I was there as a favor to my brother—actually, my older half brother—Dr. Richard Alpert, who'd joined me on that cold, gray evening in early May. Richard was Paula Devlin's internist at the university's low-income clinic. He liked Paula and hated how not knowing her son's fate was tearing her apart. He hoped I could shed some light on the kid's disappearance.

I'm not sure why Dr. Marsh was there. Maybe as Paula's therapist she thought she could protect her patient from someone like me.

So, there I stood, in the middle of Paula's modestly furnished living room, trying to soak up vibes that might tell me the little boy's fate.

Paula waited in the doorway looking fearful as I examined the heart of her home, which she'd transformed into a cottage industry, distributing posters, pins, and flyers in the search for the boy—all to no avail. Vacuum cleaner tracks on the carpet showed her hasty cleanup prior to our arrival. Too thin and looking older than her 32 years, Paula's spirit and her determination to find her missing son had sustained her over the long months she'd been alone. The paper had never mentioned a Mr. Devlin.

"I don't know if I can help you," I told Paula.

She flashed an anxious look at Richard, then back to me.

"Where would you like to start, Mr. Resnick?"

"Call me Jeff. How about Eric's room?"

A 60–watt bulb illuminated the gloom as the four of us trudged down a narrow hallway. Paula opened the door to a small bedroom, flipped a light switch, and ushered us in. "It's just the way he left it."

I doubted that, because the bed was made and all the toys and games were neatly stacked on shelves under the room's only window—not a speck of dust. A racecar bedspread and matching drapes gave a clue to the boy's chief interest—so did the scores of dented, paint-scraped cars and trucks. I picked up a purple and black dune buggy, sensing a trace of the boy's aura. He'd been a rambunctious kid with the beginnings of a smart mouth.

"He was a very lively child."

"He's all boy, that's for sure," his mother said proudly.

She hadn't noticed I'd used the past tense. Either that or she was in deep denial; I'd known little Eric was dead the moment I entered the apartment.

I gave her a half-hearted smile and replaced the toy on the shelf. There wasn't much else to see. I shouldered my way past the others and wandered back to the living room. They tried not to bump into each other as they followed.

A 4–foot poster of Eric's smiling face dominated the west wall. He'd been small for his age, cute, with sandy hair and a sprinkle of freckles across the bridge of his nose.

An image flashed through my mind: a child's hand reaching for a glass.

I hitched in a breath, grateful my back was to Dr. Marsh. A mix of powerful emotions erupted as though my presence had ignited an emotional powder keg. Like repelling magnets, guilt and relief waged a war, practically raining from the walls and ceiling.

Composing myself, I turned, a disquieting depression settling over me.

"Ms. Devlin———."

She stepped forward. "Call me Paula."

"Paula. Did Dr. Alpert tell you how this works?"

"He said you absorb emotions, interpret them, and that sometimes you get knowledge."

"That's right." More or less, I thought. "There's a lot of background emotion here. May I hold your hand for a moment? I need to see if it's coming from you, or if it's resident in the building."

Without hesitation, she held out her hand, her expression full of hope. And that's what I got from her: Hope, desperation, and deep despair. She loved that little boy, heart and soul. And there was suspicion, too, but not of me.

I released her hand and let out the breath I hadn't realized I'd been holding.

"Paula, ever heard the expression about a person taking up all the air in the room?" Her brows puckered in confusion. "You're broadcasting so many emotions I can't sort them out. I know you want to stay, but I can't do what I have to if you're here."

"But he's my son," she protested.

Dr. Marsh stepped closer, placed a comforting hand on Paula's shoulder. "You want him to give you a true reading."

I turned on the psychiatrist. "I'm not a fortune-teller, Dr. Marsh."

"I didn't mean to offend," she said without sincerity.

"I'll go if you say so, Krista." Paula grabbed her windbreaker from the closet and headed for the door. Once she was gone, my anxiety eased, and I no longer needed to play diplomat.

"What're you getting?" Richard asked.

"The kid's dead—been dead since day one. He wasn't frightened either, not until the very last minute."

"You're talking murder," Richard said. "Not Paula."

"No. I'm sure of that."

Dr. Marsh eyed me critically, brows arched, voice coolly professional. "Are you well acquainted with sensing death, Mr. Resnick?"

"More than I'd like." I glanced at Richard. "What's this about a pervert in the neighborhood?"

His eyes narrowed. "It hasn't been reported in the media, but Paula told me about the cops' prime suspect. A convicted pedophile lived three units down at the time the boy disappeared. They've had him in for questioning five or six times but haven't been able to wring a confession out of him. How'd you know?"

"From Paula just now. She's afraid he took her kid."

Dr. Marsh frowned. She probably figured I was just some shyster running a con. I can't say I was sorry to disappoint her.

"You got something else," Richard said. He knew me well.

"I saw something, but it doesn't make sense." I told them about the vision.

"Close your eyes; focus on it," he directed.

I shot a look at Dr. Marsh, saw the contempt in her gaze. Skepticism came with the territory.

My eyes slid shut and I allowed myself to relax, trying to relive that fleeting moment.

"What do you see?" Richard said.

"A kid's hand reaching for a glass."

"Is it Eric?"

"I don't know."

"Describe the glass."

I squeezed my eyes tighter, trying to replay the image. "A clear tumbler."

"What's inside?"

"Liquid. Brown—chocolate milk?"

"Look up the child's arm," Richard directed. "Can you see his clothes?"

The cuff of a sleeve came into focus. "Yeah."

"The color?"

I exhaled a breath. Like a camera pulling back, the vision expanded to include the child's chest. "Blue . . . a decal of—" The image winked out. "Damn!"

"Give it a couple of minutes and try again," Richard advised.

Uncomfortable under Dr. Marsh's stare, I wandered into the kitchen again. I couldn't shake the feeling of . . . dread? Whatever it was surrounded me, squeezing my chest so I couldn't take a decent breath.

Hands clenched at his side, Richard studied me in silence. We'd been through this before, and his eyes mirrored the concern he wouldn't express for fear of embarrassing me. He knew just what these little empathic forays cost me.

Turning away from his scrutiny, I went back into the boy's gloomy bedroom. Though banished from the apartment, Paula's anguish was still palpable. How many times had she stood in that doorway and cried for her child?

I ran my hands along all the surfaces a kid Eric's age could've touched. After 8 months there was so little left of him. His clothes in the dresser drawers, neatly folded and stacked, bore no trace of his aura. I pulled back the bedspread, picked up the pillow, closed my eyes, and pressed it against my face. Tendrils of fear curled through me.

Airlessness.

Darkness.

Nothingness.

Death.

A rustling noise at the open doorway broke the spell. Dr. Marsh studied me as she must have once looked at rats in a lab. Her appraising gaze was sharp, her irritation almost palpable. Even so, she looked like she just walked off the set of some TV drama instead of the university's Medical Center campus. I'd bet her brown eyes flashed when she smiled. Not that she had.

"I understand you've done this before," she said.

"Define 'this,'" I said.

"Helping the police in murder investigations."

"Once or twice."

"Are you always successful?"

"So far," I answered honestly and replaced the pillow, smoothing the spread back into place.

"And what do you get out of it?"

Her scornful tone annoyed me.

"Usually a miserable headache. What is this, an interrogation?"

"I'm merely curious," she said. "My, we are defensive, aren't we?"

"I can't answer for 'we,' but I'm certainly not here to fence with you, doctor. If you'll excuse me."

Brushing past her, I headed back to the kitchen. The smooth walls and ceiling were practically vibrating. Eric's childish laughter had once echoed in this room, though nothing of him remained there. I frowned; I still didn't have the whole picture, and Dr. Marsh had rattled me.

I opened all the cupboards. The remnants of Eric's babyhood—plastic formula bottles and Barney sippy cups—had been stowed on the higher shelves. No Nestle's Quik.

"Any conclusions?" Richard asked.

"Whatever I'm getting seems strongest in the kitchen." I leaned against the counter, stared at the refrigerator covered with torn-out coloring book pages attached with yellowing scotch tape. Something about it bothered me. I opened the door.

Paula wasn't taking care of herself. A quart of outdated skim milk, half a loaf of sliced white bread, a sagging pizza box, and three 2–liter bottles of diet cola looked lonely in the full-sized fridge. No chocolate milk. An opened box of tater tots, a sprinkling of damp crumbs, and a couple of ice cube trays were the only things in the freezer. Everything looked completely innocent, yet something was terribly wrong.

"Think all the apartments are set up the same?" I asked Richard.

He shrugged.

Pushing away from the counter, I walked through the rooms one last time just to make certain—and then paused in the kitchen before heading into the building's entryway. No trace of Eric, but something else lurked there.

Hands thrust into her jacket pockets, Paula waited by the security door, looking pale and frightened. I couldn't even muster a comforting smile for her.

"Chocolate milk," I said.

She blinked.

"Did Eric drink it?" I pressed.

"He loved it, but was allergic to chocolate. I never had it in the house."

I glanced up the shadowy staircase. A wounded animal will always climb. Eric hadn't been wounded, but something had lured him up those stairs. I took three steps and staggered against the banister when a knife thrust of pain pierced the back of my head—fierce, but unlike the skull-pounding headaches these intuitive flashes usually brought.

"You okay?" Richard asked, concerned. Was he feeling guilty for roping me into this?

I leaned against the wall, closed my eyes, and tried to catch my breath. "Who lives upstairs?" I asked Paula through gritted teeth.

"Mark and Cheryl Spencer in apartment D. A retired widow, Mrs. Anna Jarowski, lives on the other side."

"Did they see Eric the day he disappeared?"

Paula shook her head. "No."

I took another step. The heaviness clamped tighter around my chest. I'd felt something when I first entered the building, but I'd assumed it belonged to Paula.

I'd been wrong.

"I want to talk to them."

"They've been cleared," Paula insisted.

I didn't budge.

She bristled with impatience. "You came here to find answers about my son, not waste time questioning my neighbors. They've been cleared by the police, and badgered by the press."

"Paula," Richard said gently. "It can't hurt."

Finally she tore her gaze from mine and stormed back for her apartment, letting the door bang shut.

Richard took the lead, leaving Dr. Marsh and me to follow. He went to knock on the first apartment door, but I shook my head. He gave me a quizzical look and I nodded toward the opposite door.

Richard crossed the 10 or so feet to the adjacent door and knocked. We waited. Were Richard and Dr. Marsh struck by the unnatural quiet in that building?

The door opened on a chain. Steel gray, no-nonsense eyes peered at us. "Yes?"

"Mrs. Jarowski, I'm Doctor Alpert and this is Dr. Marsh," Richard said with authority. "We're from the university. May we speak with you?"

Mrs. Jarowski blinked in surprise. "Did Dr. Adams send you?"

Dr. Marsh gave Richard an inquisitive look, but he said nothing.

Mrs. Jarowski looked at us with suspicion. "Can I see some identification?"

"Of course," Richard said, and reached into his coat pocket.

"I left mine in my purse," Dr. Marsh said.

Mrs. Jarowski scrutinized Richard's hospital security badge. "Please come in," she said at last.

I didn't want to. I wanted to go home. I wanted to be anywhere but this place that smelled of mothballs and sour cabbage.

She ushered us inside, stepping into her kitchen. Anna Jarowski was a compact woman in her mid-sixties. Her short, silver hair was caught back from her forehead with a barrette, like something out of the 1950s. Dressed in a faded housecoat, no makeup brightened her wan features, leaving her looking colorless and ill.

She glanced at me. "I'm sorry, but I didn't catch your name."

"Jeffrey Resnick," I said, forcing a smile, and shoved my hand at her.

The woman eyed my outstretched hand, hesitated, and then took it.

Our eyes locked. Her hand convulsed around mine. Peering past the layers of her personality, I looked straight into her soul.

A tremor ran through me. I pulled back my hand, my legs suddenly rubbery. Sweat soaked into my shirt collar and I took a shaky breath, hoping to quell the queasiness in my gut.

"Mind if I sit?"

She gestured toward the couch in the living room, but I lurched into the kitchen and fell into a maple chair at the worn Formica table. The others followed, leaning against the counters, looking like wallflowers at a dance. Mrs. Jarowski moved to stand in front of the refrigerator, arms at her side, body tense. The open floor plan allowed me to look into the apartment. Like the kitchen set, the rest of the furniture was shabby but immaculate. Mrs. Jarowski's faded housecoat was freshly ironed. She probably spent her days scrubbing the life out of things.

I looked around the sterile kitchen, an exact replica of the room directly below us—the floor, the counters, the cupboards, everything—right down to the white, plastic switch plates. Three embroidered dishtowels lined the oven door pull, Mrs. Jarowski's only concession to decor. The tug of conflicting emotions was even stronger than downstairs. We looked at one another for a few moments in awkward silence.

Mrs. Jarowski cleared her throat. "Are you a doctor, too?" she asked me.

"You might say I'm an expert on headaches. Tell me about yours, Mrs. Jarowski. Migraines, aren't they?"

The old lady's sharp eyes softened. "I've had a lot of tests, even a couple of CAT scans, but they've all been inconclusive. I've been told they're due to stress. One doctor said they're psychosomatic."

"I doubt that," I said, winning a grateful nod. "They get pretty bad sometimes, don't they?"

She nodded again, looking hopeful.

"I can sure identify with that. I got mugged last year by a teenager with a baseball bat cracked my skull. Since then I get some really bad ones. I'm working up to a doozie right now."

"What does that have to do with me?" she asked, an odd catch to her voice.

"Nothing. Tell me about Eric Devlin."

Her back went rigid. "I've already told the police; I don't know anything about his disappearance."

"His mother said he was 'all boy,' but I get the feeling he was a little hellion: a noisy kid; kind of a brat, really."

Dr. Marsh glared at me as if I'd blasphemed God Almighty. The whole city had developed a reverence for the missing child.

Mrs. Jarowski didn't share that feeling.

"He used to ride up and down the sidewalk on one of those big plastic tricycles for hours at a time—up and down, up and down. They make one hell of a racket, don't they?"

Her lips tightened. The tension in that kitchen nearly crackled.

My nausea cranked up a notch and I loosened my tie. On the verge of passing out, I rested my elbows on the table to steady myself.

"When I have one of these sick headaches, I have to lie down in a dark room with absolute quiet. Otherwise I think I'd go insane. That ever happen to you?"

Mrs. Jarowski's gaze pinned me.

The vision streaked before my mind's eye: Eric, eyes round with anticipation, his small hand clutching the tumbler of chocolate milk, something his mother would never let him have; Paula calling to him from somewhere outside; the half empty glass falling to the spotless floor, shattering; chocolate milk splashing the walls and cabinet doors.

"It's peaceful and quiet these days," I said. "Like a morgue." My gaze drifted to the full-sized refrigerator and then back to her. I swallowed down bile. "You want to show me?"

Her cheeks flushed. She wouldn't look at me.

Dr. Marsh and Richard looked at me in confusion. Mrs. Jarowski seemed to weigh the question, her solemn gaze focused on the floor.

"The freezer, right?"

Mrs. Jarowski's anger slipped, replaced by a tremendous sense of guilt but not, I noticed, remorse.

"Dr. Alpert, maybe you should have a look."

She held her ground.

Richard brushed past me to cross the room in three steps. His eyes bored into hers and she backed down, moving aside. The freezer door swung open. A heavy, black plastic garbage bag filled the space. He worked on the twist tie, pulled back the plastic. His breath caught and he slammed the door, suddenly pale.

"Holy Christ."

The quartz wall clock ticked loudly, but time seemed to stand still.

At last Richard moved to the phone and punched 911. "I'm calling to report a body at 456 Weatherby, apartment C."

Richard swallowed as he listened to the voice on the other end of the phone. Dr. Marsh blinked in confused revulsion.

Stony-faced, Mrs. Jarowski turned, her slippered feet scuffing across the vinyl floor as she headed for the living room. She sat down on her faded couch, picked up the remote control, and turned on the television.

Finally Richard hung up the phone.

"Dr. Marsh, can you watch Mrs. J until the police get here?" I asked.

She nodded, still looking shell-shocked.

I squinted up at Richard. "Maybe you could help me to the bathroom. I don't want to barf on Mrs. J's nice, clean floor."

Breathing shallowly, I sat back against the lumpy couch, a hand covering my eyes to blot out the piercing light. After more than an hour, two of my pills still hadn't put a dent in the throbbing headache.

The cops had already taken Mrs. Jarowski away. The medical examiner arrived, and the crime photographer was still flashing pictures in the kitchen. The place was full of cops, and the murmur of a dozen voices drilled through my skull.

"Can I get you something, Mr. Resnick?" Lieutenant Brewer of the Buffalo Metropolitan Police stood over me. The chunky, balding cop still seemed taken aback that his case had been broken by an outsider.

I squinted up at him. "Yeah. Assure my privacy—don't give the press my name. The last thing I want is publicity."

"Okay, but answer me this: How'd you know?"

"I don't know how it works, it just does."

"The old lady waived her rights. Said she'd heard Ms. Devlin had signed a new 2-year lease and decided she'd had enough of the noise. She lured the kid up here and made him quiet—permanently."

"And the chocolate milk?" Richard asked me.

"The lure of a forbidden treat. Mrs. J ground up sleeping pills, had him drink it," I said. "When he was dopey, she planned to smother him."

I thought about it, and remembered what I'd seen when I'd touched her. Fury gave her the strength to hold the boy, who'd struggled in those last minutes. She'd sealed his nose and mouth with a wad of freshly pressed linen dishtowels, pinning him against the floor until his body slackened, his small chest no longer heaving. Then she'd heard Paula Devlin frantically calling for her son. Anna Jarowski sat beside the dead boy for a long time triumphant in the knowledge she'd finally silenced her intolerably noisy neighbor.

I looked up at Brewer. "I take it you haven't searched the place yet."

"Call me paranoid, but I'm waiting for a warrant. No way do I want this thrown out on a technicality."

"You'll find what's left of the tricycle in one of the closets. She's got a hacksaw. Been cutting it up and sneaking it out in the trash for the past 8 months."

Dr. Marsh elbowed her way through the crowd in the kitchen. She'd been gone about an hour—breaking the news to the boy's mother, no doubt.

"How's Paula?" Richard asked.

"I gave her a sedative. Now that her mother's here, I think she'll be all right." She looked at me. "How are you, Jeff?" Her icy veneer had melted, her best bedside manner now firmly in place.

"Sick."

"But you've got to feel good about what you've done."

I frowned. "I made two women miserable. Why would that make me feel good?"

She seemed puzzled by my answer, but I didn't have the energy to explain it to her. "Dr. Marsh, you said another psychic came here. What did she tell Paula?"

"That the boy was well and living in a small town down South, anxious to be back home with his mother."

Poor Paula.

"You need me anymore?" I asked the detective.

He shook his head. "Go home before you keel over."

I glanced at my brother. "Now would be a good time, Rich."

I moved on shaky legs. Richard and Dr. Marsh steadied me on the stairs. We ducked under the crime scene tape and they pushed me through the throng of press as we headed for Richard's Lincoln Town Car.

Dr. Marsh crushed her business card into my palm. "Call me." Her voice was husky, excited, like a rock star's groupie.

Reporters and camera persons swarmed as she slammed the car door. Richard left her to deal with them, taking off with a squeal and leaving rubber on the asphalt.

"Sharks," he muttered.

I leaned against the headrest and considered my first consultation—by all counts, a royal success.

Then why did I feel so dirty?

Chapter 3

Hidden in Plain Sight

By Skye Alexander

Sebastian Avery never learned which toes to step on and which to dance around. This time, the bad boy of the art world had gone too far.

"Avery's talent as an artist was surpassed only by his talent for making enemies," the reporter concluded as Charlotte McCrae aimed the remote at the TV and clicked off the morning news. But the picture of the lumpy body bag being wheeled from the crime scene lingered painfully in her mind. Even worse was the vision her imagination conjured up of Sebastian's body the way the police found it: tied to a wooden post in his loft apartment and pierced by dozens of arrows. Her stomach churned, threatening to eject the breakfast she'd just eaten, and she took a few deep breaths to calm herself.

With a shaking hand, she picked up her coffee mug and went into the bedroom, which also served as her office. Above a paper-strewn desk hung one of Sebastian's early paintings. He'd given it to her when she'd graduated from art school and he hadn't. Like most of his work, it blended contemporary satire with Old World technique, expressing the artist's opinion in a manner that was wickedly funny to everyone except the object of his black humor. After two decades, the picture still irked her every time she looked at it, reminding her that she wasn't a better artist than he was; she was just better at jumping through hoops. She'd kept it for the first 10 years because she refused to admit how much the truth hurt; for the last 10 because it had become valuable. Now, she realized in the wake of his death, the painting's worth had probably doubled.

As sadness and a sense of loss began to replace the initial shock, Charlotte sat down at the desk and sipped her coffee, trying to imagine who Sebastian could have pushed to the point of murder. Provoking people was his specialty—in fact, he believed art *should* provoke, not lull you to sleep. Oddly enough, though, he often seemed surprised at the furor his work created. Like many people born under the sign of Aries, Sebastian possessed a childlike naiveté that prevented him from seeing his "pranks" had a cruel edge that cut deep into his subjects' weak spots.

If only I'd stayed in closer touch with him recently, Charlotte thought ruefully, maybe I'd have known he was in trouble. Lately their contact had degenerated into hasty e-mails and the occasional 2 A.M. phone call when he needed "urgent" astrological advice from her about a new lover or risky money-making scheme. Friendship was like a garden: If you wanted it to blossom, you had to tend it regularly. And both of them, it seemed, had become too busy to keep up the necessary maintenance.

At least she could try to find his murderer. Pushing aside her guilt, she focused on the only question that mattered now: Who killed Sebastian Avery? She checked her watch and booted up her computer. For cases like this, she found horary astrology more effective than natal or electional astrology. She often used it to answer a specific question, calculating a chart for the date, time, and place of the question rather than for the event itself; with any luck, the chart would reveal the answer. Occasionally, she helped police solve crimes this way, and although initially some detectives were skeptical about dealing with an astrologer, her success usually won them over.

She keyed in the necessary data and waited while the computer crunched numbers that would've taken her half an hour to work out by hand. After a few moments, the chart popped up on the monitor. Charlotte studied the peculiar symbols within the circular diagram until the pattern began to make a disturbing kind of sense.

* * *

"Oh, Charlotte. Isn't it just *ghastly?*" Diana Lucas wailed, holding out her manicured hands to grasp Charlotte's.

The art gallery owner wore a short, black, silk dress that accentuated her Nautilus-trim figure and a gold necklace that looked heavy enough to anchor a small ship. Although Charlotte was only a month older than her former college roommate, Diana's plastic surgeon had created an illusionary gap of several years between them.

Located on one of Boston's most fashionable streets, the Lucas Gallery reflected its owner's panache and prosperity. Diana possessed only modest talent herself, but with her business acumen and driving ambition she'd managed to turn her love of art into a lucrative enterprise. In recent years, Sebastian's notoriety had contributed to her success. As his exclusive dealer and agent, she not only profited financially from the sale of each Avery painting, she also benefited from the publicity his controversial stunts attracted.

Diana's high heels clicked sharply on the polished oak floor as Charlotte followed her to the back of the long, white-walled room, past an exhibit of boldly textured paintings by a young Israeli woman, several large ceramic pieces on pedestals, and a collection of lithographs that Charlotte would have enjoyed looking at under different circumstances. Colorful silk-screened banners hung from the ceiling.

"I still can't believe it," the gallery owner said as she showed Charlotte into a small, private office crowded with furniture and artwork in crates.

Settling herself behind a glass-topped desk, she motioned for Charlotte to sit in a red, plastic chair that vaguely resembled a bird in flight.

"It's quite a shock," Charlotte agreed. "He died just like his patron saint."

"Actually, St. Sebastian survived being shot full of arrows," Diana corrected her. "He was beaten to death later."

The thought made Charlotte shiver, even though the claustrophobic office was warm and close. "You knew him better than just about anyone. Was he in any kind of trouble? More than the usual, I mean."

"The police already asked me that. They wanted the names of everyone who ever bought one of Sebastian's paintings from me. I told them my clients insist on confidentiality, for security reasons—some of these pieces are extremely valuable. Even museums aren't safe from thieves these days. They still haven't caught whoever robbed the Gardner Museum back in 1990."

"A murder investigation usually trumps client confidentiality," Charlotte pointed out. "Do the police suspect one of your customers?"

"They wouldn't say. They just asked questions and gave orders. Not everyone who owned Sebastian's paintings was a fan, you know. Some of his enemies bought his work to keep it from being exhibited publicly."

"Do you know anyone who wanted him dead?"

"Sure, dozens of people—not counting his three ex-wives."

"I mean anyone who'd actually do it. Usually they just sued him. I know Sebastian could be abrasive and he made people angry because he always said what he thought, no matter who it hurt. He was an Aries, after all—the word *tact* wasn't in his vocabulary."

Diana tossed her blond hair and laughed hollowly. "That's putting it mildly. Unlike most of us, though, Sebastian said what he thought in such a flagrant way. Remember José Javier, the Chilean neo-surrealist that Sebastian thought was a big fraud?"

"I remember Sebastian did a picture of a toddler painting an exact replica of one of Javier's pieces and titled it 'My Kid Could Do Better Than That'."

"And he exhibited it at a very well-attended show," said Diana. "The critics loved it, but Javier swore he'd kill Sebastian. Or how about 'Corporate Welfare'?"

Charlotte shifted position and adjusted her skirt, trying vainly to get comfortable on a chair designed to be looked at, not sat on. "That's the painting he did of some of the city's biggest business persons with the bodies of pigs, feeding at a trough filled with taxpayers' money."

"Right. One of them bought the painting and burned it. I doubt those guys are shedding tears over Sebastian's death."

Reminiscing about her old friend's audacity made Charlotte smile in spite of her sorrow and she realized, poignantly, how much she was going to miss him. "He always admired Manet's ability to shock the stuffy and the self-righteous. 'Olympia' and 'Déjeuner sur l'herbe' were two of his favorite paintings. I think if Manet could've seen Sebastian's work, he might have admired it, too."

"He was a good painter, even if he did go too far sometimes," said Diana. "Like the time that woman at the photo lab tried to get him arrested for child pornography because he took some nude pictures of his 6-year-old daughter. Sebastian did a lovely, Rococo-style painting of three little naked cherubs who had the faces of that woman's children. It's one thing to lampoon public figures, quite another to use children to get even."

"I suppose Sebastian's death makes his work even more valuable, especially with this sensational media coverage."

"It should," Diana answered. "Sebastian would've loved all the publicity he's getting. Too bad he's not around to enjoy it." Suddenly, her flawless face seemed to crumble and tears sparkled in her eyes. "Damn it, I'm going to miss the bastard."

Charlotte nodded, fighting back tears of her own. "Me too."

* * *

The problem with astrology, thought Charlotte as she walked the few blocks from the art gallery to the Boston Public Library, is that it's not acceptable as proof in court. That meant she had to find solid evidence to corroborate what she'd seen in the horary chart; and she certainly didn't relish that chore.

Holding her jacket closed against a brisk, late-March wind, she considered the key factors contained in the chart: The planet Jupiter figured prominently in it, falling in the sector astrologers connected with hidden enemies. Considering the manner in which Sebastian died, that wasn't surprising. After all, Jupiter ruled archers. But it also ruled out lots of other things including higher education, long-distance travel, foreigners, horses, religious leaders, judges, publishing, and the sign Sagittarius, which tended to complicate matters.

Maybe she should go to the police and tell them everything she knew, washing her hands of what promised to be a very messy situation. But what if she'd made a mistake? Astrology spoke in symbols and symbols could be misinterpreted. Pointing a finger at the wrong person could be personally and professionally devastating to the accuser as well as the accused. In fact, she hoped she *was* wrong. Until she could confirm her suspicions—or better yet, dismiss them—she decided to keep the information to herself.

The library kept art books on the second floor and Charlotte thumbed through several before she found the picture she was looking for: Botticelli's grotesquely beautiful "St. Sebastian". Despite the arrows piercing his torso and thigh, the martyr wore an expression of haughty indifference to his plight, as if he refused to give his tormentors the pleasure of seeing him suffer. Even though Sebastian Avery looked nothing like Botticelli's handsome young saint, their attitudes were alike and Charlotte could easily imagine her friend scowling at his killer to the very end.

* * *

Benjamin Kane opened the apartment door, letting strains from a Mozart opera spill out into the hallway. His gracefully lined face broke into a sad smile when he saw Charlotte and he opened his arms to her without saying a word. For several moments they stood in the doorway, clinging to each other before Kane remembered his manners and invited her to come inside.

"The world is a shabbier place without him," said Kane, his hands dipping and soaring in the air like swallows as he spoke. "Such a travesty."

Charlotte slipped off her jacket and took a seat beside her former professor on his antique, velvet sofa. "I still can't believe he's really gone."

"What kind of a world is it where a person feels he has the right to destroy a talent like Sebastian, simply to assuage his own injured vanity?"

The same kind of world it's always been, thought Charlotte, one in which far too many people see violence as a solution to their problems. She asked, "So you definitely think the murderer is someone Sebastian offended?"

"It's a reasonable assumption, don't you think?"

"I suppose so. Sebastian made more than his share of enemies."

Kane chuckled softly. "Yes, our dear friend did have a propensity for inspiring animosity. He absolutely refused to play by anyone else's rules." His eyes shifted away from her and focused on a painting that hung above a mahogany sideboard. At first glance, it looked like a series of blue and green dots; only later did the eye adjust and discern the landscape within the pointillist composition. "The world was Sebastian's arena and he considered anyone and everyone fair game, even those of us who loved him."

Charlotte remembered the first time she'd seen that painting hanging in a Boston art gallery along with several pieces of Kane's work. It so closely resembled the professor's other pictures that, at first, even Kane himself was confused. When he finally figured out who'd actually painted it, he insisted the gallery remove it immediately—only to discover that the piece had been sold. The irate gallery owner, forced to admit the forgery and lose the sale, refused to ever handle Kane's work again and spread the word that other Kane pictures might also be fakes. The youthful Sebastian, who before he discovered his own style enjoyed flaunting his skill by mimicking other artists, had intended it as a joke on his favorite professor. However, no one in the art community found it funny—least of all Ben Kane whose reputation had nearly been destroyed by the suspicion of fraud. As Charlotte recalled, it had taken Kane years to regain his standing in the art community and to forgive his star pupil.

"I really want to find the person who killed him, Ben."

Kane slid his wire-rimmed glasses down to the tip of his long, aristocratic nose and peered over the top of them at her. "Playing sleuth again, are you?"

"I owe him that much."

"My dear, don't you trust the police to apprehend the murderer? I can't imagine why you want to muck about in this odious business."

"We Scorpios feel it's our duty to uncover the truth, even if it means digging in some dirt," she explained, knowing he wouldn't understand.

Kane shook his head and stood up. "I'm going to fix myself a drink. Would you care for one?"

"No thanks. Did Sebastian ever mention anyone who might have threatened him?" Charlotte contemplated the significance of Jupiter in the chart she'd cast for Sebastian's murder and the planet's connection with foreigners. "What about José Javier? You know him; is he capable of murder?"

"I suppose we're all capable of murder, given the right circumstances," answered Kane, taking a bottle of single malt out of a well-stocked liquor cabinet. He poured three fingers' worth into a glass and stared at it for several moments, as if trying to scry the answer in the scotch. "José's a bit of a hot head; Sebastian humiliated him publicly. It's possible."

"What about the choice of arrows?"

"It does demonstrate a flair for the dramatic, doesn't it?"

"And a knowledge of the Christian martyr, St. Sebastian. Is Javier an archer?"

"Not that I know of," said Kane, slowly pacing back and forth across a worn, Oriental rug. "But I'm really only acquainted with him professionally. For all I know, he could be a tai chi master or run the bulls at Pamplona."

"Speculate for me, Ben. Who do you think might have killed him?"

"If I were a betting man, I might put money on his first wife, Helen. "

Charlotte nodded. "She never forgave Sebastian for divorcing her just before his work started to sell. After all those years of supporting him while he was a struggling artist."

Kane stopped pacing and propped his elbow on the mantelpiece, angling himself toward her as if posing for a photographer, so that the afternoon light washed his profile. Charlotte had the distinct impression he'd practiced this stance and knew it flattered him.

"That too," he said. "But I was referring to the scandal regarding her little boy, the one Sebastian insists is his son. Her new husband, the minister, has been horribly embarrassed by Sebastian's claim—you can imagine how their parishioners reacted—and of course, the child does look exactly like Sebastian. The same flaming red hair and angular features."

"How could a minister's wife justify murdering her ex? As I recall, the fifth commandment says 'thou shalt not kill,' " asked Charlotte, considering the possibility. Although she hadn't seen Helen in years, Charlotte remembered the woman's fiery temper and vindictiveness—characteristics that seemed incongruous in a minister's wife. Perhaps Helen had undergone a religious conversion and learned to forgive and forget.

"I think you're being a bit ingenuous," said Kane, raising his left eyebrow. "Sebastian even made the child a beneficiary in his will. I'm sure that caused the good reverend a great deal of displeasure."

"Do you think Helen killed Sebastian to shut him up or so her son would inherit his money?" asked Charlotte, playing with this new piece of the puzzle. It fit: Jupiter, the villain in the horary chart, ruled religion; and Helen definitely had a motive.

"Perhaps the minister killed him," suggested Kane.

"What about wife number 3? Sebastian's blatant infidelity didn't exactly thrill her, as I recall."

Kane quit his position at the fireplace and came back to sit on the sofa beside Charlotte. "My goodness, we've developed quite a long list of suspects, haven't we?"

"And I'm sure we've overlooked a few."

* * *

Sebastian's will stipulated no funeral—probably because the artist considered himself immortal—but the will said nothing against throwing a memorial bash, explained Giorgio Parelli, Sebastian's colleague and neighbor, and he immediately set about inviting everyone who'd ever known the deceased, friends as well as foes, to a farewell party.

By seven o'clock the following evening, Giorgio's loft looked like Time Square on New Year's Eve. Artists and wannabes, critics and reporters, ex-lovers, collectors, and the just plain curious gathered to say good-bye to a painter whose death had been as unconventional as his life. Charlotte sat on the stairs leading up to a half-floor sleeping area overhead, tucked her green, silk dress modestly around her legs, and watched them all. Surely the murderer wouldn't miss the excitement he or she had created. The killer was undoubtedly in the crowd below.

Giorgio approached her, a glass of champagne in each hand. He offered her one and asked, "Are we having fun yet?"

"Why on Earth did you invite Nutley, that pompous ass from the *Spectrum?* He hated Sebastian's work, and said so in print more than once. He insisted Sebastian was merely a satirist and political cartoonist, not an artist."

"I wanted the old fart to see how many people loved Sebastian and his pictures. Besides, even bad publicity is good publicity, Charlotte. The more notice Sebastian gets, the more valuable his work becomes. I happen to own a few Avery pieces myself." He gestured at a trio of painted panels that fit together like an early Christian triptych. "And as I recall, so do you."

"I always knew you were a crass materialist underneath it all," Charlotte teased.

"To tell the truth, Nutley's criticism really bothered Sebastian. Sure he had fun skewering his enemies and lampooning people who deserved it, but he wanted to be seen as a serious artist." Giorgio propped one foot up on a stair and leaned toward Charlotte, trying to keep his voice low yet make himself heard over the din of a hundred other voices. "I think Sebastian planned to show the Nutleys of the world that he really was a fine painter. He dropped a few hints only last week. Do you know if he was working on a new picture?"

Charlotte shook her head. "He didn't say anything to me."

Diana Lucas, elegant in a custom-tailored dove gray suit, spotted them, waved, and began winding her way through the crowd toward them. Watching her, Giorgio said, "Beauty's wasted on Diana."

"Why do you say that?"

"She's not the least bit interested in men. Too independent. You know who she reminds me of? An Amazon with two breasts."

"Sounds like sour grapes to me," Charlotte laughed, but she had to agree.

"Nice party, Giorgio," Diana said. "Too bad a mutual friend had to die for me to get an invitation to your place."

"Nonsense," protested Giorgio, but Charlotte knew they hadn't spoken since Diana refused to give him a show at her gallery 5 years ago. "We were just talking about a new project Sebastian had planned to prove his talent as a painter and silence his detractors once and for all. Problem is, he never said exactly what it was."

"Surely you'd know about it, Diana, if anyone did," Charlotte prompted her.

"Sorry to disappoint you," said Diana, toying with a plum-sized red gem at her throat that Charlotte guessed was a real ruby.

"Well, I suppose we'll never know now, unless someone discovers an unfinished masterpiece in the attic." Giorgio sighed and excused himself on the pretense of tending to his guests, though Charlotte suspected he wanted to get away from Diana.

"How many Avery paintings have you sold this evening?" Charlotte asked her old friend.

Diana smiled. "Six so far, and the night's still young. I feel like a stockbroker with a hot stock—I don't know if I should sell now or hold out to see if the price keeps climbing. Let me know if you're interested in selling yours."

"I don't think so," Charlotte said sadly. Her painting was all she had left of him now. "Sebastian would've enjoyed this turnout. He loved being the center of attention."

"Unfortunately, the only way you can be the center of attention at a wake is to die," Diana pointed out.

Charlotte noticed Ben Kane talking to a very large, very handsome man with curly black hair whom she recognized as José Javier. Here, finally, was her chance to meet the temperamental Chilean painter who'd supposedly threatened Sebastian's life.

"I've got to go talk to Ben," she told Diana. "I'll catch up with you later."

"Admit it, girlfriend. It's José you really want to talk to." Diana winked and Charlotte felt herself blushing.

As she approached the pair, Kane, looking every bit the old Yankee in a navy Brooks Brothers suit, welcomed her with a kiss on the cheek. "José Javier, may I introduce one of my favorite students and dear friend, Charlotte McCrae?"

Charlotte extended her hand and Javier, instead of shaking, kissed it.

"I'm surprised to see you here," she said. "I understood you had little use for my friend Sebastian."

"For the man, no. But for the artist, that is a different story. I have more respect for his work than he had for mine. And do you agree with your friend that my paintings are without substance?"

His dark eyes flashed and his easy smile dazzled her. Even if she'd hated his work, Charlotte couldn't have brought herself to say so. "Sebastian and I disagreed about a lot of things—I like Isabelle Allende, for instance, and he liked Hemingway."

"And you, too, are an artist?"

"Not anymore."

Javier seemed puzzled. "How can that be? Being an artist is like being pregnant. You either are or you are not. No in between." He frowned, as if her confession distressed him greatly. "Have you aborted the artist from within you?"

That's a pretty accurate way of putting it, Charlotte thought, uncomfortable with the direction the conversation had taken. Instead of answering, she returned to the subject of Sebastian. "I heard you wanted to kill Sebastian for mocking your work."

"Ah, yes. I am afraid it's true. When he made that insulting picture I said I would kill him for doing so." He held out his large, paint-stained hands, palms up, in a gesture of helplessness. "I am Latino. I am passionate. We sometimes do things in the heat of the moment that we regret later."

"The police interrogated José this morning, in fact," explained Kane.

"You see? Because of my temper I am now a murder suspect."

Charlotte studied Javier's strong-boned face, trying to determine if this man could have murdered her friend. His size, his charm, and his foreign birth were all characteristics associated with Jupiter, the mark of the murderer in the horary chart.

"Only three things are worth killing for," said Javier. "Love, money, and honor." His brilliant black eyes and wide mouth seemed to be pleading with her to exonerate or at least forgive him.

"By your own definition, you had a motive for killing Sebastian," Charlotte pointed out. "He insulted you publicly, impugned your honor."

"Yes, but I would have challenged him to a duel. Honor cannot be reclaimed by an act of cowardice."

"That leaves love and money," said Kane. "If you look to your left, Charlotte, you'll notice that the object of our previous discussion is in attendance tonight."

Charlotte turned to see the former Helen Avery standing alone in front of Sebastian's triptych.

"Maybe I should go pay my respects," she said.

Kane raised his left eyebrow. His expression said he knew her reason for wanting to talk to Helen had nothing to do with sympathy.

"I'm glad we had an opportunity to meet," she told Javier.

"The pleasure was mine entirely," he answered and kissed her hand again. "I hope you do not believe I murdered your friend. The world needs all the artists it can get."

In the several years since Charlotte had seen her last, Helen had put on quite a bit of weight, and contrary to popular standards of beauty, it suited her. The minister's wife faced Sebastian's paintings, but her glazed stare suggested her thoughts were elsewhere. As Charlotte approached, Helen turned and forced a smile.

"I'm sorry for your loss, Helen."

"And yours. You knew Sebastian longer than I did."

Charlotte nodded, sorrow tying a knot in her chest. For the past hour she'd been so engrossed in her role of sleuth that she'd managed to repress her grief. Now it bubbled up in her like an underground spring seeking the earth's surface.

"We all do foolish things in our youth that haunt us for the rest of our lives," Helen said, more to herself than to Charlotte. Her gaze returned to the three paintings as she slipped into a private reverie.

Instead of responding, Charlotte retreated into her own thoughts, allowing the silence between them to grow.

"He could be a son of a bitch sometimes," Helen said at last. "Egotistical, brazen, crude, willful—sometimes I felt like I was living with a spoiled child instead of a grown man. We used to have appalling fights—of course you know all about that, Charlotte. His temper exploded like lightning and disappeared just as fast. Oh, I know a minister's wife should show more Christian charity. It's just that Sebastian never thought of anyone except himself."

"I heard he thought the world of your son."

Helen snorted. "He wanted to take my son away from me. He didn't care who he hurt in the process, so long as he got his way."

"Don't you think you're being a bit paranoid? Maybe Sebastian was just being generous."

"He never did anything for purely unselfish reasons."

"Are you going to accept the insurance policy he left the boy?"

Helen pulled away ever so slightly and eyed Charlotte with skepticism, as if she were unsure how much to say. "You've heard the rumors, too, I gather?"

Charlotte nodded. "I suppose that makes you a suspect in his murder."

"One more nasty little joke Sebastian played on me. He may be dead, but he still gets the last laugh. Yes, the police have me on their list—along with half the city of Boston." A caterer passed by with a tray of champagne glasses and Helen snatched one from it. She drank half of it in one gulp, then squared her shoulders and narrowed her eyes, elevating her chin a notch or two. "People will believe what they want to believe, regardless of what's true; and my son will inherit Sebastian's money, regardless of who his father is."

The party started breaking up around eleven o'clock. Charlotte was among the last to leave, waiting for one of the guests to show his or her hand. At 12:10 she gave up and said goodnight to Giorgio. As she walked down the hall to the elevator, she averted her eyes so she wouldn't see the yellow police tape barring the door to Sebastian's loft.

* * *

On this raw and rainy April morning—which would have been Sebastian's birthday, Charlotte recalled with a heavy heart—the atrium garden at the Gardner Museum was a welcome sanctuary. Orchids, narcissus, cyclamen, and calla lilies bloomed among lush ferns and palm trees. Water trickled from a marble fountain at the end of a courtyard paved with first-century Roman mosaic tiles. Overhead, a weak, yellowish light filtered through the skylight roof four stories above and fell on the shoulders of the ancient statues that peopled the garden. Heavy stone walls blocked out the sounds of the city, enclosing her in a world where time stood still and only beauty mattered, where murder and betrayal were subjects for paintings, not real life.

A century ago, Isabella Stewart Gardner built this reproduction of a Venetian palace and packed it full of art treasures she'd gleaned from around the world. The dark, brooding mansion housed a priceless and eclectic collection that included Roman sarcophagi and Gothic choir stalls, Renaissance tapestries and Persian carpets, rare books, and letters from famous poets, statesmen, and philosophers. Paintings by some of the world's greatest artists hung here, too: Rembrandt, Titian, Raphael, Manet, Botticelli, and—until the infamous, still-unsolved robbery—Degas and Vermeer.

Like many art students then and now, Sebastian, Diana, and Charlotte used to come here often with their sketchbooks to learn by studying the masters' work. As she made her way along the pillared cloister, which wrapped around the courtyard, Charlotte saw a young woman who reminded her of herself 20 years ago, earnestly drawing with *conté* on a pad of heavy paper.

With a deep sense of longing for those bygone days of youthful innocence and hope, she climbed the long flight of steps to the second floor of the museum and then another to the third. There she lingered for a few minutes on one of the small, open balconies that overlooked the courtyard below delaying the moment of truth, she admitted to herself. After having come this far, she felt a compelling urge to turn around and go back downstairs, rather than follow this quest to its bitter end: the Long Gallery on the opposite side of the central courtyard. If she was right, Sebastian was every bit the painter he claimed to be.

Charlotte took a few deep breaths to fortify herself, then turned and walked briskly down the hall, through the Veronese Room and the Titian Room, barely glancing at the artwork all around her. The Long Gallery ran the full length of the museum, culminating in a small chapel. As she entered it, she hesitated, reluctant to take those last few steps that would bring her face to face with the proof she needed to verify what the astrology chart had revealed. You owe it to Sebastian, she told herself firmly, and forced herself forward. Her footsteps echoed in the absolute silence that hung around her as heavy as the weight of the past.

She stopped in front of Botticelli's "Madonna of the Eucharist." The fifteenth-century panel depicted the Holy Mother and Child in the company of a young figure whose faint halo suggested his angelic nature. The angel held a bunch of grapes and shafts of wheat—the sources of bread and wine—offering them to Mary. The plump Christ child, smiling angel, figures' intricate flowing robes, and distant landscape all appeared just as the master painted them 500 years ago. Even the age-crackled surface seemed authentic. Only Mary's face gave the forgery away.

As Charlotte studied the painting, she could almost hear Sebastian's laughter behind her. She could easily imagine his impish delight as he subtly altered the Madonna's sweet features, replacing them with those of his partner in crime. Sebastian could never resist playing a joke or putting his unique stamp on whatever he created.

How many art lovers had gazed at this famous panel without noticing the alteration? Charlotte wondered. How many times had she passed it without question? Familiarity makes us blind. Day after day, we look at the world around us and see only what we want to see, what we're prepared to see. That's what makes the artists different from other people—whatever they see seems fresh and wondrous each time they look at it, and no matter how often they look at it there's always something new to discover.

"I knew if you'd figured it out you'd come here today to make sure."

Charlotte spun around as Diana Lucas stepped from behind a marble pedestal. Instead of her usual designer garb, the gallery owner wore a utilitarian black turtleneck sweater and black jeans. Her sneakered feet made no sound as she crossed the terra cotta tile floor toward Charlotte.

Diana held up a can of turpentine. "I'd hoped to destroy the evidence before you saw it."

"How could you do it?" Charlotte asked her former roommate.

Diana shrugged. "Sebastian wanted recognition for his work. He loved knowing he'd pulled one over on people who set themselves up as authorities; but what good is duping the experts if you can't rub their noses in it? He was so proud of this caper of his—it was a game to him, not a serious crime that could put both of us behind bars. Recently, he'd made several oblique references to it—and not only to Giorgio. You know how he enjoyed stirring up controversy. It was only a matter of time before he said the wrong thing to the wrong person. I couldn't take the chance."

"How did the two of you smuggle the real Botticelli out of here?"

"We didn't—one of the guards did. A guard who died shortly thereafter, I'm sorry to say."

"Are you and Sebastian responsible for the big 1990 heist, too?"

"I wish," Diana lamented. "The very thought of it makes me furious. Those half-wits didn't have the decency to cover their tracks like Sebastian and I did—they just cut the paintings out and left the empty frames. In the aftermath, the museum improved security. It's virtually impossible to steal anything now."

Even though she'd always known her old friend was smart, tough, and ambitious, Charlotte was having a hard time squaring her image of Diana the businesswoman with Diana the criminal. "What happened to the real Botticelli?"

"It's probably in a vault somewhere. I sold it to a Japanese collector. The people who buy these things do it as an investment, not because they love art. You can't hang a picture like that on your dining room wall, you know."

Diana moved closer to Charlotte who instinctively backed away. She glanced furtively down the Long Gallery, searching vainly for a guard or even another visitor. Now that she thought about it, Charlotte realized she hadn't seen another person on the entire third floor.

"I'm curious. How did you know it was me? Did you see it in the stars?"

"Initially, yes. But I had to get hard evidence to back it up," Charlotte answered, still wishing she hadn't found the proof she'd been searching for. Losing two of her oldest friends in one week seemed almost more than she could bear. "I didn't know you were an archer."

Diana laughed and took another step toward Charlotte. Trying to keep some distance between them, Charlotte backed out onto one of the balconies that overhung the courtyard.

"Didn't you? I'm a Sagittarius, after all. And I'm named for the goddess of the hunt."

"Yes, that's how I eventually figured it out. Jupiter, the ruler of Sagittarius, showed up as the enemy in the chart I did for Sebastian's murder," said Charlotte, wondering if she, in her low-heeled pumps, could outrun Diana, the swift huntress in sneakers. They were both about the same size, but due to her daily workouts at the health club Diana was definitely in better shape.

"Of course, any reasonably clever individual could follow the money trail," Charlotte continued, stalling for time. She glanced around, hoping to spot a guard—where were they when you needed them? "All you'd have to do is determine who stood to gain the most from Sebastian's death and who stood to lose the most if he stayed alive. In this case, they both happen to be the same person."

"You always were a smart girl," Diana said sarcastically. "If you had as much talent as you have brains, you'd have been a damn good artist."

Charlotte had been watching Diana's eyes the way self-defense instructors always told you to do, but Diana's steady gaze didn't change a bit as she dropped the can of turpentine and lunged at Charlotte, slamming her against the stone railing of the balcony. The sharp pain in her lower back made her gasp; tears sprang to her eyes. The impact stunned her momentarily, long enough for Diana to clench her hands around Charlotte's neck and force her shoulders back so that the upper half of her body arched precariously over the rail. Charlotte clawed at her assailant's fingers, trying to loosen Diana's grip, but the gallery owner held on tight, digging her long, polished nails into Charlotte's skin.

Choking and unable to scream, Charlotte kicked frantically at Diana's legs—a mistake, she realized, that threw her off balance and allowed Diana to lift her partway over the railing. The gallery owner knocked Charlotte's other foot out from under her and leaned down heavily on Charlotte's chest. Dizzy from fear and oxygen deprivation, Charlotte saw the courtyard floor

30 feet below as a white-and-green blur that swayed from side to side like a landscape viewed from a swing, not comprehending that it was her own body teetering as Diana bent her backward over the railing.

In every life-and-death struggle there comes a point when the conscious mind relinquishes its command and the instincts take over. No longer aware of her actions, Charlotte stopped trying to dislodge Diana's hands from her throat and grasped the railing instead. She stopped straining against the pressure Diana was exerting on her body and let herself go limp.

Now, with Charlotte's body providing no resistance, Diana's weight and thrust worked against her. Before the gallery owner could compensate and adjust her balance, Charlotte brought her knee up between Diana's legs and pulled back as hard as she could.

Diana pitched forward, her arms flailing as if she were a fledgling bird on its first flight. She almost seemed to be floating as she slipped toward the courtyard below. For a moment, Charlotte believed her old friend might simply drift down gently as a feather and land unhurt among the lush greenery.

A shriek, then a dull thud brought Charlotte back to reality. As she dragged herself to safety and slumped onto the floor of the balcony, she heard cries of alarm far below. Running feet clattered on mosaic tiles. She leaned her hot forehead against a cool stone baluster, gasping for breath, unaware of the blood dripping onto her collar, and gazed down at the commotion. A black figure lay face down in a white stone pathway. Museum personnel and visitors streamed from the cloisters surrounding the courtyard and gathered around the crumpled figure. A man knelt, touched the figure's neck tentatively, then drew back his hand and shook his head. As if that were their cue, the other people in the courtyard turned their faces upward and stared at the spot from which Diana had fallen.

Moments later, Charlotte heard someone speak softly to her, but the words made no sense. A pair of strong arms lifted her to her feet. She was vaguely aware of being led through the museum and down the stairs to a quiet room on the ground floor where someone placed a cold, damp cloth on her burning neck. A young woman brought her a glass of water; a balding man made a phone call.

When she could talk again, Charlotte said, "The Madonna has her face." She repeated it several times.

The man and woman stared at her as if she were speaking in tongues and told her an ambulance would arrive soon.

* * *

If you want to hide something, leave it in plain sight. That way, no one will think it important enough to warrant any interest. When something is readily available, it loses its mystique. We don't want things to come easily, not really, and just to make sure, we go to great lengths to complicate our lives, obscuring the simple truths with our fervent struggling. Easy answers are often the right ones, though, as any Zen master will tell you. All we have to do to find them is open our eyes.

Charlotte sat beside Ben Kane, waiting for the auctioneer to begin the bidding. Sebastian's now notorious forgery of "The Madonna of the Eucharist" rested on an easel before a crowd of dealers, art collectors, and scandal followers eager to see the small painting that had caused such a big fuss.

Tragedy and controversy are the best forms of publicity, she thought, listening to the frenzied bidding that crackled around her like a brush fire. People aren't just buying art, they're buying a story. For a chance to tell that story to their friends, to make it a part of their own less colorful lives, they are willing to pay a sum that could feed half the hungry children in Africa. In the end, the simple answer is almost always the same: greed; Diana's greed for wealth, Sebastian's greed for fame, and the public's greed for titillation.

The auctioneer's gavel fell. Charlotte stood up and said goodnight to Kane. As she walked out of the brightly lit auction hall and into the purple night, she couldn't help thinking how much Sebastian's painting had cost her and what a bargain the collector, who only paid money for it, had gotten.

Author's Note: The burglary of the Isabella Stewart Gardner Museum in Boston actually occurred in 1990; at the time this story was written, the crime remained unsolved. The other events and characters in this story are the product of the author's imagination and have no basis in fact.

Chapter 4

The Bag Lady Caper

By Margaret DiCanio

An added burden of being homeless, for a psychic, is the necessity of wearing other people's discarded clothing. Resting on a bench in the Boston Common, Octavia O'Sullivan debated her options. If she took off the jacket she was wearing, the East wind, combined with the rain, might send her to the hospital with another bout of pneumonia. Octavia felt strong enough to withstand the physical pain experienced by the jacket's owner during the last moments of her life—a couple of years of homelessness had built up Octavia's tolerance—but the woman's fear and grief threatened to overwhelm her.

Octavia closed her eyes and whispered, "I wish I could help you." Immediately, the turmoil inside her subsided. She sensed rather than heard a voice in her mind say, "Stop him before he kills them."

"Stop who?"

The voice in Octavia's mind did not respond, but she still could feel the urgency. "I'll do what I can," promised Octavia.

With a sense of purpose, she stood up, pulled the jacket's hood over her head, and set out for My Sister's Place. When you're homeless, a concrete task, even one that might be hopeless, provides a diversion from the constant daily struggle to find food and shelter.

My Sister's Place, better known as Sis's, is a shelter for homeless women on Beacon Hill. The former home of a wealthy woman whose periodic episodes of schizophrenia throughout her life had kept her wandering the streets of Boston, Sis's offers homeless women a few beds and a variety of services.

Octavia went straight to Sis's clothing room, where she had been given the jacket she was wearing an hour earlier. The clothing room is presided over by Janice Winslow, a former accountant whose son left her homeless. After Janice's son sold her home and cashed in her pension annuity by forging her name, he left town.

"You're back," said Janice. "What is it this time? You don't like the smell of the perfume the owner used?" She paused, "For someone homeless, you are awfully picky." Janice waved her hand in the air to negate her words. "Scratch that. You have just as much right to be a pain in the butt as anyone else."

"Janice, do you know who owned this jacket? If so, are you allowed to tell me?"

"Of course I can tell you. Why do you want to know?"

"Please don't ask."

Janice stared into Octavia's face. Recognizing her distress, she patted Octavia's hand resting on the counter. Janice pulled a ledger from beneath the counter and turned the pages.

"Here it is," she said. "The woman's name was Emily Bonaventure. She's given us stuff for years."

"She didn't give you this. She's dead," said Octavia.

"Right, she died a couple of weeks ago. Her son brought it in." Janice shook her head at the memory. "Normally, I let the contributor set the price on the tax receipts, but this guy put down $600. I told him the jacket is at least 10 years old. I reduced it to $200. He pitched a fit."

"Janice, do you know where she lived?"

"I know she lived here on the Hill. *The Globe* had a long obituary on her."

"Do you have a copy of the paper?"

"I doubt it. The recycle pile is low because of the rain; women use the papers to pad their shoes. Wait while I look."

After Janice came up empty-handed, Octavia trudged across the Common and the Public Garden and down Boylston Street to the Public Library. BPL is a warm refuge on bad weather days for Boston's homeless. Its only drawback is zealous guards who wake up anyone who falls asleep.

The Globe obituary was long and detailed. Emily Bonaventure had been born into wealth. At 18, she married Carl Partridge, a philanthropist much older than herself. At 22, when her son Jeffery was 2, Emily became a widow, only to remarry 6 years later, at 28-once again to a philanthropist, Daniel Bonaventure. Emily's second husband died 10 years after they married, when her daughter Betsy was 8 and her son Jeffery was 18. Carrying on the tradition of both her husbands, Emily spent the remainder of her adult years raising money and lobbying on behalf of the poor. She'd used her enormous assets as a lever to pry loose private and public funding for people and programs. She died at the age of 57.

A librarian provided Octavia with a file of newspaper articles about Emily. After a couple of hours of reading, Octavia felt satisfied she'd learned as much as she could about the woman who had owned the jacket. Reinforced by a cheese sandwich at the Paul Revere soup kitchen in Chinatown, Emily trudged up the steep streets of Beacon Hill to stand in front of Emily's home.

"What do I do now?" she whispered.

Words formed in her mind. "Tell them I promised you a job as a maid and told you to report this afternoon."

Being homeless had only partially overcome Octavia's natural shyness. She straightened her shoulders, clenched her fists to keep her hands from trembling, and climbed the granite stairs to Emily's front door. Behind her, she dragged her shopping cart of possessions.

A red-haired woman dressed in black wool slacks and a black cotton sweater answered the door. "Can I help you?" she said.

Octavia took a deep breath and said, "My name is Octavia O'Sullivan. Miss Emily told me to report for work this afternoon."

"To do what?"

"To be a maid."

"Mother didn't believe in maids."

In her last job before becoming homeless, Octavia had been an excellent maid. She'd been fired when she felt impelled to tell a guest not to go on a trip. The maid's job was just one in a long line of jobs Octavia had lost for similar reasons.

"Mrs. Bonaventure changed her mind," Octavia said. "I convinced her that being a maid was a worthy profession."

Tears welled in the young woman's eyes. "My mother was buried last Friday." She wiped her eyes with a tissue; Octavia said nothing. The woman shook her head as if to dislodge her grief.

"If mother promised you a job, she'd expect me to honor her commitment. Come on in. Let me help you with your cart. I'll put it in the utility room off the kitchen."

Octavia followed the woman down the hall into a bright kitchen that overlooked a garden. After she put away Octavia's cart, the woman returned to the kitchen and said, "I'm Emily's daughter. My name is Betsy Bonaventure Griffin." She helped Octavia shed her jacket. "Mother had a winter jacket like that. She was wearing it the last time I saw her."

"When was that?"

"On the night she died. I left my office late. I was so tired I was walking slowly through the Common along the path that runs up the hill from the Park Street subway to Beacon Street. Mother was running toward the steps across from the State House—the ones that lead up from the Common to the street."

"Was she a runner?"

"No. Mother didn't need exercise. She ran because she was always overscheduled. I assumed she was late for an appointment, so I didn't call out to her. If I'd known I'd never see her alive again . . . "

"You couldn't have known that. Could she have been running away from someone?"

"You mean a mugger?"

"I don't know. The park can be scary sometimes."

"I don't think so. What's puzzling is that the police said when she fell she was headed down the stone stairs into the Common."

"Which stairs?"

"The ones across from the State House—the ones I watched her go up. After a meeting at the State House, she would not have been going in that direction. That would have been away from home."

"She might have had another meeting, or maybe she'd lost a glove or a scarf or something like that. She might have gone back to retrace her route and lost her balance on the steps."

"I wish I knew that."

Betsy glanced around the kitchen. "I'd offer you some tea, but I'm a terrible cook. I don't know where anything is."

"Sit down. I'll get it."

Octavia bustled around the kitchen, opening and closing cupboards. Instinctively, she knew where the tea, the cups, the teapot, and the kettle were. In the refrigerator, she found milk and a plate of unfrosted cupcakes. When her fingers closed on the plate, the voice in her head, said, "No." She released the plate and found a loaf of bread and a jar of jelly.

When Octavia put tea and toast in front of Betsy, the young woman looked up at her, her eyes filled with tears.

"Mother always gave me tea and toast when I was upset. I can't believe I'll never see her again."

Octavia put her arm around Betsy's shoulders and laid her cheek against the top of the young woman's head. The quiet was broken when a boy of about 6 burst through the door and said, "I'm hungry, Mom." He nodded to Octavia and rushed to the refrigerator. He hauled open the door, examined the contents, and took out the cupcakes.

"I wish these were frosted." He turned to look at Octavia and said, "Mom's the only one who likes them unfrosted."

"Put those back," said Octavia. "You'll spoil your supper. You can have an apple."

Betsy laughed. "You sound exactly like Mother."

The boy set the cakes down on the counter. He examined Octavia's face to see if she were serious. Behind his back, a tiny mouse scampered out from between the canisters lining the counter. The mouse took a quick bite of a cupcake and started back to its hiding place.

"Oh God, Mother's been gone only a few weeks and the Hill mice have taken over," said Betsy.

With an agonized squeal, the mouse had a convulsion and toppled over dead. Betsy clapped her hand over her mouth. "There's something wrong with those cupcakes. I'd better throw them in the disposal." She snatched up the plate.

"Don't do that," said Octavia.

Betsy paused with the plate over the sink. "Why not?"

"Because they should be tested in a lab."

"For what? We already know there's something wrong with them. The mouse is dead."

"Mice seldom eat food that's gone bad. And even if they did, no one dies that quickly from food poisoning."

"Octavia, are you suggesting some other kind of poison?"

Octavia shrugged. Betsy's face lost its color. "How do we find out?" she said, holding her hands under running water, while she stared at the mouse.

"We'll send the cupcakes to a lab, Mom," said the boy. "That's what they do on the TV cop shows."

"We can't call the police because a mouse died. They'll think we're crazy."

"Send them to a private lab," said Octavia. "There must be some in the phone book."

"But if they find poison, they'll have to report it to the police, won't they?"

"I imagine so. Isn't that what you want them to do? If this child . . ." Octavia looked at the boy.

"Wilson," he said.

"If Wilson had popped one of those cakes into his mouth, he might be dead by now."

Wilson opened a drawer in the cabinet beneath the wall phone and handed Octavia a Boston directory. "Is it okay to eat any of the food here?" he asked.

His mother rushed to the sink and vomited the food she had just eaten. Wilson hurried to his mother's side and awkwardly patted her hip. Octavia took a small towel from a drawer, ran it under the cold water, and wiped Betsy's face.

A door slammed at the front of the house. Footsteps sounded along the hall. Betsy and Wilson stopped moving.

Octavia shoved the mouse and the cupcakes in the freezer. She dropped the partially eaten cupcake down the food disposal and turned on the water. The noise of the disposal masked the sound of footsteps and the opening of the kitchen door.

"Who are you?" demanded a man's voice.

Octavia turned to look at a tall, auburn-haired man in his late thirties. He was dressed in a black, cashmere suit.

"I'm the maid."

"My mother didn't believe in maids."

"I convinced her she was discriminating against maids."

"That sounds just like her. Well, she's dead now so she doesn't need a maid." He reached into his pocket.

"How much did she plan to pay you?"

"One hundred dollars a day."

"That's $24,000 a year. That's ridiculous."

"That's what she promised."

"You've been here what? An hour? Two hours?"

"An hour and a half."

"Here's $25."

Octavia folded her arms across her chest. "I want 2 weeks' notice."

"Take the $25 and count yourself lucky that I don't throw you out the door."

"Two weeks' notice, Mr. Partridge. Otherwise, I walk over to the *Herald* and tell a reporter I know that Jeffery Partridge, the son of Emily Bonaventure, is too cheap to give me a proper notice."

"That's blackmail."

"Blackmail is an offensive word. I'd rather call it extortion."

Betsy pushed herself away from the sink. "Keep your money, Jeffery. Octavia will work for me."

"Not in my house."

"This is also my house—Mother left it to both of us. Octavia stays."

"Fine; tell your maid I want a sandwich, some coffee, and dessert in the study. I have an appointment at the bank in an hour. Tell her to be quick about it."

Octavia put on a pot of coffee and made a roast beef sandwich. The only dessert available seemed to be the cupcakes; but, after a search, she found some stale pound cake in a canister and a box of instant pudding. After she whipped up the pudding with ice water, she arranged the stale cake in a sherbet dish and poured the pudding over it.

When Jeffery's lunch was ready, Octavia said, "Wilson, show me where the study is." The boy led her down the hall. When he put his hand on the study door, he whispered, "Will you be okay?"

"I'll be fine. Go take care of your mother until I get back." Wilson opened the study door and hurried back to the kitchen. When Octavia returned, Wilson and his mother were holding hands. He whispered, "Octavia, what if all the food in the house is poisoned?"

"Something tells me that it is not."

The yellow pages lay open on the table. "There's so many labs, I don't know which one to choose," said Betsy.

"Let's wait a little while. After your brother leaves, we'll figure out what to do. Is your brother a slow or a fast eater?"

"Uncle Jeffery eats as if someone is going to take it away from him," said Wilson.

"I'll give him 10 minutes, and then I'll pick up his tray."

A mantle clock ticked in the silence as the three sat waiting. At the end of 10 minutes, Octavia rose and returned to the study.

Jeffery barely glanced at her.

"I hope you liked the dessert, Mr. Partridge. I made it with some pudding and some unfrosted cakes that were in the refrigerator."

"You what?"

Jeffery Partridge leaped to his feet, his hands to his throat. He said, "Hospital. I have to get to Mass. General." He raced out of the study, flung open the front door, and rushed out.

For Betsy and Wilson, the closed kitchen door blunted the sound of Jeffery's scream as he plunged down the granite stairs of his childhood home, but Octavia heard it clearly. When the scream stopped, the voice in her head said, "Tell my daughter and grandson I love them."

"I'll take good care of them," Octavia whispered. She sensed she would hear no more from Emily Bonaventure and felt a deep sense of loss.

Artwork by Chris Pugh, Copyright 2002

Chapter 5

Sara Morningsky

By Lee Driver

It crouched in the dense underbrush and watched the scene unfold behind a boarded-up packing plant. The moon cast silhouettes of two figures as they emerged from a dark-colored vehicle. As the driver opened the trunk, a police car arrived tailed by a black limousine.

The gray wolf's keen sense of smell detected fear. It watched with the same intensity as it would a prey, head lowered, ears raised. Instinct told it that danger was near. The wolf took two steps forward, then back, unsure whether to react to the scent of danger. Two muffled pops startled the animal. Quickly it moved from its hiding place toward the body bleeding on the ground, toward the man with the raised gun. The men were too startled to react. With teeth bared, the wolf leaped at the policeman who yelled for his friends to shoot it. The wolf rushed back to the forest with its trophy in its mouth, but it didn't feel safe. It could hear the men in pursuit—the men with guns.

Swiftly, the wolf leaped 12 feet up to a branch. What had been thick paws changed into sturdy talons, and the 100–pound body of a wolf transformed into a 2–pound gray hawk. It watched the men run under the tree branch still in pursuit of the wolf.

Gripping the trophy with its hooked beak, the hawk took flight, soaring silently, its wings flat and graceful. It made several quick beats of its wings as it followed the limousine, noticing with acute eyesight the license plate number.

The hawk flew across town, over lit streets that crisscrossed subdivisions, and the narrow creek that ran along the expressway. The hawk saw rabbits and ground squirrels from its high altitude, but had no interest in feeding. With wings level, it glided down over a forest to a remote house in a clearing and then through an opened balcony window. It landed gracefully on two feet—human feet. Dropping the trophy to the floor, the figure climbed into bed weeping. The object the men had chased the wolf for, its trophy, was the policeman's badge.

* * *

"I don't understand you, Dagger." The attractive woman paced the tiled floor on stiletto heels. Flipping back errant strands of platinum hair, she gazed disapprovingly at the 15–by–20–foot office located above a downtown shot-and-beer joint. "You can't attract high-paying customers in a dump like this."

Dagger eyed his fiancée from her well-turned heel to her shapely thighs, past the short hemline of her skirt.

"I'm just interested in customers, Sheila. I couldn't care less how rich they are." He snapped the newspaper open and turned to the second page of the headline story.

Sheila inhaled deeply, grimaced, and quickly changed her mood. "That's okay. No problem. Daddy's going to have a spot for you at his newspaper; maybe as an editor. You won't need to do anything but proofread."

"I like being a private investigator." He returned to the article. Changing the subject, he asked, "How could your father print this crap about Lieutenant Fazio?"

Sheila stopped pacing and jammed her fists onto her narrow hips. "You haven't listened to a word I've said."

A shrill sound came from inside a cage in the corner of the room. "Awk. Wicked witch of the West. Awk." A scarlet macaw lifted its colorful wings and fanned out its tail.

Sheila tossed a disparaging glance over her shoulder at the macaw. "Shut up you poor excuse for an oversized crow."

"Awwwkk, sticks and stones."

"Leave Einstein alone, Sheila."

"He only repeats what you tell him." She pulled a cigarette from her purse.

"And don't smoke around him." Dagger placed the newspaper down and stood, stretching his tall, muscular body.

Reluctantly, Sheila returned the cigarette to the pack. "I really think you should find a new home for the feathered rodent. You know I can't have him around with my allergies."

"Allergies?" Dagger laughed. "Since when?" He backed away when she playfully ran a hand through his thick, brown hair.

Pressing her body against his she said, "There are women who would kill for your cheekbones." She stroked his chiseled jawline, admiring his rugged good looks enhanced by a five o-clock shadow. With a flirtatious smile she added, "And you're all mine."

"We've done this little dance before." He gently pulled her arms away. "I am not giving Einstein away."

As Sheila brought her lips up to Dagger's, he saw her gaze drift to the doorway. A slight arch of one eyebrow told him Sheila had seen something distasteful, beneath her standards. He had seen that look many times. Her father patented the look of disdain, down the tip of his nose, as if everyone in the world was his subordinate. It was one trait Dagger disliked in her; and the list was getting longer as the wedding date grew nearer.

Dagger turned toward the doorway to see a waif of a girl in a faded but clean flowered dress and sandals. Her eyes were the color of Caribbean waters. Her waist-length hair had so many sun-streaked shades it was difficult to tell its true color. If he had passed her on a street he would have expected her to be begging for a crust of bread—not that she looked emaciated, just fragile and timid.

"I'm sorry if I'm interrupting," the girl said. "I'm looking for Chase Dagger."

"That would be me," Dagger replied.

Sheila leaned toward him. "Get payment up front." She bussed Dagger on the cheek before pushing briskly past the intruder.

"Awk, good riddance," Einstein squawked as the door closed.

Turning to the girl, Dagger clasped her hand as she said, "Sara Morningsky." He detected a brief tremble in her handshake.

Sara's gaze quickly turned to Einstein. "Aren't you a handsome fella?" She took long, graceful strides toward the cage. "And so smart. No wonder your name is Einstein." The macaw bobbed his head in agreement.

Dagger was drawn to the girl's exotic features—her almond-shaped eyes and olive complexion. She looked like she should be rising out of the waters of some South Pacific island, but the name Morningsky and her features told him she was probably Native American.

He watched her reach into the cage. "I wouldn't do that. Einstein nips everyone but . . ." His voice trailed off as he watched Einstein climb onto Sara's arm and nuzzle her chin. "Well, I'll be." Dagger ran a hand across the back of his neck. "He always had good taste." Einstein let out a whistle.

"Some macaws can live to the age of 100." Her eyes were mysterious, distant, like a door that cracks open slightly and then closes shut. She looked at Einstein's cage. "A bird this size should have an aviary or, better yet, a bird room."

"He did back at my apartment, but my landlord had too many complaints about the noise so I brought him here. It's only temporary."

"Your girlfriend has no intention of letting you keep Einstein." She didn't wait for him to reply. She was inspecting Einstein's nostrils and listening to his breathing. "He has a respiratory infection." Dagger looked closely at Einstein's face as Sara gazed up at the vent above the cage. "He's getting a draft from the vent. You should bring in a heat lamp and also give him some weak chamomile tea sweetened with glucose. Keep track of how much he eats and drinks."

"You know a lot about birds."

"A little."

Dagger found himself watching her mouth as she spoke, the movement of her lips, how her tongue touched her teeth. It was as if he was searching for flaws in a Monet painting but couldn't find any. She was refreshingly natural, like an unspoiled river or pristine beach. Her face was untouched by the pounds of makeup that masked Sheila's features.

"I'll do that. But I'm sure you didn't come here to make a house call on Einstein. How can I help you, Miss Morningsky?" He took Einstein from her and placed him back in the cage. Einstein shook his feathers as if irritated at being disturbed. "Please have a seat."

Sara glanced at the newspaper article about the detective found in the back of an abandoned building, shot twice in the back of the head. Twenty-five pounds of uncut heroin were found in the trunk of his car.

"My God," Sara gasped. "It wasn't bad enough they killed him. They planted drugs on him, too."

"You knew Mick Fazio?"

"I," Sara hesitated and then took a seat next to the oak desk cluttered with stacks of file folders and two half-empty coffee cups. Dagger pulled out a notepad and pen. "Mr. Dagger," she started.

"Just Dagger will be fine."

Sara smiled weakly. "I'm not sure where to start."

"Wherever you feel comfortable."

"I guess I can start with this." She placed the badge on his desk. "This belongs to the cop who killed Detective Fazio."

"Cop?" Slowly Dagger leaned back and studied his mysterious visitor. "Mick Fazio and I didn't always see eye to eye, but I believe we respected each other. I spoke with him last night; unfortunately, he wouldn't elaborate on what he was into other than to say he was close to solving a major crime. Mick would never have anything to do with drugs."

Sara continued to describe in detail how the cop had walked up to Fazio and shot him in the back of the head. Dagger made a quick call to a friend at headquarters to verify the badge number.

Hanging up the phone, Dagger said, "This badge belongs to Sergeant Ed Rollins, the police chief's son. You're saying he's involved in drugs?"

"Awwkk, Rollins. Crown jewel," Einstein blurted out, but Dagger ignored him.

"They weren't drug dealers. Sergeant Rollins was on some Gang Task Force, but he actually had the gangs working for him. I can't say how I know what I know. In a way, I was Detective Fazio's informant." She handed Dagger a piece of paper with the license plate number of the limousine.

"You could only know all this if you were there. How did you . . . ?"

"Detective Fazio has mentioned your name several times. That's how I knew to look you up."

"So you have met him." She shook her head no. "Then, how . . . ?" Dagger's voice trailed off. "Look, Miss Morningsky———."

"Sara, please."

"Sara, I wish I could help, but unless you are completely honest with me . . ."

"He mentioned an S and R Warehouse. Something is being stored there. I saw Detective Fazio make a number of audiotapes documenting his undercover work and conversations he's had with Sergeant Rollins."

Dagger shook his head in total confusion. She was skirting his main question. "Saw? But you said you've never met him."

"That's not the issue. What's important is finding out what Sergeant Rollins is keeping at the S and R Warehouse." The phone interrupted them.

"Awk. Hello, hello," Einstein mimicked from behind the bars. He used his powerful beak to climb to the top of the cage.

"Yeah," Dagger barked into the phone. It was Sheila, calling to say she bought him an Armani suit to wear to the rehearsal. "Sheila, I'm fine with blue jeans. You didn't have to————." He listened to her ramble, and then said, "I'll call you later." When he turned back to Sara, she was gone. She had left as silently as she had arrived.

He opened the door and ran down the rusting, white, wrought-iron stairs to the street just in time to see the belching fumes from a battered cab. Returning to his office, Dagger yelled out, "Cab company, Einstein."

"Awwkk. 555–9854."

Dagger made the call and was told Sara had been picked up at a coffee shop, not her residence—and they were to return her to the coffee shop.

Einstein bobbed his head several times as he looked around the office.

"Sorry, Einstein. She's gone." Dagger looked up at the ceiling over Einstein's cage and went to work taping a piece of cardboard around the vent to divert the draft. He then called a friend at the Department of Motor Vehicles to trace the plate number on the limousine only to learn that it belonged to Mayor Benton Sawyer. The waters were getting murkier. Standing at the window, Dagger gazed out at the dismal skies, plump clouds ready to dump their moisture.

"Hey, Dagger. How's your bird?" The rhythmic tone and deep laugh belonged to Simon. Hefting his mailbag onto a chair, Simon walked near the birdcage, noticing several feathers lying on the floor. "Looks like he's giving himself a haircut."

"Einstein is in love and upset that his lady left." Dagger held out a cheese curl, which Einstein ignored. "Cheese curls used to be the only things that made him feel better." Einstein continued to preen himself, tossing several more feathers. "If you keep that up," Dagger warned, "you'll be bald and that young lady won't ever look at you again." Einstein fluffed all 36 inches of his body and tail, shaking out a couple more brilliant scarlet red, blue, and yellow feathers.

Dagger took the bundle of mail from Simon and laid it on the desk. "You know just about everyone in town, don't you, Simon?"

"Everyone on my run, sure. Who ya' looking for?"

"A young woman. Native American, I think. Long, brown hair, blue-green eyes."

Simon rubbed a beefy hand across his chin. "Gotta name?"

"Sara Morningsky. She disappeared before I had a chance to get her address."

"She's not on my run, but there is reservation land down near Cedar Junction—about two or three hundred acres. " He gave his bulky shoulder a shrug. "Some large automotive company was building a shmanzy showroom and service facility out there years ago before the county realized the land wasn't anyone's to use."

Dagger entertained the thought of exploring the reservation land after Simon left, but his computer search through the town assessor's records completed its report on Mayor Benton Sawyer.

He leaned back in his chair, plopping his feet on the desk. "Well, Mayor. Exactly how do you fit in with Sergeant Ed Rollins?"

"Awk. Crown Jewels." Einstein's vocabulary came mostly from mimicking and word association; and what he said finally struck a familiar chord with Dagger. It had something to do with a conversation he had had with Mick Fazio months ago, but his memory was still hazy. His eyes instead locked on the computer screen where it mentioned S and R Warehouse—Sawyer and Rollins. Mayor Sawyer and Chief Rollins owned S and R Warehouse. Exactly what was stored there Dagger had no idea. But he was going to find out.

*　*　*

"I tried to explain it to him, grandmother. But there were so many questions I couldn't answer." Sara sat next to a white-haired woman whose face was weathered with lines of age and wisdom. Her veiny hands were clasped around Sara's.

"You must listen to your heart, my child. What does your heart tell you to do?" Ada Kills Bull patted her grandchild's arm. "You want to help him?"

Sara nodded. "Although maybe I shouldn't. I tried helping Detective Fazio and look where it got him."

"It wasn't your fault he was killed. But you can help find his killers."

Sara thought for a moment. "You are right. I'll just go to the warehouse myself."

*　*　*

Dagger lowered his night vision binoculars. S and R Warehouse had been quiet since he arrived an hour ago. From his post behind a boulder on a cliff near the site, he had a good view of the main entrance. He gathered his black leather coat around him to ward off the damp chill the rains had brought.

Headlights appeared down the road. A semi lumbered up to the freight door and a youth with a long ponytail jumped from the truck and unlocked the door. The driver got out and entered the warehouse through the side door. Lights turned on. Another figure stepped out of the rear of the semi. He was thin with ferret features and a receding hairline. It was Ed Rollins. Soon several youths started unloading items, which looked like paintings, sculptures, and velvet bags the size of pouches.

Dagger saw a movement along the side of the building. He scanned the area with his binoculars and zoomed in on a figure. It looked like a dog. Its coat was multicolored, its eyes and mouth surrounded by white fur; but it wasn't a dog. It was a wolf. Wolves in Indiana? Dagger thought.

"Hey!" Rollins yelled. "That's the same mutt that took my badge." The wolf growled and took a lunge toward Rollins. When Rollins pulled a gun from his belt, the wolf rushed into the woods.

Through the binoculars, Dagger watched in horror as Rollins pulled off two quick shots. The wolf howled in pain.

"Let's get moving," another man ordered.

Crouching down, Dagger moved away from the boulder. When he was a safe distance away from sight of the warehouse, he pulled out a flashlight and searched through the dense forest for the injured wolf. From the amount of blood on the trail, it appeared that Rollins had made a direct hit. The blood trail was easy to follow. Dagger found the wolf whimpering, lying on its side, its front legs trying to drag itself to safety.

"Good God!" Dagger shined the flashlight on the wolf's missing right leg, shot clean off. He bent down and examined the wound. The wolf trembled under his touch. Heaving a sigh, Dagger stood up and pointed his gun at the wolf's head. "Sorry about this, but you'll be better off, believe me."

The wolf looked up at him with the strangest colored eyes; they looked blue-green. His hand shook as he started to pull the trigger. Then the strangest thing happened. The wolf changed shape. The multicolored fur coat became hair, the legs long and muscular, the body human. It was Sara. She looked up at him with those dazzling eyes.

"For the love of . . . " Dagger breathed, returning his gun to his holster and shaking his leather coat off. "I have to get you to a hospital."

"No!" Her hands gripped his arms as he wrapped her in his coat. He stripped out of his shirt and tied it tightly around her injured leg that had been shot off just below the knee. "You have to take me to my grandmother. She's the only one who can help. Please, Dagger."

"You need a doctor, Sara." There was some underlying fear and desperation in her voice. Her eyes pleaded—and he was a sucker for those eyes.

The door to the downstairs bedroom was slightly ajar. Curious, Dagger peered through the opening at Sara's sweat-soaked body, which was covered in a sheet. Sara's grandmother had not seemed the least bit excited about her granddaughter's condition. She had just instructed Dagger to lay her on the bed and thanked him for bringing her home. For some reason, he couldn't tear himself away without getting some answers.

As the grandmother pulled back the sheet, exposing the injured leg, Dagger was shocked to see that half of it had already grown back. The bleeding had stopped, almost as if it had been cauterized. A cold chill crept up his back. Dagger's gaze moved up the sheet, watching Sara's chest rise and fall with each ragged breath. His gaze settled on her face where her opened eyes, filled with tears, were staring right at him. Startled, he pulled away and pressed his back against the wall. Five years as a PI and he had never seen anything that so shocked and bewildered him. His mind was numb, unable to digest what he had seen.

He moved away from the bedroom and surveyed the house, which looked like the showroom and automotive repair facility Simon had talked about. There were stone walls, tiled floors, numerous windows, and skylights. Other than area rugs and what looked like garage sale furniture, there didn't seem to be anything extravagant in the living room. There was one wall of shelving loaded with books, a television, and a VCR. Stairs lead up to a second floor that probably once housed offices that overlooked the downstairs and there was a catwalk that dissected the width of the living room.

He located the kitchen and with shaky legs dropped down onto a kitchen chair. From the looks of all the fresh vegetables gathered on the counter, it would be his guess that they had a large garden out back.

Sara's grandmother appeared out of nowhere and poured two glasses of cognac. She reminded him of Yoda with her stooped appearance and heavy-lidded eyes. His hand shook as he brought the glass to his lips and gulped the hot liquid. She refilled it quickly.

"How is Sara?" Dagger asked in a raspy voice.

"She will be fine," Ada replied. "I can't thank you enough for being there tonight and bringing her back to me." Her eyes had a milky veil and her head shook slightly as if she had a mild case of Parkinson's disease. It was difficult to tell her age.

"What . . . how did . . . ?" But Dagger couldn't seem to get the words out. He dragged a hand through his long, damp hair.

"Sara is a shape-shifter," Ada explained. "Some say it is just Native American folklore. It was believed elders could shift into animal forms in order to spy on their enemies. Others believed there were those with more bestial natures who would kill the farmers' cattle. I first witnessed Sara's shape shifting when she was 6 years old, when her parents died. That was 12 years ago on a reservation in Montana. She withdrew from her human form to deal with the grief. She didn't know how to change back. I took her to a powerful medicine man who had been outcast from the tribe because he was a shape-shifter; they were afraid of him. He took us in and showed Sara how to control her shifting. To some, it is a curse. But to us, it is a magical gift. Sara shifts into two distinct forms."

Dagger paused, his glass near his lips. He was already feeling the effects of the liquor. "There's another shape besides a wolf?"

"Yes," Ada said with a hint of pride. "Besides the gray wolf, Sara also shifts to a gray hawk, a beautiful creature with a wing span of 40 inches."

No wonder she couldn't tell me how she got the badge, Dagger thought. "And," he glanced toward the doorway, "her leg. How does she . . . ?"

"A shape-shifter has regenerative powers. Bleeding stops quickly and the body begins to regrow parts and close wounds."

Dagger shook his head, feeling something rattling between his ears, losing equilibrium. He wondered if this was how people felt right before passing out.

"I know this is all very hard to understand."

"Ma'am," Dagger said as he stood up. "You don't know the half of it."

"Yes, I do," was her parting remark.

"Grandmother?" Sara opened her eyes as Ada patted Sara's face with a cool washcloth.

"You must rest, Sara."

"He saw, Grandmother. Dagger saw."

"I know, dear. He's gone now."

Trying to lift herself up from the bed she said, "But the wolf will kill him. There can be no witnesses. The wolf will kill."

"Shhhh. Be still, my child. I am safe from the wolf because you and I are connected by blood. According to legend, he is protected because he saved the wolf." Ada fingered the necklace hanging from her neck. It was a black leather cord with a sterling silver wolf-head pendant; its eyes were made of two bright turquoise gems.

* * *

A package was waiting for Dagger the next day when he arrived at his office.

"Awwwkk. You're late; you're late," Einstein scolded as he flew over and clamped his talons onto the back of a chair.

"I know, Einstein." Dagger tore open the envelope and spilled audiotapes on the desk. They were from Mick Fazio with a note instructing Dagger to listen to them if for some reason something happened to him.

Crown jewel. Mick had made that comment in Dagger's office 6 months ago. That was how Einstein associated Rollins' name with crown jewel.

Dagger listened to the tapes and then made two phone calls—one to Ed Rollins, and the other to a friend with the FBI.

* * *

Sara stood on her upstairs balcony inhaling the clean, crisp air. Her thoughts turned to Dagger and how it felt when he held her. She was afraid for him. What if her grandmother were wrong? Legend is just that—legend. They really had no way of knowing what would happen the next time the wolf saw Dagger. There weren't any rulebooks and no one to confide in. Just like in the past, they might have to run again, get the wolf as far away as possible so it wouldn't be tempted to protect Sara's identity. She would never be able to forgive herself if someone else died because of her.

She stepped out onto the balcony. Night was fast approaching, bringing with it a damp mist. There was unfinished business. That was the problem with having the instincts of the hawk and wolf: Sara could hear things other people couldn't hear, go places and see things not humanly possible. She owed it to Mick Fazio to bring his killers to justice. Smiling, she silently called upon the spirit of the hawk, bowed her head, and felt the spirit enter her. Her dress fell away, shed like some unwanted skin, a cumbersome annoyance. And the hawk took flight.

* * *

A semi pulled up, the freight door lifted, spilling the light from inside. When Rollins stepped out of the warehouse, Dagger emerged from his hiding place. Dagger's earlier telephone conversation with Rollins had hinted that Rollins might be in need of someone to replace Mick.

"Are you Dagger?" Rollins asked, his beady eyes studying Dagger. Rollins was joined by a stocky man wearing pounds of gold and an expensive-looking suit that would meet Sheila's approval.

"You must be the fruit of Mayor Sawyer's loins," Dagger quipped. Mick Sawyer took a step forward. Three youths jumped down from the back of the truck, positioning themselves around Dagger. They sported black berets and armbands. The grips of guns could be seen in the waistbands of their jeans. He felt surrounded by three fire hydrants. The best he could hope for was that they had poor aim.

"Calm down boys," Rollins instructed. "Let's hear what the gentleman has to say."

Dagger pressed the play button on the recorder. Mick Fazio's voice was heard clearly, explaining how he had first suspected something when valuables listed on theft reports were showing up in Rollins' possession. Ed Rollins, head of the Gang Task Force, was using gang members to steal expensive artwork and jewelry from rich suburbanites. The items were then smuggled out of state to fences in New York and Miami. Mick had been working with Internal Affairs to bust the theft ring.

"Pretty lucrative business you two boys have masterminded." Dagger clicked off the recorder as he stepped closer.

"We're not in need of any more partners," Sawyer barked, pulling out his gun. "But we'll take those tapes."

"Not so fast." Dagger held up Rollins' badge. "Lose something, Sergeant?"

Rollins lit a cigar and tossed the match at Dagger's feet. "Think you're pretty brave coming in here?"

Dagger noticed a hawk circling overhead. He saw leaves rustling and the shadow of a figure lurking. Snipers? He had suspected as much and wondered exactly how many were out there. Then the hawk moved to another tree to his right, circling over another shadow lurking in the dark. Dagger smiled slowly and shrugged. "Maybe I'm not alone."

Things happened quickly. FBI agents arrived in four, unmarked cars, storming the warehouse as Dagger shot two of the snipers. High-beam lights flooded the area. The youths were inexperienced, not knowing where to run or where to shoot first.

"You okay, Dagger?" The gray-haired agent asked after the dust settled.

Dagger nodded, patting his bulletproof vest. He watched as the hawk lighted on a nearby post, it's blue-green eyes shining brightly. Dagger thought he might be reading into it but he could swear the hawk seemed to wait to make sure he was all right before gracefully swooping over the area and disappearing into the shadowy forest.

* * *

Dagger sat at his desk listening to another call from Sheila. There were already three on the recorder. It was 1:30 in the morning and he didn't feel like going home where there were probably even more messages—and he definitely didn't feel like talking to Sheila.

"Dagger, honey. Where are you? I know I should be mad at you, baby." She started out sounding hurt that he had missed the rehearsal, trying to sound understanding; but then her true character came through. "You son of a bitch. Where are you? Daddy is so upset. But I made excuses for you, again." There was silence for a few moments and then an exhaustive expletive. Sheila hung up.

"Awk. Good riddance," Einstein bellowed as he paced back and forth on his perch.

Leaning back in his chair, Dagger propped his legs on the desk and rubbed his hands across his face feeling the dirt and grit from the gravel lot.

"You never liked Sheila, did you Einstein?" Einstein shook his head frantically back and forth. Dagger smiled. He should give Sheila a call, but he didn't know yet how to tell her he wasn't going to make it to the wedding either.

All he could think of was Sara: her naked body lying on the ground in the forest, her shape-shifting abilities, and the way her leg had regenerated. He had just come across a magical, undiscovered island, and he had to explore it first.

"And what about Sara? Do you like Sara, Einstein?"

Einstein let out a whistle.

"I don't know why I ever agreed to marry Sheila. This should be a lesson, buddy. Never have more than one martini." Dagger closed his eyes, pressing his palms to his forehead to ward off the headache that was developing.

He felt the air move, and opened his eyes to see Einstein, wings spread, landing on the desk. Einstein plodded over to Dagger and dropped something in front of him. It was a cheese curl.

Dagger smiled as he picked up the treat. "Thanks, but I think it's going to take more than a cheese curl."

In the morning, after a restless nap, Dagger showered and drove over to Sara's. He rapped lightly on the back door. After a few moments, he peered through the screen at the empty kitchen. Somewhere inside he heard someone crying. Pulling lightly on the door, it opened and he stepped inside.

On the kitchen counter was a sheet of paper with his name printed in shaky lettering. Beside the notepad was the leather cord necklace Sara's grandmother had worn yesterday.

Dagger followed the soft cries to the downstairs bedroom where he found Sara, her arms wrapped around her grandmother. Ada was a light shade of gray, and her face had the most serene look.

"Sara?" Dagger sat on the edge of the bed.

Sara slowly looked up. "She must have died in her sleep." Sara let the tears fall freely, pressing her cheek to Ada's forehead. "She promised she would never leave me," Sara sobbed. Her hand shook as she swiped at her tears.

Dagger felt Ada's skin. Rigor was beginning to set in.

He kept Sara busy gathering Ada's possessions that she might want buried with her while he dug a grave on a flowery knoll overlooking Thornton Creek. Sara carried some of Ada's favorite plants to the gravesite.

After pounding a makeshift cross into the ground, Dagger returned to the house to find Sara sitting cross-legged on the couch, sobbing quietly, her hands clenched tightly. He sat down next to her.

"It's as if Grandmother knew." She unfolded the note and handed him the necklace. "I think she wanted you to have this."

Dagger took the necklace from her and touched her arm. Her body recoiled like the frightened wolf he had found in the forest. Sara, too, was afraid of all humans except her grandmother. It would take a lot to quell her fears of living in a world as an outcast.

For a moment when he had met Ada yesterday, he had wondered if she was Sara's great-grandmother, not grandmother. If he counted the folds of skin as anyone would the rings in a tree to determine age, she had to have been over 100 years old. It was as though she had been waiting for someone to take her place as Sara's protector. Once Dagger came on the scene, Ada seemed grateful finally to be able to rest.

His gaze drifted toward the skylights and he took in the enormous size of the house. The property was isolated, safe, and secure. He walked over to an adjacent room that was sparsely dotted with floor plants. By the looks of the floor drains, it might have been planned as the service center for the car dealership.

Glancing over at Sara he saw a frightened child in many ways but a unique woman in others. Although Ada Kills Bull had been able to be a companion and confidante to her granddaughter, there was very little she taught her about the outside world, his world.

"Come here, Sara."

Slowly Sara approached, still keeping her distance, her hands trembling.

"Einstein and I have been kicked out of our apartment and office. I think this area would make a great bird room. I can take over your grandmother's bedroom and," he turned toward the living room, "I can cordon off a portion of the living room to set up my office." He studied her face as she nervously chewed on her bottom lip. "What do you think?"

"You mean you want to move in here after you are married?"

"No, Sara. There isn't going to be a wedding."

"Oh."

"That relationship was on shaky ground from the start."

"Oh," Sara repeated.

"I can pay you $1,000 a month for the room and office space."

"That's way too much," Sara protested.

"You need to make a living, Sara. You can't live on vegetables and hand-me-downs all your life." At least she didn't say no, Dagger thought. "Seven hundred and fifty and that's my last offer." Sara forced a smile. "Dagger Investigations could also use a partner."

"Me?"

Dagger smiled. "I could use someone with your unusual . . . talents." Sara's eyes filled again. He cautiously reached out, wrapped his arms around her and held her until she stopped shaking. "You're going to be fine, Sara," he whispered. "Your secret is safe with me."

Chapter 6

The Storm

By Jon Fabris

Barret listened to the clopping sound of the carriage team's hooves splashing repeatedly in the mud. An occasional loud thunderclap broke the monotony. He didn't mind though; in fact, riding in a carriage was a luxury he could seldom afford. This trip was made possible by his friend and benefactor, Thomas Moorefield. He had urgently summoned Barret to his home and provided this carriage for the 10–hour ride. The sullen messenger would not tell him the nature of the errand—only that Mr. Moorefield wished his presence immediately. In addition to being his friend, Moorefield was a man who one seldom would dare disobey. Moorefield's new wife, Lavonia, had died suddenly 4 months ago; Barret suspected that her death was at the center of his errand.

At last he entered the outskirts of Randolph, Moorefield's estate that was located on the other end of town. He used his sleeve to wipe a circle out of the foggy window and watched the town slowly pass by. Everyone looked up as the carriage passed. It was a rare occurrence to see a fine, two-horse-drawn carriage riding through the poor farming community and it was taken for granted that he would be heading to Moorefield's, the wealthiest man in town.

Barret felt that a strange, heavy mood hung over the town. Every face he saw was grim, almost fearful. Something bad was happening here; he could sense it. And his senses were unusually sharp. Some people called him a clairvoyant or a mystic; others even claimed he was a warlock, although never to his face. In fact, it was this interest in the occult that drew him and Moorefield together at a séance several years ago.

The horses whinnied and seemed to hesitate when they passed through the gates of Moorefield's estate. The carriage stopped and the driver had to shout at his restless team to be steady. The driver opened his door and pulled out the ramp. Barret stepped down, gave him a coin, and the driver hastily departed.

The iron knocker echoed in the damp air. It was several moments before the door opened and a servant grimly led him inside. The servant took his baggage and led him into the parlor. A fire was lit and Barret stood there warming himself.

"Barret!" Moorefield called out warmly as he entered the parlor. The two men embraced.

Barret noticed a definite change in his old friend. He looked much older than when they last met at his wedding 6 months before: Streaks of gray ran through his hair; new lines were clearly etched into his face.

"Come to the dining room; there is some food already prepared."

They sat at the table eating, drinking, and reminiscing about old times. The laughter was subdued, however.

Barret heard footsteps in the hallway behind him. Moorefield called out, "Gentlemen, come meet our new guest."

Two men entered the room: a distinguished looking man of 50 with graying hair and a young man barely out of his teens. The two men had a clear family resemblance.

"This is Mr. Barret, an old and dear friend of mine. He will be staying with us for a few weeks. This is Richard Feltcher, Lavonia's uncle, and his son Donald," Moorefield introduced.

"So you are the expert who has come to solve our supposed ghost problem." Richard shook Barret's hand. The man had a distinct arrogant air about him.

"I take it you do not believe in ghosts?" Barret replied.

"I stopped believing in fairies when I was a child," Richard answered.

"Pleased to meet you." Donald said as he shook Barret's hand. The boy was somewhat quiet and sullen.

The pair left the room.

"The boy is alright, but Richard is a conceited bastard if you ask me," Moorefield said quietly.

"Have they been staying here long?" Barret asked.

"They moved in after the marriage along with Lavonia's grandmother, Lady Feltcher. She was infirm and died 2 months ago. They will be leaving soon I hope."

"I am sorry about Lavonia," Barret said.

"Thank you." Moorefield lowered his head.

"Is it about her that you asked me here?" Barret gently asked.

Moorefield took a breath, then spoke what was on his mind, "Lavonia is not at rest my friend. She is tormenting me. I believe she blames me for not being here for her when she took ill."

"I did not know her well, but I took her as a kind and gentle soul. Her illness was sudden, was it not?"

"Yes—very sudden. I didn't even know she was ill until the morning she died. I rushed home but was too late."

"Then how could she fault you?"

"I don't know, but since her death, there have been restless spirits in this house. The servants have seen her pacing the hallway. Now she will not even allow me to enter her room; when I enter, it is as if I am attacked by unseen forces."

"And the house was free of spirits before her death?"

"I lived here my entire life and have never felt a presence." Moorefield grabbed Barret's hand with a cold, clammy grip. "You must find a way to set her spirit to rest, my friend."

"I will do my best. I promise." Barret was struck by his friend's almost craven manner. He had always projected such confidence and strength.

The hour was late now, and Cynthia, one of the servants, showed Barret to his room.

"Where was Lavonia's room?" Barret asked.

She looked uncomfortable, but as a loyal servant she obeyed and led him down the hall. "I will show you, but no one is permitted to enter."

Cynthia stopped in front of a closed door. "Here was her room."

Barret opened the door and stepped inside as the servant gasped. The room was decorated exquisitely with a tasteful feminine touch. He stepped toward the bed. With suddenness, the calm was broken. The mirror on her bedstand was splashed with blood, forming the words *get out*. Almost in the same instant long, invisible fingernails viciously scratched his face. Unnerved, Barret rushed out of the room.

Cynthia was upset, almost hysterical, "I told you not to go in!" She dabbed at his scratches with a kerchief.

Barret thought back to when he met Lavonia. "Did Lavonia have long fingernails?"

"No, she used to chew them up short."

"I didn't think so," Barret said to himself. He dismissed the servant and returned to his own room.

The room was tastefully decorated with mahogany furniture. Above the head of the bed were two crossed swords mounted on a large, wooden shield bearing the ram's head crest of the Moorefield clan. The bed was exceptionally soft and comfortable, and after the exertion of traveling all day, combined with the influence of six glasses of wine, Barret fell asleep instantly.

Two hours later, he awoke suddenly and completely. Sensing there was someone else in the room, he sat up. Blinking, he could vaguely see a female figure next to the bed. He could not make out her face in the virtually complete darkness of the starless night. She turned and slowly walked to the door. The door opened and he followed her into the hallway. There was an oil lamp burning dimly at the far end of the hall, but still he could not see the woman very well. It was as if she walked in her own shadow. She led him through several turns, then entered one of the rooms. He followed and found himself in a dusty closet, obviously little used. The woman faced him and then turned and walked through the far wall, disappearing.

Now Barret was sure that the woman was a ghost—the ghost of Lavonia Moorefield to be specific. He examined the wall she had passed through. There were rough wooden shelves attached it. On the shelves were some books, wooden boxes, and folded linens. He left the room and returned with a lamp from the hallway. He examined the shelves closely. The dust was disturbed on part of one of the shelves. Barret felt behind it. There was a latch.

He fiddled with it and felt it unhook. The shelf and wall it was attached to swung inward. He stepped inside the secret room; it was very small—perhaps two men could fit inside—and bare except for a small shelf. Atop the shelf was a box.

Barret opened the box; inside were several small books. He recognized them as illustrated, erotic novels by the French author Detoulier, popular in Paris at the time. He understood why someone would wish to keep them hidden. They were considered obscene by polite society of the day. He almost laughed; his friend Moorefield traveled to Paris often, and he could imagine him deriving enjoyment from such books. There was also a small bottle filled with a cloudy liquid. He opened the bottle and carefully sniffed. There was no odor. He replaced the books carefully but kept the mysterious bottle. He closed the secret door and perused the room to make sure he had not disturbed anything.

He went back to bed, but now sleep eluded him.

Barret got out of bed late the next morning. He found the house empty except for a few servants. Moorefield had left a message that he would be out until the afternoon. A good time to explore the town, he thought.

Barret grabbed an apple from the kitchen and stepped out into the cold drizzle. A fine mist fell from the iron gray sky as he headed toward town at a brisk pace. Soon he could see the church. There was a crowd of people outside in the graveyard, all in black. He observed from a distance. They lowered the casket into the ground and completed the ceremony. The group began to disperse and Barret approached one of the mourners, a middle-aged peasant.

Using an aristocratic accent, Barret questioned the man, "Good sir. I beg your pardon, but I did not hear of the funeral. Who died?"

"It was Molly Scott, Jonah's young daughter."

"I am sorry. Was it an illness?"

The commoner snorted bitterly, "Aye, that's what the doctor says, but everyone knows it was no illness. She was never the same after the attack."

"I have been traveling; I did not hear of any attacks."

The man looked at Barret queerly, he obviously didn't want to talk about it. "Some devil has been attacking women. I am sorry, but I have to go."

The peasant walked away at a rapid pace. Barret headed into town and soon found an apothecary. The apothecary squinted at him disapprovingly through his spectacles. Barret showed him the vial he had found. The old man sniffed the potion, dripped some into a small saucer, and added a few drops of something else. Satisfied, he looked up at Barret, "'Tis poison—yellow monkshood."

Barret thanked the man and gave him a silver coin. His heart was heavy with thought as he headed back to the Moorefield estate.

Barret entered by the servant's door and walked into the kitchen. Cynthia bowed as she saw him, "My lord." The cook, Milla, also was there.

"That smells good; may I have some?" Barret lied.

"I will bring you some to the dining room if you wish, my lord," Cynthia replied.

"No need, I will have it right here." Barret chatted with the servants as he ate, using conversational tones in an attempt to put the women at ease.

"I was in town today and I heard there had been some attacks on women."

Initially, the women hesitated, but after some coaxing, the words quickly began to flow.

"They started about 5 or 6 months ago. There've been about nine attacks————." Cynthia said.

"No, 11 counting Nessa," the cook chimed in.

"Aye, and Tilley Morisson was killed. All the others survived but were never the same," Cynthia continued.

"Did they see their attacker?"

"He wore a scarf around his face and dressed all in black, " Milla said.

"All the attacks were at night," Cynthia added.

"Did you know Lavonia well?" Barret asked both women.

"I only knew her 2 months, but Cynthia was her handmaiden for 5 years," Milla said.

Cynthia looked sad and her eyes began to water, "I've known her since she was a girl. When she was married and moved here, she brought me with her."

"She was a fine lady I hear," said Barret.

"Aye, she was always good to me."

"How did she die?"

Cynthia wiped a tear from her eyes. "It was real sudden. When I brought her the milk, she seemed fine. Late that night she rang her bell for me. I found her in terrible pain—her stomach she said—and she could barely speak. She fainted and by morning she was gone."

"Did she drink a glass of milk before bedtime often?"

"Aye. She liked her warm milk every night to help her sleep."

Barret gulped down the stew, trying not to taste it. "What was Lady Feltcher like?"

"Ah, she was an evil, spiteful woman," Cynthia confided.

"She was ill, Cynthia; her mind was afflicted by old age," Milla said.

"No, she was always like that; she used to beat me."

"Did she get along well with Lavonia?" Barret asked.

"No, she hated everyone. Except Donald—she adored him."

"What is he like?"

"Quiet boy. Nice enough. He spends most of his time in the library," Cynthia said.

* * *

Barret was in the library, perusing Moorefield's excellent collection of occult books. One title caught his eye, *A Compendium of Herbal Remedies.* He turned to the index and found a section on monkshood.

* * *

Monkshood or Friar's Cap

The plant is a hardy perennial with a fleshy, spindle-shaped root, pale-colored when young, but subsequently acquiring a dark brown skin. The stem is about 3 feet high, with dark green, glossy leaves, deeply divided in palmate manner and flowers in erect clusters of a dark blue color.

Symptoms of poisoning include severe gastronomical distress, difficulty breathing, and a tingling and numbness in the mouth.

* * *

The sun had just set and Barret sat in the dark library, thinking.

The door opened and Moorefield stepped into the room. "I am sorry I was delayed, my friend. There have been problems with our bankers in Wakeshore. Come to the dining room; supper will be ready soon."

"Thomas? Did Lavonia keep a journal or diary?" Barret asked.

Moorefield thought for a moment, "Yes, I believe she did as a matter of fact."

"Did you read it after she passed?"

"No, she would not have wanted that. Besides I am not sure where the diary is . . . perhaps check in her bedroom."

"Thank you, my friend," said Barret.

Barret found Moorefield, Richard, Donald, and two priests he did not recognize at the dinner table.

"Ah, Barret, I would like you to meet our priest, Father Dorley, and his young initiate Seymore." Moorefield stood and formally introduced the three men who shook hands.

"Barret is investigating the hauntings that have been taking place," Moorefield added.

"As a man of the cloth, I do not approve of disturbing the dead," Father Dorley said. Barret thought his speech sounded somewhat slurred, as if he were drunk.

"Ah, but ghosts are not at rest. And sometimes we mortals are able to find a way to help them find peace."

"If a man has faith, he will find peace through God's love," Dorley responded reverently.

"Sometimes tragic events will lead even the most faithful to stray from the road to heaven," Barret answered.

"What sort of events, Mr. Barret?" Father Seymore asked respectfully.

"If the deceased has unfinished business here on Earth, or if they cannot accept their own death, or if they were murdered," Barret hinted. He did not want to fully reveal his suspicions as yet. He needed more information.

The men in the room stiffened as they digested the subtle hint.

"Do you think Lavonia was murdered, Barret?" Moorefield asked, horrified.

"I truly don't know, my friend, but we will discover the truth; I promise."

The rest of the meal passed without further mention of ghosts.

* * *

That night Barret sat up in his bed, unable to sleep. He went over the facts of the situation in his mind. Then, like the night before, he sensed a presence. The ghost materialized beside his bed, but, unlike the placid calm of her demeanor the previous night, she was obviously distraught. She urgently motioned for him to come and then vanished through his door. He got up and rushed to the door.

Suddenly, before he could open the door to follow the figure, behind him there was an enormous, explosive crash. Barret wheeled around. The Moorefield crest had fallen from the wall landing directly where his head had been resting only moments before. The weight had collapsed one of the bed's legs. The two swords had also come loose from the shield and embedded themselves 6 inches into the mattress.

The door jerked open and Moorefield was there, blinking at the spectacle.

"Good Lord! What happened?"

"I'm so sorry Barret. That shield has been there since I was a lad; I had no idea it was loose," Moorefield apologized.

Barret was examining the wall where the shield had hung. The wall had been tampered with. The brackets, which fastened the crest to the wall, had been removed. Someone had drilled a hole in the wall and a rope was all that held the shield up. Barret grabbed the end of the rope, which was attached to the shield. "What's on the other side of this wall, Moorefield?"

"Let's go see."

As the two men rushed out into the hallway, Richard was there, in his bedclothes, "What on Earth is going on? I was trying to sleep."

"That's what we want to know"

The adjacent room was another bedroom, similar to Barret's.

"Who stays here?" Barret demanded.

"No one, it is a spare room," Moorefield replied.

There were no obvious signs of tampering with the wall, but a large painting hung in the center of the wall where the hole should be. Barret removed the painting, revealing a roughly drilled hole about 1 inch in diameter. He bent down and examined the floor, "Look, there is fresh dust here from the drill."

He looked over at the bed located just next to the painting. "The rope was probably tied to this bedpost. Then, when the time was right, all that was needed was to loosen the knot and let the shield fall."

"I will question the servants; perhaps they saw something. I'll have another room prepared for you," Moorefield declared as he rushed out of the room.

Barret looked down at Richard's feet, "Always sleep with your boots on, Richard?"

Richard looked offended and paced out of the room without a word.

* * *

Barret slept badly in his new room and woke late the next morning. The storm had intensified and the rain was falling in powerful sheets. It was Sunday and he could hear the church bells ringing in the distance.

Barret found Moorefield, Richard, and Donald in the dining room having breakfast.

"Good morning. Did you sleep well, my friend?" Moorefield asked.

"Quite well."

"What are your plans for today?" Moorefield asked.

"I intend to conduct a séance today. Would you prepare the main hall?"

A shocked silence embraced the room. Moorefield, who was more accustomed to such events, looked relieved—almost happy. "Of course."

"I would like us four to attend, as well as your servant Cynthia. "

"I have no intention of taking part in such a ridiculous pageant," Richard objected.

Moorefield became angry. "I needn't remind you, Richard, that you are a guest in my house."

"Oh, very well," Richard said and stormed out of the room.

"What about you, Donald?" Barret asked.

"If you wish, I will attend," he replied.

Barret spent some time in the library, thinking over the recent events.

The iron knocker clanged. Barret could hear a crowd of people outside even over the intense rain and went to the door to investigate. Moorefield was already there, opening the door.

Father Dorley stood on the threshold with a crowd of about 30 villagers. "Half the town is flooded. We took refuge in the church, but now it, too, is flooded."

"Come in; you are all welcome. Go into the main hall and warm yourselves. I will have blankets brought down."

The townspeople filed in. The entire scope of the town was represented. There were old men, women with babies, children clinging to their mothers, and farmers. They all looked around with wonder at the opulent surroundings they had only heard about.

Barret helped the servants deliver blankets and move the furniture out of the way to make room for the townspeople. He bumped into Father Seymore in the hallway. "Father Seymore, good to see you again," Barret said.

"Good day, Mr. Barret." He replied.

"I have a favor to beg of you, Father—a small thing really. I wish you to bless Lavonia's bedchamber."

"I don't know, Mr. Barret. I don't think Father Dorley would approve.

"You want Lavonia to rest in peace don't you?" Barret cajoled.

"Yes, yes of course, but———."

"Then do me this small favor." Barret had Father Seymore by the arm and led him to Lavonia's room, stopping at the door. " If you would hold out the crucifix you wear around your neck, and say a blessing. You have a Bible with you, do you not? Yes. And, perhaps read an excerpt from Mark 9:24." Barret helped him turn to the right page. He opened the door and gently pushed the still hesitant priest inside.

Barret watched the exorcism ceremony from the doorway, hoping for success.

The priest hesitantly began to read the scriptures. Suddenly, he began walking backward toward the door.

"I feel something pushing me away, Mr. Barret," The panicky priest said.

"That's fine, Father Seymore; keep reading."

The priest continued reading but also continued moving backward.

"Almost done; keep reading," Barret called out as he closed the door, locking the young priest in. He could hear the priest still reading, then a surprisingly loud bang as he hit the closed door. All was quiet.

Barret opened the door. Father Seymore was white as a sheet and was rubbing a bump on the back of his head, but he was otherwise unmarked. "Thank you, Father; you have done well. Better go back down and see to your flock."

The priest looked confused but obeyed and left the room.

Barret took a breath and entered the room. He took a step toward the bed. He felt a surge of relief as nothing happened. He began searching the room. He looked under the bed and inside the closet. He examined her nightstand. He spotted a hidden drawer, obvious to one who knew a little carpentry. He pulled it open. Inside were a few letters and a small leather-bound book. He began reading. The letters were love letters from Moorefield. He felt enormously sad reading them, as they were obviously deeply in love. The book was a diary. He skipped to the last few pages.

Barret closed the book and put it into his pocket. The matter is clear now, he thought. But I still need more proof. Perhaps Lavonia will be able to help.

Barret returned to the crowded main hall. Moorefield was there and whispered into his ear, "The library has been prepared, my friend. I will fetch the others."

Barret entered the library and waited for Moorefield, Richard, Donald, and Cynthia to arrive. They all gathered around a circular table. The lights were dimmed very low. The double doors leading into the main hall were closed, drowning out most of the noise from the crowd of villagers.

"Now, we must hold hands and under no circumstances is anyone to break the circle," Barret commanded. "Everyone concentrate on my words. Lavonia Moorefield, we plead with you to return to us. You are not at rest; we need you to tell us why."

Barret continued in similar fashion for several minutes.

Barret was watching Cynthia intently and finally noticed a sign he was hoping for. Her eyes glazed over and she slumped slightly. She moaned softly and the others began watching her.

"Lavonia, are you with us?"

"I am here." It was Cynthia speaking, but her voice had taken a refined accent and a more elegant quality to it.

"Darling . . . " Moorefield exclaimed softly.

"Quiet. Lavonia, why do you remain here in these halls? Why can you not find rest?"

"Ooh!" She moaned, "My stomach pains me so."

"How came you to be ill, Lavonia?" Barret asked.

"Ooh—no, not ill—poisoned! Someone poisoned my milk."

"Who did this to you, Lavonia? Who poisoned you?"

"Aaah!" She was in extreme distress; it was heartbreaking to hear, "My own flesh and blood—no, it cannot be!"

Suddenly Cynthia slumped down and the spell was broken.

Moorefield turned and shouted at Richard, "You let go. You broke the circle!"

"No! My son let go." Richard said.

"On the first night of my visit here, Lavonia appeared to me. She led me to a secret room inside a closet on the third floor. Inside, I found this." Barret produced a vial from his pocket and placed it dramatically on the table. "I had it identified by the apothecary. It's monkshood, a deadly poison. According to a book on herbs—which I found in this very library, by the way—the symptoms of aconite poisoning match the symptoms suffered by Lavonia on the night of her death."

"Who would poison my wife? She was loved by everyone!" Moorefield cried.

"While in town, I learned of a series of attacks upon women which began soon after the marriage, and also soon after Lavonia's relatives moved here," Barret said.

"So you think the madman who has been raping these women murdered my wife?" Moorefield said with horror in his voice.

Barret ignored the interruption. "Thomas, you told me that Lavonia would not let you enter her room anymore. Were you able to enter her room right after her death?"

"Yes, for a few weeks I was; I don't understand why."

"I will tell you. Lavonia was not haunting her room at all. It was the spirit of Lady Feltcher. It was only after her death that you—and everyone else, by the way—were barred from entering the room."

"Nonsense! Why would my mother haunt Lavonia's bedroom?" Richard scoffed.

"Because she did not want anyone to find this!" Barret took the diary out of his pocket.

Barret could see a look of panic growing on Donald's face. Barret could sense enormous power building like a dam about to burst.

"Turn to the last page, Thomas; read it out loud." Barret said, watching Donald.

Moorefield began to read. He became choked up reading his late wife's last words:

"I am terribly upset tonight. My hand shakes as I write this. Last night was very hot and I could not sleep, so I took a walk in the gardens. There was a cool breeze and the moon was wonderfully bright. I heard someone coming and was frightened, so I hid. Then I saw a man. He was all in black and wore a black scarf around his face. He stopped and took off the scarf. It was Donald. He pulled off the black cloak and ran into the garden shed. He came out a moment later, without the cloak and scarf and headed off toward the house.

I felt embarrassed and planned to forget the matter, thinking it was some innocent prank. But today I was in town and heard that a girl was attacked. She didn't see the attacker's face, but she said he wore a black hood. Tonight I confronted him about it. He said he had nothing to do with it and was out trying to catch the wolves that were attacking our flocks dressed that way to stay hidden. I told him I didn't believe him and begged him to confess, but he wouldn't listen. I will tell Thomas when he returns tomorrow; he will know what to do."

As he read the last word, there was an enormous crash and the library doors burst open, followed by a mighty rush of wind. Women in the main hall screamed as the front doors burst open and the gust extinguished every light in the room. Lightning crackled outside like angry cannons. Everyone was terrified, as it seemed like God's wrath had descended upon all of them.

Over the racket Barret, could hear Donald rise from his chair and dash for the door. "Stop him!" Barret shouted. But no one could hear his words over the noise and Donald disappeared into the night.

The wind and lightning died down slightly and people began to calm. A search party was organized quickly and the men went into the night to search for the killer.

Donald was found under a craggy, leafless oak, hanging from a black scarf. The townspeople wondered how he could have hung himself. His feet dangled some 5 feet off the ground and the branch he hung from was impossible to climb. Barret didn't find it necessary to tell them the truth, that one last ghost had made its presence known: Tilley Morisson, the girl that Donald had killed.

Chapter 7

The File on Virginia Fairchild

By J. M. M. Holloway

Missing Person Report:

Brad Martin, IT Manager, Omnitech Corporation, San Jose, California, states that Virginia Fairchild, an employee in his department, failed to appear at work on February 12, 2001, and thereafter. Mr. Martin further states that Ms. Fairchild was a reliable and conscientious employee who could be counted on to notify him in case of absence.

Found in Virginia Fairchild's Computer

If you're reading this, it's because you want to know where I am. I could tell you straight off, but without knowing everything, you wouldn't believe me. Perhaps you won't anyway.

Those few who know me will probably claim I'm dead, but that's only because, to them, I was a ghost long before I disappeared. Truth is, I haunted my cubicle at Omnitech because I had no better place to go. At least in the office there were signs of life: Phones rang, keyboards clacked, and computers binged incoming e-mail, though rarely for me personally.

Coworkers seldom noticed my presence. When they did, it was as an ever-present fixture, colorless and drab as the walls, bowed over her work no matter how early or late they passed by.

That last night was an exception. Normally, I would have stayed long past the hour when the most ambitious departed—so late I would have missed Tim entirely—but Omnitech, like every other company in California, needed to conserve energy. In the current crisis it wasn't enough to turn off lights and heat at the end of the workweek. Every blink from an electronic sentinel had to stop.

Promptly at six on Friday, the power died. I fumbled my way down the stairs and into the parking lot. On the way home, I detoured through an old neighborhood where I loved to watch shadows move behind closed drapes—loved more to find a window someone had forgotten to cover.

I spotted one but dared not stop, much less pull out my camera. Taking another such photograph had made the police treat me like a peeper. That had been an embarrassing episode, but worth it in the end after I pasted my image among the happy group, as if I had been part of the original scene. The framed print sat on my étagère awaiting admiration from any acquaintance who might drop by. Not that I expected anyone.

Once, I had friends, but I'd met them through my job. After I changed companies, they never called. Once, I'd had my own family too, but it splintered. My father went to another wife. My mother had a new home as well—one with a headstone.

It was after she died that I started spying, living vicariously through the dramas that played out behind window screens. Tonight I slowed the car to a creep and watched a woman and a girl, parent and child, I guessed. As I peered at the pair, I wished myself one of them, either one. I'd be older sister, live-in maid, stray cat if I could be included somewhere.

Behind me, a horn bleated impatience. I sped away. At my condo complex I pulled into my assigned slot and caught the handsome, brown face of Tim Oglesby from Human Resources in my headlights. My first reaction was that he didn't belong here; my second was pleasure. His presence proved he hadn't forgotten me as soon as he entered my file into the new employee database.

He pulled my car door open. "Hey, Gin. 'Bout to give up on you."

Like a tongue-tied adolescent I couldn't respond. He didn't seem to notice but chatted all the way to the front door. As I fumbled with my key, he said, "A bunch of us are driving to the coast tonight—plan to camp on the beach. Want to come?"

I didn't leap at the offer even though it was the kind I secretly hoped for and never got—the kind my dead mother often warned against.

"Where's the bunch?" I asked.

Tim frowned at the question. "Want to come or not?"

I buried my doubts and let him trail me inside. "Isn't it too cold to sleep outside?"

"Fine. Whatever." He turned to leave. I caught his sleeve. Mother's warnings had kept me safe so far—safe and alone.

"It's just I've never been camping. I don't have any equipment. Not even a sleeping bag."

"No sleeping bag? No problem." Tim smiled, a wolfish grin that bared sharp incisors. "You can use mine."

The implication seemed clear—improbable but clear. "Can you wait while I change clothes?" I asked.

"Don't take too long." He jiggled keys in his pocket. "We need to get rolling."

After I changed into jeans topped with a down jacket, I gathered other essentials as they occurred to me: a flashlight, extra socks, and, of course, my digital camera.

In the living room Tim examined a fake photo. "Nice family," he said. "Why aren't you smiling like everyone else?"

I shrugged. It seemed easier than an explanation.

Tim led the way to an SUV parked in a visitor's space. As soon as he started the motor, the gossip began. Not having anything to contribute about the foibles of Omnitech personnel, I remained silent and wondered if his easy manner masked a rapist or a serial killer. Tim relieved my fears by pulling into a neighborhood of tract homes and stopping at the curb. He nodded at the house. "Maryanne from Marketing. Get her, will ya'?"

I walked to the door and rang the bell. A neon woman—pink skin, bright green eyes, red hair—answered. As the door closed behind her, I glimpsed a small boy and masculine hands interlocking tiny toys. I wondered why anyone would leave such a cozy scene. My question was quickly answered. At the car, Maryanne climbed into the front seat without another glance at me. I barely scrambled in before Tim started the motor. They whispered, heads together, as Silicon Valley lights slipped behind us into the vista. At least I didn't have to worry about being murdered any more.

Hard as it was to imagine why Maryanne preferred an office Lothario like Tim to her husband and child, I refused to pass judgment. Not so long as it won me company for the night. We followed a winding two-lane road over the hills toward the ocean, then turned south on the coastal highway. By the time we reached a deserted campground and parked, sea mist was moving in.

"You get firewood," Tim said. "We'll set up."

Like an obedient child, I followed a trail down the cliff side to a beach that promised driftwood but produced only storm-wrenched tree trunks too large to lift. With the beam of my flashlight, I searched out a twig here and there. Gathering a handful took forever. Meanwhile, the damp ate under my collar. I wanted to rejoin the others but continued on until I stumbled over a broken limb I could lift. I struggled back up the cliff with it and found two sleeping bags zipped together. Inside, twin masses humped and wriggled.

I dropped my prize and bolted, running until their moans grew distant. In spite of the chill, embarrassment burned my skin. The fog thickened and I slowed to a desultory pace. When my flashlight dimmed, I chucked it toward the unseen tide, far out at sea, waves like tympani pounded a rising and falling rhythm.

"Come to us. Come to us," they said.

A new instrument had joined the futile symphony. I resisted its lure. Instead, I used the sound to steer away from the cliffs. As I wandered on, I saw a brighter patch behind the shifting fog: other campers, perhaps, or a house. Whatever it was, it offered a better alternative than returning to my rutting companions.

Companions I called them, but to Tim and Maryanne, I was nothing more than a convenient dodge. My eyes brimmed with self-pity. Wiping the wet tracks from my cheeks as I walked, I headed toward the light. I scrabbled in my pocket for a tissue and touched the camera, my only reliable link to the world. Reassured, I continued forward.

Suddenly, there was nothing beneath my feet. I fell through empty air, screaming, and landed with a jolt on all fours. Broken weeds abraded my palms. When I stopped shaking, I tested the ground under my hands. I'd landed on a narrow ledge, open on all sides except one. I patted the solid wall above me to see if I could find the edge and pull myself up. Dirt crumbled into my face. I shifted around; the ledge was just wide enough to hold me safely if I didn't move too abruptly. I leaned back against the cliff face, hugged my legs to my chest, and considered my situation. I could call Tim and Maryanne, but that meant more humiliation. If they never noticed my absence, if help never came, in the morning I'd figure out a way to rescue myself. All in all, things were no worse than they'd ever been.

A draft from the ocean thinned the fog and brightened the illumination that had led to my fall. It seemed closer. I stared at the twin rectangles, gold as candle glow, before they resolved into double windows.

The windows were undraped, as if the occupants had no fear of what lay outside, no need to shut out a watcher. Transparent squares of color—purple, yellow, garnet red, and mossy green—edged on the opening. They tinted an old-fashioned interior with bouquet papered walls. When I leaned to the side, I glimpsed plates in a tall breakfront and the edge of a massive chair topped with a snowy antimacassar.

I feasted on the scene, eager to see the occupants. On command, a shaggy-haired man in a collarless, striped shirt and suspenders stepped into view. He peered out through steel-rimmed glasses. His drooping moustache bracketed a worried mouth. He looked rough, ugly even, but somehow I knew he wouldn't be put off by a diffident manner. His eyes passed over me as if I were a wraith. A girl on the edge of womanhood joined him. She looked so pallid and tissue-thin that the light seemed to pass through her. He gripped her shoulder. The concern in her face relaxed, though his remained. Together they continued to stare into the dark. As little as she resembled the man, I knew she had to be his daughter.

A third figure joined the tableau. This one was an older woman, swarthy as the man, but with a halo of gray hair around her plump face. She wiped her hands on an apron then stood with the other two, watching through the window, searching outside.

I longed to be a part of the family. I pictured myself among them; it would be a good fit: The girl looked so much like me I could easily be her mother if I'd had a child as a teenager.

To make my wish real, I stood, drew my digital camera from my pocket and raised it to my eye. Already I envisioned how I'd manipulate the image to include myself.

The shutter clicked. I shifted my grip to check the shot in the viewer, but the camera slipped from my cold fingers. Somewhere below I heard it clatter against stone, a sound like a death rattle. But why mourn a photograph when the threesome still stared through the window?

"I'm out here." My voice sounded too small to be heard, but the eyes of the older woman flicked in my direction. Her reddened hand reached for the man. No sooner had she touched him than he stepped from sight. As I cleared my throat to call again, a brighter light spilled from a new, door-shaped opening. He stepped through holding a lantern.

"Virginia?"

My name on his lips was too much. I waved wildly. "Over here. I'm over here."

Light suddenly engulfed me. A man's arm reached into it, grabbed my hand and hauled me up. "Good thing you yelled. We were about to give up looking."

Too late I recognized Tim's impatient face. I fought his strength. "Let me go! I have to get to them."

"Who? There's no one out here but us."

As soon as he set me on the ground, I wrenched around. "There. Look there," I said, but fog had obscured the door and windows. They'd become nothing more than brighter patches in the milky night. The man who'd called my name was gone, disappeared along with his mother and daughter.

Maryanne wrapped a blanket around me. "She's shivering, Tim. We should get her inside."

I let Maryanne guide me back to the campground while Tim grumbled about cutting his evening short. Every few steps I turned to stare until all trace of brightness faded.

Tim and Maryanne stowed the gear and drove me home. After they dropped me off, I spent a restless night full of half dreams of warm lights and concerned faces. The images pulled me awake again and again until at last I fell into a dreamless sleep. At noon I woke for good and dragged myself from bed.

Staring into strangers' windows, even the kindest strangers, would get me into trouble; I knew that too well. Neither could I knock on that door claiming I was the woman they sought, that I belonged inside with them. It would sound delusional, insane.

The man had called my name by coincidence. He didn't know me, hadn't been looking for me, but against all logic, the conviction that he had remained. By mid-afternoon, the idea became irresistible. I had to return, if for no other reason than to retrieve my camera.

As soon as I showered, I drove out of the Valley and over the coastal hills where thick, gray clouds closed in. At the highway I turned south, parallel to the tide line, and drove slowly along, watching for the campground entrance. I'd imagined no problem finding my way back, but every public beach between Half Moon Bay and Santa Cruz seemed identical. I followed the road, back and forth, checking for a recognizable feature. In the end, I settled on the most likely one and parked in its rough, empty lot.

Outside the car, I scanned the cliff tops for a house that would guide me where I wanted to go, but only one—an early modern structure built of glass and stone—rose from the treeless plane. Certainly not the haven I sought, but perhaps, with so few buildings along the beach, the occupants could point me in the right direction.

I headed across the barren bluff top. Only a few weeds greened by winter rains interrupted its surface. Half the distance to my goal, I came to a stream bed too wide to cross. I continued along its edge, watching a trickle of water weave through granite outcroppings far below. Before it reached the highway, the stream bottom rose almost level with ground. I crossed and approached the front door of the house. The bell summoned an elderly gentleman in a cardigan and plush slippers.

"I hope you can help me, sir. I'm looking for a house. I know it's near here, but I've only been there once and can't seem to find it again," I said.

"Do come in, my dear."

I heard eagerness in his greeting and took a step back. "I'm in a hurry. The place I'm looking for is old. Victorian, I'd guess. Do you know it?"

He leaned on his cane and smiled. "No other houses for miles I'm afraid. The Coastal Commission won't allow it—protecting the view corridor they call it. I wouldn't be here except this house is grandfathered-in."

"I said it was old. Certainly a lot older than yours." My tone was sharper than I intended. I tried to staunch my irritation. "Sorry, but I really need to find it. I know it's within walking distance of a campground just like that one." I pointed through the doorway toward a glass wall with a view all the way to the ocean. "Even if it's not near here maybe you know the family: a mother and her grown son; and a girl about 12 or so. Another woman might live there too. A woman named Virginia."

He shook his head. "Can't say I've heard of them."

"But you must have. They probably farm."

"This land is far too sandy for farming, my dear. To the best of my knowledge there's never been a farm nearby except for that one." He gestured out the window toward a tall stand of weeds. "It's an old dairy, but nothing remains of it now except pieces of the foundation."

I wilted. "I was so sure."

"Perhaps a cup of tea will soothe your disappointment. I'd enjoy one myself if you'll join me."

I recognized the need in his tone and took a step forward. "Tea would be nice."

"Excellent," he said. "While I heat the kettle you might peruse that local history on the coffee table—some interesting tales there about the area. One claims campers sometimes glimpse a ghostly house from the beach. But don't be alarmed. I've lived here most of my life and never seen anything even remotely spectral."

In spite of his denial, I felt a chill descend my spine. I remembered the warm light so unlike electricity, the old-fashioned clothes and furnishings, and how the windows faded when Tim and Maryanne came. I wasn't such a techie that I couldn't understand the implications. Others had seen what I had seen—something that couldn't be there yet was.

The old man's voice followed me as I rushed away. "Perhaps you'd prefer . . ."

I ignored him and raced across the ground until I reached the edge of the fissure. As before I tracked the stream, only this time seaward and from the opposite side. As I approached the cliff, the stream bed cut more and more deeply into the ground. Here and there along the sides, ledges protruded, one with crushed weeds. I stopped, sure it was the very place I'd fallen and looked down. Far below, at the bottom, my camera lay on a granite boulder.

I retraced my steps until I could safely lower myself. Scrambling from rock to rock I made my way back. My hands shook as I reached for the camera. Would the last shot reveal black nothing or a world of possibility?

I clicked through stored memory to the last frame: not black; not filmy apparitions either. Once more the mother, grown son, and his daughter stared out the window. I sagged with relief. The photo proved they existed. They were real; I had only to find a way to them.

I hurried back to the ruin. As the sun lowered into the ocean, the night wind picked up. It chilled me, but I forgot discomfort when I reached the stone outline of the old house. I stepped along three sides picturing the parlor as I'd seen it. Here, the breakfront would have stood; here, the top of the chair. Where the fourth side should have been, where the family had watch from the window, the foundation had fallen away.

I settled into the nearest block to await their return. Night would fall; the lights would glow; faces would stare out; a man's voice would call my name; and I would go to him.

I waited for complete darkness, the time for ghosts. It took too long—so long that I questioned my certainty. When the family reappeared, when I stepped out to join them, would I step out into a void? The entrance to the house was over the stream. Would some magical support materialize and transport me across? Or would I fall to my death on the rocks below?

If death was the price of reaching a better place, I intended to pay it, but the stone under my seat grew cold and the wind blew with a hoary chill that felt like fear. I raised the camera to my eye again for reassurance. The faces captured there said, "Trust what you know. Come to us."

When the fog rolled in, the night grew colder still. The house remained a low, stone sketch, untenanted. Tendrils of vapor swirled about me. They struggled to coalesce into forms but failed. The night held nothing but amorphous mist.

Why didn't they return? Were the dead as cruel as the living? I strained to understand until new light smoldered behind the eastern hills. Below my perch, the tide rose and backed into the chasm, covering the trickle of fresh water. I watched it, tempted to go over the edge before I steeled myself and trudged back to my car. All the way home, I told myself it didn't matter. I still had the best of them. A little digital magic and I would join them.

At home I used photo manipulation software to merge myself with the picture. I stood next to his daughter. The protecting arm of the homely man enveloped us both, but it wasn't good enough. The gray haired matron still looked concerned. My image was wrong also: too modern; too wan and disillusioned. Contentment should glow from my smile, but I couldn't achieve it not matter how many photo files I searched for a better likeness. Every picture of me showed a waiting-to-be-kicked grimace or morose frown.

Maybe I wasn't fit for happiness. Maybe that's why I failed to find it. With that thought, I fell into bed and cried myself to sleep. In my dreams, they came to me—the man, his mother, and daughter. They asked me to try again and they told me the way: I must return to the beach. I'll retrace my steps to the very spot where I fell on Friday. I'll slip over the edge and wait on the ledge. Soon the light will glow. My new family will reappear in the window as promised. When the man opens the door, lantern in hand, calling my name, I'll step into the void. On a bridge as strong as trust can build, I'll walk across.

I'm leaving this file so that after I'm gone no one can claim I committed suicide on the rocks. If you find me there, then call me crazy. Say I was driven insane by a sad, isolated life. Maybe it's true. Maybe depression made me hallucinate the whole thing, but think about this: so many people disappear and are never heard from again. Where do they go? Are they all buried too deep to recover? Do they drift far out to sea and sink into the depths? Or do some find a better place?

If you never find my body, if there's no trace of me anywhere, then don't say I went out with the tide like flotsam. Picture me safe on the other side.

Addendum to File

Summary of statements from Timothy Oglesby, Assistant Manager, Human Resources, Omnitech Corporation, and Maryanne Hoffman, Marketing Specialist, Omnitech Corporation: Mr. Oglesby and Mrs. Hoffman attest that when last seen, Virginia Fairchild appeared distracted and despondent.

Summary of statement from Thomas Fairchild, Fort Worth, Texas (father of Virginia Fairchild): Mr. Fairchild denies his daughter was suicidal, but admits he has had no contact with her in over a year.

Summary of interview with Robert Batson, Old Dairy Beach, Highway 1, Pescadero, California: Mr. Batson states that a young woman matching Virginia Fairchild's description appeared at his door on Saturday, February 10, 2001. She became agitated when unable to locate friends in the area.

Impound Report:

Toyota Camry (model year 2000) registered to Virginia Fairchild, towed from Old Dairy Beach.

Deposition:

Virginia Fairchild's disappearance ruled suicide. San Mateo County Sheriff's Department alerted to watch for the body to wash up on shore.

Chapter 8

The Worst Thing

By Helen Rhine

Joanne knocked quickly on the open office door, and walked through at the brusque "In" that came from Donald Lasko, the current owner of this office. Bonita Williams, his assistant, was standing beside him at his desk, explaining something, while Lasko signed a stack of forms. He turned to take the sheaf of papers Joanne had come in to deliver, jerked sharply, and turned his attention back to Bonita.

"What did you say?" Don's body was stiff with anger.

Bonita, looking caught, said, "I was just saying that I put the paper that was misfiled in your personal folder into the safe."

Lasko stared at Bonita. Joanne, still standing quite close to him, heard his furious thought, "I'll kill you, you bitch!"

Joanne stared at Lasko until he remembered she was there and took his fixed glare away from Bonita.

"Was there something else?" he asked.

"No, no, I'm leaving." Joanne said quickly and left the office.

Her knees were a bit wobbly as she made her way back to her desk, wondering what, if anything, she should do about what she had just "heard."

Joanne had never thought of herself as anything but ordinary. Okay, she dreamed of fame, fortune, and saving the world, but doesn't everyone? See, perfectly ordinary—an ordinary research clerk in an ultrahigh-security lab. Sure the lab thing might be a little out of the ordinary, but she was a clerk. Well, her actual title was Executive Assistant, but her duties were those of a clerk—so very ordinary.

When Joanne had been a child, she had realized that if she had one of those adrenalin moments—times when you suddenly remember that you were supposed to pick up your baby brother after school and school was out an hour ago—any thoughts she had at that time would be audible to anyone close to her. She knew this because she could hear those mental exclamations from others.

When she was older, and educated, she thought that perhaps the adrenalin surge people experience boosted the brain's transmission power, allowing the thoughts occurring at that moment to travel a longer distance. Certainly the thoughts she heard were seldom useful. What she got were things like, "Oh, my God!" mostly. Although, there had been that one time she accidentally had scorched the carpet in a bed and breakfast, and when she told the nice lady owner that she would love to come back someday, the nice lady owner thought, "Oh, I hope you don't!"

She had definitely never overheard anything like a declaration of impending murder.

Maybe there was no need to worry; after all, people do think of killing others and sometimes even speak the threat out loud, but it doesn't mean anything other than a passing frustration. But he had been furious, coldly furious, when that thought escaped, and Bonita was a friend; she couldn't just ignore it.

* * *

Joanne stopped by Bonita's desk just before lunch and they walked down the two flights of stairs to the employee cafeteria. Because the lab was fairly isolated, most people had lunch in the cafeteria. This suited their employers, who always worried when all the lab's secrets walked out the doors, nestled comfortably in the heads of the workers. So they graciously provided good food at reasonable prices and a very comfortable place to eat.

Joanne chose a table with a view of the duck pond and settled in.

"Oh, what a morning! Don has been both moody and jumpy, which I would have thought was impossible," Bonita said.

"Yeah, he was pretty annoyed when I was there this morning."

"But he was perfectly normal before that. I have no idea what set him off."

"Maybe it was me," Joanne speculated.

Bonita grinned. "Well, I really don't think so. But come to think of it, the first time Don got mad was while you were there."

"Yeah, you were telling him something he didn't seem to like."

"But he shouldn't have been mad about that." Bonita leaned closer and whispered. "Because I covered for him."

Joanne whispered back, "Some file he had left in the wrong place?"

Bonita nodded. Having secret files in your possession imposed lots of rules and regulations, one being that the file must be either in your immediate control or in the safe. This particular rule, however, was not followed as strictly as the rule makers would like, so it was puzzling that Bonita's boss would have been upset about that. After all, if he wanted the file, all he had to do was sign it out of the safe again.

"You signed it in, right?" Joanne asked.

"Sure."

"I've heard some things about Don."

"Probably mostly true, if they're bad," Bonita grinned. "There are a lot of people in the lab who despise him, but he's never really done anything really bad to me—probably because I'm not important enough. And I get good performance reviews."

Joanne decided to push a bit. "When I was with you this morning, he was so angry he scared me. I was scared for you too."

"He can be a little scary when he's angry," Bonita admitted. "But he's not going to kill me."

Joanne jumped, startled. Had Bonita heard the threat too? Maybe there was finally someone who shared her . . . what, talent?

"Has he threatened to kill you before?"

"What do you mean, *before?* He has certainly never threatened to kill me!" So she hadn't "heard."

"And anyway, you never see him except at work, so even if he did want to kill you, there wouldn't be a chance."

"Joanne, you are being very peculiar today. Now I'm going to change the subject." And she did.

* * *

Joanne had to decide whether to tell Bonita about the threat. She knew from bitter experience what the response would be. It would be the same as her sister's response when Joanne had told her about the "talent." First laughter, thinking it was a joke and then other explanations: "Maybe they are actually saying it really low, and you just hear it" or "You're just imagining you hear it." No matter how completely insulting those explanations were, how utterly stupid a person would have to be to become confused that way, they still said it.

No, Joanne would patiently explain. It doesn't come through the ears. It comes in right in the middle of the forehead. And, of course, if I am insane, then I might very well be imagining it, but because I manage to function quite well, I'm probably not completely looney! This was always followed by lots of "But how could that be?" questions. Joanne's logical explanation of adrenalin-boosted transmission never cut any ice.

Then the worried look would come. Obviously, poor Joanne is having some kind of mental problem. With her sister, she had had a further difficulty: Why, her sister had demanded, didn't you ever tell me about it when we were kids? I told her that if Mom had told us to wash up for dinner and we were both standing right there, I didn't turn and ask her if she had heard Mom's instructions. I just assumed she heard when anyone spoke, and assumed she also heard the thoughts I heard. Her sister dealt with the issue by completely ignoring it, but it created a rift between them nevertheless.

However, if Bonita was going to be killed, what then? Would saving her reputation as a levelheaded person be worth that? She and Bonita had been friends a long time. They were both in their thirties, divorced with no children, and had lost the big house in the divorce, but had been able to buy something small. They mostly cried at the same movies, and traded books and books on tape constantly. No, Joanne was going to have to confess; she had no choice. She just hoped she didn't lose Bonita's friendship over it.

* * *

The next morning, Joanne was startled to see Bonita in the hallway, walking stiffly and with bruises and scraped-looking places on her arms and chin. Bonita paused to cough, a nasty dry cough that went on and on.

"Bonita, what in the world happened to you?"

"On, Don had me working late last night. Why I do not know because nothing I did was urgent. Anyway, driving home last night, the brakes went out on my car. I was driving toward the traffic light at Parker and Custer. The light turned and I tried to brake to stop, but just went right on through the red light and off the edge of the road into a ditch. Good thing it was late, because no one was coming through the intersection."

"Oh no! Were you hurt?" Joanne smacked her forehead. "Well, duh. Obviously you were hurt. Bruises that big don't come without pain."

"No, not really. I am now a fanatical believer in airbags, though. The car is totaled." Bonita coughed hard. "This cough bothers me the most."

"You have a cough from a car accident?"

"It surprised me too. It's the air bags. They have to pack them with stuff like talcum powder—maybe it is talcum powder—to keep the plastic from sticking together. When they deploy, the whole car is filled with it. That's what's making me cough. The doctor says it will go away."

"Do you know what happened with the brakes?"

"No, and since the car's totaled, probably no one will bother to check. It is strange though. I just had the car in for service a couple of weeks ago."

Joanne felt the tug of fear.

"Bonita, can we meet somewhere after work? Have dinner maybe? I really would like to tell you something."

* * *

Well, surprise, surprise. Bonita didn't believe her either, although she earned Joanne's everlasting gratitude by not asking insulting questions and she seemed to understand the concept.

"Clearly something is happening, but I find it hard to believe that this kind of talent exists and no one has ever documented anything like it," Bonita finally said. "And, why would Don want to kill me? Have you thought about that?"

"Yes, of course I've thought about it. The only thing I can come up with has to do with that file. I was standing there with the papers; he was only half-listening to you, and was perfectly calm until you mentioned the file. Then he exploded."

"But I was covering for him. Surely he wouldn't get mad when I was covering for him."

"Bonita, that file that you put back in the safe, was it signed out?"

"I assume so; I didn't check. But even if it wasn't signed out, it's just a technicality. Don can look at those files as much as he wants."

"I know you can't tell me what you saw on the file, but was it very sensitive?"

Bonita frowned. "Yes, very sensitive. But Don isn't stupid, and I don't think he's a traitor. Well, except on a smaller scale: He cheats on his wife."

"But if he was a traitor, then he might want you dead if you could expose him!"

"But he's not a traitor."

"Okay, you don't really believe me. But could you just humor me and pretend like you might be in danger and take some sensible precautions?"

"If it will make you feel better, I will be extra cautious for a few weeks, but no longer than that."

Joanne sighed in relief. "Yes, that would make me feel so much better. What kind of precautions?"

Bonita laughed. "You never give up, do you? What do you suggest?"

"Well, keep your security system on all the time. Make sure your car, I guess your rental car for now, is locked at all times. Don't park where you usually do at work, over under the shade of the trees. Park under a light in the main section."

Bonita looked at Joanne. "Is that enough?"

"It doesn't feel like enough. Okay, also pay close attention to Don. He probably wouldn't do anything to you at work, but don't be alone with him outside the lab."

Bonita said, "Well, that's easy. I have never been alone with Don outside the lab."

"Oh, and just look around you, especially when you're between places;—like when you park your car, check around before you get out."

"You really, really are worried about this, aren't you?"

Joanne nodded. "I really, really am."

* * *

Joanne had to stop herself from calling Bonita every half hour to check on her and she couldn't restrain herself from hovering just a little bit at work. She knew she was being a major pest. For instance, if she got to work ahead of Bonita, she would wait in the car as long as she could until Bonita came in, then Joanne would walk in with her. Joanne made a few trips to Bonita's territory every morning and in the afternoon, often not even speaking to Bonita, just observing that she was alive and well. It was a strain for both of them. Still, Bonita gamely continued practicing her extra safety precautions.

One further piece of evidence appeared a few days later. The check for Don's expenses for a short trip to see a demo of some new equipment had arrived in Bonita's *In* basket, but when she tried to put the check into Don's personal folder, as usual, she found the file drawer containing his personal stuff had been locked.

"So I think he was mad about my looking in his personal folder, but I've never seen anything in there that was so private I shouldn't see it," Bonita said.

"Just that secret file," Joanne countered. "And for what reason would he have a secret file in his personal folder in a drawer that was not usually locked?"

"There isn't any good reason; I just assumed that he had the file in his hand along with something else that was going in his personal folder, got distracted, and put both there."

* * *

At the end of the first week of the siege, as Bonita started referring to it, she made a trip upstairs to Joanne's office.

"We can stand down from general quarter's now, Sir," Bonita sharply saluted Joanne.

"We can? Why?"

"Don just told me he'll be out the rest of the week and all of next week. And not just at work, but out of town."

Joanne was surprised at how relieved she felt. She had really been wound up.

"Oh, good. Maybe he's going to that seminar in Las Vegas; a couple of people in my lab signed up for it."

"Maybe. I don't know his exact plans yet, but the travel office will copy me on his itinerary." Bonita sprawled in Joanne's guest chair. "I didn't realize until I heard about his trip just how uptight you have made me about this."

"I'm sorry, I . . . " Joanne started.

"No, I would have done exactly the same thing. And I do appreciate your concern." Bonita sat up. "You know, this has been a really good thing. I see now that I have been taking lots of foolish little chances."

"Like what?"

"Oh, like leaving the house doors unlocked when I'm home. I don't go in and out a lot most of the time, so it's been easy to keep them locked. And, although most of the time it's perfectly safe to leave them unlocked, the time and amount of extra work required are far outweighed by the risk of leaving them open. And," Bonita continued, "I keep my cell phone handy and turned on, which I never did before. But what really brought it home to me was paying attention to surroundings. I went to the mall the other day and noticed a group of young guys looking very much like gang members loitering under a tree in one area of the parking lot. I just drove by them and parked somewhere else. They probably wouldn't have bothered me, but why take the chance?"

"Well, I'm glad to hear that this episode hasn't been completely useless as well as an unbridled misery."

"Nope. Let's celebrate—go out to eat tonight and go to a movie." Bonita stood up.

"Absolutely, but we can't stay out late. I plan on getting some really good sleep tonight for a change."

* * *

After a quiet end of the week, and a blissfully uneventful weekend, both Bonita and Joanne were back at work. Joanne was surprised to see Liane Wang in the hallway. Joanne knew that the tiny Chinese doctor of physics had been scheduled for the Las Vegas seminar.

"Hi, Liane. Didn't you go to Las Vegas?"

"Of course I went. I find the juxtaposition of decadence and abstruse theory very stimulating. Wasn't long enough though. The seminar finished Friday, but almost everyone stayed on at least through Saturday. I certainly did."

Joanne went immediately to Bonita's office.

"Did you get that copy of Don's itinerary?"

"'Hello and how are you' to you too!" Bonita remarked, one eyebrow raised.

"Sorry, I just found out that the Las Vegas seminar was over last Friday, but you said Don was out this week too."

"Oh, well," Bonita rifled through her in box and found the itinerary, "It says here that this week he will be on vacation at his cottage in Bramford. Please do not phone except in an emergency."

"Bramford's not really that far away is it? A hundred miles or so?" Joanne was getting worried again.

"Don't know. Is it important?"

"It's just that it's the perfect alibi. If something, God forbid, were to happen to you even when he was in town, no one but me would suspect him at all. If something happened to you when he's out of town, suspecting him would be nearly impossible."

Bonita saluted sharply. "Yes, sir. Back on general quarters, sir!"

"So on a scale where blithering idiot who should be ignored is 0 and friend is 10, where do I stand now?" Joanne asked.

"Still a solid ten, friend. A friend who's just a little bit looney, but still a friend."

* * *

When Joanne got home, she got out her map and found Bramford—a small, picturesque mountain town with desperately precious few shops—to be about 120 miles away. Not a hard drive, especially when you considered that it was only about 6 miles from the interstate that ran nearly arrow straight right back to Bonita.

Still, Thursday had come and there had been no sighting of Don, much less the slightest indication that he had foul play in mind. Joanne was beginning to think that his threat had been just a really severe fit of pique that Don had dealt with by locking Bonita out of his personal file drawer.

Bonita dropped in on Joanne during the afternoon coffee break.

"I finally checked the log book," Bonita said, sitting down in Joanne's guest chair and taking a sip from her coffee mug. "That file hadn't been signed out."

"Not signed out," Joanne sighed. "But that alone isn't such a big deal. He'll have to explain how a file which hadn't been signed out was signed in, but it's not like that doesn't happen to everybody now and then."

"I know," Bonita shrugged. "It really doesn't tell us anything new, except that Don, who is usually so scrupulous with his files, messed up once."

"Okay, stay on alert until the end of next week. If he hasn't done anything by then, he probably never will," Joanne said, although she really wasn't 100 percent sure it was a good idea for them to let down their guard. But it was this week that was ideal for Don to try something, so if he didn't, then he likely never would.

* * *

That night Joanne couldn't sit still, but couldn't accomplish anything either. She started five or six household chores and abandoned each minutes later. Finally, she decided to go for a walk to use up some of the excess energy. Out in the fresh air, Joanne felt much better. Walking didn't require much mental attention so her thoughts could ramble around unfettered by details, which is what her thoughts had wanted to do all evening.

Because her mind was so deeply occupied with her mental ramblings, it was surprising that she noticed the car, especially because it wasn't a very noticeable car. Perhaps it was the silhouette of the driver's head that flashed so strongly as the car went through a shaft of evening sunshine—Don's silhouette—but it wasn't Don's car. Oh well, might as well make a side trip to Bonita's house. It wasn't far.

* * *

The car was parked on the last side street before Bonita's house. Joanne's heart jumped. But it was such a common car, a rental, she noticed, as she got closer. Still she was nearly running by the time she reached Bonita's. Then she was shocked into stillness by the sight of Bonita's door, standing slightly open. Joanne went through the door as quietly as she could. The light in the foyer was not on, but there was light coming from the living room further down the hallway—light and sound, the sound of voices, Bonita's and Don's.

"Just don't try anything stupid," Don was saying.

"Don, please don't shoot me. Please." Bonita's voice quivered.

Oh God, No! What do I do now? Joanne was sick with terror. She patted the pockets of her jacket, but she already knew that she had stupidly left her cell phone at home. The only thing she could do was to leave before she was discovered and try to call from a neighbor's house or run into the street screaming.

Then she heard the unmistakable sound of the gun's slide being racked. Don wasn't going to give her enough time to get help.

She walked softly down the hallway. When she reached the doorway to the living room she saw Don aiming the gun at Bonita, intent on pulling the trigger.

"Why, Don, we were expecting you much sooner," she said loudly.

Don whirled around bringing the gun to bear on Joanne. Then in the next heartbeat, he turned back to Bonita, who had risen from her chair.

"You, Bonita, stand right there!" He turned back to Joanne. "You! Get in here!"

Joanne went through the door, and as she neared Don, she heard him think, "These damned bitches are gonna' ruin my life!"

Joanne turned to him and said, "Don, these damned bitches have already ruined your life. So just put that gun down."

Don was taken aback, but was still holding the pistol level.

"As I told you, we've been expecting you," Joanne said coolly. Although terrified, she had never thought more clearly in her life.

Don's next thought came through loud and clear, "This woman is a stupid clerk!"

"Umm, not really a clerk and not stupid either."

Don went a little pale. His next thought betrayed his fear and confusion, "She's reading my mind!"

"Got it on the first try! Congratulations! May I introduce myself, Joanne MacAndrews, Commander, Psi Corps," Joanne held her hand out mockingly. If Don took it to shake, she had an advantage; if not, well, she was no worse off. Don was rattled, but not enough to lessen his grip on the gun.

"Psi Corps. Yeah, right, lady," Don rasped. "Now get over there next to Bonita."

Joanne didn't want to do that because she probably wouldn't be able to hear his thoughts that far away. She stalled a little, looking at her watch and saying, "I don't know why we aren't hearing sirens yet, the police know to come here."

"Yes, they know to come to my house," Bonita said forcefully. "And they know you have a gun."

"The police! Why would the police be in on this, it should be lab security." More confident now, Don again gestured with the gun. "Now, get over there!"

This is really the crunch. Joanne would just have to gamble that she knew enough of the true story to keep bluffing. Crossing her mental fingers, she said, "Don, Don, the lab doesn't want anyone to know that one of its respected scientists is selling secret information. They want you arrested on a criminal charge, like attempted murder, which will put you away without the embarrassing information coming out."

Don almost bought it. "Nonsense, they can't send me to a regular prison—my talents would be wasted and all the secrets I know could 'accidentally' get out," he smirked.

"And that's why you wouldn't get sentenced to a regular prison," Joanne was getting onto some pretty thin ice here, but she remembered a fragment of conversation she had overheard at the lab once. "You'd go to Dagmar."

Don visibly paled. He thought, "There really is a Dagmar."

"Yes, there really is a Dagmar." Joanne was deeply grateful that she had once again caught one of his thoughts, just to keep the heat on him. But what was she going to do? Wait until she drove him crazy and then take the gun away? That didn't seem like a viable option. She wished she could think of what to do next.

"This is insane. There is no such thing as a Psi Corps! It's impossible!" Don was sweating despite his protestations.

"Of course there is, and I can prove it," Joanne said calmly. "I can read your mind, you know that, and I work at the lab. I don't have to convince you how much it would mean to lab security to have a group of people who can read minds, do I?"

Suddenly, all three people in the room became aware of lots of sirens, and they seemed to be coming nearer. Joanne saw Bonita mouth a fervent "Thank God." But surely these sirens were not coming to their rescue.

Don, however, was convinced. He grabbed Joanne and started for the door. Joanne went limp and dropped to the floor, becoming a dead weight. Don kicked her viciously in the side and on the leg, but dropped her and once again headed out. Immediately, outside the door were policemen. Don ran right into their arms.

Bonita jumped up and ran over to help Joanne up from the floor and assist her to the sofa. "That bastard kicked you! I'll ask about paramedics."

"But how did they know to come?"

Bonita picked up her cell phone from the table and started speaking into it. "The police are here, thank you so much! Yes, my friend is injured . . . No, I'm fine, just scared. Oh, good . . . yes, thank you. Good-bye."

Bonita grinned hugely. "Remember, I told you I was leaving my cell phone on and handy at all times? When you sneaked in and scared the pants off Don, I had time to call 911. I couldn't say anything, but I was just hoping to keep the line open so they would know to come."

"And that's why you said they knew to come to your house, so they would know where you were! Oh, and the gun, you mentioned the gun too! You're brilliant!" Joanne enthused.

Bonita started to cry. "Oh, dammit! As soon as the worst is over, I start to bawl like a baby!"

"But, Bonita," Joanne asked, "how did Don get in?"

Bonita wiped her eyes. "My new laptop came, and I had to sign for it. There's no place to put it down in the hallway, so I took it into the dining room and put it on the table." Bonita grinned ruefully. "Then I had to open the box and see it, and then I just had to see if it worked. And the door was unlocked and the security system was off."

"What rotten luck. The one time the door is open is when Don comes by!" Joanne exclaimed.

"Oh no! Don told me after he came in that he had been by every day. He accused me of being paranoid for keeping myself so well locked up!"

"Did he tamper with your car? Did he say why he wanted to kill you?"

"Yes, he cut the brake line. He was extremely exasperated with me because I didn't die in the car crash. He said he had just started making really, really big bucks by selling stuff, and I ruined the handoff method by prying into his private personal folder. I assume that a security guard or one of the cleaning crew was picking the stuff up, then bringing it back after copying it."

Joanne shook her head. "Why couldn't he just fire you?"

"He said it would take too long. Since my record was spotless, he had to first report me for some infraction, give me my warning lecture, then cite me for something else before he could even begin to get me fired. The people he was working for only gave him a couple of weeks to get rid of me."

"But it's over now," Bonita sighed. "Except, what are you going to tell the police about your talent? That is going to be one strange 911 tape!"

Joanne shrugged. "I'll just tell them it was lucky guesses. They'll believe that a lot easier than they'll believe the truth."

Joanne was right. The police were only too happy to believe that she had just been guessing and had been lucky enough to stall Don until help could arrive.

But Bonita was wrong; for Joanne, the worst was yet to come.

* * *

The next morning, Joanne was intercepted as she went through the front door of the lab building and was escorted into a part of the lab she had never even known existed to speak to two men she had never seen before. Before she was completely seated in her chair, the older of the two said, "Welcome, Joanne. You will be spending some time with us at another facility. We need to know some things about you."

Artwork by Chris Pugh, Copyright 2002

Chapter 9

After the War

By David Terrenoire

In every class picture, Rose was the tall girl trying to disappear in the back row. She wore round glasses, her clothes were secondhand, and she had a small spot on her cheek that, on a pretty girl, would have been considered a beauty mark, but on Rose was a mole. When she spoke, which was not often, her voice was hushed and hidden behind her hand.

Alton Baker held a trophy in nearly every one of his school pictures. He pomaded his hair and owned a flask. He drove a green Hudson Hornet recklessly and dated laughing girls who sat next to him with the gearshift between their knees.

Then the war came and that changed everything.

When Alton returned home he had a stillness that whispered to Rose like a sad song on a distant radio.

It rained often that following spring and when it did, the streetcar filled with men and their smell of Old Spice, cigarettes, and wet wool. One morning Alton sat next to Rose. When she slid closer to the window, she dropped her glove. Alton picked it up and said, "You have nice hands."

"I'm a typist," she said, "at the mill," and immediately felt too clumsy and stupid to live.

He took one of her hands and held it, gently. "They're beautiful," he said. "You could be an artist."

Alton was smiling, but all Rose could see was his face: unshaven, dirty, streaked with blood.

"Do you live around here?"

"What?" She took her hand from his.

"Do you live in the neighborhood?"

"Up on Third Avenue. Just me and my father." Her hands were still now, folded like nesting birds in her lap. "My mother passed on."

"I'm sorry," Alton said. "My father died while I was overseas."

"I remember," Rose said.

"It's just me and my mother."

"I know," Rose said.

A large man carrying a package pushed Alton against Rose. Instantly, her head filled with explosions and shattering pines.

"She's been sick," Alton said. "I love her, of course, but sometimes a guy could use a break, you know?"

"If you would like," Rose started the sentence before she could think of all the reasons why she shouldn't, "you can come to dinner at our house. It's nothing special, though, so if you'd rather not . . ."

Alton surprised her by saying yes.

That evening Rose insisted her father wear a clean shirt.

"I'm not wearing a goddamn tie," he hollered from his bedroom. "The way you're running around, you'd think he was the goddamn Pope."

At Alton's house, Alton was telling his mother about the girl he'd met. "It was strange. There was this instant connection. I've never met anyone quite like her before."

Alton's mother tried to picture the tall girl on Third Avenue, but couldn't. Finally, she said, "She must be very nice."

"Then you don't mind? You'll be all right?"

"I'll be fine," she said, and tried not to let him see how breathless the words made her.

In all but the heaviest rains, Alton rode a 1936 Indian motorcycle that could be heard all over town. When Alton pulled up to Rose's house, her father got up from his chair and stood, the screen door locked between him and Alton. The father stared at the motorcycle. "You ride that thing?"

"Yes, sir."

Rose's father turned that over. Then, with a grunt, he let Alton come inside. Alton sat on the edge of the sofa, his hands clasped.

Rose's father talked about the Pirates and their chances for the pennant. "Good to have real men playing ball again," he said. "Not 4–F's, hit like a bunch of goddamn girls." When this didn't get a response he said, "You still play?"

"No," Alton said. "Not anymore."

"Too bad. You were damn good."

Rose announced that dinner was ready. She placed Alton at the foot of the table and she took the chair closest to the kitchen. As they ate, Rose watched Alton, and her father watched Rose.

Untrained in dinner conversation, Rose had no idea how to fill the quiet that settled over the dining room. Her father, his forearms on the table, knife and fork in either hand, said, "Men down at the VFW said you got a medal."

"Yes, sir."

"Bronze star?"

Alton prodded his chicken with his fork. "Yes, sir."

"Pretty rough, huh?"

Alton folded his napkin and placed it next to his plate. His lips seemed to form a word, then stopped. He picked up his napkin again, placed it in his lap, and said, "I liked Germany. I mean, after the shooting stopped." Alton tried to smile, but it didn't reach his eyes.

"I bet it's pretty. Prettier than here," Rose said. "A person could choke to death on the smoke."

"Nothing wrong with smoke," her father said. He speared a buttered red potato, pushed it into his mouth, and chewed. "Puts food on the table." He pointed the fork at Rose. "When the smoke stops, that's when you worry."

After dinner, Rose refused Alton's help clearing the table. As she removed the plates, her father tilted his head, curious as an alley dog, and said, "What the hell's that noise?"

Rose stopped, a woodland creature caught in the open. "It's me, Father. I guess I was singing."

"What the hell for?"

"I don't know," Rose stammered. "I'm sorry."

"I thought I'd had a stroke."

"You have a beautiful voice," Alton said. "You should sing more often."

If her hands had not been full of the good china, they would have fluttered about her face. Instead, she backed out of the room, her eyes glistening with tears of gratitude.

Rose's father eyed Alton. He knew of only one reason why a good-looking guy like this would flatter a plain girl like Rose, and it wasn't for her roast chicken and red potatoes.

Alton and Rose worked at the steel mill and their lives, like all the lives in the valley, were regulated by the hard voice of the mill whistle: Their days were overcast. At night the furnaces lit the clouds until they smoldered like live coals. The air smelled of kerosene, and the river, red as a wound, carried barges of slag downstream. Everywhere smoke clung to the valley and snagged on the branches of dead trees.

Rose worked in the mill's front office where she heard Alton's name in the mouths of other women. Alton had done things, they said, that other men would write books about. They stared at Rose in wonder and resentment, unable to connect the golden war hero with this shy giraffe of a girl.

Unlike the others, Rose had no desire to talk about the awful things Alton had done. She didn't have to wonder; she could see them, every time he touched her.

They spent most evenings either at his house with his mother or at her house on the front porch. Alton rocked back and forth in the metal glider and remembered night skies so clear he saw God in the stars. He talked of rivers in Germany that glittered with fish.

In their second week together, Alton kissed Rose good night. It was a quick kiss with lips closed, but it rocked Rose and she had to break away, gasping from the pain that roared through her body.

"I'm sorry," Alton said.

"No, no," Rose said. "I wanted you to."

"I'd better go," Alton whispered.

Rose gulped, needing Alton to kiss her again but not sure if she could take the pain of it. "Maybe so," Rose said.

"See you tomorrow night?"

"Oh, yes," Rose said. "Yes."

The next day in the mill's front office, Rose misspelled a word. She stared at it and knew it was wrong, but the letters could have been Russian. So she let it go. She didn't look it up in the big dictionary on the plant manager's desk. She didn't ask Millie Larsen, the office grammarian. She just put the invoice in the out basket and quietly experienced a light-headed rush, as if she was falling from a great height.

From April through October Alton and Rose talked of movies and books and what it must be like to live in California. She longed to see the Pacific Ocean, but only if she could see it with Alton. At the end of every night, Rose would close her eyes and let Alton kiss her, and every night she saw new horrors.

It was a Saturday, and Rose's father had gone to bed. Alton and Rose sat on the sofa listening to the radio, when Alton spilled coffee on his shirt. Rose insisted he take it off so she could soak the stain.

Alton unbuttoned his shirt and, standing under the kitchen light, he held it out to her.

Without thinking, Rose reached past the shirt and laid her trembling fingertips against the hard, white scar on Alton's chest.

Instantly, her hands and feet were frozen. She saw snow-flecked red and men in rags thrown about the ground, their limbs twisted in odd angles. She heard screaming and then, as if an invisible hand had swung a hammer, something hit her chest and she gasped, her eyes blinded to everything but the sudden flash of light.

Alton mistook the gasp for passion. He held Rose tighter against his skin and whispered into her ear, "I need you, Rose. I want you more than anything."

Rose backed away and said, "I can't, Alton. I just can't."

Alton glanced upward toward her father's bedroom. "We can be quiet," he said.

"No, Alton—it's not that."

Alton reached for her again and she retreated to the sink and pressed her back against the counter. "Please," she said.

Alton stood beneath the kitchen light. After a moment, he nodded and said, "Okay. I'd better go."

"Alton, I need to tell you something."

"No, no," he said. "You don't have to explain. I understand."

"No," Rose said, "I don't think you do."

Alton took his shirt and for the first time in months, left without touching her.

The next day marked the beginning of a week without Alton. For Rose, it was the longest week of her life. Unable to stand his absence any longer, she went looking for him.

It was late morning on the last day of October, and sometime in the night an inversion had capped the valley trapping the smoke and soot inside like a giant kettle. A dry mist covered the town, thick as a wool blanket, throwing the streets into twilight and leaving the sun no brighter than a lamp in the fog.

In this darkness, the children's Halloween parade moved down McKean Avenue. People lined the curb and watched children appear, small wraiths drifting in the swirl, then disappear wrapped in the mist. Wagons rolled by, their crepe paper colors leeched to a funeral gray by the haze. Parents were unable to identify their own children and mothers, panic in their voices, called out their names.

Rose thought she saw Alton's shape, the hunch of his shoulders, on the far sidewalk. He seemed to shimmer there a moment and then was gone. She ran through the parade, between a sheeted spirit and a pale cowboy on a broomstick horse. She looked up the street, in the direction she thought Alton had disappeared. She checked every store window, the pool hall, and the barbershop. She turned toward the green neon glow of the Shamrock Tap and there, by the curb, stood the Indian motorcycle.

She stepped inside, thankful for the familiar smell of Camels and work clothes. She looked around for Alton's blond head above the crowd. When she saw him, Alton was sitting at the bar, his hand around a cold Iron City beer and his arm around Angela Toracelli's waist. Angela was laughing, her black hair thick and shining, her lips red, her teeth bright.

Alton looked up and saw Rose standing in the doorway. Her eyes were wide and wet behind her glasses. When she turned and ran, Alton threw a single on the bar, grabbed his jacket, and went after her.

Rose ran in front of the car that carried the Pumpkin Princess. The driver didn't see her until it was too late: The Cadillac's bumper caught her and threw her to the ground. On her skinned hands and knees, she groped for her glasses, found them, and staggered off before anyone could reach her. The Pumpkin Princess coughed and said, "Why did we stop?"

Alton caught up to Rose and pulled her around to face him.

"Please, Alton! Please, let me go."

"Are you all right?"

"No," she said. "You hurt me."

"Where?" Alton looked for a fracture or the dark blossom of blood. "Where?"

"Here, Alton." She touched her chest. "Right here."

"You saw me with Angela."

Rose tried to pull away.

"Angela doesn't mean anything to me. She's just a girl I know."

Rose tried to fix the twisted frame of her glasses, gave up, and put them on her face, skewed and missing a lens. With one eye blind and the other trying to focus on Alton she said, "And what about me, Alton? Am I just a girl you know?"

Alton said, "No, Rose. You're different."

"I don't want to be different, Alton."

"But the other night . . ."

Rose looked away. "I'm sorry." Then, her eyes on his, she took Alton's hand and placed it to her breast. Rose saw bright flashes in darkness and heard men cry out. Holding tight to the terror that skittered beneath her skin, Rose lifted her face to Alton and said, "Take me home."

"But your father . . ."

Rose swallowed the pain and said, "He's a marshal in the parade. He'll be gone all day."

Together, they climbed the hill to Third Avenue. Once inside the house, Alton kissed her and Rose was taken to another place: For the first time, it wasn't a battlefield. She was in a small bedroom and Rose saw a woman with dark hair and bottomless eyes, her ribs close to the skin. Rose gripped Alton and kissed him back, opening to him. Dreams of California flew away. Visions of glittering rivers vanished. All that was left was a hunger and the hope that she would survive this day.

Holding onto one another, they stumbled toward Rose's bed. Each button undone was accompanied by thunder; each piece of clothing was stiff with sweat and blood. Although Alton was gentle and slow when he entered her, Rose bit her lip to keep from screaming out, and by the time Alton rolled away, Rose had died a hundred times.

Alton sat on the edge of the bed and said, "You were speaking French."

"I know," Rose whispered.

He touched her shoulder and Rose saw the dark-haired woman lying beneath a table, her legs tucked beneath her, her arms outstretched, her palms as open and as sightless as her eyes.

Rose began to cry.

"I have to go," Alton said.

Rose listened to him dress. When she felt him close to her, about to touch her again, she said, "No, please. Not now; I don't think I could bear it."

Alton sighed once, then left without speaking. After the noise of the motorcycle had died away, Rose curled up under the covers. She smelled Alton's hair tonic on the pillowcase and felt his warmth in the sheets. She pressed her hand against her face where his lips had been and felt her skin flushed and hot as if from fever.

That evening Rose's father woke her. He was standing in her bedroom door. "You're in bed early. You sick?"

"No," Rose said.

"Where's Alton? Have you seen Alton?"

"No," Rose said.

Her father stood by the bed and touched her forehead. "You sure you're not sick?" But as soon as his fingertips touched his daughter's skin, he stepped back as if burned. His voice was different now, dark with rising blood. "Where is he?"

"I don't know. Maybe at his mother's."

"At his mother's," her father repeated. "His mother's dead."

Rose sat up, holding the blanket against her, unable to breathe.

"Eighteen others are dead, too, on account of this . . . this . . ." her father waved his hand, "this poison. It's all over the radio."

Rose slumped back against the headboard.

Her father shook his head like he was shaking water from his face. "She died while you two were dirtying this house. I thank God your mother is gone," he said. "I'd rather she be in her grave than to see you now."

"It's not like that, Father."

"Get dressed," he said. "You're staying with your Aunt Ruth."

"But, Father————."

"Don't argue."

Rose could feel the heat of his anger fill the room. She packed a small bag and let her father drive her across the steel bridge and upriver to Monesson and her Aunt Ruth's. She spent the night in the small guest room. In the living room below, she heard the radio report the tragedy. No one knew how this happened or why; they just knew that it had, and never again would the valley be comforted by mill smoke. Never again would someone answer a complaint with the joke, "It smells like money."

Rose returned home late the next evening. The mist had lifted leaving a blood-red sunset behind her house. She surprised her father in the garden. He had turned the earth in a new section of the yard and had planted a young peach tree in the corner. When her father saw his daughter crying, he hugged her, his soiled hands on her back. "He's gone," he said. "He left town before I could catch him."

When she didn't answer, he said, "You're better off, Rose. He was no good for you. I saw how he hurt you, night after night."

Rose nodded and wiped away the tears with the back of her hand.

"I planted a nice peach tree," her father said. "We'll have fresh peaches now, any time we want. Won't that be nice?"

Rose nodded again. "Yes, Father."

"And we won't think about this other thing no more, will we?"

"No, we won't."

In 4 years, just as her father had promised, three peaches ripened. The next year it was an even dozen. By 5 years, the branches sagged with fruit. Rose never ate the peaches from the tree, but she canned them for the winter and packed them in her father's lunch.

When the steel company closed the mill, Rose took her pension and watched from her front porch as her neighbors moved away or went on welfare. Three years later she nursed her father through lung cancer until he died, suffocated in his bed at the new hospital in Pittsburgh.

The day after he was buried, Rose hired a boy to clean out the garage. Unlike many of the young men in town, he worked hard and was honest. He came to her, his cap in his hands, and told Rose that the old motorcycle in the back of the garage was worth a lot of money.

Rose told him he could have it as payment for one more job. The boy agreed, and the next day he cut down the peach tree and split the limbs into firewood.

That winter, Rose sat on the floor close to the fire. She saw his face in the flames and heard his promises in the whispers of steam. The scented smoke filled her hair, and when she pressed her hand against her cheek, it felt hot, as if from fever. When the fire died and the house grew cold, she went to bed in darkness, closed her eyes, and waited once more for the dream she knew would come.

Chapter 10

Future Imperfect

By Nicholas Knight

I was 11 when my world first flashed black and white. My parents and I had been driving by a perfectly normal, brown brick house surrounded by green shrubbery and a faded cedar fence when everything lost its color. Everything, that is, except for the cement porch. It had been grayish to begin with, but for that brief moment, while the rest of the world had turned black and white, the gray porch was covered in bright red blood.

I looked at my parents in the front seat. My mother, who normally freaked out if a bird was smooshed on the road, was smiling and humming along to a song on the radio. My father, who demanded no distractions whatsoever while he drove, looked just as blissful as Mom.

We were on our way to an open house, searching for a new place to call home. I'd seen the listing, and the house had seemed perfect for us, what with the three bedrooms, three bathrooms, and a backyard hot tub for Dad's bad back. Perfect, that is, until I'd had my vision of the death house. Now there was no way I could live in that neighborhood.

My world flashed black, white, and red again as we returned to the main road the same way we'd come. I screamed that time, but my father yelled something about shortening my life expectancy and that was that—end of subject. Not that I was surprised; they were probably a little skeptical of my sanity after I'd told them at the open house that the neighbors would murder me if we moved in there.

To my parents' credit, they did look at dozens of other homes over the next couple of months. We'd already sold our house though, and eventually they had to buy something. They bought the house two blocks over from the death house.

I begged them not to, but they never saw the blood on the porch like I did, and I was afraid they'd send me off to live somewhere with padded walls if I told them about my visions. Of course, the funny farm didn't scare me as much as the death house, but what could I do? I was only an 11-year-old girl.

Still, I argued with them right up to the day we moved in. I even told them that I would run away, but nothing worked.

* * *

During my school years, I had to pass by the death house a minimum of twice a day. Of course, anytime I went anywhere—to the movies, shopping, dancing, skating, *anywhere* outside our neighborhood—I had to pass by it both ways. At first, I tried closing my eyes, but that didn't stop the flashes. Over time, I learned to deal with the visions like they were a hay fever allergy with no antihistamines to stave off the sneezing fits.

As if those drive-bys weren't torture enough, a girl my age lived in the death house. Her name was Ellen, and we went to school together. If I got too close to her too soon after she'd left home, I'd get the flashes as though I were standing in front of her house. I thought I could just avoid her, but when she learned where I lived, she tried to befriend me. I pretended to be a shy loner, but she persisted until I finally had to make up a lie. In a panic, I blurted out, "You smell!" Some boys nearby heard and called her names such as Elle Smells and Smellin' Ellen. She was ostracized, and I somehow became popular. I felt awful, but I didn't dare go near her again. She hated me ever after.

* * *

Although I was sad to leave my family, the day I moved away for college— moved away from the death house—felt like the happiest day of my life. With the aid of distance, class deadlines, and a new love interest, I nearly forgot all about the house and my bloody visions. After college, I married my boyfriend Chad. We moved back to my hometown, but miles away from the old neighborhood, and I always insisted that my parents came to our place for visits.

My life seemed wonderful—normal. Until two nights ago that is, when my husband came home late from work.

"Where've you———." I started to ask as he came into the living room where I sat reading a book. The book dropped from my hands as the vision of the death house flashed before my eyes.

Chad rushed over to me. "Honey, what's wrong? You look like you've seen a ghost."

"You must have been in *the house.*"

"What house? I came from the office."

"Why did you go there?" I searched his face for answers. He was flushed, like he'd recently exerted himself. His desk job didn't require manual labor; was there another woman? Oh my God! "Ellen! You slept with Ellen. She still lives there?"

Chad's face dropped. "How . . . how did you know?"

I leapt out of my chair. I wanted to claw his eyes out, but I had another strong flash, and backed away in mental anguish.

"I'm so sorry," Chad said. "I never even looked at another woman before. She came on so strong . . . I said no, but she wore me down. She made me feel like I was the most important man in the world. She said it was our destiny to be together, but if you know her . . . Was this some kind of revenge? Did you steal her boyfriend in high school or something?"

I glared at him through tear-blurred eyes and said nothing.

Chad picked up the phone up the end table and punched in a number. "I'm so sorry," he said to me again while he waited for a response.

I didn't know if I could ever forgive his betrayal, but he earned some good favor by what he did next: He'd called Ellen. When she answered, he told her he'd made a mistake and that he never wanted to see her again. I couldn't make out her words, but I could hear her strident voice well enough to tell that she argued vehemently, begged, and finally hung up on Chad.

* * *

Yesterday, the phone rang and the death house flashed before my eyes. I didn't want to answer the phone, but I did anyway.

"Hello," I said through chattering teeth.

"Hi, this is Ellen Para—remember me?" Whore, I thought. "Is everything okay? You sound scared."

"I'm fine. What do you want?"

"Look, I know I'm probably the last person you want to talk to right now."

Oh, why's that? I thought to myself, You're just the whore who slept with my husband in your death house.

"But I'd really like to talk to you—try to make things right."

Another flash. This one lingered, as if the image had been burned into my retinas.

I knew before she asked that she wanted me to go to the death house.

"Please come over," she said, "so we can clear the air face to face."

I wanted to refuse, to give her a believable excuse—not that I owed her one—but my mind was blank. "Okay, I'm on my way." It seemed as though fate had given me no choice but to go.

"Thanks."

I hung up the phone and then dialed a new number. I considered calling the police, but what could I say? "Uh, hi. I'd like to report a murder that's going to happen in the near future." No, they wouldn't believe me, but there was someone else I could call . . .

* * *

I parked my car a block away and walked up to the death house. The visions seemed to flash across my eyes with every step. As I drew closer to the house, the rapidity of the flashes increased. When I stepped onto Ellen's property, my world lost color altogether. I averted my eyes from the porch, so everything I saw was in shades of black and white.

I snuck along the side of the house, and peaked in an open window with a view of the front foyer. I fully expected to see Ellen standing there with a gun pointed at the door, waiting for me.

I didn't see a gun or Ellen—just some paintings, a ladder, and some tools. I was about to turn away, when I noticed a stone statue atop the ladder. There was a ledge above the door, which was probably the statue's final destination, but why hadn't she finished the job? Something about the way the statue perched precariously sent a shiver down my back.

The doorbell rang and I jumped.

"Come on in; the door's not locked," I heard Ellen call from somewhere out of sight within the house.

I watched in black and white as the door swung open. The door hit the ladder and the statue came crashing down on the visitor's head—Chad's head.

I rushed around to the front of the house.

The force of the blow had knocked Chad off the porch, and I saw the bloodstain of my visions. My world regained color as Chad died.

Had I cheated fate, or sent my husband to his death . . . or both?

Chapter 11

Chance

By Elorise Holstad

"Reading glasses." Madame Wanda winked as she settled half spectacles on her nose. "You'll pardon the pun."

Sophie Olsen had to smile. Wanda was nothing like she'd imagined. At any rate, there was absolutely no aura of occultism about the plump woman seated across the table. Glancing around the psychic's living room, Sophie viewed a comfortably cluttered area. The room's front bay window, brazen in the shifting October sunlight, framed an ordinary suburban street lined with maple trees.

"I charge $30 for a tarot reading," the older woman continued. "If you want your palms done as well, the total will be 45."

Sophie nodded, pleased the quoted figure was well within the allowance provided by her editor, Scott Carr. She bit her lip, and tugged at the sleeves of the old sweater she'd worn today in order not to look like an investigative journalist. "How much for . . ."

"Gazing?" Wanda laughed as she touched the crystal ball cushioned on a velvet pillow on the table. "Sorry. This is only for atmosphere. I could stare into it for hours and see nothing more than reflections."

Sophie leaned forward to look down into the glassy, brilliant ball. A miniature copy of a green van crept like a bug across the smooth orb—an image that vanished as the vehicle passed Wanda's house. Sitting back, Sophie pulled a gold charm bracelet from her pocket.

"I'd like you to give me a reading on this," she said, dropping the bracelet on the table.

Wanda eyed her skeptically. "If you intend to catch me up, Miss Olsen, you haven't chosen wisely," she groused, pointing at two dangling trinkets on the bracelet: a perky mouse and a pair of scissors. "Any fool can deduce you've been to Disneyland and like to sew."

Sophie stiffened, abashed. She hadn't considered those associations when she'd asked Dana, her friend and co-worker, to lend her a piece of jewelry.

"I don't want my personality profiled," she said. "Just give me any impressions you receive."

Wanda singled out another tiny ornament. "Who's this one? He looks like Lenin. Have you been to Russia?"

Sophie peered at the charm's pointed beard for a long moment before recalling that Dana had visited Stratford.

"No, that's Shakespeare."

Wanda gave her an oblique look. "You like words."

Sophie smiled wanly.

As planned, her feature assignment, scheduled for a two-page spread in Sunday's supplement, would be a broad debunking of various topics falling under the subject of Parapsychology, especially forms of divination. The article would explore aspects of extrasensory perception ranging from astrology and clairvoyance to runes and tarot cards. Sophie felt confident that the paragraphs she'd write about Madame Wanda would expose the woman's inability to reach accurate conclusions about the bracelet's *real* owner.

Wanda pushed the gold bracelet firmly to one side, and reached for an illustrated deck of cards. "I'm not very good psychometrician," she said with a regretful smile. "My best results always come from tarot. The guiding principle behind tarot is similar to the *Book of Changes.*"

Sophie blinked. "Changes?"

"Also known as the *I Ching*," Wanda clarified. "It predicts using yarrow stalks, or the toss of a coin."

Sophie's expression turned incredulous. "Are you serious? Like, head or tails?"

"Exactly," Wanda answered, shuffling the colorful cards. "To the Oriental way of thinking, whichever side of a coin turns up in any given moment, is right—absolutely correct—because it is of that moment."

"That's absurd."

Wanda shrugged, her plump face serene. "Tarot spreads are also random. How the cards fall, and how I interpret them, point to a moment in time yet to come."

Momentarily forgetting her assignment, Sophie shook her head. "Cards can't predict the future," she scoffed.

"You don't have to believe me," Wanda returned as she dealt out three cards, face down. "The beauty of the tarot is that it allows you to access your own intuition." Curling an index finger under the first card, she flipped it over. "For instance, tarot gives clues about different influences surrounding you. It's up to you to accept, or reject, the suggested symbolism."

Sophie didn't reply immediately, distracted by the wail of a far-away siren. The sound faded, intermingling with a sudden breeze whispering against the windowpanes.

"Come again," she said, narrowing her eyes at Wanda.

Madame Wanda turned over the next card. "Sometimes, the message isn't even intended for the future. Tarot speaks to the present in many cases."

"I still don't get it."

Wanda tapped the first card, which pictured a young boy leaning on a staff. "Drawing information from this card—the reversed Page of Staves—

one might conclude the present situation has something to do with travel. Travel for your work, perhaps. Business travel."

"I have nothing scheduled along that line," Sophie told her, looking triumphant. "No vacations, either."

"The card's reversal indicates a problem. It's next to the Knight of Swords—a restless card. Take care."

Sophie pushed Dana's bracelet toward the other woman. "What do you think about this?"

"Swords," Wanda murmured as if she didn't hear. "The Knight of Swords."

"Listen, I don't want a tarot reading today," Sophie insisted. "Try to get something from my charm bracelet."

Wanda exhaled a sigh. "Very well, then, fifty dollars. In advance please."

Sophie removed the cash from her purse, handed it over, and slouched back in her chair, arms folded.

"Gold," Madame Wanda whispered, coiling the bracelet in the palm of her left hand.

Sophie nodded. "Yes, it's gold. Not an alloy."

"No," Wanda responded. "I meant the color. Gold is falling around you in a kaleidoscope. There's confusion, a golden color, a sense of shock and————."

Breaking off, the psychic closed her eyes and brought her hand to her forehead.

"Well?" Sophie prompted. "What else do you see?"

"Nothing." Wanda opened her eyes, blinked away a tear. "Only sadness and gold, filling a space."

As Sophie slipped Dana's bracelet in her pocket, she felt disconcerted; Madame Wanda actually seemed to believe her own outlandish pronouncements.

* * *

As hardly enough of the afternoon remained to justify returning to her office, Sophie drove straight home.

The telephone was ringing as Sophie unlocked her door, but she couldn't reach it before the caller hung up. After gulping down a quick cup of instant coffee, she sat down with her laptop to finish her article.

At first, nothing flowed, but Sophie grinned when the words finally began to click.

Perhaps she didn't have the credentials to judge the more esoteric, metaphysical themes, like reincarnation, but she knew what was bogus and what wasn't.

Her pager vibrated; she ignored it.

Her fingers flew over the computer keyboard, composing and revising sentences, rushing to discredit Madame Wanda's personal point of view.

The telephone shrilled, interrupting. Sophie picked up the receiver.

"Where have you been?" Scott demanded over the line.

"I went to interview that psychic woman," Sophie told him. "Don't worry; the article will be on time. I'm almost finished here."

"Never mind. Isn't it terrible?"

"Isn't what terrible?"

"You haven't heard!" Scott's voice took on the jerky tempo associated with catastrophe. "Dana had an accident."

"What?"

"I was busy with the press. I sent her out."

"Calm down, and tell me what happened."

"There was a pile-up on the expressway," Scott cried. "A chain reaction, involving six cars."

"Were you driving?"

"Me, driving? No, no. I told you. Dana. I sent her on a last-minute interview. She was driving my car."

"She's okay, isn't she?"

Scott let a long silence pass as his answer.

Sophie's mind fluttered with fearful suppositions, as she demanded to know if Dana was hurt badly.

"Dana is g-gone," her editor stuttered out, and then managed to speak sensibly. "I'm sorry. She died in the accident—killed instantly." His voice faltered. "We'll run her obit tomorrow. It will say where and when her funeral will be held. Will you attend with me?"

"Of course," Sophie promised, feeling the paralyzing reality of her friend's death creep into her body. Knees buckling, she sat down and hung up the receiver, without saying anything more.

* * *

Four days later, Sophie slipped the charm bracelet in her jacket pocket, planning to return it to some member of Dana's family after the funeral service.

Scott picked up Sophie in his car and drove her to the funeral home. After parking beside the curb where fallen autumn leaves were piled for disposal, he pounded the steering wheel.

"Dana would be alive if not for me," he moaned. "Why did I have to send her out on that interview? It could have waited."

"Enough, Scott," Sophie cried, jerking the car door open. "It wasn't your fault."

She caught her breath as a sudden gust of wind blew brittle, golden-hued leaves inside the car's interior, where they spun and eddied, filling the space.

She closed her eyes. "If anything, it was chance. Pure fate, written in the cards."

Chapter 12

A Lover's Understanding

By Patricia Harrington

The two of us trudged through the snow, the forest silence broken by dripping icicles that dangled from tree limbs, warming in the late afternoon sun. Jim and I were returning from the lake's shore. Nature had frolicked there the night before, making its own snow persons by piling snowdrifts over trees and shrubs.

In reality, though, there were three of us on the walk: Jim, his wife Emelda, who had died a year ago, and me. Her presence seemed to stalk us, and I could sense her anger spreading, her sick unhappiness sullying the air. I knew she was miserable because Jim had found a new life with me. She wouldn't let him go, even in death.

I glanced at Jim. Did I dare tell him about Emelda's presence? Jim knew nothing about my gift of second sight, and I feared he would disapprove. He might say I was being fanciful. It had been a long time since such a sense of dread had come over me. Usually, the rising tide warned me of something terrible about to happen. Other times I had been wrong, swayed by an overwrought imagination. The last medication prescribed by Dr. Pendergast at Harmony Glen had blocked those feelings. After my stay at the hospital, I had shut that part of me away, never allowing my premonitions to prey again.

But I'd forgotten my pills before we left for the weekend, and I could feel my mind spiraling, trying to draw my body upward with it as it reached toward the heavens. So I stifled my fear and turned my head away from Emelda. The aura around her had become blood red.

When Jim and I met 6 months ago, he told me that his wife had died the prior year in a fire while he was out of town on business. They had been married for 25 years, and it was understandable that her death had left him a crippled man. He had shown me a picture of the two of them taken when they were a young couple. When I studied it, they had beamed back at me, their enduring love shining about them. Later, Jim began telling me little bit about himself, and when he talked, I could feel his misery and see the starless night of his soul in his eyes. We had met at a Rotary meeting. Afterward, he had discuss business. I'd just been named Entrepreneur Woman of the ..., and he congratulated me and listened while I talked about my franchise plans. One latte led to another, and our late night dates led us to becoming lovers. All the advice columns caution to wait a year before dating again after a divorce or the death of a spouse, but Jim had needed me. His hunger for closeness, his need for my body was all consuming. When he held me in his arms, I knew I was Jim's true destiny. No words were necessary for us to communicate. With the keen insight of lovers, we seemed to know the other's thoughts. They were printed in bold letters on our minds and hearts. We understood each other.

That's why I had to hide from Jim that I had seen Emelda watching us.

We had been plodding over the rough path for almost an hour, and even in the cold, I was sweating inside my parka. As hard as I tried not to, I kept glancing about, catching glimpses of the red haze that hung around Emelda. It told me that she was still following us, flitting in and out of the trees. A throbbing pain in my head had begun, making it hard for me to think, and I answered Jim's questions with monosyllables to save energy.

When we reached a creek, we stopped and listened to it bubble merrily where it had broken through the ice. Jim turned to face me. Taking hold of my hands, he said, "I have something to ask you tonight. Something I've wanted to say so many times over these last few months." He smiled. "Finally, the time is right."

Happiness flooded my heart. This was the moment that I had waited for all my life! Finally, the man of my dreams wanted me to be his forever. He's going to ask me to marry him.

I pulled my hands from his grasp, clasping them together. "And just what might that be, good sir?"

I gazed into Jim's eyes. They were so alive, with nothing hidden. The anticipation of his answer caught my breath; my head filled with a crescendo of sound. Lights, brilliant as stars, seemed to flash. I could see into the depths of Jim's soul—see all that he was and would become—but the sight sent me stumbling backward. I looked around wildly, calling out, seeking something— anything—that would prove me wrong, would show me that my mind was playing tricks again.

"What's the matter?" Jim asked.

I clenched my hands at my sides, digging fingernails into flesh to bring reality into focus. A cry of horror and then pain stuck in my throat. I had looked into my lover's soul and read its wicked intent: It was fun to get rid of Emelda, and you'll be the next. You and your insurance will be easy pickings, you dumb bitch.

I turned to run from what I had seen, had learned and saw Emelda on the path behind me. Her anger was gone, her aura no longer blood red. Instead, a halo of dull mourning gray hung over her. She looked at me with pity and sadness, and then nodded twice before fading into the snow-fringed trees.

Artwork by Chris Pugh, Copyright 2002

Chapter 13

Animism

By George M. Scott

When Professor Laurie Dickinson heard the knock, her gaze jumped from the computer screen to the door. She frowned and then saved the chapter she'd been working on and walked over. She hated not being able to just open it.

"Who is it?"

"Officer David Robbins, ma'am. Campus Police. May I come in? I'd like to talk to you."

She sighed and turned the knob. His bulk filled the opening and his round, boyish face seemed to pinch his eyes into two brown slits. He ran the fingers of one hand through his wispy brown hair while holding his cap with the other one. Why, he was almost blushing, she thought. An endearing trait one didn't see much of these days.

She smiled in spite of herself. "Come in."

He followed her inside, and he left the door open behind him.

"Professor, you shouldn't———."

She held up her hand to cut him off. "I know. I shouldn't be in my office at night. Alone." She shrugged. "But I have a deadline to meet on my book."

"It's kinda dangerous, ma'am. You know what's been goin' on."

"Everyone knows what's been going on, but I can't help thinking that maybe it's over. There hasn't been another murder in the last 3 weeks."

"You mean . . . uh . . ."

She rested her hands on her hips. "Okay. How about rape, *then* murder?"

Robbins looked down, and this time there was no mistake about the redness on his face.

She cleared her throat. "I'm sorry. I shouldn't have . . ."

"That's all right. We're all kinda stressed these days."

She forgave him his condescension and asked, "Any new developments?"

"The LAPD's no closer to catching the psycho than they were after the first victim. No forensics, no witnesses, and no suspects. But today the coroner gave us his MO: first, a small shot of An-An, uh, Anectine to make his victim weak but awake while he . . . uh . . . undresses her and ties her up. Then he waits 'til she gets her strength back to . . ."

"That's all right," she said, touching his arm. "I know what happens next. Let me get my things, and you can walk me to my car."

As she gathered up her papers, he said, "That's some mask you have on the wall there."

She didn't bother to look; she'd explained it many times before. "It's a spirit mask—from Sri Lanka."

"Kinda scary lookin'."

* * *

The next day several of Professor Dickinson's students paid her a visit in her office. On such a small campus, word had traveled quickly that the professor was defying the police by continuing to work in her office at night.

"Can't you work at home?" one of the female students asked.

"Nope," she replied, with a shake of her head. "Too many distractions—especially Toby the feline. I can work only in complete solitude, and the publisher wants my book by next week."

"But this guy attacks his victims in their offices at night," the student pleaded.

The professor started to speak but only shrugged.

"What about a gun?" another student asked. "Do you own one?"

A young woman rolled her eyes. "Oh, Derek, what good is a gun gonna do?" Others in the group murmured in agreement.

"Look, Mary, nothing like a bullet to stop that wacko in his tracks." The murmurs now turned to loud derisive protests.

"I agree with Mary," another student said. "I-I don't think a gun's such a good idea."

"Oh, Howie, you would————."

Professor Dickinson had put up her hand to cut off Derek. "All right, that's enough. I don't own a gun, and I don't plan to own one."

Derek sighed and shook his head. "Not even if your life depended on it?"

"I don't need a gun when I have my *arakshakadeiyo,* the Professor replied, looking at the mask hanging on the wall. "My protector-spirit."

"Yeah, right!" Derek blurted out.

"Do you really believe in animism?" Mary asked. "That's what it's called, right? The belief in spirits?"

"Yes, that's right. Well, I've, uh, seen some strange things . . ." Professor Dickinson's voice trailed off as she looked away from the students. After a few tense seconds, she blinked rapidly and said, "But I don't know if I really believe in it." Suddenly she stood up. "What I do know is that I have to prepare for my next class."

The students took the hint and began to file out of the office. The professor followed them to the door. When she was about to close it, Mary and Howie stuck their heads back in. "Please be careful," Mary said. "Yeah, watch yourself," Howie added.

Professor Dickinson smiled. "I will. Now, get out of here. I have work to do."

After closing the door, the professor, still smiling, went to her desk and sat down. She took the lecture notes out of her file and started reviewing them, but after the first page, she found herself looking at the mask. It was an old one, genuine, not at all like the garish, assembly-line masks now sold to tourists. It had been hand-carved in one piece from a block of wood. The eyes bulged out above the long, hooked nose. The hinged jaws were lined with flat, brown teeth. Long whiskers of buffalo tail hair flowed downward from the chin and framed the mouth from the upper lip. Giving the mask its identity, a hooded cobra arose from the top of the head, flanked by long ears. The red, yellow, and blue colors had faded, and it exuded a musky, primordial smell. Yet there was something reassuring about its outwardly menacing mien, at least to Laurie, whether she believed in animism or not.

She leaned back in the chair and gazed out the window, letting the memories flow in like a warm spring breeze. The old *kaparala* had given her the mask on her last fieldwork visit to Sri Lanka. She knew it represented a *nagaraja,* a king cobra-spirit, one of the most powerful ones, but the shaman had assured her that he had tamed it. She remembered his words as if he'd just spoken them. "Madam, he will not hurt you. He will protect you. Keep him with you, and you will never be harmed. To summon him, all you have to do is call out his name—*Nagaraja*." The old man had then paused, and a stern expression unfolded on his leathery face. "But do not summon him unless you truly need his help. For he will not appear again if you summon him frivolously."

"Maybe you'll have your chance soon," she spoke to the mask. As usual, it remained just a mask. It was all a mystery to her. She smiled, shook her head, and went back to her lecture notes.

* * *

Another week passed with no further attacks. The university community relaxed some, but the investigation continued. Then the killer claimed his third victim. A physics professor, Chitra Patel, had gone to her office at night without police protection, and her bloody body was found the next morning. Fear tightened its steel grip on the campus once again.

Although the entire campus grieved for the well-liked Professor Patel, no one mourned more intensely than Laurie Dickinson, for she and the latest victim had been close friends.

Laurie stayed home for 2 days, with Toby trying to comfort her and only partly succeeding, and then returned to her teaching duties. She'd decided work was the best treatment for grief. Her first day back she was seated at her desk, staring blankly at the lecture notes before her, when she suddenly put her hands over her face. Her body jerked with sobs as she rocked back and forth in the chair. She leaned forward, beat her fists on the desk, and moaned, "Chitra. Why? Why?" Her mouth agape with sheer anguish, she put her head on the desk. The tears stained her lecture notes; she didn't care.

Soon grief morphed into fear. With a jolt, she realized she wasn't safe. For the first time in her life she was truly afraid. Now she knew she'd been in denial. She looked at the mask, but remembered the shaman's warning and decided not to summon the spirit. Then she felt foolish for even considering it—now wasn't the time to depend on the mystery of animism.

* * *

Over the next week, Professor Dickinson hurried to and from class, often with a cautious glance over her shoulder. Several times she stopped in the middle of a lecture and covered her haggard face with her hands as the students whispered among themselves and looked on with concern. But she always recovered before any of them dared go to her.

Then one night she decided to leave the campus library without a police escort. It had been 15 minutes since she made the call, and she'd grown impatient. She had to get home and feed Toby, especially because she'd forgotten his breakfast. Poor guy was probably meowing his head off. Besides, it was a short walk to her car. Halfway there, she thought she heard footsteps behind her. She turned; all she saw were students walking in the distance, but the shadows immediately behind her seemed to pulsate with a foreboding menace. She shuddered and hurried away, only to hear the footsteps again. She spun around and caught a glimpse of her pursuer just before he ducked behind a hedge. Could it be? It almost looked like Howie Burns, her student. Ripples of panic ran up and down her spine. A shot of adrenalin got her feet to move, and she started to run. The footsteps pounded behind her. Faster, faster—gaining on her. Her heart thudded in her chest. Ahead, a light— safety? She turned the corner of the parking structure and ran headlong into a large man.

"Help me," she panted. "Please, help!" She looked up and saw the uniform of Officer Robbins. "He's following me."

"Who?" he asked, holding her shoulders as she turned around to look behind her.

"A student."

"Wait here, and I'll go see." He jerked loose the strap securing his pistol and disappeared around the corner.

Laurie trembled and felt the tension force tears down her cheeks.

In a few seconds, Robbins returned. "I didn't see anyone, ma'am. Are you all right?" He peered at her with concern.

She wiped her eyes with her hands as a shudder racked her body. "I'm sure he was there!" she screamed. "I saw him! He was after me!"

Robbins fidgeted with his belt and looked down.

"Why are you just standing there? Don't you believe me?"

He looked up and a nervous smile played across his face. "Yes, of course I believe you, but he's gone now. Please, you don't have to be afraid anymore. I'm with you."

She nodded and her breathing began to slow. "I'm sorry for yelling."

"Not a problem. Did you recognize him?"

She started to speak but hesitated.

"Do you want him to do it again?"

She shook her head and folded her arms across her chest. "No. No, I don't. It was Howard Burns. He's in one of my classes."

Officer Robbins took out his radio and called in the information.

"He may not be the killer," the professor said when he'd finished.

"We'll find out when we take him in. Now, if you don't mind, I'll walk you to your car."

"Mind?" She looked at him and smiled, then took his arm.

* * *

A few days later, Professor Dickinson discovered the police had released Howie for lack of evidence. The next thing she knew he seemed to be everywhere she went: He looked, he stood, he watched—from the end of a row of stacks in the library, behind a bush as she walked to her car, at the end of the hall as she entered and left her office.

She called the campus police. The dispatcher connected her to Officer Robbins.

"He's following me again."

"Has he threatened you?"

She didn't answer.

"Professor?"

"Not really."

"Then we can't———."

"I want to buy a gun." There, she'd said it, but her trembling belied any bravado in the statement.

"I could help you with that."

* * *

Later that afternoon when she was about to open her car door, she saw Howie's reflection in the window as he approached her. She clenched her fists and spun around.

"Professor Dickinson, I———."

"Stop following me," she screamed. "Stop! Just stop it, you hear me!" She felt the tears come, this time hot and angry.

Howie took a step toward her with his hand out.

"Get away from me!"

"I-I only want to———."

She shook her fist at him. "Go away, Howard!"

Sadness clouded his eyes. He hung his head, turned around, and walked off.

* * *

Professor Dickinson didn't see Howie again for the next few days. Then she discovered he had dropped out of school. The guilt was a small voice in her continuing storm of fear, for terror still infected the campus like a raging virus.

As the days passed, the professor all but forgot about Howie. She was besieged with another problem. She hadn't been able to work on her book. At Officer Robbins' behest, she tried to write at home, but just as she feared, between Toby and the noisy neighbors, it proved impossible. Finally one night in sheer desperation, she got in her car and sped toward the campus. Her new gun was in her purse on the seat next to her.

As soon as she'd parked, a campus patrol car pulled up next to her. The officer got out and asked where she was going. It was Robbins. She found his smile comforting.

"To my office to do some work."

"I'll escort you, if you'll wait 'till I call it in. It'll be just a minute."

He returned to his car and used the radio. After a few seconds he lowered his passenger window and said, "I'm sorry, ma'am, but I've been called to another part of campus. Wait here with your doors locked, and I'll send another officer. He'll be here in a few minutes. Be sure to wait for him before you go to your office."

"Fine," she said, but her body prickled with impatience. She rolled up the window and locked the doors. As she waited, she felt the hardness of the gun against her leg. This is ridiculous, she thought. What am I, a little girl? I have a gun and I have every right to walk around this place. To hell with this waiting.

She abruptly got out and hurried toward her office. The campus seemed deserted, typical of a Saturday night. Normally, she would relish the quiet darkness, but now it pressed against her like an ominous, heavy blanket.

When she neared her building, she ran. Her heart pounded; her chest heaved. She reached the door and fumbled with her keys. Finally, she let herself in, and the heavy glass door snapped shut behind her. She turned to see if anyone had followed her. "Ma-major victory," she chuckled to herself.

She took the elevator up to the third floor and walked to her office, but her hand was still shaking so badly that she dropped her keys. She looked up and down the hallway, picked them up, and opened the door. She quickly closed it and stood with her back to it, trying to catch her runaway breath. Then she went straight to the computer and turned it on. "My anchor," she said as she patted the monitor.

Professor Dickinson had been working for about an hour, smiling with relief at finally being able to do what she liked best, when she heard a knock on the door.

Her skin crawled as she slowly approached it. "Who-who is it?"

"Officer Robbins, ma'am."

"I-I'm all right."

"How much longer will you be here?"

"Oh," she sighed, "several more hours."

"I'll try to wait for you out here."

Impatience resurfaced, this time a finger tickling her guts. "Do whatever you like, but please don't disturb me again. I'll come out when I'm ready."

"Yes, ma'am."

It took her a good 15 minutes to convince herself there was nothing to worry about with Officer Robbins stationed outside the office. She stretched out her arms and flexed her fingers and went back to typing.

After 2 more hours of work, the professor was ready to call it a night. She was removing her work from the printer when a loud ruckus erupted out in the hallway. Papers flew as she bolted upright. Groans and thuds penetrated the wall and attacked her mind. And then there was silence, broken only by the professor's ragged breathing. She strained to listen and gasped when she heard a loud knocking.

"Professor Dickinson, open the door. I need you to identify someone." It sounded like Officer Robbins, but his voice seemed higher-pitched.

She found herself reaching for the knob with a shaking hand.

"Open the door!"

She jumped at the words and turned the knob.

Howie stood in the doorway. He had grown a beard and was wearing a knit cap, but it was him. She inhaled sharply, holding her hand over her mouth, and backed away. His wild eyes seemed to brim with depravity. All at once, he rushed toward her. She fell back, trapped between her desk and her attacker. She screamed and pushed him away. He collapsed to the floor. A knife handle protruded from his back, and around it redness spread.

Then Officer Robbins stepped into the room and closed the door behind him.

Professor Dickinson, eyes wide with fear, stood gaping at him. Her mouth moved but no words came out. The boyish face had aged and hardened. The smile that spread like a stain meant only one thing. On impulse, she started to put up her hand but knew it wouldn't work now. She remembered her gun and lunged for her purse sitting on the desk. He was on her before she could reach it. He clamped one hand over her mouth and the other around her waist, gripping one arm and pinning the other against her side.

"You can call me Dave," he purred. "Ma'am."

The professor grimaced and tried to turn away from his hot, foul breath. She struggled and kicked and writhed and tried to bite his hand, but he was too big and strong.

"Bitch!" was the last thing she heard before he jabbed the needle in her neck. Her eyes blurred, and she melted down to the floor.

She wished he had given her something that knocked her out completely, because she was perfectly awake but couldn't feel or move her arms or legs. Nor could she move her mouth or see very well—but well enough to know he was undressing her, slowly and carefully, exploring with his hands and murmuring to himself as he went along. It occurred to her that it was just as well that she couldn't feel what was happening. Still, she wanted to scream and kick and punch, but she couldn't. Now he was tying her wrists underneath her. When he finished he spread her legs apart and tied her ankles to the legs of a heavy chair.

Feeling crawled back into her body, and her eyesight cleared. She blinked several times.

"Good. Your feeling's comin' back."

His big hand again choked off her scream. Then he covered her mouth with a strip of silver duct tape. She squirmed against the ropes.

"You're not goin' anywhere. Got you tied up real good. Now that you're gonna be able to feel it, we can begin. You're gonna like it." He giggled as he ogled her body. He reached over and pulled the knife out of Howie's back and wiped the blade off on his pants. He grinned and held it up so she was sure to see it.

The professor's heart raced, but she gave up struggling. A coldness crept over her skin, and her stomach churned. She tasted the bile rising in her throat.

Officer Robbins unbuckled his belt and unzipped his pants. She whimpered and strained to look up to the wall where the mask was hanging. She looked back at Officer Robbins and began pleading, with her mouth and eyes. She hoped suggestively.

"You wanna say something, darlin'?" he snickered. "Maybe talk dirty?"

She nodded avidly.

"I'm gonna take off the tape, but if you scream, I'll cut you." The long blade of the knife gleamed in the light.

He ripped the tape off. She squeezed her eyes shut against the pain and tried to speak.

Robbins leaned close to her face and listened. "What the hell are you tryin' to say? If this is some kind of a trick———."

This time she managed to mumble a word.

"Speak English, Laurie honey," he hissed through clenched teeth.

She smiled hopefully and said clearly, *"Nagaraja."*

"Whatever." He laughed and slapped the tape back over her mouth. Then he stroked her hair. "A blond, but no bimbo, huh? That's why I like you professors so much. Y'all think you're so damn smart." He snorted and moved back between her legs, leering toward the business before him. He reached down and, with a groan, pushed toward her.

A loud hissing stopped him. The professor's nostrils flared and her eyebrows shot upward. Robbins twisted around, and she saw a blur of two red eyes, a forked tongue, and two gleaming fangs rushing toward him. She squeezed her eyes shut, but she couldn't block out Robbins' guttural scream.

When she opened them and looked at the mask, it was back on the wall, impassive in its wooden vigilance. Officer Robbins crawled over her leg toward the door and reached up for the knob. He tried to pull himself up, but his hand slipped off, and with a rattling sigh he collapsed to the floor, rolled over on his back, and lay still.

As her body relaxed, the professor's mind escaped to the pleasant green warmth of Sri Lanka where animism was not a mystery. And neither would it remain a mystery to her. She glanced up at the computer and thought of her book and all the hard work she'd put on it. What a slave she'd been to it. Now, that's where the real mystery lay.

Chapter 14

The Thirteenth Hole

By Lee Driver

Be careful what 'ye wish for.
Emma Sullivan

There was a bounce to Ben's step as he crossed the foyer. Things would be different now. Things would be done the right way, his way. Then that familiar tingling caught him in midstride. In the past, whenever that icy chill crept up his spine, he would turn to find Emma leaning against a wall, arms folded, a disapproving scowl etched across her face. Or she would be peering around a doorjamb, just half of her face visible, lurking like some grade school principal. However, she wouldn't be lurking around corners any more. Emma Sullivan was dead. Ben had practically danced a little jig when he heard the news weeks ago: heart attack. Little strange for a woman he was sure never had a heart.

Slowly, Ben turned, seeking the cause for the cold that was gripping his body. Emma wasn't lurking around any corners or standing in any doorways; instead, a new addition had been added to the foyer. Ben took a step back and assessed the portrait. Thick, ornate mahogany framed the large painting of Thomas and Emma Sullivan. Emma was built like a sequoia, with red hair and blazing green eyes. She stood just a scant 2 inches shorter than her husband, a stick of a man with a wisp of a gray mustache.

Ben stepped to his right and noticed that her eyes followed. It was only his imagination, he was sure. As if challenging their control, he cautiously moved left, but still her gaze was locked on him like a heat-seeking missile.

Casually walking to the far corner of the foyer, Ben's fingers twirled the diamond-studded ring on his left hand. Before him was an elaborate staircase, like something out of the movie *Titanic,* branching out at the mezzanine level. He could imagine his executive office on that floor with a perfect view of the course. And he would generate more revenue by renting out the meeting rooms. The place was a gold mine.

He returned his gaze to the portrait. Emma's heat seekers bore a hole through him as his fingers twirled the ring until his skin felt raw. With hands shoved in his pants pockets, he strolled back to the wall where the possessed portrait hung. He could almost hear Emma's voice, the last words she had spoken to him in her rich, Irish brogue: "Be careful what 'ye wish for."

Shamrock Isle Country Club was an 18–hole golf course tucked behind a palatial clubhouse. The first generation Sullivans had been of aristocratic stock, owning castles in Europe and passing jewels and property holdings down the family tree. The properties served well for the five-star golf courses they built. All of the clubhouses had the trademark castle design. They also carried one other tradition: They were exclusively for men.

This was never a problem until Thomas married a professional golfer. Emma had tried for years to get the rules changed; she even filed a discrimination suit. The court ruled that, because it was a private club, the owners could make their own rules. When she set out to change the minds of the members, she ran into a solid brick wall known as Ben McAfee, Scott Jessic, and Jim Turner. They were members of the board who continually voted against the other two members, one of which was Emma's husband, Thomas.

There was a lot to say about being a board member at one of the most prestigious country clubs. It permitted Ben access to any country club in the world, garnered him invitations to parties held by the rich and powerful, and made his opinion carry weight; all the members would nod in agreement to whatever he suggested.

Ben walked through the empty restaurant to the French doors, which opened onto a flagstone patio. It was Monday and the course was closed. This was the day all the maintenance work was performed. He stood at the opened doors and admired the lush landscaping, professional layout of the course, and flowering gardens. Inhaling the fragrance, he smiled. Soon it would all be his. Thomas Sullivan was financially strapped.

Ben's trip to Europe wasn't just to oversee a computer-networking project, but to gather financing to buy Thomas Sullivan out, make him an offer he couldn't refuse.

Ben's gaze drifted back to the entrance, to the foyer where the portrait hung. Emma's stare was penetrating and there was something about it that kept the chill pulsing through his body.

He stepped out onto the patio where a gaunt black man was working a hand trowel through the dirt in the flowerbed. Their eyes met, sending another icy chill up Ben's spine.

Otis nodded, eyes downcast as he returned his attention to the flowers. His gnarled hands worked the trowel, jabbing at the dirt, then dropping the day lilies into the hole, the bright yellow trumpet petals contrasting sharply with the purple irises.

"Surprised you're still here. Thought with Emma gone you'd be looking for another job." Ben pursed his lips and did nothing to hide the sneer that was becoming as much a part of his features as his thick eyebrows. Whenever he looked down his aquiline nose at the working staff, his eyebrows formed a *V* at the bridge.

Otis rubbed his hand across his shirt and stood. Beads of sweat clung to his forehead.

Ben plodded on. "I know Thomas let Emma golf on Mondays when the course was closed, but that kind of preferential treatment for any of the wives is going to stop. Emma isn't around to carry their banner any more."

The black man stared for a few beats, then in a Cajun accent, voice barely above a whisper, said, "Be unkind to talk about the dead dat way. It be disrespectful."

Ben smiled. "I don't think she can hear us."

"Ben!"

He turned to see Thomas Sullivan walking toward him, a Shamrock crest emblazoned on the breast pocket of his navy sports coat. Tired gray eyes blinked against the sunlight as he pulled a straw hat from his head.

"You're back."

"Just flew in." Ben turned back to view the course. The workers were cutting a path across one of the fairways. The two men stood in silence as if the Monday cutting were some reverent ceremony. In the background, the trowel continued to beat at the earth.

"I take it your trip was successful," Thomas said.

Ben turned slightly toward the elderly man. The loss of his wife had aged him even more. The corners of his eyes sagged as if pulled downward by some imaginary strings.

"I know you've been running around Europe the past month trying to get financing to buy me out." Thomas kept his eyes on the tree line behind the first tee. His fingers played with the brim of his straw hat.

"Really am sorry for your loss," Ben said.

Thomas finally turned to look at him. They both knew he wasn't one bit sorry. "We found out about your plans for Shamrock Isle; just about tore Emma's heart out. That's what killed her."

So now it's my fault? Ben thought. "It was destined, Thomas. You aren't managing the place like an entrepreneur. Membership dues should have been raised years ago."

"People shouldn't have to pay close to a year's wages to join. That wasn't our tradition."

"Prices go up, Thomas. Food, wages, maintenance." Ben nodded toward the fairway. "You saw fit to purchase state-of-the-art lawn equipment. Someone has to pay for it."

Thomas sighed heavily, his shoulders sagging further, revealing a man outmaneuvered whose fight left him when Emma died.

"Changes need to be made. I will have to meet with Jim and Scott to discuss the bylaws."

Thomas just stared. "You haven't heard?"

"Heard what? I came right from the airport."

The trowel clambered to the walkway as Otis straightened. He retrieved more plants from the back of the cart.

"No one has heard from either of them."

Ben thought for a moment. Jim was an architect. It wasn't unusual for him to make a quick trip to a job site, sometimes clear across the continent. He unclipped his cellular phone from his waistband and dialed Jim's office only to be told that they assumed Jim was in New Zealand.

"Strange." Next, Ben called Scott who was an optometrist. His office told him they hadn't heard from him since last week but it was possible he was at a convention in San Diego. Ben called Scott's wife. Unfortunately, they were recently separated and she, in her words, "couldn't care less if he dropped off the face of the earth."

"Do what you gotta do." Thomas settled his hat on his head and strode off, pausing briefly to pat Otis' bony shoulder.

Ben's gaze trailed after the man then drifted back to Otis. "What are you staring at?" He watched as Otis placed his hand tools in the cart overflowing with impatiens, lobelia, creeping phlox, and an assortment of other annuals. "And just what are you doing with all those flowers?" Ben asked. "The old lady isn't here anymore. We don't have to clutter the course with those feminine decorations. Flowers belong only around the clubhouse."

"It's how Mizz Sullivan wanted it. Mizzer Sullivan, he say it was her last request, dat her favorite hole be designed in her honor."

Ben jammed his fists onto his hips. It was bad enough he had to put up with Emma when she was alive, but now she was dead. He was about to be one of the new owners and he'd be damned if he was going to have any reminders of her anywhere on the course.

"Really! And exactly what else did she request from her deathbed?" He waved a hand at Otis, as though swatting a fly, and looked in the direction Thomas had walked. "Forget it. I'll just go ask Thomas." He started to walk away.

"Dey were here," Otis announced, turning to add more tools to the cart. "Mizzers Jim and Scott."

Ben turned. "When?"

"Mizzer Scott, he play last week. Nobody saw him after dat." His chocolate eyes held Ben's gaze. "Mizzer Jim, he play the week before. Ain't nobody seen him since."

Ben cocked his head, a chill drying up the perspiration dotting his forehead. There had always been something about Otis that made him uneasy. Maybe it was the fact that he came from the land of voodoo. He once saw Otis talking to an arrow dangling from the end of a string, and then chanting in some strange language. Ben had watched as the arrow changed direction, as though Otis commanded it.

Otis and Emma always had their heads together. Word was when she would come out on Mondays to sneak a round of golf, she would take Otis with her and give him lessons. Ben had complained that Emma was taking Otis away from his work, but it always fell on Thomas's deaf ears. Otis was untouchable employment-wise. We'll see about that, Ben thought.

"Really strange," Otis said, "how dey just up and be gone." He pressed his dark fingers together and spread them quickly, whispering, "Poof."

"What are you saying?"

"Saying nothing, Mizzer Ben." Otis climbed into the cart and it lumbered down the cart path.

Unable to find Thomas, Ben headed for the locker room, shrugging out of his shirt before he reached the entrance. The locker room was a veritable oasis. A man could have a massage, play cards, get a drink or snack, or soak in a whirlpool. It was spacious with tall lockers large enough to hold a week's worth of clothes and shoes. He jammed his key into the lock and sat down on the bench, kicking off his shoes. Damn, if Emma could play on Mondays, I sure as hell can, too, he thought. He'd have the course to himself. Checking his watch he figured he would only have time for a quick nine.

His golf shoes, cleaned and polished, lay on the top shelf of his locker. He quickly changed and checked his reflection in the mirror hanging on the inside door. It was time for a touchup. More gray was sprouting at the roots and he didn't like the deep creases around his eyes—wouldn't look good in *Golf Digest* magazine.

Slowly his gaze drifted to the lockers across from his. He often golfed with Jim and Scott, and at times they would leave papers in their lockers regarding the buy-out of the golf course. After stashing his clothes in his locker, he picked up his key ring. They each had a duplicate set.

He searched through the keys for Jim's and inserted it in the lock. It clicked open. Inside were golf shirts, pants, extra tees, and balls. Ben checked the pants' pockets. Nothing.

He turned to Scott's locker. A handful of cigars had been left in a box on the floor of the locker. Shirts were jammed together. Two golf hats hung on the clothes hooks, and a knot of golf gloves were clumped on the top shelf. Ben entertained the thought of mandatory monthly locker inspections. He was just about to close both of their lockers when he realized something was missing. Shoes. Every golfer he knew owned more than one pair and Jim and Scott always left a spare in their lockers; it was customary. After golfing you leave your clubs with the caddy to be cleaned and stored and drop your shoes off with the attendant to be cleaned.

Ben walked along the plush green and navy plaid carpeting to the attendant's storage room. It contained shelves, like mail slots, where cleaned shoes would be left for pickup. Jim's and Scott's slots were empty.

He walked downstairs to the pro shop. "Larry."

A bronzed face framed in sun-bleached hair peered over a clearance rack. "Ben, when did you get back?"

"Just now. I wanted to hit a few balls at the driving range." The less Larry knew the better.

Larry reached under the counter and pulled out a basket of striped balls. His gaze drifted toward the window. "Nice day as long as those clouds stay away." Large, dark clouds loomed in the distance.

Nodding toward the schedule, Ben asked, "Could you tell me the last time Jim Turner and Scott Jessic played?"

Larry's freckled hand flipped through the pages. "Those guys were always good for at least three to four rounds a week. Don't know what happened to them." His index finger traced a jagged trail as it checked several columns. "Scott played last week Thursday and Jim . . ." He flipped several pages back, "Jim played 2 weeks ago Monday."

Ben noticed a detailed drawing on the wall behind Larry. "What's that?"

"That? It's an artist's drawing of the thirteenth hole. The renovations are just about complete."

"What are they doing?" Ben peered closely at the drawing.

"We redesigned the sand trap so it's shaped like a shamrock, identical to what we have on the first and tenth holes." The shamrock was the trademark of Shamrock Isles and could be found on the shirts, sweaters, and jackets in the pro shop. Larry continued. "The pond has a waterfall, some pond fish like koi and calico fantails, and a lot of foliage and flowers."

Ben grimaced. "Who the hell's idea was that?"

"Emma Sullivan. The thirteenth hole always was her pet project, and Mr. Sullivan wanted to implement some of her last requests."

"I go away for a month and the place goes to hell," Ben muttered. "Well, we'll see what happens at the meeting Saturday." He studied Larry, a retired semi-pro at the young age of 36. "Tell me, Larry. Wouldn't you rather this course stay a men-only club? Don't you enjoy not having to wait for slow players and having the fairways chopped up?"

"More men tear the course up with their divots and there's nothing slower than a man sizing up his putt," Larry said as he returned to the clearance rack. "To tell you the truth?" He leaned his forearms on the glass top above the circular rack. "I would love to host a pro golf tournament like Cog Hill does the Western Open, but we never will if we keep our exclusionary rules." A smile crinkled the corners of Larry's clear blue eyes. "I guess Emma got the last laugh. She said if she couldn't be a member, she'd make sure her presence would always be here. And she did it: The crafty lady had her ashes strewn on the thirteenth hole."

Ben rushed outside where the warm air could relieve the chill in his bones. He scrapped the idea of teeing off on the back nine and drove his cart directly to the thirteenth hole to see what kind of appalling changes were made to his course.

He passed Otis near the driving range and for a brief moment wondered if he had some dolls in the likeness of Jim and Scott tucked away somewhere with pins sticking out of them. He chuckled at the thought, but the smile faded as he watched Otis slowly lift his head, his eyes following Ben. For a brief moment, it again reminded Ben of Emma's picture with her piercing glare.

The dark clouds followed as Ben brought the cart to a halt at the thirteenth tee. Shamrock Isle was a beautiful course with manicured fairways and picturesque scenery. The front nine had rolling hills with sand traps to challenge the best of golfers. The back nine had less hills and more 90–degree doglegs and trees.

At first Ben didn't notice that many changes. A brook churned along the left side following the bend in the fairway. On the opposite side where the rough bordered the forest, a field of wildflowers stood like sentries. There were enough problems with bees in the fall without attracting them during the entire golf season. "Absolutely hideous," Ben said. "Next we'll have park benches to sit and rest."

The dogleg prevented his view of the green or sand trap, and although he couldn't see the pond, he could hear the waterfall.

Ben left the cart on the path and walked down the middle of the fairway. He often wondered why people had their ashes strewn anywhere. Once it rained, the ashes would soak into the ground; on windy days, they would be blown to kingdom come; and when dumped into the lakes and oceans, they were nothing more than fish food.

He strolled toward the forest and wished he had brought a club to whack at every flower he saw. As if flowers weren't bad enough, there were large tufts of tall grass. As long as your golf ball didn't sail too far into the forest, you had a chance of hitting it out. But now, if it got tangled up in the tall grass or flowers, it would easily be a penalty shot.

"Why didn't you just put a damn gazebo out here, you nutty lady?" Ben yelled as if Emma could hear.

The sun dipped behind a large cloud dropping the temperature several degrees. A gust of wind rustled through the foliage. The tall, grassy reeds reached out for him like long tendrils. Ben turned away, gazed briefly at the sky. The clouds had picked up their pace, threatening to transform what was supposed to be a bright, sunny day.

The wind howled through the trees and a whisper was carried on the breeze. "Bennnnnnnnn."

Ben spun around and peered at the forest, his gaze darting through the trees. Was it his imagination? Was someone in there?

"Bennnnnnn." There it was again. It had to be the wind, he thought, playing tricks on him. Or was it Otis? Playing some dumb game Emma told him to play—another one of her stupid requests.

He retreated, the soft cleats on his golf shoes getting caught in the thick, bent grass fairway, but he was afraid to turn his back on whatever was in the forest.

His gaze scanned the shadows as he continued his retreat, finally mustering enough courage to turn. He charged down the fairway fueled by fury and fear. Rounding the bend, he heard the rush of water and came to an abrupt stop. Water flowed from a 6–foot tower of polished stones. The soft thumping of the water pump sounded like a heartbeat. Water lilies floated and frogs leaped to avoid the koi fish that had come up to the surface to study him. Purple phlox snaked its way over and around the flat rocks bordering the pond. A portion of the waterfall veered off sending water spilling into a pot that, when full, slowly tilted, pouring its contents into the pool.

Then Ben saw them—two of them. They stood on either side of the pond: One was leaning against the rock tower; the other one stood watch over the pot. Leprechauns. Bronze sculptures so lifelike Ben almost expected to hear them speak.

"Be careful what 'ye wish for." Emma's comment swirled in his head as the wind picked up. Ben had always told Emma that one day he would get that pot at the end of the rainbow.

No, Ben thought. Those weren't his exact words. Emma knew Ben, Jim, and Scott were cooking up something. His exact words were, "One day we will get that pot at the end of the rainbow."

Thunder groaned and lightning streaked across the sky. Ben willed himself to turn and run, but his legs felt like rubber. Could this be happening? Or had he finally lost his mind?

His breath caught as he felt his heart slam against his rib cage. Stumbling, he turned and ran blindly. Leaves were whipped from the trees and funnels of dirt curled and twisted along the grass.

He could barely see where he was running until he found himself in the middle of the sand trap. It was just an ordinary sand trap, but to Ben it felt like a pit of wet cement. He couldn't lift his feet, couldn't move his legs.

The cloud continued its move, slinking silently across the sky, sparked by the lightning.

Ben screamed. Would anyone hear him? The maintenance crew was gone for the day and Otis was God knows where. His screams were like blowing into a wind tunnel, his words rushing back at him like a blast of hot air.

He felt a rumbling under his feet and then the hungry earth opened up, sucking him down farther. His arms flailed in the sand as if he were slapping at the surface of a pool. "Nooooo," he screamed again.

Emma's words echoed. "Be careful what 'ye wish for."

The sand rippled along his legs as though the trap had come alive. With one last gulp, Ben's body disappeared. The wind kicked up, swirling the tiny grains of sand and erasing any trace of an intruder from the surface of the sand trap.

The sun blazed in the calm sky on Tuesday morning. Butterflies played tag among the wildflowers and the frogs teased the goldfish in the pond. Otis pushed the dirt around the roots of the yellow coreopsis and bright red poppies. He plucked dead leaves from the day lilies and redirected the path of the creeping myrtle.

The renovations to the thirteenth hole were finally complete. Satisfied, he picked up his tools and tossed them in the cart. Easing behind the wheel, he gave one last glance at the pristine fairway, colorful wildflowers, and the picturesque pond. Emma would be pleased. Otis smiled secretly as he drove away.

During the night, a third leprechaun had been added to the scene. This one sat on the side of the pond, his hand on the pot of gold where water flowed. The fake gold coins shone brightly in the sunlight, and if you crept close enough and the light was just right, you could see the sparkle of a diamond-studded ring on the leprechaun's left hand.

Chapter 15

Art Eternal

By Nicole Burris

Bill Harlan shut the door behind him and quickly took the parcel to his study. He could hardly wait to open it and see what he'd been hunting for over 3 years.

"What is it?" Kate looked up from the piano.

"This," he began unwrapping its brown covering, "is one of the most infamous pieces ever created."

"It's nice." Kate admiringly ran a hand over the young woman shown in the portrait. "But she looks so sad."

"Yes, I suppose she does."

"What makes it so famous?"

Bill's eyes sparkled as he began the history. "Over 200 years ago, a Parisian artist was so grief-stricken by his young wife's death that he had her body cremated and mixed the ashes in with his paints. This is not only a depiction of the woman, but is the only way the artist could see keeping her with him."

"You mean there's a dead person on here?" She wiped her hands on her pants.

Laughing, Bill hung the art on a nail he'd reserved right above the fireplace. "That look straight to you?"

"Yes. Bill, was that story true?"

"Of course it's true."

"That's a little morbid, don't you think? I don't know if I want it in my house."

"It's not in your house. It's in my study. You hardly ever come in here. Besides, I think it's fascinating. I'd like to have it done to me."

"You aren't serious?"

Bill turned from the painting and walked to his wife. "Think about it. To be preserved forever like that? Now come on; let's get something to eat."

As the pair walked toward the kitchen, a light scent of orchids formed in the study.

* * *

Later that evening after Kate had gone to bed, Bill sat on the sofa in his study, sipping a glass of brandy and admiring the painting. The fire he'd lit crackled and popped, and the flames lapped against each other, forming shadows in the room. The more the shadows danced and the more he studied the woman, the more she seemed to come to life.

A floral cloud took Bill's attention from the painting. Carefully, he twisted around.

There was nothing behind him. Placing the snifter on the end table, Bill looked back to the fireplace and his heart leapt. Clad in the gauzy, white dress he'd studied all night, the woman stood in front of him. Her hair hung long and straight, and the expression on her face was a thousand times more sad and dismal than in the portrait.

For what seemed like an eternity, Bill stared at her. He wasn't afraid, but rather overcome by her melancholy beauty.

"Please. You have to help me."

Her words were barely audible, but the fact that she spoke jarred him from his trance.

"How?"

She moved across the room, nearing him. "I've been trapped with this painting for several centuries. My soul cannot rest until I'm buried."

"You've been stuck with it for hundreds of years?" His heart pounded violently.

She lowered her head. "Paul loved me dearly. That's why he put me here; he didn't want to be without me. But he's been gone for a long time, and I've had to exist without him."

Bill stared, innately sensing how a man could love her so deeply.

"I need you to burn the painting and bury its ashes. That's the only thing that shall set me free."

She wanted him to destroy the painting? Already her beauty had drawn him in so intensely that the thought of losing her seemed almost sacreligious.

The apparition looked past him. As the smell of orchids disappeared, she vanished, leaving Bill with a leaden heart. He'd never experienced such love, such an overpowering need. Not even with Kate.

* * *

For over a week, Bill's life continued with each night's visit intensifying his love.

During her second visit he learned her name, the most beautiful name in the world: Sarah.

On the third visit, she again begged him to set her free, claiming that she could never love again and that the only thing she could love was her freedom, which Bill wouldn't bring himself to give her.

By the fifth visit, he was thinking about her so often that she even invaded his dreams, filling his subconscious travels with orchids and love—a love so strong that neither would ever need again. She'd become a drug and he the anxiously awaiting junkie.

By the morning after the seventh, thoughts of her preoccupied him to the point that he couldn't concentrate on anything: not work; not his wife. Though their conversations consisted of Sarah begging Bill to do what, in his mind, seemed like murder, he felt the bond tightening. She was what he'd always sought.

On the tenth morning, Kate angrily slammed her cup of coffee on the breakfast table. Bill didn't even look up from his newspaper and corn flakes.

"I can't stand this. There's something not right about that painting. If I didn't know any better, I'd swear you were in love with it."

"Don't be silly," he answered absently.

"You spend all of your free time locked in your study with it."

"You're jealous?" He laughed sarcastically, knowing Kate had every right to be jealous.

"Bill, I mean it. If you don't get rid of that painting and start acting like a husband, I'm going to leave you."

Bill said nothing. There was nothing to say, for nothingness was how he felt about everything except Sarah.

* * *

After a typical day of board meetings and phone calls, Bill returned to an empty house. Kate had left a note, which he quickly crumpled into a ball, saying she was staying with her mother until he disposed of the painting. Rather than call her and try to save his marriage, he entered the study.

His ghostly love pleaded with him. "Please. You have to help me."

"You know I can't do that." Bill smiled and poured himself a glass of brandy. Even if he wanted to, his need for her had grown so great that he didn't think he'd be able to let her go.

Her expression darkened. "Consider yourself warned." Sarah vanished, taking the smell of orchids with her.

Bill spent the rest of the night thinking back to what she could mean by the threat. He knew little about the previous owners, only that the most recent had suffered a fall off the stairs that broke his neck. Could Sarah be so desperate for freedom that she is somehow responsible?

Walking to the piano, he sat down to play, to relax through music. He poised his fingers over the keys and immediately the lid slammed down, crushing his knuckles. Bill withdrew his bleeding fingers and ran to the bathroom to wash his hands. By the time he got there, the pain had disappeared. So had the blood.

Bill knew it was Sarah's doing, but he couldn't give in—not if it meant losing her. He returned to the study to have another glass of the calming brandy.

As he lifted the bottle, it flew out of his hands and against the wall, crashing into a thousand shards right below the painting. Hideous giggles assaulted his ears and the room began spinning violently.

He dropped to his knees, covered his hands with his ears, and cried, "This isn't funny!"

The spinning stopped and the voices hushed.

"I mean it, Sarah. I'm not destroying the painting. I need you too much."

Suddenly Bill became aware of the bottle, intact, that he held by its neck. Sarah was playing an illusionary game with him, one that he didn't like one bit.

A wind blew through the room that sent a chill down his spine. He decided to get out of there, before she could further mess with him. Let her have some time to calm down.

As he closed the study's doors, the grandfather clock in the foyer chimed midnight.

Bill, tired and a little shaken, crept upstairs to try to get some sleep.

* * *

Sometime before dawn, Bill awoke to the sounds of horrible screams—not just Sarah, but hundreds of distinctly individual voices. He covered his ears and slowly, squintingly, opened his eyes.

Even in the darkness he could see her, staring at him with hatred. She crossed her arms and held her head back, cackling at him. The screams ceased.

"Sarah, please. It doesn't have to be like this." If only she'd try to understand.

"Give me my freedom." Her eyes flickered, orange with rage and pain.

"I can't. I need you."

As he adjusted to the light, she began to fade, and he flipped on the lamp. Sarah was gone.

Fully awake, Bill walked to the bathroom and yanked the string to turn on the mirror's light. Leaning down, he splashed some cool water on his face and debated whether he should destroy the painting, but he knew he couldn't. It would take time, but she'd get over her anger and learn to love him. Bill squinted, dried his face with a hand towel, and jumped.

In the reflection, Sarah stood behind him. He quickly spun around to see that she'd disappeared.

Sarah's anger frightened him. Unlike a scary novel, which he could put down for another day if it got too intense, he couldn't take a break from his life.

You need a smoke, old man, he told himself.

Bill had quit smoking years before, when his grandmother succumbed to a nasty case of emphysema. Only rarely did he partake, and he was positive there was an opened pack of Camels in the junk drawer in the kitchen.

Sure enough, as he rummaged through the drawer, his hand soon found the cellophane-covered box. Bill removed one cigarette and used a burner on the stove to light it. Inhaling the stale smoke, he smiled, relaxing for the first time that evening.

From the doorway he could see the study. While the fireplace should have gone out, he could hear through the barely open doors the unmistakable sound of flames popping. Limply, as if caught in a spell, he neared the room.

The study awaited him ominously. Pausing before he opened the door, Bill wondered if he was walking into a trap. The worry quickly subsided as he realized that maybe lighting a romantic fire signaled that she'd finally come around. He grabbed for the knob but quickly retracted from its searing heat. Flinging the doors open with a pajama-covered hand, he saw the room enveloped in flames.

The inferno was rampant and spreading quickly. Over the crackling, Bill could make out Sarah's maniacal laughter. So panic-stricken that he didn't even think to try to save the painting, he ran toward the foyer, wheezing from the thickness of the air.

Could it be another trick against his perceptions? Surrounded by flames, he didn't stop to wait and find out.

Though he stumbled, Bill continued toward the door, resisting the force that pulled him. His feet didn't want to move. Determined, he continued on, fighting her psychic lure.

Inches before he reached the door, Bill's knees buckled and he fell, hitting his head on the floor with a resounding thud. Blackness overtook him.

In the kitchen, a cigarette absently dropped joined with the kitchen drapes and began to smolder.

* * *

"Mrs. Harlan? If I may ask, what made you decide to do this?" the young painter asked as Kate handed him the urn.

Kate looked up through puffy, guilt-ridden eyes. "He would have wanted it this way."

The painter poured the ashes into the tray of acrylics and propped up the picture of Bill that Kate had provided. As he began his first stroke, Bill stood invisibly, watching and silently screaming in horror.

The scent of orchids floated to him, and he heard the whisper, shrouded in laughter, mocking him, "Eternal life is yours." When the house fell, Sarah finally got her freedom.

The floral cloud faded, leaving Bill alone in his limbo.

Chapter 16

Guilt

By Sarah E. Glenn

I am beginning to think that, after 20 years as a psychologist, it's time to quit. I could retire; I have investments and could get along nicely without an office to maintain. It's not that I'm burned out or sour on people. I just don't think I could ever trust my judgment the same way again—not after Phyllis Longcamp.

One of my other patients, Alexa Hatton, referred her to me a few years back. She felt that Phyllis needed counseling after the death of her husband; she was listless and had lost weight. When I met Phyllis at our first appointment, however, I realized that her problem was more complicated than a sudden loss. There was the usual air of sorrow around her, but it was contracted around something deeper inside. It was a dark kernel that I couldn't reach.

Grief counseling is one of my specialties. My first encounter with it came when I was not quite 11. My mother gave birth to an infant with severe health problems, and despite everyone's best efforts, he died at 6 months of age. Father handled it with the stoic style most men are boxed into using, but my mother was devastated. She wept daily, and I became aware of an effect around her like gray mist, heavy and clinging. I didn't realize then that I was seeing something others didn't. I learned that if I hugged her the right way, though, something would go out of me and the mist would break up, replaced by a warm, pleasant feeling. I had to hug her a lot before it went away for good.

That was the beginning of my journey into psychology. Making my mother better made me feel like a real hero, especially because even Dad couldn't do what I could. Over time, I learned that what I had done wasn't considered real by most people, but I knew better. I had a powerful gift, and I would use it to help others.

My office was comfortable, with a large, high-backed chair for me and plush couches and easy chairs for my clients. Boxes of tissue were within easy reach from every seat, and soft, colorful pillows were scattered about for hugging and pounding. I lined the room with books like *Codependent No More,* *Life After Suicide,* and *Please Understand Me,* but this was mostly to impress and gain the confidence of my patients. The real key to my therapy was drawing the patient out in conversation and bringing their feelings to the surface where I could deal with them.

Every Wednesday Phyllis would come to my office, and we would talk about her husband and how she was coping with things. She had a graceful, athletic build, but she would slump in her seat, taking up as little room as possible. She had flat affect as well; her clear pale eyes would stare mutely at me as I spoke to her about adjustments and acceptance. I loaned her some of my best books and we talked about them during session, but nothing seemed to impact that dark center.

It was over a month before any sort of rapport began to form between us. By then, I was attuned to every subtlety of her moods. When I felt the first flicker of emotion during our sessions, there was a rush inside my chest, and all I could hear for a moment was the blood rushing through my ears. I quickly focused on the dark center, and the flicker came again: guilt. What were we discussing when it started? We had been talking (again) about how she missed her husband. Something one of us had said had triggered it.

"I think that maybe we've spent enough time talking about life without Darwin," I told her. "Perhaps, in order to let him go, you need to examine your life with him. I think you may have some unresolved feelings." The surge of anxiety told me I was on target. "What was your marriage like?"

"It was . . . well, it was a marriage, Dr. Bahr." Phyllis shrugged. "I don't really know if it's the sort of thing one can rate."

She was playing dumb, and we both knew it. "You know if you were happy with him. That's an important indicator of the quality of a marriage. Were you happy?"

"I . . ." The sound died away and things became quiet for several minutes. I sat frozen in position, unwilling to break the moment with a sudden movement. She stared out the window, fingers tracing the edges of the sofa arm. I waited, willing her to speak.

"No," she finally answered and stared at her knees. A tear formed at the corner of one eye, then slid down her face.

I gave her one of the tissues and put a hand on her shoulder. Yes, she blamed herself for his death; I couldn't help but pity her. "The death of someone with whom we have issues is often the hardest to bear. Once they're gone, those issues can't be resolved and we have to work them out on our own."

She clutched my hand with cold fingers and sobbed. When her tears had dried, the hour was almost up. "Can I leave a little early? I have a headache, and I really think I'm too tired to go on."

I radiated as much warmth and reassurance as I could. "Of course, Phyllis. We won't go any further or faster than you're willing to travel."

Afterward, I was exhausted. It had been a long time since a session had tired me so. During that year when my mother was grieving for my brother's death, I was continually tired. I also suffered more colds and accidents than at any other time in my youth. The doctor recommended vitamins, which seemed to help, but I knew that if I were going to become a counselor, I would need to find new and better ways to handle people's emotions. When I went to the university, I studied the traditional therapies diligently, looking for ways to make myself more effective.

In graduate school, I also began developing a more remote, less hands-on method of altering people's feelings. Too much body contact is generally discouraged in therapy, and learning to do what I did from a distance made me stronger and more detached, leading to less exhaustion on my part. My goal with my gift was to learn how to permanently change how my clients felt about their situation, to recast their reactions into healthier patterns—in other words, to cure them. It took me years to get really good at it, but those years brought me great success. I was able to go into private practice very quickly with all the referrals my pleased patients brought me, and I never had a shortage of clientele.

It had been awhile since treating anyone had drained me so, but when Phyllis entered my office for our next session, I decided it was worth it. Her posture was more erect, and she had added earrings to her usually understated outfit. They peeped out from the short blond hair, which showed signs of recent styling. She took her accustomed seat and we began the session. This time, she had more to say about her marriage.

"Darwin was unfaithful," she told me, clenching her hands together in her lap as she clutched internally to emotions that desperately wanted to be freed. "He was involved with Janice, one of his coworkers. I found out about it about 2 months before his death."

"That must have been hard on you. I imagine you were very hurt."

She began turning her wedding ring round and round on her finger. "I was furious!" Her face filled with color. "Ten years of marriage, always trying to look my best for him, always supporting him in his dreams, not mine, and he decides this 20–something girl is more his style." Her movements became jerkier and I was afraid she would hurt herself. But the dark kernel had loosened, and glimmers of her internal conflict were beginning to come to the surface at last.

"You confronted him?"

"You know it!" She grinned fiercely. "We had a couple of awful fights over it. He tried to deny what he was up to, but I had hired a detective. I had pictures; he couldn't argue with that."

"When did these fights take place?"

"I showed him the pictures about 6 weeks before the accident. He said he was offended by my mistrust, but he promised to end the affair."

There was still more to the story than she was letting on. I could tell by the marks the twisting ring had begun to leave on her finger. "Did he?"

Instead of answering, she gazed at the baroque border along the ceiling, moisture glittering in her eyes. "No. He might have withdrawn from her for a week or two, but he didn't end the affair. I hadn't dismissed the detective; I guess I wasn't very trusting. Going to Hawaii was my idea. I thought getting away would be good for us. It could be sort of like a . . . a second honeymoon. I didn't realize I was trying to revive the dead."

The guilt was strong in her now; we were getting very close to the cause. "Hawaii was where the accident happened."

"Yes!" She broke down and sobbed again. "It was my fault, Doctor. We were taking pictures at Kilauea when Darwin told me that he had decided to marry Janice and he wanted a divorce. I began screaming."

I moved closer and touched her shoulder; inside, the kernel had opened into a porcupine blossom. "What makes it your fault?"

"We were shouting at each other. There were some other tourists around, but they quietly left the area. He told me I was humiliating him by creating a scene. Ha! That was why he told me where he did. He hoped I would just quietly agree if he did it in front of other people."

"You believe he staged it that way."

Her eyes, brilliant blue with emotion, met mine. "Exactly! I told him that, too." The connection was there now, strong. I could feel both her rage and her guilt; they pounded me.

"What happened, Phyllis? What is your fault?"

"I hit him in the stomach. I was so mad that I punched him. There were rope barricades, but . . ."

Comprehension dawned. "But he fell through." She began to sob again, and this time I did pull her close. The poor woman had equated a mistake with murder. My gift flowed into her, blending into her guilt, shifting it. "It's not your fault. You were very upset and he had provoked you. You weren't thinking; you were beyond thought. Forgive yourself . . . let the guilt go." The relief of her confession worked very well into what I was doing: I broke down her self-blame and recrimination, shifting them into feelings of forgiveness and self-worth. "You were not to blame. He provoked you, and you were beside yourself. Let it all go." Every last bit of guilt finally dissolved under my catalyst, and she pulled away at last.

"Thank you, Doctor. I feel free for the first time since he died."

Not long after, Phyllis left therapy for good. She was wearing sky blue that last day and it was wonderful to see it on her. I felt proud of the way she had learned to look to the future with hope—with a new sense of the path that lay ahead of her—instead of the pain in her past. The guilt was gone, and I was confident she would make a new life for herself. I heard later that she had remarried, and I was happy for her.

Over the weekend, I read an obituary in the paper for one Frederic Adair. He was the husband of Phyllis Adair, twice widowed. The obit said that he and his wife had been involved in a traffic accident, and I had to wonder. When I helped Phyllis overcome her guilt, was it for an act of impulse or something more deliberate? Even if the death of her first husband been a true accident, did I contribute to the death of her second husband by removing her natural remorse? I wondered if she and Adair had been having marital trouble, too. What if, because of me, she felt that lethal acts were acceptable when done under certain circumstances?

I didn't sleep well last night and was still sluggish this morning when Phyllis called to set an appointment. "I was in the car with him when it happened, Dr. Bahr. Even though I wasn't driving, I'm suffering from those old feelings of guilt again. Fortunately, I knew just the person to call."

This is why I'm considering retirement.

Artwork by Chris Pugh, Copyright 2002

Chapter 17

Switching Chairs

By Amanda Marie

After the dream was over, Sandra awoke as she had conditioned herself to do. Even with the disturbing images still real enough to keep her heart thumping, she forced herself to follow her routine. First she switched off the small EEG machine, stopping the chattering of the pens caused by her movements and the overflow of chart paper onto the floor. Then she grabbed her dream journal from her bedside table and began to write.

Already early dream elements were disappearing like the morning mist. One image remained vividly and Sandra knew it would continue to bother her for the rest of the day. Although only a few of her dreams came true each month—a fact that would seem to reduce the odds that this one fell into the precognitive category—almost no disaster in her life, no matter how small, had come without her presentiment.

Sandra could hardly dismiss this morning's dream. After all, she made her living taking spectacular photographs for the local newspaper using clues from her dreams to always be at the right place at the right time. Her walls were decorated with dozens of amazing shots she'd captured on film.

With the speed that comes from experience, Sandra disconnected the web of electrodes she'd pasted on the night before. As she showered and dressed, she couldn't help her thoughts from wondering back to a familiar question: What was the point of seeing the future if you couldn't change it? That consuming concern still distracted her as she left the house with the box of EEG paper under her arm.

Sandra crouched to inspect the rows of felled snapdragons that some rabbit had feasted on and she mumbled, "Oh, will you look at that?" As she stroked the remains of the chewed stems, one seemed to squirm to life and whip out at her. Sandra dropped back on the porch steps with a duo of punctures burning into her palm.

* * *

"At least it was just a harmless garter snake." Dr. Jennifer Marien patted Sandra's bandaged hand, and then she spread Sandra's EEG record from the previous night on her desk.

"I wouldn't call it completely harmless. It smarts like the dickens."

"Oh, don't grump." Jennifer smirked at her longtime friend. "It serves you right for not heeding your dream's warning."

"I didn't see the snake or I would have known better than to put my hand down there. Besides, if I was destined to be bitten, then no amount of precaution could have prevented it."

"You don't really believe that, do you?" Jennifer dug into the pocket of her lab coat and pulled out a clear ruler to measure Sandra's brainwaves during her last period of REM. "Certainly you must have had some dreams about the future that didn't come true because you altered some factor."

"Well, if it never happened, how do I know it was ever more than just another dream?"

Jennifer glanced up from the record. "After all this time, haven't you begun to get a feel for which dreams might be predictive before they come true?"

Sandra shrugged. "Sometimes. Sometimes not."

"Next time when you really get a strong feeling it might come true call me and we'll test your unchangeable destiny hypothesis."

* * *

Sandra gripped the steering wheel. That was all she could do: She couldn't step on the gas to move out of the intersection; she couldn't lean on the horn; she couldn't even draw a breath to scream. All she could do was watch the car come at her.

The impact into her driver's side door shattered the world—or had it just been she that splintered into a million pieces?

* * *

"Sandra!" Jennifer shouted over the phone. "Calm down. You sound hysterical. What happened? Have you been crying?"

"I'm dying!" She sobbed, "I'm going to die."

"What? What happened?"

"I saw it. I'm going to be killed in a car accident."

"Listen to me. Make yourself some tea or something and I'll be right over."

Forty-five minutes later Jennifer sat down on the couch with her arm reassuringly wrapped around Sandra's shoulders. "Now, don't you worry. We won't let you die in a car accident."

"How? Am I going to walk everywhere from now on? Take the bus?"

"I'll drive you."

Sandra snorted, "Everyday? For the rest of my life?"

"I'm sure it won't come to that."

"But what if I'm supposed to die? Then nothing can save me."

"You are not supposed to die." Jennifer poured more tea into Sandra's cup and handed it to her.

"Are you saying that as a **friend** or as a scientist?"

"Both." Jennifer patted Sandra's knee. "First of all, it could have just been an ordinary, run-of-the-mill nightmare."

Sandra shook her head. Her fingers rubbed the cup in her hands as she gripped it too tightly; it reminded her eerily of clenching the steering wheel in her dream.

"Okay. For argument's sake, let's say it was a premonition. Can you remember any details? What street were you on?"

Staring into space, Sandra tried to summon the memory. "I don't know. It was at an intersection with a traffic light. The other car slammed head-on into the driver's side of my car."

"You were driving?"

"Yes."

"You're sure?"

Sandra nodded.

"Were you in the car you own now?"

"I don't know. I think so."

"So we'll change the circumstances. I'll drive you to my house. I've got an old tank of a pick-up truck that probably could survive a train wreck. You can drive that as long as you like."

Sandra looked up at Jennifer knowing that the uncertainty was obvious on her face.

"Come on." Jennifer stood up, pulling Sandra to her feet as well. "We'll go now before the morning traffic gets going. Then I'll follow you to work."

Sandra couldn't relax as Jennifer drove. They both wore their seatbelts and Sandra had pulled hers extra tight. The way she gripped the armrest until her hand hurt reminded her of the first time she rode on an airplane and felt that she had to literally *will* them to reach their destination without crashing.

"We're almost there."

Sandra glanced over at Jennifer, trying to force a smile, when she saw the car speeding toward them. "Look out!"

* * *

"The seatbelt and side airbags probably saved your life." The emergency room doctor checked the plaster on Jennifer's cast to see if it was dry yet.

"I'm so sorry," Sandra said. She'd walked away with little more than shaken nerves, while Jennifer had a concussion and a broken arm. "It should have been me in the driver's seat."

"Nonsense." Jennifer smiled. "At least we were able to disprove your destiny theory."

"What are you talking about? We didn't stop the accident from happening, even with the changes we made. Different time, different car, different driver—none of that helped."

"At least you didn't die."

"But you could have."

"Not a chance." Jennifer pretended to knock on her head. "Too hardheaded."

"You're in far too good a mood for someone whose car just got totaled."

"It's insured and, more importantly, it had airbags. Your car does not." Jennifer took Sandra's hand and squeezed. "See? You are not a slave to destiny."

* * *

Sandra bolted upright in bed. Her scream stifled in her throat and sweat tickled down her cheeks and arms. She trembled all over and the more she tried to stop the harder she shook.

The light spilling in her window was from the street lamp, not sunlight. She still had some time. At least she hoped she did.

Sandra flipped off the EEG and unplugged the wires. She wouldn't waste time pulling off the electrodes. From the closet, she snagged the first pair of jeans and sweatshirt she touched and found her sneakers under the bed. Sandra carried them with her as she crept silently down the darkened hallway. Her keys and purse were by the door. As quietly and quickly as she could, she scooped them up too.

Sandra scanned the darkened corners of the house for movement or the figure of a man, but saw only pitch. From here, she could see into the shadowy kitchen, and even though she saw nothing there she would not go into it now for all the money in the world. Sandra even thought she could feel a malevolent presence in the kitchen, felt it ready to bolt after her.

Carefully, Sandra peeked out of the peephole. The street lamp illuminated the front yard. All seemed deceptively still.

Keeping her eyes trained on the kitchen all the time, Sandra turned the deadbolt. It clicked open, loud enough for anyone hiding in the house to hear.

Her nerve broke. Sandra yanked open the front door, hit the handle of the screen door wrong and rattled it uselessly. Grappling wildly, Sandra nearly screamed.

He was coming for her—she knew it. She even thought she could hear him breathing now, he was so close.

The screen door opened. Sandra ran out and slammed the door closed behind her, hoping to create an obstacle for any pursuer, then she raced to her car. Any second she expected to hear the front door open again.

Her sneakers slipped from her grasp, banged off her pumping legs, and tumbled onto the lawn. The rough texture of the concrete scrapped her bare soles, but Sandra didn't even slow down.

The driver's side door was already unlocked. Sandra tossed in her clothes and purse and dived in. Belatedly cautious, she checked the backseat, but no one was there. She locked her door. As she started, the car she glanced back at the house. The screen door banged in the breeze. There was no one coming out of the door; no faces peered from the darkened windows.

Sandra backed out of the driveway as fast as she could, nearly hitting the mailbox.

* * *

"Gosh, Sandra. You've been having an epidemic of bad dreams this month." Jennifer tried to effect a light tone of voice, but it was obvious that this time she was as scared as Sandra.

Sandra huddled in the corner of the couch in the lab's break room. Despite the blanket Jennifer had given her, Sandra's bare feet were still icy from sitting in the car half the night. She still wore the T-shirt and shorts she'd slept in under her sweatshirt and jeans.

Using acetone, Jennifer removed the electrodes dangling from Sandra's head. "Tell me exactly what happened. Maybe we can prevent it from happening."

"Like the car accident?" Sandra frowned at Jennifer's cast.

"We'll do a better job of it this time. I promise."

Sandra wasn't reassured, but she said, "It begins outside my house."

"Are you sure it was your house?"

Sandra nodded. "Massacred snapdragons and all, so it has to be soon."

"Go on."

"I go up to the door, but it is already open. I walk inside; there is a noise in the kitchen. I don't see anyone, so I go to check it out."

"So far so good."

"There is someone in there, hiding behind the refrigerator, but I don't see him in time. He stabs me in the back with a huge knife." Sandra rubbed her lower back. "I can still remember the pain of it. In the dream, I knew I was going to die."

Jennifer detached the last electrode. "Why don't you take a soothing shower? I want to think on this one a bit."

* * *

"Ready to face the future?" Jennifer asked when Sandra returned from the bathroom.

Sandra took a step back. "No. You aren't thinking of going to my house are you?"

"Why would you see the future if you're not supposed to do something about it?"

I've been asking myself that my whole life."

"We were able to change it before."

Sandra, now dressed in only her jeans and sweatshirt, stuffed her night-clothes into her purse. "I've been debating and I don't think we did change it."

"What do you mean?"

"It's like . . . chairs."

Jennifer blinked. "What do you mean?"

Sandra pulled out two chairs from the kitchen nook. "It's like we all have a chair to sit in. The chair I was assigned was supposed to be hit by that car. All we accomplished was to switch chairs. For whatever cosmic reason, my chair seems to have a target painted on it, and I get to see the wrecking ball before it hits." Sandra shook her head. "I won't let you sit in my chair again."

"You're talking nonsense and you're feeling sorry for yourself. I'll prove to you that you can be the master of your own destiny."

Sandra shook her head again.

"Fine. I'll go without you." Jennifer walked out.

Sandra stared after her for a moment, muttered, "We both must be crazy," and hurried after her.

* * *

Jennifer parked across the street from Sandra's house. The morning sun shone cheerily on the green lawns and neat houses of the nice neighborhood, but at this time of day most of the homes stood empty—no one around to hear her scream.

"There are the shoes you lost," Jennifer said. "You ran out so fast, you didn't even bother to close your front door."

Sandra tried to speak, but only managed a strangled squeak.

Jennifer looked at her friend. "You closed the door, didn't you?"

Sandra nodded.

"Don't worry. I came prepared."

Sandra grabbed Jennifer's arm. "Don't go in there—call the police."

A car pulled up behind the rugged pick-up truck, and the man driving it stepped out.

"I already did." Jennifer grabbed her handbag and hopped out of the truck.

"Jennifer, no! Wait." Sandra ran around the truck, but Jennifer had already pointed the man toward the house.

Jennifer stopped Sandra from following. "Let the detective check it out first."

"No. Don't you see? I can't keep sending others into the dangers meant for me."

"Sandra, don't be silly. He's a professional. He can handle it."

Sandra twisted free of Jennifer's good hand. With the screen door hanging open and the front door left ajar, Sandra was able to creep quietly into the house. Ahead of her, she could see the detective entering the kitchen. Sandra reached out for him and whispered, "Be careful."

A flash of motion slammed into him. The knife blade glint as it cut through the back of the cop's jacket. Sandra screamed.

Twisting around, the detective and attacker tumbled onto the kitchen table. The knife clattered to the floor. Sandra picked it up just as the pair of combatants stumbled toward her, forcing her backward and ramming her into the wall.

In the next moment the attacker fell away from her, the knife sticking out of his back. The detective tripped him and, once he had him down, cuffed him without showing any caution to the knife still plunged in his back.

"Sandra, are you all right?" Jennifer rushed into the kitchen.

Sandra caught Jennifer before she could get too close to the intruder. "I can't believe the officer is unhurt."

He raised his jacket, revealing a bulletproof vest. He knocked on the imbedded metal plate. "I came prepared."

Sandra nearly collapsed with relief.

"Now, I have a question," the detective began. "What's the story with this guy?"

Jennifer glanced at the knife, then at Sandra. "It looks like he sat in your chair."

Chapter 18

Special

By Jordan Carpenter

Ever since she moved into the new house, there had been a pool of blood on the floor of Alice's bedroom that no one else could see.

At first, she was so proud! She had a puddle! None of the kids from school had a puddle; Mrs. Johanssen didn't have a puddle; Mommy and Daddy certainly didn't have puddles, and they were so jealous! "Alice is doing her thing again," they'd sigh in response to her gloats. "It's because she's *special*," they'd add whenever anyone else was around.

Special! Boy, what a thing to be. "I'm Alice the Special!" she said whenever she met anyone new. She didn't exactly know what the word meant, but she knew it was something not everyone was, something to be proud of. "Look it up in the dictionary," her mother said once, but who cares about boring old books. She felt like such a baby with her little kiddy dictionary anyway, with its big letters and colorful pictures.

Everyone always treated her like a little baby, like she still slept in that crib. She barely even *remembered* that stupid crib. She was way old enough for the big-person stuff; but still, everyone talked to her like a diaper-baby— Mommy, Daddy, Mrs. Johanssen, even her pool of blood.

"Don't forget to wear your jacket," it would say; or, "That sugar cereal is bad for you."

When it talked, it would change shape, rippling like that octopus in that movie. Even though it talked just like Mommy, she liked the puddle better because it made her special and because it was so pretty. So shiny! Sometimes, she stepped on her puddle, squishing happily, and she could see herself stomping down on the soles of her own feet. "Hi, Upside-Down Alice!" she exclaimed sometimes, and Upside-Down Alice said the same thing back. Then the pool would interrupt, "Be careful you don't slip, honey," which Alice hated, because she was too careful to slip, and besides, even if she did, Upside-Down Alice would catch her.

Sometimes she argued with her puddle, which Mommy didn't like at all, especially when she was trying to work in her office downstairs, which she always was. Once, Mommy yelled for her to shut up, which is a bad thing to say and was so scary, since it had never happened before. Even when Mommy apologized, Alice was still afraid, so she went upstairs and sat with her puddle, which said, "Mommy didn't mean to yell. She loves you."

But that didn't help much, because downstairs, she could hear Mommy and Daddy arguing. "—just an imaginary friend," Daddy said. "Like that rabbit in the closet at the old house, remember?" (Oh! Alice had forgotten dear Prince Mopsy. She hoped he was happy with his new family.)

"But *blood,* Harold!"

"The doctor said . . ."

"BLOOD!"

Daddy sighed, something he only did during arguments with Mommy. "The doctor said a hundred times that didn't mean anything. Do you want me to call him again?"

Then Mommy started talking about something else and using a lot of big words and Alice stopped listening. She looked down at the pool of blood and sighed like Daddy, just to see how it felt.

"Are you imaginary, puddle?"

The pool of blood shimmered, "Yes, but I won't always be."

"Oh." Alice sighed again; it was kind of fun. "What's *imaginary* mean?"

"Look it up."

Alice growled in annoyance and stomped off to the other side of the room. That puddle could make her so mad sometimes! But it was always nice, and, all in all, she liked having it in her room.

Except at night.

At night, it would grow.

Sometimes it grew out so that it covered her whole floor. Sometimes it grew up until it touched the ceiling, like the tower of blocks Jimmy at school said he made once.

One night, she tried to get out of bed to touch it, but it stopped her. "Don't!" it screeched. "Don't, don't, don't, don't, don't! My *head!!*" And Alice hid under the covers, but it wouldn't stop. "Don't, don't, don't!" all night long. It stopped being scary after a while, but Alice still didn't like it.

And even when she was good and stayed in bed, it would glow and whisper to her. Even though she couldn't understand what it was saying, she could tell it wasn't being nice.

But then the morning would come, and it would shrink back to being a pretty, red puddle, and it would apologize for frightening her. "Sometimes things are scary," it said once. "But you're brave, right?"

Alice wasn't sure, but she nodded and said yes anyway. "Good," the puddle said then, sounding more like Mommy than ever, "it's important for you to be brave."

Alice never told anyone what her puddle did at night. She liked being special, but she hated how sad Mommy always looked when she heard about the pool of blood. Maybe she was just jealous, but Alice still didn't like it. Mommy only smiled around Daddy and around her friends, never to Alice. Daddy almost never smiled, and the puddle didn't have a mouth, and Upside-Down Alice always looked sad, too.

So things weren't perfect, but Alice still loved her pool of blood.

One night, Alice woke up and something was strange. The room looked normal, but *something* was missing. It was like looking in the mirror and realizing you don't have a nose; things just looked *wrong*.

Alice looked around the room, hugging her blanket to her neck. The chair was there, and the shadow behind the closet door, and the toy chest, and the bookshelf . . .

Then she realized what was missing, and she almost shrieked in horror. There was no glow; there was no whispering. The pool of blood was gone.

Alice's mouth hung open wide. She felt like crying, but she was too surprised. The puddle was scary at night, but she missed it terribly now that it was gone.

She went over the night's events in her head, like the detective in those stories she had tried to read once. She had gone to bed at 9:00 P.M., just like always. The pool of blood had been there then; she knew it. She had lain in bed, watching it grow outwards until it flooded the entire floor.

She remembered hearing voices coming from downstairs. Mommy and Daddy were fighting, not about Alice being special but just boring adult stuff. Daddy had stomped around and then the front door had slammed.

Mommy was crying or laughing—probably crying, Alice realized, but laughing is more fun so she hoped she was doing that. Then Mommy had walked to the kitchen and stayed there, and Alice had gone to sleep.

The puddle had escaped while she was asleep! Alice almost got out of bed to look for it, but realized it could be hiding. Maybe it was going to jump out at her and start yelling again! That would be really scary, even for a special girl like her.

She crawled to the edge of the bed and stuck her foot over the side, listening carefully. She couldn't hear anyone, not even Mommy or Upside-Down Alice.

Alice almost started crying again. What if she had woken up in the wrong house! She pulled the sheets over her head and tried not to cry, because whoever owned the house might hear, and they'd get mad at her for being there. But then she realized, they'd be even madder if they found her in their bed in the morning!

She clearly heard a loud voice bellow something about someone eating porridge, but she knew it was just her "imagination playing tricks on her". She didn't know what that meant, but Mommy said it sometimes and it always made her feel better.

Thinking about Mommy made Alice a little more brave, so she sat up—slowly, quietly—until her legs dangled off the edge of the bed, an inch from the floor. She listened again—still nothing. She looked up at the door on the far side of the room. If she could make it there, she would be all right.

A huge, bear-shaped shadow huddled in the corner of the room. "And someone's been eating *my* porridge!" it said. Alice squeezed her eyes shut and made a blind dash for the door. Even though her eyes were closed, she could picture the bear coming after her.

And then it was over. Alice opened her eyes. She stood in the hallway. There was no yelling, no bear, no "Don't!"—just Alice and her panting breath.

This *was* her house, after all! But then, where was Mommy? Where was the pool of blood?

"Mommy?" Alice called. Nothing changed; the silence stayed. Alice softly tiptoed down the hall to her parents' room, but no one was there, either. The bed was made up, too.

Alice went downstairs, completely brave now, but confused. Where was everyone? Maybe . . . maybe the puddle finally went to talk to Mommy, and Mommy could see and hear it now. She hoped so; they were so much alike.

The living room was empty, so was the dining room, the den, the bathrooms, the kitc—

Alice froze in the doorway to the kitchen. There was something strange beneath her feet. The weird linoleum was still there, but there was something else, something familiar.

Alice hugged herself with joy. Her puddle wasn't gone, it had just gone downstairs for a snack! She quickly jumped up and turned the lights on to tell her puddle how brave she'd been.

When the light flooded the room, Alice noticed something else that was weird. Her pool of blood was right there on the kitchen floor, but it wasn't alone. Mommy was there, too.

"Mommy!" Alice said. Mommy didn't move; she just kept lying there in the puddle. Alice noticed something else on the floor, a broken wine bottle. There was even glass sticking out of Mommy's foot, which was gross. "Mommy? What's wrong?"

Mommy didn't answer, but the puddle did. "She's hurt, honey. She fell and hit her head. See?"

Alice also looked above Mommy's head and saw more blood—but not the nice kind; not the shiny, puddle kind—on the edge of the counter. "Do you remember what I told you to do whenever someone is hurt?" the puddle asked.

Alice looked down and saw her upside-down self with a telephone in her hand. Alice nodded and ran to where the phone was. "Do you remember what number to call, honey?"

"Uh-huh," Alice called back, and then another lady's voice came out of the phone and Alice said, not crying at all, "Mommy's hurt! Send an ambulant!"

Later, a lot of strange men came and took Mommy away and made Alice sit in some room all night. One of them told her she was very brave, but she already knew that. Then Daddy came and, the next night, they all went home together. Someone had cleaned up Alice's pool of blood, and she knew it was really gone forever.

She went up to her room. Mommy and Daddy talked for a long time downstairs, but Alice didn't start listening until she heard her own name.

"What about Alice?" That was Mommy. "She'll be traumatized! She had to see that, and the paramedic said there was so much blood . . ."

"She's fine," Daddy said. "And she knew just what to do. She wasn't scared, even at the hospital. She really is a special girl." Then they started talking about not-Alice stuff and so she went and lay down in bed.

Alice missed her puddle, but she was glad Mommy wasn't hurt anymore. She closed her eyes, but she couldn't sleep.

She sat up in bed, sighing like Daddy. A sudden thought struck her. She stood up, tiptoed over to her bookshelf, took out her dictionary, and looked up the word *special*.

Chapter 19

Emily Sees Red

By J. M. M. Holloway

Tinkling prisms fractured the morning sunlight into rainbows and beamed colors into the crib. Emily stretched up chubby arms and babbled her frustration. Tiny fists opened and closed in demand. The pieces rattled on their wires before several separated and rained around her. When she reached to claim her prize, she felt a pinch on her toe.

"Bad girl. Emily shouldn't make the pretties fall down."

Such cruel treatment from her kindly old nanny made her hold her breath. Then she cried.

* * *

Emily's first word was doggie. Long before she said Mommy, who kissed her in the morning then left for the whole day, or Daddy, who seldom appeared before Emily closed her eyes at night, or Nanny, who was always there, she called to a young stray. The puppy answered by wiggling through the bars of her playpen and licking her face. One day as she watched, he discovered something to eat at the edge of the yard. He choked it down like all the other scraps Nanny put out then started to moan. He crawled to the edge of the playpen and stopped; his tongue hung limp.

"Doggie?" Emily reached for the mutt and pulled him to her. No matter how she poked his side, he wouldn't move. As she hugged him, she started to cry. "Doggie, doggie."

She wished he could play like he did before. She wished hard—so hard the puppy coughed and wriggled. "Doggie!"

Nanny ripped him from her grasp. "Good girls leave dead things alone!" Nanny's rough hands snapped the dog's neck before putting him into a trashcan.

Emily wailed.

* * *

146

"Tell Mommy what color you see."

Emily stared at the cardboard square. She liked to please her mother, who smiled when she got the answer right, but she only knew red, yellow, white, blue, black, green, purple, and sometimes orange, which looked a lot like red and a little like yellow. The color on this card was an ugly color, like the color on Nanny's face when she hugged and had to sit down. Emily didn't know its name.

"I'm on hold," her mother said into the phone between her shoulder and ear. She gulped her coffee. "Come on, sweetie. Mommy has to leave soon."

Emily fretted. She hated to disappoint her mother who'd stayed home specially to teach her the things she needed to know.

"You remember, precious. We learned it last week. What's the name of this color?" She shook the cardboard in a way that meant hurry up.

Emily guessed the color was orange. That was the one she'd learned last time they'd done the color cards. She didn't want to disappoint Mommy. She needed to peek to make sure. In the kitchen Nanny stood cutting bananas. Emily closed her eyes and wished hard. The opposite side of the color card wasn't orange at all.

"Purple," Emily said.

"Right, baby doll." Her mother smiled and showed the backside of the next card. "Now what is this?"

Emily wished again. "Yellow."

Mommy stared at the squares in her lap. The phone dropped to the floor. "Emily, I had the cards backward. You named the colors without seeing them. How did you do that? Try this one."

Emily didn't want to say the card was white because Nanny was sure to hear. Her mother flipped to the next card. "Nanny, come in here. You won't believe what Emily can do. Show her, baby. What's the next color?"

Nanny's face turned red. Emily refused to wish for a peek with her looking so mean.

"Don't encourage her, missus. This is witch stuff. I know—seen it in my own granny, devil take her evil soul."

"For God's sake, Nanny, nobody's believed witches are evil for eons. This is a special talent. If Emily can see things that are hidden, imagine what else she might be able to do. I have to go, but I want you to keep flashing these cards." Her mother handed the stack to the nanny and pocketed her phone. "Keep track of how many she gets right. I want some documentation we can show to experts."

Her mother headed for the door. "Now be good for Nanny 'til I get home, Emily."

Emily held out her arms, but the door had already closed. She looked into Nanny's angry face.

"Child, this'll hurt me worse than it'll hurt you, but we got to stop Satan in his tracks." The woman held up the back of a card. "Now tell Nanny what color you see."

Emily closed her lips tight.

"Come on, child. It's for your own good. Tell Nanny."

Emily blinked and the color came clear. "Black."

"No! It's gray. Only a demon would say black." The flat of Nanny's palm slapped Emily's face. "You got to learn. A good girl only sees what's in front of her eyes."

Nancy raised another card. "What's this one?"

She'd never been hit before. The pain confused her. Which color did Nanny want her to say? Gray on the front? Or red on the back? She couldn't figure out the right answer.

"It's a pretty color. Tell me it's name," Nanny coaxed.

"Red?"

The old woman raised her arm to strike again, but quickly lowered it to her chest. Her face lost all color, turning grayer than the cardboard. "Help me, child. I know you can."

Emily shook her head.

Nanny dropped to the floor. "Emily, please," she said and then went silent.

Emily approached her cautiously. The old woman's tongue lolled like the dog's; her eyes stared; she lay very still. Emily reached out a pudgy hand.

Just in time she remembered: Good girls leave dead things alone.

Chapter 20

Haunted

By Scott Nicholson

"Do it again, Daddy." Janie's coloring book was in her lap, forgotten.

Darrell smiled and thumbed open the top on his Zippo lighter. He struck the flint wheel, and the flame burst to life. The dancing fire reflected in each of Janie's pupils. Her mouth was open in fascination.

"It's pretty," she said.

"And so are you. Now back to your coloring. It's almost bedtime." Darrell flipped the silver metal lid closed, snuffing the orange flame.

Janie put the coloring book in front of her and rolled onto her stomach. She chose a crayon: gray.

Darrell frowned and placed the lighter by the ashtray. Rita tensed in her chair beside him. She reached out with her thin hand and gripped his arm. "Did you hear that?" she whispered.

Darrell listened: Janie was humming to herself. The wax of the crayon made a soft squeak across the paper. The clock on the mantel ticked once, again, three times more.

He tried to hear beyond those normal sounds, but his hearing was shot. Too much Elvis, Rita always said; too much Elvis would make anyone deaf.

Darrell stood, his recliner groaning in relief. He looked down at the hollow impression in the woven seat of the chair. Too much food; too much food, and too much Elvis.

Can't go back; can't get younger; can't change things. He shook his head at nothing.

"From the kitchen," she said. "Or outside."

Janie heard the same noise Rita was hearing. She cocked her head, the crayon posed above the page and she stopped kicking her feet, the heels of her saddle shoes nearly touching her back.

"Mice most likely," he said, too loudly. He was head of the household—it was his job to put on a brave face. The expression fit him like a glass mask.

Why didn't the damned dog bark? Dogs were supposed to be sensitive to spirits from the other side. He put down the newspaper, paper crackling.

Mayor Loeb and Martin Luther King, Jr. looked out from the front page. Black and white.

"Terribly loud mice," Rita finally answered. Darrell shot her a glance, then rolled his eyes toward Janie. Rita was usually careful in front of their daughter, but having those noisy things around had been stressful.

"Sounds like it's coming from the kitchen," he said with what he hoped was nonchalance. He pulled his cigar from his mouth. He rarely smoked and never inside the house, but they were a comfort, with their rich, sweet smell and tangy taste and the round weight between his lips.

He laid the cigar carefully beside his lighter, propping up the damp end on the ashtray so the dust wouldn't stick to it. The ashtray was shaped like a starfish. They'd gotten it on their honeymoon to Cuba, back when Americans were allowed to visit. He could still see the map of the island that had been painted on the bottom of the glass.

"Don't bother, honey. The mice won't hurt anything." Rita chewed at the red end of her index finger.

"Well, we can't let them have the run of the house." It was their secret code, worked out over the long, sleepless night. Janie didn't need to know; she was too young to understand. But the things were beyond anybody's understanding, no matter what age a person was.

Darrell glanced at the big, boxy RCA that cast a flickering shadow from one corner of the room. They usually watched with the sound turned down. Barney Fife was saying something to Andy, his Adam's apple twitching up and down like a turkey's.

"Get me a soda while you're up?" Rita asked, trying to pretend everything was normal.

"Sure. Anything for you pumpkin?"

Janie shook her head. He wished she would go back to coloring. Her eyes were wide now, waiting. He was supposed to protect her from worries.

She put the gray crayon back in the box. Fifteen other colors, and she almost always used gray. Freud would probably have made something of that. Darrell hoped she would select a blue, even a red, something vibrant and found in rainbows. His heart tightened as she chose black.

He walked past her and turned up the sound on the television. Beginning to whistle, he headed across the living room. No tune came to mind. He forced a few in-between notes and the music jumped track somewhere in his throat. He began again with "I See the Moon," Janie's favorite.

Where was that dog? Always underfoot when Darrell went through the house, but now nowhere to be found. Nothing like this ever happened back in Illinois, only in Tennessee.

He was in the hall when he heard Aunt Bea's aria from the living room: "An-deeeee!"

They used to watch *The Outer Limits* and sometimes *The Twilight Zone*— never again. They got too much of that sort of thing in real life. Now it was nothing but safe, family fare.

Darrell eased past the closet. His golf clubs were in there, the three-wood chipped where he'd used it to drive a nail into the kitchen drawer that was always coming apart. Cobwebs probably were stretched between the irons; par for the course, these days.

He stopped outside the kitchen. A bright rectangle of light spilled into the hallway. Mice were supposed to be scared of house lights. Well, maybe mice were, but those things weren't. Then why did they only come at night?

There was a smudge of fingerprints on the doorway casing. Purple. Small. Grape jelly.

He tried to yawn, but his breath hitched. He checked the thermostat, even though it was early autumn and the temperature was fairly constant. He looked around for another excuse for delay, but found none.

The kitchen floor was off-white linoleum, in a decorative sort of pattern that disguised scuffs and stains. Mice would find nothing on this floor. The Formica counters were clean too. Three soiled plates were stacked in the sink, but he didn't blame Rita for avoiding the chore. No one wanted to be alone in the kitchen, especially after dinner when the sun had gone down.

A broom leaned against the little door that hid the folding-out ironing board. He wrapped his hands around the smooth wood. Maybe he could sweep them away, as if they were dust balls.

Darrell crossed the kitchen slowly, the broom held across his chest. As he crouched, he felt the bulge of his belly lapping over his belt. Both he and his cross-town hero were packing on the weight in these later years.

Where was that dog? A few black-and-white clumps of hair stuck to the welcome mat at the back door. That dog shed so much; Darrell wouldn't be surprised if it was invisible by now. But the mess was forgivable, if only the mutt would show up. A good bark would scare those things away.

He parted the curtain on the back door. The grass in the yard had gotten tall and was a little ragged. George next door would be tut-tutting to his wife. But George was retired; he had nothing on his mind but lawn fertilizer. There was a joke in there somewhere, but Darrell wasn't in the mood to dig it up.

A little bit of wind played in the laurel hedge, strong enough to make the seat of Janie's swing set ease back and forth. Of course it was the wind—what would those things want with a swing set? The set's metal poles were flecked with rust. He didn't remember that happening. Gradual changes weren't as noticeable, he supposed.

In the dim light, the world looked colorless. Nothing else stirred. If they were out there, they were hiding. He almost expected to hear some corny organ music like they played on the *Inner Sanctum* radio program.

He was about to drop the curtain and get Rita's soda, and maybe a beer for himself, when he saw movement: two shapes, wispy and pale in the faded wash of the backyard. A trick of moonlight; yeah, had to be. They didn't exist, did they?

He looked forward to the beer bubbling in his throat. The bitter sweetness wasn't as crisp as it used to be back when he was young. Maybe everything got flatter and less vivid as a person got older. Senses dulled by time and timelessness.

The big General Electric was nearly empty. The celery had wilted. Something on the middle wire shelf had separated into layers. He didn't dare open the Tupperware container to see what was inside. Half a dozen eggs roosted in their scooped-out places. One had a hairline crack, and a clear jewel of fluid glistened under the fluorescent light.

He fished out the drinks and closed the door. There was a hiss as the motor kicked in and sucked the seals tight; a fluff of lint shot from the grill at the base of the appliance.

The drinks chilled in his palms. Sensation. He pressed a can to his forehead, a great way to cure a headache. Too bad he didn't have one.

He went back to the living room. Janie was still coloring, the tip of her tongue pressed just so against the corner of her mouth. Her eyes were half closed, the curl of her lashes making Darrell's heart ache. He sat down.

Darrell gave Rita the soda, then pulled the tab on his beer. The can opened with a weak, wet sigh. He took a sip. Flat.

"See any mice?" Rita asked, trying to smile.

"Not a single Mickey Mouse in the place. Saw a Donald Duck, though."

Janie giggled, her shoulders shaking a little. Her ponytail had fallen against one cheek. Darrell hated lying, but it wasn't really a lie, was it? The lie was so white; it was practically see-through.

He settled back in his chair. The newspaper had slipped to the floor and opened to page 7, where the real news was located—more stuff on Johnson's mess in Vietnam. Right now, he had no interest in the world beyond. He looked at the television.

Gomer was doing something stupid, and his proud, idiot grin threatened to split his head in half. Barney was waving his arms in gangly hysterics. Andy stood there with his hands in his pockets.

Television was black-and-white, just like life. But in television, you had problem, then problem solved, sprinkled with some canned laughter along the way. In life, there were no solutions and not much laughter.

He took another sip of beer. "You want to visit your folks again this weekend?"

Rita had gulped half her soda in her nervousness. "Can we afford it?"

Could they afford not to? Every minute away from the house was a good minute. He wished they could move. He had thought about putting the house up for sale, but the market was glutted. The racial tension had even touched the midtown area, and middle-class whites didn't want to bring their families to the South. Besides, who would want to buy a haunted house?

Even if they did manage to sell the house, where would they go? Shoe store managers weren't exactly in high demand, and he didn't want Rita to work until Janie started school. So they'd just have to ride it out for another year or so. Seemed like they'd been riding it out forever.

He put down the beer and jabbed the cigar in his mouth. "Maybe your folks are getting tired of us," he said around the rolled leaf. "How about a trip to the mountains? We can get a little cabin, maybe out next to a lake." He thought of his fishing rod, leaning against his golf bag lost somewhere in the back of the closet.

"Out in the middle of nowhere?" Rita's voice rose half a step too high. Janie noticed and stopped scribbling.

"We could get a boat."

"I'll call around," Rita said. "Tomorrow."

Darrell looked at the bookcase on the wall. He'd been meaning to read so many of those books. He wasn't in the mood to spend a few hours with one, even though he had all the time in the world.

He picked up the Zippo and absently thumbed the flame to life. Janie heard the lid open and looked up. Pretty colors: orange, yellow, blue. He doused the flame, thumbed it to life once more, then closed the lighter and put it back on the table.

Rita pretended to watch television. Darrell looked from her face to the screen. The news was on, footage of the sanitation workers' strike. The reporter's voice-over was bassy and bland.

"Do you think it's serious?" Rita asked, with double meaning.

"A bunch of garbage." The joke fell flat. Darrell went to the RCA and turned down the volume. Silence crowded the air.

Janie stopped coloring, lifted her head, and cocked it to one side. "I heard something."

Her lips pursed. A child shouldn't suffer such worry. He waited for a pang of guilt to sear his chest, but the guilt was hollow, dead inside him.

"I think it's time a little girl went beddy-bye," he said. Rita was standing before he even finished his sentence.

"Aw, do I have to?" Janie protested halfheartedly.

"Afraid so, pumpkin."

"I'll go get the bed ready, then you can come up and get brushed and washed," Rita said, heading too fast for the stairs.

"And Daddy tells the bedtime story?" Janie asked.

Darrell smiled. Rita was a wonderful mother; he couldn't imagine a better partner. But when it came to telling stories, there was only one king. "Sure," he said. "Now gather your crayons."

The promise of a story got Janie in gear. Darrell heard Rita's slippered feet on the stairs. Her soles were worn. He'd have to get her a new pair down at the store.

He froze, the hairs on his neck stiffening.

There—that sound again. The not-mice.

Where was that damn dog?

He got to his feet, stomach clenched. Janie was preoccupied with her chore. He walked to the back door and parted the curtain, wondering if Rita had heard and was now looking out from the upstairs window.

The moon was fuller, brighter, more robust. Why did they only come at night?

Maybe they had rules, which was stupid. They broke every natural law just in the act of existing.

There, by the laurel at the edge of the backyard: two shapes, shimmering, surreal, a bit washed out.

He opened the door, hoping to scare them away. That was a hoot—him scaring them—but he had to try, for Janie's and Rita's sake.

"What do you want?" he said, trying to keep his voice level. Could they understand him? Or did they speak a different language in that other world?

The shapes moved toward him, awkwardly. A bubbling sound flooded the backyard, like pockets of air escaping from water. One of the shapes raised a nebulous arm. The motion was jerky, like in an old, silent film.

Darrell stepped off the porch. Maybe if he took a stand here, they would take what they wanted and leave his family alone.

"There's nothing for you here," he said. "Why don't you go back where you came from?"

A sudden rage flared through him, filling his abdomen with heat. These were the things that bothered Janie, made Rita worry, and were the fountain of his own constant guilt. These things had no right to intrude on their space, their lives, their reality.

"I don't believe in you," he shouted, no longer caring if he woke up Neighbor George. If only the dog would bark, maybe that would drive them away.

The bubbling sound came again. The spooks were closer now, and he could see they were shaped like humans. Noises from their heads collected and hung in the air. The wind lifted, changed direction. The noises blew together, thickened, and became words—Darrell's language.

"There's where it happened."

A kid. Sounded like early teens. Did their kind age, or were they stuck in the same moment forever?

Darrell opened his mouth, but didn't speak. More words came from the world of beyond, words that were somnambulant and sonorous.

"Gives me the creeps, man." Another young one.

"Three of them died when it burned down."

"Freaky. Maybe some of the bones are still there."

"They say only the dog got away."

"Must have been a long time ago."

"Almost 30 years."

"Nothing but a chimney left, and a few black bricks. You'd think something would grow back. Trees and stuff." A silence. Darrell's heart beat again, three times, more.

"It's supposed to be haunted," said the first.

"Bullshit."

"Go out and touch it, then."

"No way."

A fire flashed in front of one of the shapes, then a slow curl of smoke wafted across the moonlit yard. The end of a cigarette glowed. Smoke, spirit, smoke, spirit—both insubstantial.

Darrell walked down the back steps, wondering how he could make them go away. A cross? A Bible? A big stick?

"I only come here at night," said the one inhaling the fire.

"Place gives me the creeps."

"It's cool, man."

"I don't like it." The shape drifted back, away from the house, away from Darrell's approach.

"Chicken."

The shape turned and fled.

"Chicken," repeated the first, louder, sending a puff of gray smoke into the air.

Darrell glanced up at Janie's bedroom window. She would be in her pajamas now, the covers up to her chin, a picture book across her tummy with the pages opened to a story that began, "Once upon a time . . . "

Darrell kept walking, nearing the ghost of shifting smoke and fire. He was driven by his anger now, an anger that drowned the fear. The thing didn't belong in their world. Everything about them was wrong—their bad light, their voices, their unreal movement.

He reached out, clutching for the thing's throat. His hands passed through the flame without burning, then through the shape without touching. The shape froze, shuddered, then turned and fled back to its world of beyond.

Darrell watched the laurels for a moment, making sure the thing was gone. They would come back; they always did. But tonight he had won. A sweat of tension dried in the gentle breeze.

He went inside and closed the door. He was trembling. But he had a right to feel violated, outraged. He hadn't invited the things to his house.

He had calmed down a little by the time he reached the living room. A Spencer Tracy movie was on the television. The glow from the screen flickered on the walls like green firelight.

Rita was in her chair, blinking too rapidly. "Was it . . . ?" she asked.

"Yeah."

"Oh, Darrell, what are we going to do?"

"What can we do?"

"Move."

He sighed. "We can't afford to right now. Maybe next year."

He sat down heavily and took a sip of his beer. It was still flat.

"What do we tell Janie?"

"Nothing for now. They're just mice, remember?"

He wished the dog were here, so he could stroke it behind the ears. He thought of those words from beyond, and how they said something about the dog getting out. Getting out of what?

He reached for his cigar and stuck it in his mouth.

After a moment, he said, "Maybe if we stop believing in them, they'll go away."

The clock ticked on the mantel.

"I can't," Rita said.

"Neither can I."

The clock ticked some more.

"She's waiting."

"I know."

Darrell leaned his cigar carefully against the ashtray. He noticed his lighter was missing. He shrugged and went upstairs to read Janie her story. He wondered if tonight the ending would be the same as always.

Artwork by Chris Pugh, Copyright 2002

Chapter 21

The Believers

By Didier Quémener

"Do you come here often?"

"More or less . . . I like their fried sweet potatoes," she said without raising her eyes from the counter.

She was spinning the olives attached to the wooden stick in her drink. It was the first time she had ever gone to that bar downtown. Usually she wouldn't talk to strangers, but for whatever reason, his voice sounded kind of amusing and ordinary at the same time.

"Another one? Two martinis, please," he told the bartender.

"I've never been to this place. It's pretty nice. I'm Paul," he said, looking her in the eyes for the first time.

"And I'm Mae," she replied, brushing her hair to the side of her face. Her cheek had the slight rose hue that often follows a first drink.

"The place is packed tonight," she continued. "But it'll soon be quieter again. The tourists are ready to head south as always at this time of the year. She took a sip of her drink. She hadn't been feeling overly comfortable, but his presence changed that. His scent—rather sweet and light—reminded her of the wild honeysuckle that had been creating a long wall of wild bushes along the shore.

"I couldn't tell—I've never been to an empty bar before!" he said, laughing. She noticed that he had a slight accent.

"Where are you from?" she asked, glancing at him briefly.

"Paris originally . . . " he said, then hesitated for a moment. "But it's been many years since I came to the U.S.," he added grabbing his glass. "Would you care to join me outside? The air is so cool. It's very pleasant out there."

He offered her his arm.

The dimmed lights of the city were starting to glow as they left the bar. She felt a chill on her bare shoulders. The breeze was light, but she shivered passing through the harbor.

"Are you cold, Mae?" he asked. "Here, let me put my jacket on you. You'll feel more comfortable."

"I'm fine," she replied. "It's just the wind. I guess what they say is right. It does get colder once September begins around here."

"You're not from the city?" he said, intrigued.

She couldn't help but notice that his pace had slowed quite a bit. The last thing she wanted to do was to stand in the cold looking at the ocean. What does he want us to look at from the pier? There is nothing to see, she thought to herself.

"Uh, no . . . I came a few months ago. That's all————" she told him.

"Follow me! I want to show you something over there. It's very interesting, you'll see!" He seized her hand.

They were walking quickly on the bridge and she almost tripped. She could barely keep up with him.

"Slow down!" she yelled. "I'm going to twist an ankle————."

"Come on," he said, ignoring her words. "We've almost arrived, Hurry up!"

As they stooped at the end of the bridge, the wind picked up strength—nothing violent, but enough to swirl her hair close to his face. He looked up and pointed to the other side of the coast. The waves were breaking on the bridge's poles and roaring underneath.

"Maybe we shouldn't stay here too long, Paul," she said softly. "The water's kind of rough, and I don't trust the wood of this bridge."

"Don't worry; I come here often and it's safe," he told her. "Now come closer over here. You see that house all lit up on the right?"

She couldn't care less about any of those houses at this point. She was freezing, and her hair was turning into a mess.

"Which one?" she asked, trying to hide the bitterness that had welled up within. "I can't really see anything! It's dark."

"The big one there—full of lights, can't miss it!" he said, guiding her to the side.

The house was imposing. Built on three floors, its big, beige columns were letting some of the light through so that one could see the size of some of the rooms. The flower garden in front of it was strictly designed, but the gray, marble statues here and there gave an impression of fake movement.

The shadow of a woman walking slowly within the house appeared from time to time as Mae looked between the columns. A wide, white veil covered the woman's face completely, but one could still distinguish the darkness of her eyes at times. Her steps appeared weightless as she was walked through what seemed to be the living room.

What am I supposed to look at, Mae said to herself. It's just a woman in her house—nothing that extraordinary!

Mae was getting a little annoyed. The wind was piercing through her body, and she felt as if her ears were about to snap off.

"Tell me, Paul: Are we going to spend the whole night staring at this ghost of a woman walking back and forth in the house?" she finally asked, her voice sarcastic. "I'm freezing here! Can't you see?" Obviously, if he were to look at me instead, he would notice that, she thought with annoyance.

"Funny you mention that, Mae . . ." he said, gazing at her for a second.

"Do you believe *they* exist?" he asked, staring at her intensely.

Paul suddenly came closer to her. As she was holding onto the railing, she realized his hands were touching hers. I'm so cold. My fingers are about to break. I don't even feel his hands!

"What are you talking about?" she asked, her eyes still on the house. "What kind of a question is that? I don't know. What do you mean anyway?"

She stared at the house for a moment. She wanted to play his game for a moment and see where it would lead. Mae caught his eyes now, and moved toward his chest.

"Well, I've never seen any!" she said finally with a sarcastic laugh.

"You shouldn't laugh too much, Mae," he said. "Take a look ahead and make sure you keep both eyes open." He put his arm around her shoulders.

The bright light inside the house was fading away. It now was switching to a gloomy, orange color, which became unexpectedly difficult to perceive. The woman, so clear earlier, was becoming a shadow and when she finally vanished entirely, the house lost all light.

Mae couldn't quite figure it out. What kind of illusion was that? Should I be scared, she thought, trying to process what she had seen.

"What was that all about?" she asked.

"I come here every night," Paul said. "And I've seen her every single night."

Mae was a bit disturbed. At first, she considered him to be just another weirdo—the type she attracted much too often—but she felt somewhat different this time, and it started from the minute she saw him at the bar. Why would he come up here every night to look into someone's house? He's got to be strange.

As she was staring at the house left in darkness, she sensed her heart beating so loudly that she felt light-headed.

"There's a story behind what you've just seen, Mae," he said, catching her eye. "It's quite fascinating, you know."

"Well I'm sure it is," she said, softly. "After seeing a trick like that, I'd like to know what this tale is all about!"

"They say she is waiting for her lover to come back and take her to the other place with him," he said. "Something tragic happened awhile ago, and since then, her soul wanders where she used to live, and she waits—waits for him."

"Who is he?" she asked. His words were piquing her interest. "And what exactly happened?"

"I heard many versions of her story. I guess her death was extremely difficult to deal with for the one she loved because he couldn't save her life or something like that. People say he arrived too late at the scene, and he found her gone even before anyone could call for help or anything. After that, he literally disappeared. No one ever saw him again, but her soul remained here. She lingers in that empty house that was theirs before the accident."

Mae was speechless. Glancing at the house from time to time and trying to figure out what to do, she felt uncomfortable and she didn't even know why. She stepped back for a moment.

"Do you really buy into that?" she asked. "I mean, every old town has legends like that, you know. I just don't know what to tell you. I've seen the lights, the shadow, and all that, but it's just a bit too much for one evening."

"Well, I———."

She interrupted him. "Let's go," she said curtly. "I'm really cold and it's getting late. I should head back to town."

Paul didn't try to convince her otherwise. He knew that she was feeling tense. They walked back to the downtown area, which usually was almost empty at this hour. As they neared the bar where they had met earlier, he stopped.

"I'm going this way, Mae, but I can walk you home if you'd like . . ." he said.

"I'm fine. Shall we meet again in a different place sometime soon?" A place more human next time, she wanted to add.

"Why not?" he said gently. "Absolutely! I think I know where to reach you."

"Okay then, good night." she said as he turned down a side street.

Mae quickened her pace. It was late, and she really was worn out. As she approached the corner, she noticed a great commotion coming from the direction of the bar. The blue and red lights from police cars and ambulances sporadically illuminated the scene. A group of curious onlookers were gathered on the sidewalk, giving officials their stories.

"The car came out of nowhere," someone said. "Thank God those stools were empty in the bar—it could have a real disaster if people were sitting there!"

"I knew it was going to happen one day!" said an old man in a deep, raucous voice. "They all come to town, drink like fish, drive like maniacs, and almost kill us afterward! This city's got to do something about it. We've seen enough accidents like this one."

The old man shook his head and waved his hands madly.

"For heaven's sake, a woman was killed here years ago! Don't they learn anything?"

It took a couple of minutes for Mae to fully realize what was taking place before her eyes. She and Paul were having their drinks earlier at the exact spot where the car finished its wild course. The stools were now chunks of wood and leather scattered across the hood of the car. Mae felt nauseous. Pieces of glasses on the ground, people talking at the same time, the odor of broken bottles of alcohol everywhere in the air. She sat down on the sidewalk and tried to regroup.

A police officer was hauling off the drunk driver, who had nothing but a few cuts on his hands and certainly a serious hangover coming in the next few hours.

"You can't stay here, Ma'am," another officer said to Mae. "Are you all right?"

"Yeah, uh . . . I'm fine," she said, looking up at him emptily. "Was anyone hurt?"

"Just the driver of the vehicle, nothing bad this time," he told her. "Do you need a ride home?"

"No . . . thanks. I'll be okay. I'm leaving now."

Mae couldn't even remember how she returned home that night. The following day, she woke up with one of the worst headaches ever. Still in the middle of organizing things in her mind, she spent the day at home. That evening, she decided to find some answers. She didn't exactly know what she was searching for, but she figured that she would understand things better by going back to the bar. Maybe she would run into Paul again.

Only a few stragglers remained. A square piece of cardboard on the front door said that the bar would be closed for a week. There was no sign of Paul anywhere. Maybe I'll see him in a couple of days, she thought.

But she had to find out. She couldn't sit around with all of those unanswered questions eating at her mind. Pushed by a strange feeling, she walked toward the pier.

I'm crazy. Why do I even bother thinking of that, she asked herself. As she arrived at the end of the pier, she stood still and looked up. The air was quiet, and the ocean was unusually calm. Mae turned in the direction of the house. She didn't actually know what she wanted to see or what to expect, and she wished for an explanation more than anything else.

The house remained dark. Light never appeared. None of what she had seen before with Paul happened again—and it never would.

Vanished. The silhouette had disappeared and so had Paul. Mae understood that, even when coming night after night. Many things within herself had changed. She was given something she didn't expect, and couldn't explain. Irreplaceable, this single, unique experience had altered her beliefs. That was the only thing that was certain.

There were nights when she would hear Paul's voice in her sleep; the distinctive French accent and the unchanged words he told her while at the pier, almost like a leitmotiv: Do you believe they exist?

Chapter 22

Unique Tours, Ltd.

By Michele Lassig

"Pearl Harbor! Shit, that's gonna be fucking boring!"

Delia flushed with embarrassment and inwardly cringed, while out-wardly she only gave a tiny, nervous giggle. The entire room of couples at-tending the hotel's activities presentation had heard Pete's deep Missouri twang rumble through the room as he had pronounced one thing after an-other as a "rip-off". He had shown interest in only one brochure placed on the table before them and that was the glossy images of the evening luau at the neighboring hotel. He had made it profoundly obvious to everyone there that he particularly wished to see those exotic native ladies clad in their scanty hula costumes that were pictured in the brochure. "After all," he'd said, "this may be a honeymoon, but I ain't dead yet." This had been accompanied by a loud guffaw, and a forceful nudge in the ribs of his startled neighbor, who hap-pened to be an accountant from Bangor, Maine. Delia thought that he and his wife seemed to be a nice couple, but she was not surprised when they excused themselves and moved to another table. That had happened a lot here. Come to think of it, it happened a lot everywhere, but back in Missouri she just hadn't noticed it as much.

Delia had hoped that the grand wedding, the beautiful garden reception at her parent's home, and all the established trappings of tradition would change Pete. Well, not change him, but soften the edges, bring out the posi-tive points in him that could override his more grating qualities. He could be so nice, even charming, when he was doing exactly what he wished to be doing, and after all, he was 28 now. Certainly old enough to be married and accept responsibility, and he had seemed agreeable to the union. Though it had been hurtful of her family to hint ever so gently that their prosperous auto dealership and status in their small town had been more of an influence than any of Delia's charms.

Looking back on it now, she felt less sure of her own enticements and more certain of her family's instincts, but she was a long way from home now, and only 4 days into her honeymoon. Ironically, though, as she spent more and more time poolside with her new husband, she found she had the dubious luxury of time in which to recount the past, and to realize that in the 10 months since Pete had come to work for her father as a mechanic, she probably hadn't explored his character as thoroughly as she might have. She had also been acutely aware that at 33 she had better get a move-on. It wasn't as if there were a lot of prospects in her neck of the woods, and considering that she was carrying an extra 40 pounds of flesh around her hips and thighs had always made her hesitant to make any male friendships. If it wasn't for Pete's enthusiastic overtures to her every time he came up to the customer service department of the lot where they both worked, she would be sitting at her desk right now instead of in the middle of this large room, next to her large, handsome husband, with his large mouth.

The Pearl Harbor remark had been in reply to her timid suggestion that they pay the historic spot a visit. She had been there once before with her parents as a teenager and had found it a profoundly moving experience. She was, therefore, more than a little shocked at her husband's reaction. She thought all Americans should see it, and said so. His answer had been to belch loudly and dismissively. And that had been the end of that—or so it seemed.

That was before the perky activities director had given them the news that all the available spaces for the luau had been sold out. Delia inwardly braced for the colorful response that this latest bit of information would elicit in her spouse. She and the rest of the room were rapidly treated to a verbal treatise, in which the words *cocksuckers, Jews,* and *timeshare gimmicks* were sprinkled liberally. Though Delia was confused as to what the first two had to do with the last, she had to agree that she could do without a tour of the resort, however beautiful, if it meant she had to listen patiently while an initially fawning salesperson did a gradual metamorphosis into a rude, sneering snob.

Embarrassment aside, Delia knew, and with only the barest hint of resentment, that there had been several openings only minutes previously (she had gotten a good look at the sign-up sheet), and that she couldn't really blame the hotel staff for any half truths in the name of guest satisfaction. After all, these people were here on their vacations and they, unlike Delia, had not paid good money to put up with a loud, vulgar, semi-inebriated bumpkin. There was the argument that this was her honeymoon, but for all intents and purposes, she had experienced very little in the way of amorous contact that so many of her girlfriends had boasted about both before and after their nuptials. For someone who spent every afternoon poolside, visually devouring the tanned, tumescent bodies of the many female sun-worshippers while knocking back Mai Tais, Pete had been surprisingly disinterested in any advances Delia had made, prompting her already fragile self-esteem to plummet. Where, she wondered, was the frenzied, feverish coupling all the romance books so promisingly described? The theme of all these works of literature, she believed, had been that with patience there was someone for everybody, whether you possessed a lush, corset-bursting bosom or not. Observing the reactions that Pete was capable of eliciting in strangers made her question (only momentarily, of course), whether Pete was really meant for anyone at all, let alone her. These musings were brought to a halt by Pete's ham-sized hand smacking the table and his churlish command to her to "Get up! We're outta here!"

Delia clumsily rose from the too-tight fit of her tropically upholstered chair as Pete glared around the room dramatically then, without another word, ushered Delia out of the room. Delia was familiar with this particular behavior of her husband's. It was, she knew, an attempt to convince the salespeople in the room that they had made a colossal mistake in mismanaging their booking schedule. Because of their folly, not only would they miss out on a huge opportunity to do business with "Sweet Pete" as he sometimes referred to himself, but the remaining guests would be sadly deprived of his company. As Delia glanced back at the small crowd, she thought that in light of the gravity of this situation they seemed to be soldiering on quite nicely. In actuality, throughout Pete's tirade the level of conversation and laughter in the room had dimmed somewhat, but that was due to the natural, if uncomfortable, desire of most people to watch uncouth behavior. Once they had been moving toward the door, the conviviality of the group seemed to restore itself, and with the relief of a potentially disastrous situation averted, the resort personnel returned enthusiastically to their willing victims. Delia noted, not for the first time, that her husband's tantrums never seemed to work on anyone but her.

"Well, now what the hell are we gonna do?" Pete was saying as he tried ineffectually to slam the heavy, spring-loaded door that Delia had just scuttled through. He lifted a finger accusingly at her. "I hope you know this is your fault—you and your damn history. If you hadn't been askin' questions left and right about the friggin' Pearl Harbor tour we could be signed up for a real luau. Now, because of you we ain't gonna be doin' jackshit. Well, you ain't at least. I'll find me something to do" And he smiled that charming smart-ass smile of his.

Delia had been about to summon up the courage to make a tart reply when a rustle from what sounded like a newspaper in the nearby lounge area let her know that they were not alone. She saw a wizened face peek from the partially lowered Honolulu Herald. A pair of startlingly blue eyes was focused on her and her spouse. She lightly touched Pete's arm and glanced meaningfully at the direction of the still frankly staring old man. Pete, who had been about to inform his wife of his own as yet unformed plans for the evening, seemed to think better of his next sentence. Not for the same reason as Delia, though. Still, he could tell she was starting to get her priorities straight.

"Good thinkin' hon," he murmured approvingly as he patted her kindly on her bottom. "It's about time for another cold one." She'd been left to follow in his wake.

As they sat at the bar, Delia could feel the gaze of the old fellow on them. It amazed her at how the elderly could sometimes disregard all pretenses at good manners. He was really starting to make her uncomfortable. She was just about to ask Pete for the room key when the man got up, came over, and actually spoke.

His voice sounded deep and well modulated, the tones of a more youthful man. "Pardon me for intruding" he began, "but I couldn't help but overhear."

This Delia could well believe. She would only be mildly surprised if the inhabitants of other islands had not called to complain about the noise level.

"Am I correct," he continued, "in assuming that you two are interested in the Pearl Harbor tour?"

"No, you are not." Pete retorted in his best do-you-believe-this-fag voice.

Delia, always taught to show respect to the elderly, hastily intervened. "Actually, I had wanted to see it, but the tours are all booked. I saw it when I was younger, but I . . ." she trailed off.

The old man was looking at her keenly now, and Delia suddenly felt that it was absolutely essential that she remain silent. She had a sudden flash of those scenes on nature shows where the predator decides who is the easier prey to choose from, and the decision is made based on which of the Thompson Gazelles decides to linger at the watering hole a little too long.

She turned to Pete who, never at a loss for words, was demanding another beer. She looked back at the old man, aware that he continued to study her, and she stared back, desperately afraid that in some indefinable way she had been found wanting. Suddenly, the moment was over, and he smiled and looked exactly like any other elderly gentleman: fragile, weak, and benign. Delia was ashamed that for even a mere second she had thought him, of all things, sinister.

"Yes. Yes, we do want to see the Pearl Harbor tour!" she pronounced in what to her seemed like ringing tones in the almost empty bar area. But the old man did not seem shocked at her sudden decisiveness. He merely inclined his noble-looking head in a slight tilt to indicate Pete. Pete, who by this time was completely engrossed in the dual occupations of drinking and staring intently at ESPN racecar highlights, paid them no mind. "Yes," she nodded, "Pete will want to see it."

The old man beamed. "Excellent." He produced a finely engraved card from his jacket pocket. It read

> Unique Tours, Ltd.
> History Repeats Itself
> Hans Belfont, Proprietor

Delia studied it carefully. There was no address or phone number. As if reading her thoughts, Mr. Belfont murmured that he had several offices globally. After assuring her that he would be in the lobby waiting at eight that night to take them on their own private tour of the Pearl Harbor Memorial, he took leave of her, but not before, as if anticipating any difficulties with her spouse, he bent to whisper in her ear that the limousine would be stocked with an open bar.

* * *

The ride to the memorial had proved uneventful, and for that Delia had been extremely grateful. Pete had given in to her—not because she had stressed that Mr. Belfont was going out of his way for them, and that they shouldn't be rude. Certainly not due to her pleadings that this was something she really wanted to do. As a matter of fact—and she couldn't believe that she had really resorted to it—it was the result of her simply mentioning to him that it was her honeymoon too; and perhaps she should phone her father and inform him of the lackluster time that Pete was having, and that the expensive treat he had so generously given to them was largely unappreciated by both his daughter and her new husband.

After flinging the television remote control at the wall, leaving a sizable impression that would have to be explained to housekeeping, he agreed to accompany Delia on the tour, but not before exclaiming that, "Yeah, we all know that your daddy always bought you everything—including all your favorite candy bars by the case."

Now they were sitting in a small outboard motor boat expertly piloted by Mr. Belfont who, mindful of his duties as tour guide, had begun by asking both Delia and Pete what they knew about the U.S.S. *Arizona* memorial itself. Before she could answer, Pete, who up to this point had sullenly refused to speak, decided to enter into the spirit of the adventure. Relaxed and buzzed, his basic nature to be the center of attention took over, and airily waving his cut-crystal scotch glass (compliments of the limousine), he began to hold forth authoritatively.

"Japs got the drop on us, surprise attack. Sneaky little bastards had their diplomat up visitin' that gimp Roosevelt and all the while the subs and Kamikazes are on their way here to bomb the shit out of us. Bad idea havin' a crippled guy for president—made the whole world view us as weak. We set 'em straight, though. Kicked some serious Jap ass before we were through. One of them Japs called us a sleeping giant. Said they hadn't ought to woke us up. Hell of a wake-up call for those poor bastards, though!" He gestured out to the slowly approaching Memorial.

"Indeed, Pete. May I call you Pete?" A magnanimous sweep of the Scotch glass gave assent. "Indeed, Pete, you seem to know the general story of the attack, albeit rather blurry on the details. Why then, would you consider such a place of tribute to be boring?"

"Well, Hans, it ain't as if those guys are doing anything exciting now are they?"

Delia all the while had been scanning anxiously ahead, unsure of what was different from her previous visit to the memorial. As they grew closer, she realized what it was: There was not a uniformed guard in sight. She could distinctly recall a guard—Navy or Marine, she wasn't sure which—at the dock to greet visitors, but as they pulled alongside there was no one.

As if he could read her mind, Mr. Belfont leaped lightly to the dock, and with an alacrity that belied his advanced years; he swiftly tied up the boat. Extending his hand to assist Delia out the small, bobbing craft, he whispered assuredly that he had an "arrangement with the guardians in residence." Delia suddenly, inexplicably, felt a stab of fear that was not allayed by the tightened grip and menacing start her host gave her. Then, as if aware of her state, Mr. Belfont gently squeezed her hand and led her up the darkened gangplank to the well-lit concrete arc that covered the expanse of the U.S.S. *Arizona*.

Oblivious to the silent communication that passed between his wife and their guide, Pete swaggered behind them upward into the bright whiteness of the structure.

Releasing Delia's hand, Mr. Belfont turned to them and commenced the tour, his mellifluous tones filling and echoing eerily off the bare emptiness of the room.

"We are now in the entry room. The memorial itself is built over the mid-portion of the sunken battleship, U.S.S. *Arizona*. On the morning of December 7, 1941, seven of the Pacific Fleet were tied up along Battleship Row. Keeping serene company with her were the *Utah*, the *West Virginia*, the *Maryland*, and the *California*. The *Tennessee*, the *Oklahoma*, and the *Nevada* were there too. Those "poor bastards" that you referred to Pete, were not limited to the *Arizona*. The *Utah*, a training ship, capsized with more than 50 of her crew trapped inside. Let us now proceed to the center area."

Dutifully, they trailed after the old man. Delia turned to observe her husband's reaction to this historical treatise but was rewarded by the bottom of his upended glass.

"At this point, you are now directly over the final resting place of 1,177 of the crewmen of the U.S.S. *Arizona*. Some might refer to them as the most valiant sailors since Ulysses, but one would have to have known Ulysses." Here, Mr. Belfont paused to emit a low, throaty chuckle that seemed to hold no real humor in it.

It was then that Delia, who had approached and was leaning over the side, saw something that did look familiar. As she peered downward into the gently lapping water, she saw it. The swirling, pearlescent colors that lazily and gracefully caressed the rusted metal of the gun turrets. She could remember as an imaginative and, even then, overweight kid the pretty hues had looked remarkably like the sheeny opalescent bubbles that one could get out of the bottles at the K-Mart. She turned to Pete and laughingly repeated this.

Her husband's reaction was typical. "If that's the kind of shit you told the guys in high school, it ain't amazing that you never got laid. I'm just glad that no one from my school knows I settled for you. Back then I had a reputation to preserve. The things we do for money, eh' Hans?"

Delia's face burned and she could feel the tears make their way down her smooth cheeks where they dropped almost invisibly into the dark but clear waters. She was mortified at what a gentleman so obviously from another era must think of Pete and his treatment of her. But, as if he hadn't heard, Mr. Belfont was ushering her into the Shrine Room telling her it was a good place to reflect. Obediently, she went feeling only a little disconcerted when she heard Mr. Belfont urging Pete to come and see something he knew only he would appreciate.

It was dark and quiet in the Shrine Room. As her eyes adjusted to the light from the tastefully appointed insets, she could read all the names of the dead: a father and son; brothers. She began to weep again as she read the corresponding ages of the fallen. So many young—babies really. She turned to call to Pete, wanting him to see this. Even his heart could not be so hard. He certainly liked action pictures and here was evidence of men who had given the ultimate sacrifice for their country. She started to walk toward the doorway when she saw it: The same iridescent tendrils that swirled through the water surrounding the rusted hulk were now unbelievable undulating over the top of the guardrail and slithering across the floor of the memorial. Neither Pete nor Mr. Belfont seemed aware of this, however, because their backs were turned.

Their guide was generously refilling her husband's glass with a small flask produced from inside his natty sport coat. Pete was pontificating loudly that "some real changes" had to be made to "this place."

"Such as . . . ?" His host prompted politely.

"Well, Hans," he began, "for starters, I'd put a glass bottom on this thing. People love gruesome shit, and I for one would pay a hell of a lot more for this tour if I thought I was in for a glimpse of a corpse or two."

The smile on Mr. Belfont's face was positively beatific as he murmured, "Pete, my boy, you already have."

Delia saw her husband was puzzled by this ambiguous remark, but there was no time for him to voice this. Suddenly, the center part of the memorial was the shiny gray deck of a battleship and smoke was everywhere. The cries of the dead and the dying filled the air. Pieces of mangled bodies rained down on the sinewy youngsters and grown men alike as they rushed about the deck in a vain effort to aid their fallen comrades, blown sky high from the blast of the 1,760 pound armor piercing bomb that had slammed through the *Arizona*'s deck and ignited the forward ammunition magazine.

Delia could not see Pete or Mr. Belfont through the haze and, from somewhere deep inside, she knew she was not meant to. She turned away, closed her eyes, and prayed that it would stop. Then suddenly it did. She was by herself in the Shrine Room standing in the dark. She knew she was safe, without knowing why.

When she turned around again, only Mr. Belfont was there and the last of the swirling shapes were disappearing over the guardrail. Silently, she joined her guide and they left the memorial together.

As they drove back to the hotel, Delia watched the lights of the harbor recede behind them. She accepted the neat Scotch from her host, and decided she would look into getting in on some pleasurable island experiences. A nice, authentic luau sounded like just the ticket. After all, she thought, I am from the Show Me state.

Chapter 23

Burden of Guilt

By Rosemary Edghill

"You ever kill anyone?" Royce asked me idly.

It was April, and the two of us were working late at the Bookie Joint. There hadn't been enough work for weeks to keep it open with a full staff in its daytime incarnation as Houston Graphics, the graveyard of freelance book design, and there were rumors that Mikey was thinking of closing us down for good.

I wasn't sure how I felt about that. I'd known for years that this was a dead-end job, but my other life took all my time and energy. In that life, my real life, I'm a member of—to use a strictly anthropological definition—the adult-conversion, non-pastoral polytheism known as Wicca. But my particular side road of the Path has strict injunctions against taking money or recompense for the practice of my art, so I've got to do something to pay the rent. For quite some time now, freelance book design has been it.

"Kill?" I said. "As in murder? No." But I've tripped over an entirely unwarranted collection of corpses in my life, and come far too close on several occasions to being one myself. I glanced over the top of my worktable at my fellow inmate. Royce is one of the few Bookie Joint regulars who shares my outside interests, though in a tangential way: Royce is a Christian mystic whose path is the achievement of the Holy Grail. "You haven't started believing all those ugly rumors about us, have you?" "Us" as in witches, of which I am one.

He grinned at me. "No. It was a rhetorical question. I was trying to imagine what it must be like."

"I know what it's like," I said. Once I'd known a murderer very well, though I hadn't known he was a murderer until too late. "When you kill, you cut yourself off from everything that came before. And I don't know if you can ever go back to being what you were."

Royce looked at my expression, and his smile faded. "It must be like being separated from God, as Lucifer was when he fell."

I shrugged, but I understood. The gods are always with me, their presence a part of my world. I suppose the same holds true for any devout believer, which can lead to trouble, if what your gods tell you is to get rid of all the others. Fortunately, witches, as a tribe, don't tend to have that problem.

"You're going back there, aren't you? Tonight?" he added.

I sighed. Of course Royce knew the story, at least some of it. When you have to testify in a criminal case that gets newspaper ink in the *Times,* it's hard to keep it a big secret from your day job.

"Back to Gotham County, anyway. But I'll be miles from Paradise Lake. I'll be fine." I don't know which of us I was trying to convince. Maybe Royce believed me.

Because business was slow, I'd been looking around for alternate sources of revenue, and my good buddy Lark—now manager of the Serpent's Truth (the Snake), the largest and tackiest occult shop in Manhattan and possibly the world—had found me one. I still recalled the tact and decorum with which he'd pitched it to me.

* * *

"There's this moronic collection of woo-woo bliss-ninnies who're going off for a weekend of getting fleeced at a conference of big name New Agers in upstate New York. Geez, Bast, just check out this pamphlet—*all* the heavy-hitters, and you know they don't come cheap! Twelve hundred bucks for the weekend! Christ!"

"Well," I said, taking the glossy four-color pamphlet out of his hand and inspecting it, "it *does* include room and board. And it's indoors." But at a thousand and change, it was one festival I wouldn't be attending, even for the pleasure of going on a guided spirit quest and gaining my very own animal totem.

"The thing is, I know the organizer, Sister Moonwomon Divine———."

I stared at him.

"We slept together a couple of times a few years back—nothing serious," he added hastily. "Anyway, there'll be a books and supplies table at the conference, so the participants can buy the organizers' books and the ritual supplies they'll need, and T-shirts and souvenirs and shit, and her girlfriend usually runs it, but she broke her leg and can't do it this year, so Sister called me up and asked if I knew anyone local and responsible she could get to take care of it. She'll pay . . ."

He put on his best wheedling expression and batted his big blue eyes at me.

"What do you get out of it?" I asked, because with Lark it is always more restful to cut to the chase.

"She says I can send up some appropriate stock. She'll pay you $750 for the weekend, plus the same room and board that the rest of the festival attendees get. No workshops, of course."

"Thank the gods for that," I muttered, looking at the list of delights. Seven hundred and fifty dollars would go a long way toward easing the current financial crunch at chez Bast. "I'll need to borrow the van," I said.

* * *

Which was how, late on a Thursday night, I found myself heading back to a part of the world I'd sworn I'd never go near again.

I'd brought an actual suitcase full of my most upscale New York blacks, as from all accounts this was a very fancy event indeed, aimed at the post-yuppie New Age–end of the Aquarian Frontier, the sort of folks who didn't mind writing $1200 checks for a weekend of sage smudges, crystals, Tibetan crystal bowls, and chanting. I didn't expect to fit in and I didn't expect to have fun: what I expected to do was earn a large enough paycheck to keep the wolf from the door for another couple of months. Maybe it really was time to quit Houston Graphics and go find something a little less marginal.

There were four boxes of the Snake's fluffier high-end merchandise in the back of the ancient Ford van, along with a couple uniques that Lark thought I might be able to unload on the feckless wannabes. He might even be right; he had a good eye for what sold—under his management, the Snake was doing better than it had in years.

My destination, according to the paperwork and maps on the seat beside me, was the Tamerlane Conference Center, an idyllic rural retreat located on 50 landscaped acres in beautiful Gotham County.

The SpiritJourney QuestWithin Retreat officially began Friday afternoon with a Bonding Tea, but apparently Sister Moonwomon Divine was already on-site, and I'd be spending tomorrow morning getting the QuestWithin Mall of the Mysteries unpacked and set up.

According to the brochure, attendance at the SpiritJourney QuestWithin Retreat weekend was restricted to 500 seekers, none of whom could probably spell their chosen *noms de fluff* any better than Sister.

Gotham County is about 3 hours north of the city, between Dutchess and Columbia Counties. I'd driven to Hallowfest every year for the last several, and the Paradise Lake Campground where it was held was just down the road from Tamerlane, so I didn't see much problem with reaching the area before I got lost. I concentrated on practicing my bright and perky, something I'm not good at the best of times.

With only a few unplanned detours, I arrived around nine.

There was a bright new sign out front of the conference center, painted and gilded wood and expensively floodlit, that proclaimed this to be the Tamerlane Conference Center. A pair of iron gates, pegged back between a set of tall fieldstone posts, led me up a blacktopped, thoroughly landscaped drive. The building itself wasn't visible from the road.

When I got to the top, I got a mild surprise. I'd thought the building would match the sign—new, trendy, and smart as paint—but it didn't. It had been cleaned and refurbished to within an inch of its life, and was extensively floodlit, but the building itself was old—turn of the century, at least. It looked vaguely institutional. I wondered what it had been before it became a conference center.

I parked the van next to a little red car that screamed airport rental, picked up the big tote that had everything I'd need for tonight, and walked up to the side door wondering how I was going to get in. The door said service entrance, and there was a buzzer. I pushed it and heard it echo all the way down inside. At least the lights were on. I could see a hallway done in early corporate.

About the time I was considering digging out my phone and calling Sister's phone, a woman in a business suit appeared. Aside from the eye makeup, which would have done credit to Liz Taylor circa *Cleopatra,* and a lot of trophy wife jewelry, she was a good match for the building, being done in early corporate herself: designer suit, killer heels, very manicured nails. Her hair was expensively, unnaturally blond, and elaborately secured at the back of her head in a sweet disorder.

She peered uncertainly through the door.

"Lark sent me," I said, raising my voice to be heard through the glass.

Her expression cleared. She twisted the lock and swung the door inward.

"Hello," she said. Her voice matched the package, expensive and professional. "I'm Sister Moonwomon Divine."

I'd been practicing perky and nonjudgmental for so long that my face felt frozen, which was a good thing. I don't think I gave away any of the disbelief I felt. I'd thought she was some sort of corporate facilitator that came with the building. She didn't look anything like the wild-haired wolf-running maenad in the brochure's publicity picture.

"I'm Bast," I said, stepping inside. She locked the door carefully behind me again.

"Is that all you brought?" she asked, looking from my leather jacket, T-shirt, and jeans, down to my Doc Martens, and back.

"The rest of my stuff's in the car. I didn't think I'd need it for tonight. I just wore this for the unpacking and the heavy lifting."

She looked relieved. "You understand, we want to provide a certain experience here," she said delicately.

"I clean up very well."

She smiled and patted my arm reassuringly. "I know you've had a long drive. It was so good of you to agree to do this on such short notice. Would you like something to eat? I've been here since this morning, making sure everything would be ready, so the water's hot and the elevators work. You can shower if you want."

A room with a private bath. I was beginning to understand why these weekends cost $1200 bucks.

"If I could get a cup of coffee or something, that would be great," I said.

"Sure! I just put up a fresh pot! All our meals at the SpiritJourney Quest-Within Retreat are fully organically catered, of course, but the food service won't be starting until tomorrow afternoon, so I picked up a few groceries to tide us over until then—nothing fancy, just cold cuts and eggs. Lark told me you eat meat?"

She looked worried, and I hastened to assure her that I was fully canni-bal. "So do I, sometimes," she assured me, her voice dropping as though she was telling secrets. "Not beef, of course; you can never tell what might be in it. But I don't think there's any harm in chicken or pork, do you?"

I assured her I found both perfectly harmless, and she led me off to the Tamerlane Conference kitchen. You could have dropped down all of Houston Graphics in the middle of it and had room left over for my apartment. I opened one of the industrial-sized refrigerators at random; empty.

"The caterers arrive tomorrow morning to drop off the food and the ser-vice staff," she said. "Just sit anywhere."

I found a stool and seated myself at the long, center food-prep counter, while Sister proceeded to serve me with her own fair hands, setting out filled mug, sugar, milk, and spoon with brisk efficiency. I suspected that in a pre-vious life she'd been a very good waitress.

"You really ought to eat something," she said, peering into another of the cavernous refrigerators. "A sandwich is no trouble, really. What would you like?"

"Anything," I said feebly. It was easier to go along with her than to argue, which was undoubtedly the secret of her success. I doctored my coffee and took a sip. If this was what she was going to be serving all weekend, this might actually be painless.

By the time I'd taken my first sip and set the cup down, she'd assembled a sandwich with lettuce, tomato, two kinds of cheese, and several different kinds of cold cuts. My stomach rumbled, reminding me that I'd skipped din-ner and hadn't stopped to eat on the way up.

"See?" she said triumphantly. "You *are* hungry. You just didn't know it."

I leaned forward to pick it up, and as I did, my pentagram slipped out of my shirt and dangled free.

Most witches and pagans wear them, the upright star-in-circle that's the badge of-allegiance of our particular patch of the Aquarian Frontier. It's a harmless symbol, about as neutral as Ivory soap. Mine's about the size of a dime; it's the thought that counts.

"You're not going to wear that, are you?" she asked, wrinkling her nose and pointing to my chaste, silver pendant.

"I'll keep it inside my shirt."

"Some of our seekers find it Satanic."

I looked at her to see if she was joking. She wasn't.

"I'll be careful," I said blandly.

But our budding rapport had cooled, which puzzled me. She knew Lark, and he wasn't even a little quiet about his religious beliefs. She spent the rest of our time together covering the things I'd need to know for tomorrow: in-ventory control, credit card validation (there'd be a modem hookup and an electronic cash register set up in the bookstore), and what to do with the cash at the end of the day.

Then, to my surprise, she gave me an envelope.

"Here's your check for the weekend." The envelope wasn't sealed. I looked inside. A cashier's check for $750, just as Lark had said. I tucked it into my purse.

"I'll show you to your room now."

* * *

The room was small, and looked a little more like a dorm room than a hotel room, but it was stone luxury by the standards of a pagan festival. She handed me the keycard, and said she'd like to get started on the setting up by nine, if that worked out for me. I said that wouldn't be a problem. She said if I was up earlier, I should feel free to come on down to the kitchen and make myself breakfast and that she'd be up doing a dawn meditation.

"Look, Bast," she said as we both stood in the doorway. "About the pentacle . . ."

I waited.

"I didn't mean to come down on you so hard. I know it's not a Satanic symbol—I'm a witch myself, you know—but the people coming here this weekend . . ."

"Aren't," I finished for her. "They won't see a thing." In more ways than one, I was sure.

She smiled, looking tired beneath all that makeup. "We have to be so careful. Where there's money, there's litigation. Sleep well."

Oddly enough, I didn't remember seeing that phrase in my *Book of Shadows.*

She left. I closed the door.

She'd been up here earlier, making sure the room was ready for my arrival, I guessed. She'd left a book on the bed. I picked it up: *Chasing the Moon: A Spiritual Journey by Sister Moonwomon Divine.* I looked at the author's color photo on the back—Sister standing in front of Stonehenge wearing several enormous amber necklaces and coiling bracelets up both arms. Her hair was a flowing leonine mane and a gauzy white caftan that seemed to be composed of several layers of artful tatters. Both hands were raised to the sky, and a probable wind machine off-camera fluttered the tatters dramatically. She looked like the chief druidess in an MGM epic.

I consulted the flap copy and discovered that Sister was an Initiated Priestess of the Arkan Sonney Wicca Tradition, of which I'd never heard—that didn't mean anything other than if she were a witch, she was at the far end of the bell curve from my kind. But I hadn't come up here to find friends and co-religionists.

The bathroom was on the same scale as the bedroom—small and Spartan—but it had a walk-in shower, and the water was hot. I did my best to exhaust the Tamerlane Conference Center's hot water supply and got into bed.

I'd brought a book, but Sister's offering seemed more entertaining. I read a few chapters about her spiritual journey until the day and the drive caught up with me, and then I slept.

* * *

My travel alarm jarred me awake at seven, and for a few moments I could not imagine where I was. I'd left the curtains open as an aid to consciousness, and the green leaves and blue sky I could see when I looked out were actively disorienting. I am an urban creature at heart. Eventually I remembered about the retreat, and then the lure of coffee was enough to get me up, dressed, and moving. I slipped my pentacle off over my head and looped the chain through a bra strap, tucking it down out of sight.

The kitchen was deserted when I reached it, but the coffee was brewed and waiting in a warming carafe beside a cup and fixings all ready, set out on the table. I took in-depth advantage.

There was still no sign of Sister, so I decided to go empty the van next. By the time I was done stacking the boxes and my suitcase inside the service entrance, she'd reappeared.

Today she was in a transitional state between the corporate avenger I'd seen yesterday and the druid priestess of the book cover. She wore a pale mauve, silk jogging suit with an aqua silk T-shirt beneath the jacket, and hot pink espadrilles. Her hair was caught back in a loose ponytail. The makeup was still the same, as were the rings, but the rest of the jewelry had been given a rest.

"Why don't you take your suitcase upstairs and we can get started?" she said brightly. It was nowhere near nine, but she was the one calling the shots this weekend.

Fortunately, other unseen minions had been here before me to assemble the selling booth; my function was merely to stock and run it. It was big—the sort you'd find at major trade shows—emblazoned with the SpiritJourney QuestWithin Retreat logo in full purple and gold on the back, with power strips, phone hookups, lights, a counter for the cash register, and racks and shelves for the merchandise.

I'd dealt with her type before, so there weren't any surprises in finding that her contribution to the work that followed was restricted entirely to telling me where to put things.

There was a resident conference staff. They arrived promptly at 8:45-I checked my watch—and began bustling. I did not pay excessive attention to them, but Sister did. Around ten, she told me I'd have to move my van because the catering trucks were here. I did, taking care to park it in the hinterlands of the extensive parking lot, where I probably would not be called upon to move it again until I left Monday.

Or so I thought then.

At intervals during the morning Sister interrupted her administrative duties to welcome the conference presenters. The majority of them were women with, shall we say, carefully managed public personas. Some of them I knew by reputation: There were Coyote Dawn, the spirit woman who'd built one-sixteenth Cherokee ancestry into a major career, and was now a genuine member of the Wannabe Tribe of the Marabou Nation; Harper Merrow, a B-list novelist turned gen-u-wine Priestess of the Old Ways from the hereditary royal line of Boudicca (assuming, of course that Boudicca had stopped by Marin County, California); and several more that I didn't recognize.

And one I did.

"Bast! What are you doing here!"

I swung around fast with my arms full of books and nearly collided with probably the one genuine witch queen here this weekend: Lady Freya. Freya is my former HPS Belle's Queen—meaning the woman who brought her into the craft and to the point of running a coven of her own—and in her other life, a social anthropologist of some note and writer of popular books on the feminine images of the Divine. In her tweed jacket and jeans, she looked like a postcard from normalcy and very much like the college professor she still is sometimes.

I had to think for a moment before I could change gears enough to remember her legal name, Sheila Steinmetz, Ph.D.

"Um. Working?" I suggested.

"So am I. *Channeling the Goddess Within.* New book. Tour. Lecture. It's a good lecture. You should come."

"I'm just running the bookshop. I think I'll be pretty busy."

"Oh well, maybe next month. Lark's trying to get me to do it down at the Snake." We both laughed. A lecture by Sheila Steinmetz is not inexpensive to book, and we both knew the Snake couldn't afford her.

"Maybe you could do a signing there?" I suggested. Over her shoulder I could see Sister bearing down on us, intent on her prey and looking disgruntled that I'd connected first.

"I'll call you," she said. "Blessed be!"

I waved. Freya turned to Sister. They exchanged happytalk noises. I got back to work.

It was a good 4 hours before everything that could be shelved was shelved, and the rest of the stock and boxes were stacked behind the kiosk to open later. In the process, I'd come across Freya's new book, which looked interesting. The displays of the presenters' books were assembled and arranged outside the booths, and I knew without being told that I'd be spending every spare minute reorganizing things. So much for sneaking off to any lectures, even if doing that weren't on the forbidden list.

"It's a good start," Sister said, coming back. She dug through a box of SpiritJourney T-shirts and handed me one. "Here. For you. I think you've earned this."

She was watching me. I got the sense she was expecting something, but I wasn't quite sure what.

"Thank you." I channeled sincerity.

"Time for lunch. There's a pick-up buffet set up in the dining room. Nothing fancy. And then I think we'd better both get cleaned up. The rest of the presenters will be arriving soon—and then the guests!"

Translation: You'd better look a lot less New York. I knew the kiosk wouldn't be opening for business until noon tomorrow, but I'd have plenty of work to do to get it completely ready to go by then.

I moved all the displays I'd just set out back inside the kiosk and turned off the lights. Sister pulled the flexible plastic security mesh across the front of the opening and locked it, then handed me the little ring of keys to the various locks.

"This is yours for the weekend. And this. Don't lose it."

"Thanks," I said. She'd given me a nametag. It said Staff in large, friendly letters.

"I wasn't sure what name to put on it."

"This is fine."

I stuffed the key ring into my jeans, then took my T-shirt and headed for the elevator. I was looking forward to lunch, but somehow on this occasion I thought personal grooming might just take precedence.

I checked my copy of the schedule: Registration opened at three, the tea ran from 3 to 6 (none of the presenters attended that, I noted), dinner was at 7, opening ceremonies were at 9, and something called a Chthonic Mysteries Spiritwalk was scheduled for midnight. The bookshop wasn't open until tomorrow. It had intermittent hours: Open from 8 to 10 A.M., from 4 to 7, and again from 7:30 'til 9.

I unpacked my suitcase and put myself more sartorially in tune with SpiritJourney QuestWithin Retreat's presumed demographic, then went back downstairs. By now it was coming up on noon.

I collected a plate and ate quickly, then took a cup of coffee and got back to work at the kiosk. There were 10 presenters here this weekend, plus SpiritJourney QuestWithin, Inc., plus the Snake, and they all had inventory lists that had to be kept in order and checked off each time an item was sold. I'd made sure everything was here and matched the inventories when I'd unpacked them, but keeping up with them all weekend was going to keep me busy.

While I was working, the conference center staff came in and started setting up registration at the other end of the room, right across from the front doors, and soon enough, the attendees began to arrive.

I'd been curious about what these people might look like. Most of them weren't pagans, as I understood the term: They weren't religious to the extent of offering their devotion to a specific pantheon of gods or even to a school of philosophy. They were spiritual, that vague, ill-defined impulse toward, well, something that my stretch of the Aquarian Frontier often defines, rudely, as "thinking happy thoughts." As they began to arrive, I watched them covertly.

As I expected—considering the price tag of the weekend—the median age for the group was high thirties. Three-quarters were women, with a lot more makeup than you'd see at an equivalent pagan festival; expensive "natural" clothes; souvenir T-shirts from similar festivals, including previous SpiritJourney QuestWithin Retreats; beads, crystals, feathers, and pendants; and a lot of Southwestern jewelry, mostly on the men. A few Coach bags and business suits suggested an early leave-taking from the day job. A lot of them knew each other. I caught scraps of talk. They were looking forward to this event the way I'd looked forward to my initiation.

It made me sad for them. They were eating goblin fruit. These people wanted to be happy. They wanted connection and validation as much as anyone else who goes seeking outside the established traditional faiths and teaching of our, or any, culture. But unlike others, no better-trodden path had caught their feet. They wandered, like Kai Lung, through a garden of bright images, attracted by the soft and bright, the pretty and formless. And so they never found anything that truly changed them that they could take back with them into their own lives to keep and use. They had to keep coming back for another fix.

Or maybe I was just jealous.

* * *

"Is the shop open yet?"

I looked up from my paperwork.

A woman with tumbled blond curls—bleached and permed—was standing in front of the counter. She was one of the business-suited ones and had an indefinable Midwestern look about her. She'd been through registration, so I could see that her name was Marcie Wheeler and that she hailed from Lexington, Kentucky. Above the name printed on the badge, she'd written Dawnchylde in flowing purple letters. There was a rhinestone unicorn pin on her lapel.

"Not 'til tomorrow," I said.

"Oh," she said, looking dismayed. Her suit was a businesslike violet; her blouse was pink; her lipstick coordinated. If I looked over the edge of the counter, I was willing to bet she was wearing pumps and that they'd match the suit. I wondered what Dawnchylde did in real life—sold real estate? Probably.

"I really wanted to buy a T-shirt."

"We open at eight tomorrow," I said, trying to sound kind. "I'm still setting up."

She deflated completely, one of those people it didn't take much to crush. "Sorry. I'll come back." She picked up her suitcase and teetered off. I peered over the edge of the counter. I would have lost my bet; the shoes were brown.

I wish now I'd sold her the damned T-shirt. What harm would it have done?

* * *

I got the kiosk as organized as it was going to get, tucked everything back inside, locked it up again, and realized I still had a couple of hours to kill before dinner—after which I'd have several more hours to kill. I thought briefly about driving down into Tamerlane proper in search of the local nightlife and decided I wasn't quite that desperate.

For now, I thought I'd go for a walk.

The conference center grounds were nicely landscaped with extensive pathways leading here and there and intermittent benches. I walked most of the way around the conference center. The parking lot was full of cars by now, a number of which possessed declarative bumper stickers: Magic Happens, The Earth Is Our Mother, I'm Sorry My Karma Ran Over Your Dogma. Hearts, pentagrams, yin-yangs, roses, unicorns, pegusai, fairies, and other mystical symbols abounded. I wondered what Sister would say about the pentagrams.

I still couldn't figure out what the conference center used to be.

Eventually it was dinnertime, so I dined. The food was both vegetarian and organic. The meals were served buffet style, with the tables going up by number. I was seated at the main table, with the presenters, so I got to go first. At least this settled the question of how I'd be able to get out to the kiosk in a timely fashion in the morning.

"How is everything going?" Sister asked. Sister was in her full she-druid garb now, and clanked when she walked. I liked the woman I'd met last night in the kitchen better.

"Just fine," I said, remembering to be upbeat. "And you?"

"Oh, the usual. You didn't tell me you knew Sheila."

I blinked. There was an undercurrent here I'd have to be deaf to ignore. Had I been supposed to tell Sister Moonwomon Divine about every mildly famous person I knew? I certainly wasn't going to mention our craft connection, even though Sheila is a fairly public witch. One of the rules of my branch of the craft is that you never make a fellow witch's affiliation public knowledge. "We have mutual friends. I wasn't expecting to see her here."

"I had a last-minute cancellation and she was able to fill in. Isn't it wonderful?"

"She's a great speaker," I said.

Again I got the sense that Sister was waiting for something, and I'd fluffed my lines. But whatever it was, she let it go, and I was left in peace.

After dinner, I retreated to my room again. According to the glossy brochures I'd picked up at the business office during my afternoon rambles, the Tamerlane Conference Center wasn't even full at the moment ("offering a fine selection of dormitory-, single-, and double-occupancy accommodations for every need", it said here), and as far as I could tell, I was still the only occupant of the fifth floor. It hadn't occurred to me I'd be so isolated here, though it was only a problem for tonight; tomorrow I'd be busy long after the kiosk closed. I opened the window and leaned out. Oh, to be in Gotham, now that April's here.

I went back to reading Sister's account of her spiritual journey, wishing I'd thought to bring a copy of Freya's book up from downstairs.

If you were a properly jaundiced reader, with sufficient practice in reading between the lines, it was fairly easy to separate the truth from the poetically crafted image building, but I doubted her core readership had either the experience or the critical tools for that—or the desire, for that matter. They wanted to believe what she told them, and she was smart enough to know what they wanted to believe. And so she unreeled a tale of detailed past-life experiences, long conversations with the Sidhe, and spirit animals of all nations. The message, when you peeled away all the gingerbread gilding, was a comforting one: I used to be wonderful in a previous life that doesn't bear too close examination, and probably you can make similar claims if you try; and no matter what's wrong with your life now, you don't need to fix it, because it's all part of a purpose and a plan; so just relax and feel good about yourself, because you used to be somebody important, and people should treat you as if you still are.

It's a seductive message. The temptation to live in the past always is. But there's no oxygen there.

From my current mood, there was no oxygen here, either.

I gave up and went to sleep.

* * *

I hit the kiosk bright and early Saturday morning, and it was just as well. Apparently half the attendees had been waiting all year just to shop here. After the first few transactions, I found out why: There'd be a party tonight after dinner where everyone could get their books autographed. I'd thought, when I'd been opening and checking everything, that there were way too many books here. Now I thought we just might run out.

I didn't see Marcie Wheeler anywhere.

At 9:55 A.M. I started shooing people out of the kiosk, telling them we'd open again at four. Fifteen minutes later, the last of them had drifted off to their workshops.

I did the financial housekeeping and took the cash over to the conference center safe.

When I came back, trouble was standing in the middle of the entry hall, looking for someone to tell its problems to. Trouble was a white-haired lady who looked like she was dressed for a couple rounds of golf. She looked ill.

"Young woman, could you help me?" she asked. "There's . . . I think there's a problem."

"What kind of a problem?" I asked, guiding her over to one of the benches along the walls. Her nametag said Samantha Collins, Asbury Park, New Jersey.

"I think a young woman may be ill. Back there. I got lost looking for my workshop, and . . . I think she's hurt."

"Samantha, why don't you wait right here and let me go take a look?" I said. "Can you do that for me?"

She nodded.

"I'll be right back. Stay here."

I took off, not running. Not where anyone could see.

The brochure had a layout of the floor plan of the center. All the meeting rooms were on the first floor. The retreat was using only a few of the larger ones on this side of the building. The ones back in the direction Samantha had pointed were small, and there were a lot of them. The conference center was much larger than it looked from the outside.

I started running as soon as I was out of sight, for a lot of reasons—the way she'd looked, the way she'd sounded, the way she couldn't make up her mind whether the woman she'd seen was ill or hurt.

As it happened, she was neither.

Marcie Wheeler was never going to be coming back for her T-shirt.

I stood in the doorway. Marcie lay doll still on her back in the middle of the floor, tumbled as if she'd fallen. She was wearing a dress instead of the suit I'd last seen her in, something pale purple that sparkled, suitable for evening. She would have changed after I'd seen her. Her eyes were wide open and quite dry.

Her face was much the color of the dress, a color no face gets under natural circumstances.

I took a step back, feeling the world go pale and cold. Part of me wanted to walk away, get in the van, drive, and keep driving. Part of me knew I couldn't, and I was thankful that . . . what? I'd stumbled on so many bodies before?

What to do first? I took a deep breath. Find Sister and tell her, then call the police.

I went back out to the foyer. Samantha had disappeared—so much for my bedside manner.

* * *

I opened doors until I found Sister's workshop. Seventy people were seated on the floor, om-ing in unison with their eyes closed. She looked up when she saw me. I beckoned.

"That's right, just keep on. Feel the energy," she said. "Pull it up from the earth beneath you; let it flow through you. Breathe. I'll be right back."

She came outside. I closed the door.

"One of your attendees is dead," I said. "Marcie Wheeler. Another one found the body, but I'm not sure she realizes Marcie's dead."

Sister took a deep breath, indicating she'd been using her own techniques to good purpose. "When? How did she die? Where is she?" She glared at me.

"She's in one of the conference rooms in the other wing. I don't know how she died or when. And that's why we have to call the police."

For a moment I thought she'd refuse. Then she smiled. It wasn't a nice smile at all. "Fine. You handle it. You have some experience in these matters, don't you?"

At that moment I made up my mind about Sister Moonwomon Divine. I didn't like her at all.

* * *

I am a packrat. I hang onto business cards when I am given them. It wasn't hard to dig out Sergeant Fayrene Pascoe's card from my wallet. I made the call, hoping she was on days. Better the law you know than the law you don't.

"Pascoe."

"Sergeant Pascoe, this is Karen Hightower. I'm calling from the Tamerlane Conference Center on Route 6."

"Bast, you'd better not be calling to report another murder," she said. Fayrene was the deputy involved with all the trouble at Hallowfest the last time I'd been here. She remembered me. Her son, Wyler, is a pagan; Fayrene isn't sure she approves.

"I hope I'm not."

There was a pause, and when she spoke again, her voice had changed completely, to her cop voice. "Tell me."

"One of the conference attendees is dead. Her name is Marcie Wheeler. I don't know how she died exactly. I found the body a few minutes ago, after one of the other attendees, Samantha Collins, told me that a woman seemed to be sick or injured. I went to look."

"You're remarkably well-informed," Fayrene said dryly.

"They all wear nametags." I sounded bitter, even to me. I'd come up here to exorcise old ghosts and ended up replaying old murders.

"I'll be there as soon as I can."

"Come in the side. I'll wait for you there."

* * *

Fayrene was there within 15 minutes. She wore a pale tan Stetson that always seems so out of place here in the East and the rest of the usual sheriff's deputy paraphernalia: black leather belt and a truly enormous gun. She has pale blue eyes and strawberry-blond hair to which humidity is unkind. She keeps it short.

"Show me," she said, when I let her in.

It took me a couple of tries to find the right room.

"And the door was open when you came by here?"

I had to think about it. "About halfway. Samantha might have left it open, though. She said she'd gotten lost looking for her workshop."

"And you didn't go in?"

"No."

"But you closed it when you left?"

"Yes."

Fayrene stood beside me, regarding the body. "What else?" she said.

"I saw her—Marcie—when she checked in. I'm running the bookshop this weekend. She wanted to buy a T-shirt. She was wearing a business suit, so she must have changed clothes. This looks like something she'd wear for the tea, or for dinner, not for one of the late-night workshops."

"Many of those?"

"There was a SpiritWalk at midnight last night. I don't know if she went; I was in bed."

Fayrene sighed. "I think I'll take a closer look." She walked into the room and gazed down at the body for a long moment, then pulled out her radio. "Best to call the suits now and save ourselves all some shouting," she said to me.

If she was calling for a detective, that meant she knew for sure what I hadn't wanted to let myself believe: It was murder.

I backed up to where I could lean against the opposite wall. I wasn't frightened, and I wasn't angry. I was tired. I would have been indignant if I'd had the energy.

Fayrene was talking into her radio, doing all the things I remembered from the last time I'd participated in this little dance. Soon we'd have the M.E., the crime scene, and the rest.

"Can they try to keep this low key?" I asked when she'd finished.

"Tamerlane Conference Center is the local cash cow," she said. "They'll do their best. Now why don't you make yourself useful and stand right here for about 5 minutes?" She came out and closed the door.

In fact, she was back in 3, with a roll of yellow tape that said *Police Line: Do Not Cross* to liberally decorate the door.

I thought about asking if I could go back to what I'd been doing—it was tempting—but Sister would want somebody at least tenuously connected with the retreat around. So I stayed, compromising by going back and hanging around by the service entrance. Fayrene stayed by the door.

More cars showed up. I checked my watch. It was a little after twelve, now. The morning workshops would be ending in another hour. If they could get out of here soon, maybe 500 people would never know what had happened.

It went fast. I stayed down the hall, where I couldn't see any of it. More old friends arrived.

Detective Lieutenant Tony Wayne is a solid, dark-haired, ordinary looking man with brown eyes, a bushy moustache, and a gold shield. Because he works in Gotham County, inevitably, his nickname is Bat.

Bat wasn't sure if he was pleased to see me.

"Why is it every time a bunch of woo-woos shows up around here I get you?" he said.

"I'm being paid to be here this time," I said.

"You running this?" he asked in mild disbelief.

"Sister Moonwomon Divine is the organizer of the SpiritJourney Quest-Within Retreat," I said, with perhaps more primness than the occasion demanded. "I'm just running the bookstore."

He went off to talk to the rest of the law. While I waited for him to come back, Marcie Wheeler left the conference, this time in a body bag.

"Why isn't she here?" Bat said, coming back. It took me a moment to remember what we'd been talking about.

"She's teaching a workshop right now." I checked my watch again. "It should be over at one. She'll be glad to talk to you then."

"I'll bet." Bat grinned without humor. "And this—whaddya Samantha Collins—she's the one that actually found the body? When?"

"I think it was about 10:30 when I saw her. She said she'd seen a woman who was ill or hurt, so I told her to stay put out in front and went looking. When I saw————" I stopped. "I went and told Sister and called Fay———— Sergeant Pascoe."

"And where is she now?"

I shrugged. "I don't know. Lunch is in half an hour," I added helpfully. "Everybody should be there."

"And Ms. Moonwomon Divine just left all this with you?" Bat asked skeptically.

"I have so much experience as a police liaison," I said.

My sarcasm didn't impress him.

"Fine. Then you can get us some coffee, find a room where I can interview a few people, pull Ms. Wheeler's registration forms, and get me the key to her room."

I started to do as I was told and stopped.

"Detective? Where was her purse? Where was she keeping her room key?"

Bat favored me with a sour stare. "Honey, leave the detecting to the professionals. Now scat."

I did. On my way to the kitchen, I picked a likely looking conference room, made sure it was set up with a table and chairs (some were; some weren't) and made a note of the number. Then I ordered an urn of coffee and set-ups for a dozen to be sent there immediately, charged to the retreat's bill.

Next I went to the office to see if I could find out who was in which room. I couldn't, but I could get a master passcard. The room assignments were with the registration information, which was in boxes on top of a desk in another office, waiting to be packed up and shipped off with Sister and her traveling road show come Monday. I paged through the *W*s until I came to Marcie's file. There were several sheets of paper in it. One of them was a sheet of trackfeed paper with a Tamerlane Conference Center watermark and Marcie's credit card information and room number.

I carried my ill-gotten spoils back to Bat, arriving at about the same time as the coffee and Sister Moonwomon Divine. She was slopping him all over with sugar—as my friends from south of the Mason-Dixen line would say— pumping out the star power and anguish in equal measure.

"Oh, *there* you are, Bast!" she said, rounding on me. She beamed at Bat and me, showing both of us how much she adored me. "So good of you to pitch right in. I don't know what I'd do without her. Isn't that right? But I can take care of things from here. I'm sure you have things you need to be doing."

It was self-aggrandizement and patronization and dismissal, all wrapped up into one expert, candy-coated package to sell to the law. Whatever I might have said to them could be discounted, because I was a mere employee, and probably not too bright besides.

I felt my face go rigid. I knew I was sending all the wrong signals, and I was going to pay for it later. The rich and powerful and insecure do not like being dissed, but I couldn't help it. She was not a nice woman. Maybe she tried to be, when it was easy, but down inside, where it counted, she wasn't.

"Here's the file you asked for, Detective. And the key. The coffee's in the room down the hall. I'm sure Ms. Divine won't mind you using it. I'd better get back to work." I got out of there fast.

I stopped in the dining room because, although I wasn't at all hungry, I wanted a great deal of coffee, and that was the only place to get it. The dining room was full of people fresh from a morning full of self-actualization and personal empowerment, and I could tell within 5 minutes that any lid Sister wanted to keep on things was doomed to failure.

I wasn't surprised that everyone at the retreat knew there'd been a death—rumor walks through walls—or even that they thought it was murder. It was the rest of it that I didn't expect.

Freya nailed me while I was loading mugs of coffee onto a tray.

"So what happened?" she asked.

"One of the attendees died," I said. "Sister is talking to the police now."

"I'm sorry, Bast. You didn't need something like this to happen. Is there anything I can do?"

"I don't think I'm on Sister's list of favorite people right now," I said, taking my tray over to the main table. Freya followed. I noticed that she was wearing her pentagram openly. Apparently it wasn't Satanic when worn by the possessor of a doctoral degree.

"She's just upset. She doesn't want any bad publicity," Freya said.

I remembered what Sister told me the first night: Where there's money, there's litigation. I wondered what kind of trouble this could lead to for the retreat. "I'm told the police are going to be sensitive." I drank coffee.

"People are saying the woman was murdered," Freya said casually.

I shrugged. "The police don't confide in me, but there's a detective over there."

"By a ghost."

She'd timed it perfectly. I had to work very hard to keep the coffee going in the right direction. Once I managed to swallow, I turned and looked at her. She kept a straight face, but there was a wry sparkle in her eye, a glint of humor at the foibles of our fellow travelers.

"A ghost," I repeated, when I could talk.

"The conference center used to be a psychiatric hospital. It closed, got bought, and was turned into this place. Therefore, it's haunted by its previous inmates, one of whom killed . . . ?"

"Marcie Wheeler. Is any of this true?"

"It did used to be a psychiatric hospital. Is it haunted? I have no idea. If you're interested, why don't you give Daffydd a call? He was talking about doing a book on hauntings of the Hudson Valley awhile back, and he might still have his notes."

Daffydd has another name when Columbia signs his paychecks. He's Belle's off-and-on working partner, and a student of practically everything.

"I'll do that. Thanks."

She clapped me on the shoulder, got up, and went off to talk to someone who looked as if he'd left his horse parked outside—one of the other presenters, I assumed. I drank coffee, and while I did, I managed to stop thinking about this morning and straighten out in my mind what had been so odd about Thursday night and Sister's behavior, then and now.

I was supposed to worship and adore, and I'd blown my lines. Here had been this great and powerful famous person waiting on me, treating me as an equal, and I was supposed to melt down into a quivering bundle of jelly. And I hadn't. So then she'd taken me up to a high place, and shown me all the kingdoms of the earth—or at least a large cashier's check—and I still hadn't caved. It must have puzzled her desperately.

But in the craft, my patch of it, we are all equals. I may be enormously impressed with Sheila Steinmetz's latest book, but that does not affect the way I treat Lady Freya.

Sister just didn't get it.

I drank my coffee, though not in peace. I was privileged to listen in on too many urban legend conversations—all running much along the lines Freya had laid out for me—and when I went back out to the kiosk to do the house-keeping I should have been doing all morning, the conversations followed me there. People were clustered in the foyer in small, excited clumps, all retailing rumor at market rates.

Item: The present Tamerlane Conference Center had been the former Gotham County Psychiatric Hospital and therefore, was full of evil vibes and the unexorcised ghosts of deranged murderers and others who had died there under evil circumstances.

Item: Because the late Marcie Wheeler was so very psychic, one of the ghosts, specifically a serial killer named Edward Madison who was committed here sometime in the 60s, killed her.

Item: The conference room in which she died was the genuine former location of the electroshock therapy lab in which Madison was tortured to death. And so on.

It is not, of course, that I don't believe in ghosts or for that matter, bad vibes and deranged murderers, but few ghosts survive as enthusiastic a renovation job as the conference center neé asylum had undergone. Fewer still strangle a victim all the way to death and then make off with her purse afterward.

* * *

I tried to put the whole matter out of my mind. A little after one, the attendees disappeared to their various workshops, and I got down to the serious business of restocking the shelves. I wondered if I could go without sleep until Monday. I wondered if I could get through the rest of the weekend without being told off by Sister, or saying anything to her that I'd regret if I were a better person. I wondered if there were any new and entertaining ways of killing Lark that I hadn't contemplated yet.

I pulled out a copy of *Channeling the Goddess Within,* paid for it, and bagged it. If I wasn't going to sleep tonight, I was going to have some reading matter to keep me company that was less incendiary than Sister's auto-hagiography.

Sister showed up about the time that I was finishing up. As an experiment, I tried on a large, meaningless smile, just to see if I could do it. It seemed to disconcert her.

"The police need to see you now," she said. "They'll want to take a statement."

"All right," I said. I got up, shut down the power to the kiosk, and locked it. I headed in the direction of the interview room. To my mild surprise, she followed.

"I want to talk to you, too," she said, when we were out of the foyer.

I stopped, obedient as any lackey.

"I don't want you talking to the presenters or spreading any rumors," she said. "We have enough trouble here this weekend."

"Fine," I said evenly. "I'll tell Sheila you told me I can't talk to her. The rumors seem to be doing fine on their own. Is there anything else?"

Her nostrils flared. I noticed with a detached interest that there was a white line around the edge of her mouth where her foundation ended and her lipstick began, but when you've faced people who were actually and literally intending to kill you, it's hard to work up a lot of interest in people who are merely irritated with you.

"I don't like your attitude."

I thought of telling her I didn't like it much myself, but restrained myself. In fact, I liked it rather too much for my own good.

"I'm sorry you're unhappy." I thought of explaining to her that Sheila was a friend of mine and that she'd approached me, but it seemed like too much trouble. I waited.

I'd expected ultimatums or at least another round of warnings. I got something different.

"Well, this has been a strain for all of us, hasn't it? Especially after your friend was murdered up here last year. I'm sorry I snapped at you, Bast. You go ahead and talk to the police. I'll see you later."

She patted me on the arm and walked off, leaving me as confused as I'd been yet, not least of all by her flip-flop from fury to conciliation. I wondered if either of them had been genuine. Her information certainly wasn't.

A year ago last October, a local hellfire-and-brimstone preacher named Jackson Harm had been murdered at Hallowfest, the NeoPagan Festival that meets over at the Paradise Lake Campground, a few miles down the road. The killer had been the Snake's former manager, Julian Fletcher, someone I'd thought I knew better than it turned out I did. Julian was alive and well, though not likely to be receiving visitors anytime soon.

I went down to where the rest of the police presence was. Bat was long gone, of course. A technician fingerprinted me—on the off-chance, I supposed, that they'd be able to get some useful fingerprints off the door or doorknob—and a deputy I didn't know took my statement and gave me a standard release to sign. He said I'd have to come down to the station to sign the final version when it was typed up. We agreed that tomorrow would be fine for that. I was uncomfortably conscious of being rather well known in these parts and somewhat too familiar with the ritual dance that surrounds a murder investigation. The deputies packed up and left. I'd been the last item on their agenda.

I went up to my room to wash the black gunk off my hands. While I was there, I decided to take the chance and give Daffydd a call.

He answered on the first ring. I told him where I was and what I was doing, leaving out the murder and police. He expressed cautious and appropriate sympathy.

"The thing is," I said, "the inmates are saying the place is haunted. Freya said you might know."

"Haunted." I could hear his ears prick up. "It used to be a mental hospital?"

"In Gotham County, just outside Tamerlane."

"Hmm." Daffydd was noncommittal. "Call me back? Fifteen minutes?"

I checked my watch. I'd be cutting it close, but doable. "Right."

I lay down on the bed staring at the ceiling and trying to make sense of my day, Sister Moonwomon Divine in particular. I don't expect to like a lot of the people I meet—Belle, my former high priestess, says I'm far too judgmental—and I'd pretty much made up my mind about Sister. I was 99 percent sure the feeling was mutual. Other than my scut-labor, which she'd already bought and paid for, I had nothing she could possibly want. So what I couldn't figure out was why she was trying to court my good opinion.

My 15 minutes were up; I called Daffydd back.

"You're talking about the Upper Hudson Psychiatric Facility," he said, once we'd established that I was me. "Built in 1913 as the Gotham County Asylum and closed in 1981 courtesy of Reaganomics. It stood empty for almost 20 years, until the Gotham County Development Board decided to turn it into a conference center a couple of years ago."

"No ghosts?" I said.

"Unfortunately, no." Daffydd sounded regretful. "It wasn't even put up on the site of an ancient Indian burial mound. The inmates all seem to have been a quiet and well-mannered bunch. No criminal records, even."

"You got all this from your notes?"

"Well, I called a friend of mine in the Sociology Department. He's doing a book."

Everybody is these days.

"You sounded like you could use the whole story."

"I could. This is a help. Thanks."

"You want to tell me what this is about now?"

"As soon as I get back. We'll have dinner—I promise."

"I'll hold you to that. Blessed be."

"Blessed be."

I turned off the phone and made it downstairs just in time to open up for the afternoon rush.

Murder and the disembodied Edward Madison were on everybody's minds. Madison's legend grew in the telling, as did Marcie Wheeler's. I discovered she was a channeler, a spirit medium; that she'd known about Madison; that she specialized in helping troubled spirits "pass beyond"; that she'd gone to help Madison "pass beyond" and he'd killed her; yadda, yadda, yadda. I also discovered that Madison had killed either 5, 17, or 23 women before he'd been caught, all blonds, and that possibly he was the reincarnation of Jack the Ripper—never mind that Saucy Jacky had liked to cut up his ladies, not neatly strangle them.

And no, the SpiritJourney QuestWithin Retreat bookshop did not stock any books on serial killers.

We sold completely out of sage smudges, incense, crystals, and anything that could possibly be construed as a protective amulet of any sort, including the Venetian masks Lark had sent up. Business was good.

The questions, however, continued odd.

"Um . . . somebody told me . . . you're a witch, aren't you? Well, couldn't you do an exorcism and make this guy go away?" The speaker waved her platinum American Express at me from atop a pile of books and T-shirts and looked expectant.

"You'll have to talk to the organizers about that," I said, taking her plastic.

I was saved from having to confirm, deny, or explain anything by the arrival of one of Sister's little helpers—the unpaid assistants who exchanged volunteer hours for a discount on their memberships and a free T-shirt—bearing a pile of flyers. She plunked it down on the counter.

"You're to hand these out," she said, and departed.

I picked up the top one and glanced at it while waiting for the approval code on the American Express. It announced that there would be a special cleansing and transitional circle tonight to harmonize the vibrations and ease the passing of the departed into the light at 10:30 tonight on the front lawn, after the book signing. I handed it to my interrogator; she seemed satisfied. The approval code came through; I was satisfied. She went away.

"I heard what she said," a man said a few minutes later.

Customers run in tides, like fish. A few minutes ago the kiosk had been mobbed. Now there was nobody around but him. He was one of the few men at the retreat, mid-forties, Hilfinger sports shirt and jeans. His nametag said Warren Shipton and Shadowking; the flourishes on the *g* had blotted out his city and state.

"About you being a witch," he added, in conspiratorial tones.

"People of all spiritual paths are welcome here at the retreat," I said in my best nurse-nanny tones. It was a line straight out of the brochure.

He actually winked. "That's okay. You don't have to say. I know. That Sheila Steinmetz—she's one too. Real witches. With power."

I did wonder whom I had to thank for this unauthorized addition to my biography. It didn't exactly seem like Sister's style.

"Can I help you find something?"

"No, I, uh . . . do you have any books on witchcraft?"

I doubted it was a legitimate question, but I treated it as one. I came up with two of Sheila's books: *Images of the Dark Divine* and *Channeling the Goddess Within*. Neither one was actually Wicca with a capital *W*, but they were closer than the rest of the stock.

"Those aren't really what I'm looking for." He sounded disappointed.

"You might have better luck with your local bookstore. Or Amazon," I suggested, because odd as it seems, not every city in the land has a large and well-equipped occult bookstore.

"Maybe you could help me. What books would you suggest?"

I suddenly felt like a drug dealer who realizes that the fresh-faced kid trying to buy a nickel bag is a vice cop.

"There's *Chasing the Moon*. Sister Moonwomon Divine wrote that," I said neutrally. I pointed to the large display at the front of the kiosk.

Warren "Shadowking" Shipton from nowhere-in-particular smirked. "She's not a witch. Edward Madison would make mincemeat out of her. You know, bringing a bunch of psychics like Marcie to a place like this, that's practically reckless endangerment. If Marcie's dead, it's practically her fault."

I wondered if Shadowking was a lawyer in daily life. I handed him a flyer. "This should take care of it."

About then a few more shoppers wandered up. They wanted to take a close look at the books, and particularly at the one last item of junque-du-Lark I hadn't been able to unload: a 6–foot wizard staff of gnarled driftwood with a 4–inch crystal ball wedged in the tip. The crystal ball was mineral quartz, and the price tag on the item was $650. I had hopes.

When I looked up again, Shadowking was gone.

* * *

I managed to get through dinner without, the gods forbid, talking to any of the presenters. Unfortunately, that didn't include the retreat's organizer, who assured me she wanted me to attend the cleansing ritual.

"I really think it would be best if *everyone* participated," she said meaningfully. "We'll chant and encircle the conference center with love, and everything will be fine. Oh, it might not be the way you'd do it, but I think it's the appropriate thing to do."

"Fine," I said.

"And each of the presenters will come forward and do a ritual of love and farewell to the powers and send them energy for their release. And you too, of course."

"No," I said flatly. My art is not for sale.

She stared at me. *No* was not a word Sister was used to hearing, I suspected.

"I came up here to run the bookshop. You paid me to do that, and I'm doing it. I am not available for other duties."

She turned quite red beneath her makeup. It was an interesting effect.

"Sheila said you wouldn't mind," she said sullenly.

I regarded her with detached interest. I didn't know Freya that intimately, but I doubted she'd volunteered my services. "I'll have to talk to her about that," I said mildly.

"Why are you so incredibly stubborn?" Sister demanded furiously, lowering her voice even further. "All I did was ask you if you wanted to participate in the ritual!" She actually managed to sound hurt, as if she were the injured party.

I took a deep breath and kept my voice even. "No," I said quietly. "You didn't. You ordered me to participate in the ritual and expected me to obey you. I am your employee for this weekend within specific limits—not your flunky."

She regarded me as if I'd just screamed obscenities at her, then thought it over for a moment and decided to be smug about it. "You don't like me, do you?" she asked. There are people for whom that is nearly as good as being loved, and suddenly I realized what it was that Sister wanted from me. She wanted me to care.

But I didn't. I thought over a dozen responses, from the flat truth to asking her if she thought she was a likable person. I wondered why people like Sister always ask when they know the answer, or hope they do.

"After Monday, neither of us ever has to see the other again," I finally said.

* * *

The kiosk was open till 9:00 P.M., but lightly visited. I restocked the shelves. The boxes behind the kiosk were almost empty now. I was facing the warming prospect of having nothing to repack on Monday, or nearly nothing.

At nine precisely, I closed down the kiosk for the night and retreated to the sanctity of my chaste and inviolate room. I decided to take a pass on the delights of the attempt to banish ghosts from the asylum after the conversation I'd had with Sister. The inmates—which is to say the retreat attendees—would still be here in the morning, which was enough to look forward to.

But the not-late-enough Edward Madison continued to puzzle me. Had there been an Edward Madison at all, or was he mere urban legend? If he existed, had he been here and when? Daffydd said that Upper Hudson hadn't had any criminal detainees, but if Madison had been judged unfit to plead due to diminished capacity or other New York State legal hoodoo—the way Julian had—he might not have shown up on Daffydd's radar. To end up in Upper Hudson, I imagined he would have had to do his work fairly locally, but I might be wrong about that. I wondered if there was any way to find out one way or the other.

Cruising the Tamerlane bars had never seemed so attractive.

Around 11:30 P.M. I heard the sound of chanting under my window. I went over and looked out.

The cleansing ritual was in full force. A candlelight procession—not everyone was carrying a candle, but enough—of attendees, in a long wavering line some three to five abreast, was walking around the conference center, chanting about the sky above, the earth below, and the light within. I could smell the faint burning-hay smell of sage smudges and hear bells and drums beating out the rhythm of the chant.

I turned out my lights and watched the candles flicker along my ceiling.

Ritual touches something deep within us. That's what it's designed to do. The elements of it—the chanting, drumming, darkness, and fire—all are designed to waken the primitive child-self, the part that comes before reason. Responsible ritualists know that the child-self is vulnerable and that what we lead into ritual must be led out again into the daylight, protected and re-armored with all the protections of the adult self.

Those who are not ethical and responsible take that vulnerable, undefended self and prey upon it, using its unquestioning acceptance to further their own ends. When adults do that to actual children, we call them predators. When adults do it to other adults who have temporarily become children through, perhaps, misplaced trust, we call their victims fools, but the mechanism is the same: predation, brutality, the despoiling of innocence, and the destruction of a thing that the human animal needs to keep in order to remain human.

It is always hard among adults to know whether this is occurring or not, and if it is, what you can do as an outsider to stop it without simply making matters worse.

I went to bed.

* * *

Sunday morning. There were many post-ritual reports of dreams and visions, all eagerly retold over breakfast. Angels, the Sidhe, and several goddesses had appeared to many of the attendees. Edward Madison had gone into the Light. So had several other dead people. Large volumes of automatic writing had been generated. Extensive past-life visions had been experienced.

But there were dissenting views. Maybe Edward Madison was tougher than they thought. He might very well be angered by the meddling of Spirit-Journey QuestWithin Retreat and be planning to kill again. There was a report of mysterious vanishing graffiti in one of the communal bathrooms on the third floor, message unspecified, and someone had seen Marcie Wheeler's ghost.

It was all terribly exciting. The victim wasn't a real person to anyone here. She was an excuse to add a little more reality-flavored drama to their weekends. Perhaps it is unfair to blame them. We all do what we have to in order to get by in a world that grows increasingly more toxic and random as the years pass. There isn't enough compassion to go around, social commentators tell us, and even civil politeness seems to be too much effort in a society where the rules that constitute propriety change daily.

I managed to get in and out of the dining room without seeing Sister, a minor victory. Or maybe she was avoiding me. It would have been soothing to know which or if this, too, was randomness.

* * *

At ten I closed up the kiosk again and spent a couple of hours restocking the shelves—everything was out of the boxes now—and getting all the inventory sheets up to date. The last set of workshops would be over at four, and then the kiosk would reopen for one last shopping frenzy until seven. Then would come dinner and the closing ceremonies. Some people would leave then. Some, Sister and I in particular, wouldn't be leaving until Monday.

I wondered how Bat and the Tamerlane SD felt about that, considering the probable fact that somewhere in this 500–plus gaggle of happy spiritual seekers was the person who'd made off with the end of Marcie Wheeler's life. However, it was not my problem, as Bat had taken great pains to remind me.

Getting my statement signed, however was, so about the time everyone was gathering for lunch, I took the Snake's van and myself off to the wonders of downtown Tamerlane.

I had a number of questions that I wanted answers to, so I made my first stop the library. Unfortunately, small-town association libraries don't generally run to Sunday hours, and it was closed. I had a second place I could ask my questions—a long shot, but worth a try.

I'd been to the sheriff's station several times the last time I'd been up here, and they hadn't moved it. I accomplished my routine business—read over the typed transcription, certified it was true and correct in all particulars, signed same—and then went looking for Fayrene.

She was on her way out the door when I caught her.

"Busy? Buy you coffee?" I suggested hopefully.

She regarded me unreadably for a moment, then nodded. "Come on."

It was the first time I'd ridden in the front seat of a police car. We went up Route 6 to the best—and, for all I knew, the only diner in Gotham County. Everyone there knew Fayrene by sight. They were willing to take me on faith. She went to a booth in the back. The waitress brought her coffee immediately and asked if she'd have her usual. I ordered a cheeseburger platter with unworthy meat-eater glee.

"I can't talk about the case. Unless you've come to confess," Fayrene said when the waitress had gone. Cop humor.

"I don't want to talk about the case. I want to find out about an old crime; it'd have to have been committed before 1980 at least. And the library's closed. How's Wyler?"

"Still a teenage boy. Still interested in that Wicca stuff. Some day he's going to burn down the trailer with those damn candles of his. Thanks for the books, by the way."

"Least I could do." From time to time I send Wyler books. I waited, drinking coffee, to see whether Fayrene was willing to be helpful.

"So, what's this old crime?"

"I want to know if there was ever a serial killer named Edward Madison working around here who would have been committed to Upper Hudson between 1960 and 1980. Apparently he strangled blond women."

Fayrene thought about that, drinking coffee. "Why?"

"Because the current inmates are saying he's haunting the place. If he never existed, it would be difficult for him to be haunting it."

Fayrene considered this. I knew she was probably putting more together than I was telling her, but cops do that. "They're saying he killed Marcie Wheeler, is that right?"

I sighed, giving up. "Yes. Of course, they're also saying he was the reincarnation of Jack the Ripper."

"And none of this was in your statement?"

"Should it have been?" I asked her, honestly confused. "I didn't start hearing any of this stuff until lunchtime yesterday, and nobody said any of it to me directly. I run the bookshop, and they were all just talking to each other across me."

Lunch arrived. Fayrene's usual was also a cheeseburger platter.

"Would you mind telling Detective Wayne the things you've just told me?" Fayrene asked. "Off the record?"

I stared at her. "You're not kidding."

She shook her head.

"Fine. Sure. Will one of you tell me whether or not Edward Madison exists?"

"Well, Tony would be the one who'd know that better than I would. You just let me go give him a jingle."

* * *

Bat showed up by the time we got to pie and coffee. The waitress had a slice and a cup in front of him before he'd finished sitting down. They have them well trained here in Gotham County.

"Sergeant Pascoe tells me you have some more to tell us about the Wheeler case," he said.

"Assuming you want pointless and idiotic rumors," I grumbled.

Bat smiled. "Actually, we do. It's amazing how useful they can be."

So I went through the entire list of tall tales surrounding Marcie Wheeler's death by ghost, including those involving her being a spirit channeler and the ones involving Madison's death by electroshock. I did not omit the vanishing graffiti or the angelic visitations; I was thorough.

"And how much of this do you believe, Bast?" Bat asked when I was done.

The question took me by surprise. "None of it," I said. "Point one: In my limited experience, post-death personality survivals , a.k.a. ghosts, don't work that way except in the movies. Point two: I checked with a researcher friend, and no one with a criminal record was ever committed to Upper Hudson. Point three: Upper Hudson has no history of paranormal activity in any of its incarnations, nor was the site a locus of paranormal activity previous to any structure being built on it. Point four: My turn to ask a question. Was there ever a serial killer named Edward Madison who operated in this area and was caught previous to 1980?"

"So the place isn't officially haunted?" Bat asked.

"No." Daffydd would have made certain.

"And there's no Edward Madison." This time it wasn't a question.

"There isn't?" I asked.

"We'd know," Bat assured me. "I checked the files. He's a figment." He looked at me. "But I'd sure like to know who started that particular rumor."

I played out the next part of the conversation, suitable for popular fiction only, in my head: Do you want me to ask? I can't ask you to ask. That would be illegal; but if you hear anything, call me.

"If you hear any more interesting conversations, call me," Bat said, in an uncanny echo of my inner monologue. He passed me his card. "My cell phone number's on the back. Gotta go."

"You have a knack for trouble," Fayrene said, once he'd gone.

"All I wanted to do was come up here, sell books, and make the rent money," I said. And not spend long afternoons chatting up the police.

"I'll run you back to your van," Fayrene said.

She told me to stay out of trouble. I assured her I would, but I no longer had any real confidence in my ability to keep that particular promise.

* * *

I fooled around downtown Tamerlane, found a convenience store, and stocked up on enough supplies that I could afford to miss both dinner and breakfast without going hungry. I suspected the less time Sister and I spent in each other's company, the better for both of us.

I wasn't completely sure how we'd managed to form such a completely adversarial relationship in less than 48 hours. I'd come up here intending to treat her with polite indifference. Obviously that hadn't worked out well. Apparently she had expected more from me for her $750. I wondered which of us was being unreasonable.

I got back to the conference center about 3:40 P.M. Shadowking was hanging around the lobby, along with a gaggle of lady admirers.

"But it was so awful for you!" I heard one of them say. "Didn't you try to stop her?"

"Well, Marcie and I had worked together for a long time. She knew the risks. When you deal with the Shadow Realm, you come to understand that sometimes only Darkness can banish Darkness. Sometimes the Light just isn't enough. And that's why he's still here."

Warren, a.k.a. Shadowking, had a well-oiled line of patter going, and his troupe of acolytes was falling for it nicely. All he needed was the black satin cape and the little goatee to become the free-range Prince of Darkness of his dreams.

"Do you really think so?" one of the women asked.

"Well, when I saw that message on the mirror this morning . . ."

Now this was all much too interesting. Warren had seen the conveniently vanishing message regarding the mythical Edward Madison's further intentions?

I opened up the kiosk. Several people drifted over. The foyer began to fill as the workshops emptied, but traffic wasn't as heavy over by the kiosk as it had been earlier. I began to fear that the wizard staff would be going home with me again. I found a few packets of fairy dust—glitter and star-shaped sequins in plastic bags—that had been overlooked in previous shopping frenzies and set them out on the counter with the last of the T-shirts to encourage trade while I thought about what to do next.

If this had been a pagan festival, I'd have known almost everybody here. I could have circulated freely and asked questions of the people most likely to know the answers. It would have been pretty easy to find out some quick and basic information, such as how well Warren knew Marcie and whether they were an item. It would have been harder, though probably not impossible, to find out when and where the Edward Madison rumors had started.

Here I had to improvise.

"I guess Warren's pretty broken up about Marcie and all?" I said. The woman standing at the counter was one that I'd seen hanging around him when I'd come in. The name on her badge was Birdwoman, in mundane life Dorothy Lester of La Grangeville, Kentucky.

"Oh, yes!" It came out *yay-us,* and I remembered that Marcie, and perhaps Warren, came from Kentucky. "They'd been coming to the retreats together for years. His wife . . . well, she's unevolved, you know? But he and Marcie had a soul bond. She said they were married in a previous life."

"How awful," I said. I wanted to ask her something else, but Warren came up right behind her, so I simply rang up her purchases and sent her on her way.

Warren hung around. It wasn't terribly obvious—everybody had to be somewhere, after all—but obvious enough to make me edgy. He knew Marcie, he was married, his wife didn't understand him, he was one of the main sources for the rumors about the activities of a non-existent ghost. You do the math. It's a sad fact of life that you're far likelier to be murdered by someone you know than by a stranger, especially if you're female.

"You know that guy's still around, don't you?" Warren said conspiratorially, when everyone else was away from the kiosk.

I regarded him with bright-eyed interest. I felt safe; the foyer was still pretty well occupied with people waiting to go in to dinner.

"Madison? I thought they got rid of him."

"They thought they did, but he's still here. Some people saw him last night after the ritual. There's going to be more trouble if he isn't stopped."

"That would be bad." I was interested to see how far he'd go with this. As for why he'd picked me, well, it was undoubtedly my aura of great Wiccan virtue. Or something.

"I think the two of us could stop it before it goes any farther," he said, leaning in a little closer. "I heard you were involved in something like this before, down in New York, that you work with the cult crimes people there."

Rumor is a wonderful thing. Belle is the one who works with cult crimes, not me. And as far as I know, neither of us has ever been involved with an exorcism.

"If we could go back to where Marcie died and get Madison to show up again, you could get rid of him for sure. And then this place would be safe again."

"It would be sort of like a memorial to Marcie's memory," I heard myself say.

I could not imagine what Warren thought he was doing. I knew he thought he was appealing to the conceit he thought I had, but of all the people here, he had to be the one who knew best that there was no Edward Madison to exorcise. Had he fallen down the rabbit hole to the point of believing his own story? Was this going to be a long, involved, impractical joke in New Age clothing? Or was he trying to set up some more corroboration of Madison's existence by providing a second victim?

"Yeah, that's right," he said, a little too eagerly. "We could do it for Marcie, because she's going to be earthbound until her killer is caught. And because, you know, I really respect Sister Moonwomon Divine, and I wouldn't want her to have any trouble over this."

He was lying outright now, and not quite putting it over. I heard in his voice what I'd heard in my own all weekend: contempt. It made up my mind for me.

"You're right. I hadn't thought of that. Sure. It's a good idea. But we'll have to do it when nobody's looking. We don't want anyone to stop us."

He practically preened, sure now that I'd fallen for his line, sure I was as stupid and as vain as Marcie, Sister, his nameless wife, and every other woman he'd ever met.

There is a particular type of fellow traveler found throughout the Aquarian Frontier, usually male, who assumes the coloration of their environment without internalizing its lessons. They are predators. They may be after sex, money, or simply uncritical adoration. They are difficult to spot, because they are so extraordinarily facile. Generally they don't want trouble. They view their environment as a shopping mall filled with the clueless who, if the right buttons are pushed, will cater to their desires and provide for their needs. But they give back nothing, and over time, they erode trust. When they rise to positions of power, as they so often do, things turn ugly very fast.

As they had here.

"Everyone's going in to dinner in a few minutes. We can go then," he said.

"Great. I've got some preparations to make. *You* know." I doubted he had the least notion, and in fact I had very little idea of what a proper banishing ritual for a murderous ghost would actually involve, but I figured it wouldn't hurt to let him fill in the blanks. "Where shall we meet?"

"We can meet right at the site. Be sure no one sees you," he said.

I smiled. It was easy, this time. "I'll be careful."

He walked away.

I sat there waiting to feel the sense that this was a very bad idea and the height of idiocy, but all I felt was a faint numb indignation at Warren's stupidity. And in fact this might all be coincidence and misunderstanding of the highest order. He might be a callous, oblivious manipulator who had nothing to do with Marcie's death, but I was taking no chances.

At seven sharp I closed up the kiosk for the last time. I took the wizard staff, figuring I might want it for a prop later, went up to my room, and called Bat on my cell phone.

"This is Bast," I said when he answered. "Warren Shipton has been spreading a lot of the rumors about Edward Madison. He was the only one who saw the mirror message this morning. He and Marcie Wheeler were an item. He has a wife back home who is not into New Age. He is very eager to have me go off alone with him to the murder site and do an exorcism of Edward Madison's spirit, to which I've agreed. It's set for 7:15."

There was a long, sharp exhalation in my ear. I sensed Bat struggling with things better left unsaid. "Stall him."

"I'm not going. I'll be in my room when you get here," I said. I'd decided not showing up at all would be about right.

I changed back into jeans and a T-shirt and started to clear the room. I could move the van up closer when most of the cars were gone and pack it with the unsold part of the Snake's merchandise tonight, and only have the SpiritJourney stuff to deal with in the morning. Lark had done pretty well out of the weekend. I figured I'd charge him hazard pay for having to deal with his ex-girlfriend, though.

About 7:05 there was a knock on my door. Thoughtlessly, I opened it.

Warren was standing there.

"I thought I'd come up and get you. Everybody's at dinner; the coast is clear."

"Hold this," I said, grabbing the first thing that came to hand—a large bottle of spring water—and thrusting it into his hands.

How had he known where I was? Nobody did, except Sister. Of course, nobody here this weekend outside of Sister and Freya was supposed to know I was a witch, either, and that seemed to be fairly common knowledge, too.

Seeing him was a shock. I felt as if I'd managed to be not as clever as I'd hoped, and I knew that the most important thing at the moment was to get us out of a small, isolated room and back to where people would hear me if I screamed. I grabbed my purse, a packet of joss sticks that I'd laid out for some reason the night before, and the wizard staff. It was big and heavy and looked impressive, something someone like Warren might think was necessary for a Wiccan exorcism ritual. "Come on."

To my great relief, he came.

We went back down in the elevator. I wondered how long it was going to take Bat to get here; I wondered what Warren was thinking, if anything; I wondered how long I could stall him, and what would work.

No one was in the foyer.

Just then I would have been happy for Sister Moonwomon Divine in all her glory to descend upon us and demand to know where I was going with one of her subjects, but no such luck. The hallway was deserted as well; as Warren had said, everybody was gathered at the farewell dinner. The conference center staff had left for the day. The two of us might as well have been alone in the building.

We got to the end of the hall that led down to the row of meeting rooms, and I stopped. Stall him, Bat had said.

"Look, Warren. You interrupted me back there. Before I do something like this, I've got to ground and center, you know. I can't just go in there cold. I've got to prepare, or it won't work."

"Couldn't you do it inside?" he said. He was starting to get nervous, looking back and forth. Halfway down the hall I could see the yellow police tape gleaming faintly. Most of the lights on this side were shut down.

"Of course I can't do it in there," I said reasonably. "The vibrations are all wrong."

Poor Warren. I doubted he believed in any of the New Age cant he'd spouted so plausibly, but he knew everyone around him did, and probably I did too. To get me to do what he wanted, he was going to have to go along with me.

And I was safe for as long as Warren maintained his fixation on duplicating the circumstances of Marcie Wheeler's murder.

I should have been terrified. Maybe I just wasn't taking Warren seriously enough. It was hard to take any of these people seriously, when you came right down to it. Maybe proper caution was a finite resource, and I'd used up my allotted share in too many encounters with unreasonable individuals. Maybe I was just too angry to be careful or too irritated. For whatever reason, I rummaged serenely through my bag for lighter and incense, lit several joss sticks and passed two to Warren, then proceeded to go through the entire Lesser Banishing Ritual of the pentagram as slowly as possible.

I know it by heart, every om and adonai. It can be very impressive, when done with proper theatrical gestures. I was properly theatrical; the wizard staff helped a great deal. It is not in the least Wiccan, so my conscience was clear.

I finished.

No Bat.

I was running out of stall.

"Come on!" Warren said impatiently. He started down the hall to the room. I followed more slowly, considering my options. Carefully.

Rule number one for urban survival: Do not enter rooms of any sort with strange murderers or possible murderers.

Warren opened the door and went inside, ducking under the tape. I followed him to the doorway and stopped.

He was standing right about where Marcie had lain, waiting for me to come in. Odd behavior in a soul mate, I thought. Shouldn't he be more conscious that this was where she'd died?

Or was he?

"Get in here," he said. The mask of civility was slipping. If he had a secretary back home, this was the side of him she probably saw most often.

"Why?" I said. I took a step backward, taking a good grip on the edge of the door. I could feel the words pushing to be said. They were the right words, and so I said them.

"You know there's no Edward Madison to exorcise."

Among the Wicca, we have some experience with masks. I felt the shimmer as his fell away. It gave me time to start to swing the door closed, but not enough to get it shut before he reached it. He ripped the door out of my hands, grabbing for me, breaking the tape. I swung the wizard staff forward. The crystal ball hit the side of his face harder than I'd expected, but not as hard as I probably ought to have hit him.

"Hold it! Police!" I'd never heard Bat raise his voice before. I heard it now. He came through a side door, pointing a gun at Warren's back.

Warren stopped and turned around, shocked, as I was shocked. I backed away, out of the line of sight, moving down the hall away from the gun. I gripped the staff and held it against me, as if it could protect me from everything that was happening here. I'd been wondering why I wasn't afraid. Now I was, as if I'd been saving it all up for this moment.

"On the floor! Hands behind your back!"

I stayed where I was, pressed against the wall, hearing thuds and clinks and random noises. I listened with a sense of unreality as Bat read Warren Shipton his rights, and heard Warren begin to cry. I kept my eyes averted. I didn't want to see anything more; I'd already seen enough. I'd seen Edward Madison—the only Edward Madison there was to see, the one that lived behind Warren Shipton's eyes—the one I'd summoned up, just as he'd asked me to do. The one I'd exorcised, just as he'd asked me to do.

Bat made a phone call.

Deputies arrived and took Warren away. I stayed where I was, leaning against the wall, clutching the ridiculous wizard's staff as though it really was a thing of power.

Bat came over to me.

"Are you all right?" he asked.

I nodded. Everything hurt—shock and its aftereffects. "He came up to my room," I said. My voice was unsteady. "I meant to stay there."

"If you'll swear out a complaint, that will be a great deal of help," he said. "You'll need to come down to the station again."

"Yeah," I said.

"Buy you coffee?" he said.

"He came to my room," I repeated, as if that were somehow important. "Nobody was supposed to know where it was."

"Come on," Bat said.

* * *

In hell and police work, the paperwork goes on forever. I spent the evening down at the Tamerlane Sheriff's Station, sitting in a chair beside Bat's desk as he came and went. He bought me coffee, as promised. He also bought me dinner, though I wasn't hungry.

I made a full confession. I wasn't charged with anything, but the statement I made still felt like one. I told what I'd heard and what I'd done. He already knew how it ended.

"If you keep doing stupid things like this, you're going to get yourself killed," Bat said sternly around eleven o'clock as I signed the typed version of my statement and complaint against one Warren Matthew Shipton of Lexington, Kentucky. "Let us do our jobs; that's what we're here for. We might not have caught him tonight, but we'd have caught him. Ms. Wheeler was his girlfriend. Apparently they were having an affair. The M.E. said she was pregnant when she died."

I regarded him with a wary "why are you telling me all this" expression.

"Mr. Shipton has waived his right to counsel and is in the process of making a full confession. As a member of the Bar, we must presume he knows what he's doing. Apparently you scared him half to death and he's afraid you'll put a curse on him if he doesn't," Bat said. I decided to take that as more cop humor.

"Will it stand up in court?"

"It's a place to start."

Eventually there were no further services I could perform for the Sheriff's Department of Gotham County. Ultimately there would be a trial, and I might have to come back for that. I was becoming resigned to the presence of such events in my life, though not reconciled.

Bat drove me back to the conference center. I had been allowed to retain the wizard's staff; apparently it was not considered evidential. Somewhere along the course of the evening I'd decided to keep it. I figured Lark owed it to me for services rendered. If he disagreed, we could probably work something out.

To my surprise, Bat walked me to the door. "It's late, and I want to make sure you get inside safely."

I rang the buzzer, not sure who, if anyone, would answer.

"Look," he said. "I know you're leaving for New York tomorrow, and could you do a poor overworked small-town cop a favor and stay there this time? It seems like every time you come up here, I wind up with a fresh corpse and a nutcase angle."

I rang the buzzer again. Someone was coming.

"With all due respect, the only way anybody's ever going to get me out of Manhattan again is in a straightjacket and chains."

It turned out to be one of Sister's little helpers. She unlocked the door, gazing curiously at Bat.

"See you later," I said. Bat smiled, hoping I wouldn't. I went inside.

"Sister wanted to see you," the helper said. Her nametag said Merrybeth, and oddly enough, it seemed to be her real name. "But she's gone to bed. Where were you? She's been looking all over for you."

"I was down at the Sheriff's Station. Thanks for letting me in."

"You missed dinner, and the closing ceremonies, and everything," she said, staring at me.

I remembered I'd put my pentacle back around my neck when I'd gone up to my room to change, intending to stay in for the rest of the night. It was hanging out in plain sight now. So much for the rest of my good intentions.

"I had some things to clear up that couldn't wait." Let someone else break the news about Warren's arrest. I was through liaising, as the current argot would have it, between the police and the retreat.

"Well, goodnight," I said firmly. "I'll talk to Sister in the morning." I walked past her, heading for the foyer, where the elevators were.

"What about Edward Madison?" she asked, following me. "Do you think he's really gone?"

"Oh, yes," I said. "He's definitely gone."

We got to the elevators. The foyer was dark, only a few lights on at this time of night. She got into one of the cars and waited for me. I stepped back and waved her on. The doors shut. After a moment, I turned away and walked over to the kiosk.

I wasn't at all ready to sleep. I switched on the lights in the kiosk, pulled the boxes out of the back, and got to work packing up the remains of the Snake's stuff. There wasn't much. I totaled up the amount I needed to get back from the retreat on the Snake's behalf and put a note on top of the box.

Stopping seemed like too much trouble, so I took down the rest of the kiosk, broke down the displays, and packed them, too. It was just about dawn when I finished. I figured I'd catch a couple of hours sleep, load the van, and get the hell out of Dodge.

It would have been nice if I'd remembered that Sister was an early riser. I was walking toward the elevators, staff in hand, when one of them opened and she stepped out.

She was dressed down from the way I'd seen her all weekend—more Earth mother than druid princess—but it was obvious that she was still playing to the galleries. Her outfit was calculated for effect. That was what I'd unconsciously responded to so badly all weekend. I am not a fan of calculation.

"There you are!" she said. "What are you doing up so early?"

"I got in late. So I decided to pack up the kiosk before I went to bed," I said.

"Well." She blinked. I'd thrown her off her script. "We missed you last night at the dinner."

"It was unavoidable."

"I sent someone to go and get you. I thought you might be in your room."

I just managed to keep from blurting out that if she'd sent Warren Shipton, he'd found me all right.

"I'd probably left by then. I was called away. I'm sorry I missed it." I realized we were having another one of those bizarre pointless circular conversations that were a feature of our non-relationship, one of many things I wouldn't miss about this weekend.

"The police were here again last night. I heard they caught the killer."

"I've got the whole inventory packed up and ready to go," I said, pitching my voice to make it sound as if I were answering her. "I've got the total for the things I sold for the Serpent's Truth. I could take that as either cash or a check."

The friendly expression on her face faded as she realized she hadn't gotten her answer. "What did the police want?" she said sharply.

"If you call the Tamerlane station, I'm sure they'll be happy to talk to you, but I can't."

I was only stretching the truth a little bit. Bat had encouraged me not to talk about what had happened last night, but I could reasonably have told her that Warren had been taken in for questioning, if reason and I had not parted company some hours before.

Her eyes grew round. She looked pleased and excited, as if she'd wandered into some sort of Disneyland of the mind.

"Merrybeth said you wanted to talk to me last night?" I said, prompting.

"Oh, yes . . . well . . ." We were back on the script now. "Look, Bast, I know we sort of got off on the wrong foot, but just over the weekend, and especially with everything that's happened here, I can tell you're an individual with enormous drive and capacity and great spiritual commitment, and you know, such people are very rare. I could really use someone like you in the Spirit-Journey organization to help me run the retreats. I want you to think about it, and when you're ready, you give me a call." She patted me on the shoulder and walked on toward the front door. "Oh, by the way, I like your walking stick!" she called back over her shoulder.

I got into the elevator and rode upward in silence.

Had I just had a very vivid hallucination, or had Sister Moonwomon Divine just offered me a job?

She had, of course. I don't know what I symbolized to her, or what she thought I represented, but whatever it was, she couldn't leave it alone. She had to try to win, whatever winning meant to her.

But it wasn't going to happen. I was never going to be ready to make that call. My soul and my conscience are my own. I pay on the installment plan, and the payments are high, but so far I've managed to keep them up. I had no intention of selling either one to Sister's traveling New Age bazaar.

I'd come to Gotham County to face old ghosts. That had been a mistake. Sometimes our ghosts are the only things we can keep.

_____ Please send me information on the Rhine Research Center.

_____ I would like information regarding making a financial contribution to the RRC research and education programs.

_____ I would like information about becoming a member of the **_Rhine Research Center Association._**

_____ I would like information about subscribing to the **_Journal of Parapsychology._**

Name: _____

Address: _____

Address: _____

City: _____ State: _____

Zip: _____ Email: _____

(Please print clearly)

Rhine Research Center
2741 Campus Walk Avenue, #500
Durham, NC 27705